Cover Design and Interior Format

RAFE TAKES THE HEAT

a Real Vampires novel

GERRY BARTLETT

DEDICATION

This book is dedicated to dear friends Nina Bangs, Donna Maloy and Jo Anne Banker. Their fingerprints are all over this book. Thanks for holding my feet to the fire and making my work better.

CHAPTER ONE

"**I** HATE TO TELL you this, but your place reeks, bud."

Rafael Valdez gave his brother a hard look. "What do you mean by that?"

"Hey, don't shoot the messenger." Tomas held up his hands. He looked around the busy bar. "There. See that one? He's heading for the door now." Tom leaned in. "Demon in a man's clothing. See for yourself."

Rafe was out of his chair and at the door before the man, who did carry the stench of evil, had made it to the sidewalk outside. Rafe grabbed the back of the pricey jacket and walked him around the corner and into the alley.

"Hey, watch what you're doing." The creep struggled, looked over his shoulder, then gave up pretense. Hissing, his forked tongue flickered as his eyes turned red. "Take your hands off me before I fry you where you stand."

"That the best you got?" Rafe slung him farther down the alley, where the lights suddenly died in a burst of sparks. "What do you want? Why were you in my bar?" He shoved the demon against the brick wall.

"I don't answer to you." The man, who now sported claws instead of fingers, carefully brushed at his shirt. "Keep your hands to yourself. I was minding my own business. Checking out the scene. I paid for my drink with real money."

"Demons aren't welcome in N-V." Rafe let his own eyes glow.

"Why not? You're not pure, but carry enough of the blood that I can smell our kind on you." The man snarled. "Think you're better than we are, shifter?" He glanced down the alley toward Sixth Street where people were beginning the nightly stroll toward shops open late and other night clubs. "Look out there. Take a whiff. Hate to tell you, brother, but there's a hell of a convention coming to town." He chuckled. "Yeah, Hell's meeting here and the party's already started."

Rafe moved closer. He didn't like this guy's attitude. Mocking. As if he knew a secret. "What do you mean by that?"

"Haven't you heard? Lucifer has spoken. He's offering a prize. A bounty. First one to bring the big guy a certain child will get riches and perks beyond imagining." The man polished his long nails on his lapel. "I think you know something about that kid, don't you?"

Rafe's inner demon roared to life. His humanity, even his shifter side, began to fall away, leaving him in the grip of a rage that he struggled to control. A bounty? On a certain child? He would destroy this son of a bitch. He gripped the demon's shoulders, sending him to his knees on the cracked pavement. When a hand clamped on his own shoulder from behind, he growled, ready to rip that hand from whoever dared touch him.

"Stop. You're never going to get the answers you need if you kill the son of a bitch." The soft voice was close to his ear.

"Release me. This isn't your concern, Cisneros." Rafe ignored the whimpers coming from the demon on the ground in front of him.

"When the Devil sends his minions here, it concerns all of us." Miguel Cisneros did let go but didn't go far.

Rafe spared him a glance. The vampire had a point and could be useful. Ancient, with some kind of Mayan blood, Cisneros was damned powerful. While Rafe didn't quite trust him, he knew his best friend Glory St. Clair treated the man like a long-lost brother. Which he just might be. They both had Olympus ties. Yeah, a very powerful man.

"I can help. Let me get the truth out of this devil's spawn." Miguel moved around Rafe and kicked the quivering demon with one of his fancy ostrich boots. "Tell me something, Ezra. That is your name, isn't it?"

"This week." The demon's teeth started chattering. "What are you doing to me?"

"Freezing you. It's a new power I'm playing with. How do you feel? Icy?" Miguel smiled at Rafe. "One kick between your legs from my friend Rafael here and your frozen nuts will shatter. Want him to try it?"

"No, please!" The cry was from what passed for the demon's heart. He jerked his knees together and covered his eyes, sobbing. "What do you want to know?"

"How many are coming to Austin and what's the plan? What does Lucifer want?"

The shivering demon told them everything. Greed was a powerful motivator in the demon world and Lucifer's favor was highly coveted. Dozens of demons that Rafe considered merely annoyances were already here, but some high-level characters who he knew had powers too terrifying to dismiss were also in town or on the way.

A child. Yes, he knew the child. His child, beautiful and born with enough of his demon blood to be of interest to Lucifer. He had prayed this day would never come. No surprise that his prayers had been ignored. He shuddered. He glanced at Miguel and got a nod. Sympathy? From this hard-eyed man? This was bad. A disaster.

"I'm sorry." Miguel easily read his mind. "Let me know if I can help in any way, Rafael." He spoke his name with the inflection of a native Spanish speaker.

Rafe felt sure if he broke into the language the man would never miss a beat. "Why are you helping me?"

"Why not?" Miguel smiled. "Gloriana reminds me that our kind, paranormals she calls us, should stick together, have each other's backs." He shrugged. "She has urged me to stay on what she called the right side of things. Once, I would have gone after this so-called bounty. Been willing to face Lucifer himself for a chance to gain riches."

He shook his head. "But I have plenty of money and it seems I have gone soft. Because I realize I have limits. A child? No, *hermano*, I cannot sacrifice a child. *El Diablo* goes too far."

Rafe held out his hand. "You're right about that. Thank you." Miguel was what Rafe's wife would call a handsome man—tall, powerfully built and always in black. His smiles were rare, Rafe had noticed that. He'd come into the club from time to time, ordering the synthetic blood Rafe kept in stock for his vampire friends and sitting in the balcony with Glory and her husband. But not often. He seemed to be a loner. This gesture was unlike him.

Miguel shook his hand. "You are Gloriana's friend. She will be pleased if we can protect your little one." He reached out and picked up the demon. "I will dispose of this trash." Miguel nodded, the limp demon under his arm like a bundle of rags bound for a dumpster.

"Truly, Miguel. Thanks. I won't forget this." Rafe walked back to the street and looked around. He took a deep breath and the taint was still there. More demons close by. They weren't all so easy to spot. Ezra had been low level. The elder demons with strong skills cloaked their true natures and were well-disguised. He was going to have to be constantly on guard from now on. And he couldn't protect his family alone.

He had always taken care of himself. Even spent most of his life protecting others, for pay, working as a bodyguard. But when it came to his family? He'd take any help he could get, even from a man like Cisneros who seemed to have more than a little darkness in his own soul.

Rafe headed back into the club. Tomas still sat at the table, gesturing for a refill. Rafe looked around and noticed there had been more arrivals since he'd been in the alley. The vampires Rafe welcomed into his club were up on the balcony, sitting at the table that was their usual hangout.

"What did you find out, *hermano*?" Tom took a full glass from the tray the waiter brought and took a deep swallow of bourbon. "You look rough, man. I'm not surprised. I smelled evil. Not a little bit, like you put out with a flicker of red in your eyes. No, I'm talking full-on bad ass, I'll-drag-you-to-hell-if-you-look-at-me-wrong evil, bro." Tomas shuddered

"You're right. And I'll need your help. If you keep drinking like that, you won't be able to give it to me. You remind me of our father, drowning your fear in expensive bourbon." Rafe wanted to shake Tom. "If your wife sees you, Chica will drag you out of here by your ear."

"Shut up. She is too busy shopping at your pal Glory's vintage clothing shop to bother with me." Tomas gestured for yet another refill. "I love you, bro, but this demon thing you live with every day is too much for me. It's getting on my last nerve, I tell you."

"Slow down on the booze. Come upstairs with me. I want to discuss the situation with my friends." Rafe picked up his own full glass. He waited for Tom to follow him. When he didn't get up, he grabbed Tom's sleeve. "That was an

order." He'd given his brother a job here, as
assistant manager. He didn't often issue orders but
this time he needed him to step up.

"You know how I feel about those *vampiros*."
Tomas frowned.

"Suck it up. I need you. Those demons are
threatening my family." This time Rafe did let his
eyes glow red.

"I've never seen you afraid of demons. Of
anything, bro. Me? I don't have your courage.
Suck it up?" Tom shuddered. "Would you not say
that?" He picked up his fresh drink and followed
Rafe to the stairs. "I know these are your friends.
You say you trust them, but I don't have your
demon blood, or your history with them. That
woman Florence… She is one hot tamale, eh?
She caught me looking down her blouse and
showed her fangs to me." He tripped on a tread
as they walked up the stairs. "Then she sniffed
the air near my neck. Called me *deliciouso*. I
almost pissed my pants." He grabbed Rafe's arm
when he saw Florence da Vinci and her husband
Richard Mainwaring turn to stare at him. "I'm a
dead man. They hear everything, don't they?"

Rafe stopped at the top of the stairs. Besides
Flo and Richard, Jeremy Blade was there, sipping
premium synthetic blood. No sign of Blade's wife,
Glory St. Clair, but there was an empty chair next
to Blade.

"Relax, *hermano*. I know Flo. She wore that
low cut blouse on purpose. She would have been
insulted if you hadn't noticed her beauty, right,
Flo?"

"But of course." Florence put her hand on her husband's shoulder when he started to rise from his seat at the long table. "Darling, I was teasing this shifter. Tomas, how are you tonight? Don't be scared. Relax. I am drinking a glass of something much more exotic than your common shifter blood." She got up to walk around the table and give Rafe a hug. Then she patted Tom on the cheek with one beringed hand, her diamond leaving an oozing scratch. She ran a fingertip through the blood and tasted it.

"Oh, you have been hitting the drink hard. I wouldn't mind being a little tipsy if I did take you down a pint." She leaned in closer, inhaling deeply. "This makes me sorry that I like your wife too much to lay a fang on you."

Richard Mainwaring watched this with narrowed eyes. He grinned when Tom stepped behind Rafe to use him as a shield.

"Darling, behave or I'll have to take you home and teach you a lesson in manners." Her husband picked up his goblet and sipped, eying her over the rim. "Tomas is shaking in his shoes."

"A lesson? Really, Ricardo?" Florence strutted around the table. She was dressed as usual in full seductive mode, her high heels making her a little over five feet tall. Her nails were painted black to match her tight leather skirt and she tapped those nails on Richard's head as she passed him to settle in her seat. "I will be interested to see what that could be. But Rafael is here with worry on his face. We must hear him out, I think. Before we can move on to our pleasures." She picked up Richard's hand. "And it *will* be pleasures, am I right?"

"Of course, you are right." He kissed her palm. "What's amiss, Rafe? How can we help?"

Tom rubbed his cheek. "There is evil in the air." He glared at Flo. "Maybe it's not from demons like I thought, maybe it's coming from here."

"I told you there is demon activity in the area." Blade, once known as Jeremiah Campbell, leaned forward. "Glory told me she had a minor demon in the shop last night. She managed to run him off with the holy water she keeps next to her cash register, but we all know a demon when we smell one. He damaged some clothing and lifted a piece of jewelry. Just to prove he could, I'm sure."

"I don't like to hear that. I just found out that they're here about me and my family." Rafe took a seat at the long table. He and Jerry had come to terms a long time ago. They both loved Glory, Jerry's wife. Rafe was firmly in the friend zone with Glory now, happy in his own marriage. Jerry had a jealous streak, but he'd learned to trust his wife. And the fact that Rafe was in love with his own Lacy had convinced Jerry he had no cause for jealousy in Rafe's friendship with Glory. They had even done some business deals together recently and been comfortable enough to call each other friend. Now Jerry frowned.

"What do they want with your family? As leverage against you? I know about your demon blood but what . . ?" Jerry glanced around the table. "What are you not telling us?"

Rafe could feel the concern from these people, these vampires and his brother, half-brother. He and Tomas shared a father. Lucky for Tomas his mother was one of his father's mistresses and a member of the shifter clan, not a demon. Rafe had two other half-brothers who shunned him because of his demon blood. Wise of them. Hanging out with a demon was dangerous and stupid. He should send Tomas away. Or disappear himself. Except there was a problem.

He really didn't want to tell these well-meaning people about it. But he couldn't face the coming situation alone. Not and prevail. Hell was coming to call. If he could just face it and, if he had to, sacrifice himself, maybe it would all go away. He'd die for his family. But he knew that wouldn't be the end of it. Too many demons were circling. Too many high-level demons. Obviously this bounty being offered was so huge that even the laziest demons were stirring and coming out of their lairs to see if they could win it.

"Rafe, you look like you are facing Hell itself. What is it? You've fought demons and won before, haven't you?" Tomas sat beside him. His glass was empty again and his words slurred. "What is it that has you so upset? Why are you turning to these, um, people?" He waved his hand around the table. "Do we need to send for some of our own? From the clan?"

"It would do no good. These vampires are my friends. They are strong and decent. If it comes to a fight with Lucifer himself, I would trust everyone here. Glory too, of course."

"What the fuck are you trying to drag my wife into this time, Valdez?" Jerry was on his feet. "I may have something to say about that."

"I'm sorry. You're right. I shouldn't risk anyone else. It's just that it's not for me. Not just my life at stake." Rafe put his face in his hands. He had sworn to keep this a secret. Only four people knew the truth and that was already too many. But if danger was coming, the secret was going to come out. No doubt about it.

"Jeremiah, let him tell us what has him so upset." Glory St. Clair's voice came from the top of the stairs.

Rafe looked up and met her gaze. "I'm sorry, Blondie. I really shouldn't get you involved. Jerry's right."

"I'll be the judge of whether I want to get involved or not. Tell me what has you in a bad way." She walked over and stood next to him, her hand on his shoulder. "Please. You know you can tell me anything."

"It's Daniela, Glo. My beautiful little girl. I knew the first time I held her." Rafe took a shaky breath and clasped Glory's hand. "I saw it in her eyes. She's got the demon blood. Now Lucifer is going after her, claiming her. He's offered a bounty and is determined to drag her down to Hell."

CHAPTER TWO

"I'VE GOT TO go. My family..." He hadn't taken two steps when his phone vibrated in his pocket. One look and he was afraid he was too late. "Lacy, everything okay?"

"No." The clipped way she said that, the lack of explanation, made his heart shudder.

"Speak to me." He ran down the stairs. He could feel Tomas on his heels, the vampires moving silently behind his brother. No one spoke. It was as if they'd formed an army at his back. It should have been reassuring but terror squeezed his lungs as he heard his wife breathe into the phone. "Lacy, please."

"Your mother is here. She, she says she must take Daniela with her." She sobbed, and it tore through him.

His mother, a demon who never should have spawned a child. Him. Threatening to take his baby. He struggled to speak past his rage.

"Rafe, I need you. She is too powerful for me to stop. Our baby girl is staring at her like she is her favorite Disney character offering her a season pass to …" Lacy sobbed, unable to go on.

"I know, baby. Lilith is like that, mesmerizing."

Rafe hit the door, not sparing a thought for the sight they made as he and his entourage exited the packed club. "I'm on my way. Do whatever you can to keep her from leaving. How's your family?"

"What do you think? She froze them in place. One look from Lilith and they couldn't do a thing. At, at least she spared me that. My mother was not so lucky." Her tears had stopped and Lacy was back to being furious. "Damn her to hell. No, wait, that's her happy place."

"I'm sorry, baby. I'm coming and I'll take care of this. Let me talk to her." He cursed when the phone went dead. So much for that idea. He wanted to fling his own phone to the concrete and stomp it. No, he'd need it.

"Boss?" The doorman, Ed, a shifter who made a mean gorilla when he wasn't in mortal form, touched his arm. Ed didn't try to slow him down. Good thing, since Rafe would have knocked him on his ass.

"Keep things running here. Watch for demons." Rafe hissed the word. "They're here for one of my kids. Try to keep things looking normal but feel free to take out any if you have the chance."

"You've got it." Ed nodded, eyes widening as the vampires brushed past him. "You need anything else, call."

Rafe headed down the dark alley toward the SUV he kept parked behind the club. "The cat compound. Meet you there." All the vampires but one changed and flew up and into the air. They would be waiting for him, getting there much faster than he could driving the road out to where the werecats lived in a cluster of buildings outside the edge of town. He could fly as well, but he needed the special weapons he kept stashed in the back of the heavy-duty vehicle. If his mother had reinforcements with her, he'd use the things he'd collected…in case of emergency.

His mother. God, he'd thought they'd come to an understanding. Had she really betrayed him? Come to take his daughter? But the lure of a new demon was strong. He had been afraid it would be too much to hope that Daniela's curse would stay hidden. And it *was* a curse. He unlocked the car and jerked open the door.

"Rafael, what are you going to do?" Tomas was on his heels.

"Handle it. Please stay here. Ed can't run this club alone in this situation. He's needed at the door. Lesser demons may try something as a distraction. This is my livelihood. I need…" He couldn't think, aware of the vampire who hadn't flown with the others but who had slipped into the front passenger seat. His best friend. Who wasn't crazy about shifting. He was glad for her support as Tomas, suddenly sober, nodded and headed back to the club without another word.

Rafe clipped on his seatbelt. "Thanks for staying."

"I didn't want you to be alone right now." Glory St. Clair held onto the handle set in the truck ceiling as Rafe took off, taking a corner too quickly and bouncing a back tire off the curb.

He negotiated through traffic to get out of the

congested downtown area and onto the freeway that took them toward the hills and what he called "Cat Country." He'd resisted moving there, convincing Lacy that they needed to be closer to the club and her job as manager of Glory's shop, both on Sixth Street. But the children loved their cat grandmother and Sheila was happy to keep them and teach them cat ways whenever she could. His boys and Daniela had plenty of cousins to play with there too. The children looked forward to staying with the werecat family and had spent the weekend there.

"I heard what Lacy said. Everyone on the balcony did. Your mother is a strong demon, one of the worst. Last I knew, she was in Lucifer's favor. Would she really sacrifice one of her grandchildren for him?" Her big blue eyes were shiny with tears. She loved his kids, he knew that. They had filled a hole for her. She cuddled and played with them as if they were her own whenever she got a chance.

"I don't know and it kills me to say that. She once claimed to love me but had a strange way of showing it when I was growing up, dumping me on my grandparents and taking off with my father. But then neglecting me was a blessing. I sure didn't want to become her demon protégé, following her into Hell. If she really does love me, she needs to prove it and leave my child alone."

"It seems to me she would have come after *you* years ago if she wanted to please Lucifer. Why wait to take one of your children?" Glory wasn't going to let this go.

Rafe didn't talk about this. He kept his demon half hidden as much as possible but Glory knew all about it. She'd seen him use his powers to protect her when nothing else could. He guessed he owed her the truth. They had a long and close history.

"The last time I saw her she told me she'd made a deal with the devil, Lucifer. Not sure I believe her but here's the story: She's powerful enough that she can come and go in Hell as she wants. Unfortunately, he craves her presence at his side. Even the Devil has his favorites. So, when she had me, a surprise outcome of her affair with my father, she was over a barrel. She couldn't bear the thought of her own child being raised in what she tells me is a palace of torment and pain." He glanced at Glory. She was fascinated. Sure, why not? Easy for anyone not actually thinking they might have to go down there to try to work this out.

"What did she have to give him? Lucifer. To keep you safe?" She reached over to touch his arm, stiff on the steering wheel.

"She has to spend six months of the year by his side in exchange for my freedom. She's done that for a thousand years." Saying that out loud knotted Rafe's stomach. If he believed her, Lilith had made a sacrifice for him, a big one. She'd left him alone, too. Until now.

"Wow. If that's true, she made quite a sacrifice. Give her credit for that, Rafe."

"She never should have had a child!" He slammed his fist on the wheel. "God!" Pain pierced his forehead, what always happened when he thought the "G" word. Yeah, demons weren't godly and suffered when they called on Him. Too bad his shifter half couldn't stop trying.

Rafe saw his freeway exit and took it with a squeal of tires. "I have to fight the evil side of my nature constantly. And now my little girl…" He couldn't bear the thought. "What is Lilith going to do with her? I won't have it. She's not taking my baby anywhere." He'd turn himself in first. Become Lucifer's plaything. He gripped the wheel so tightly he heard the plastic crack.

"No! There's got to be a better way!" Glory put her hand to her mouth. "You can't think you're going down to Hell. I won't let you."

"Quit reading my fucking mind, vampire." He let up on the gas. Getting a ticket for speeding on this country road was the last thing he needed, particularly with the odd weapons he had tucked in the back. "I have to do something. You see Daniela all the time. Haven't you noticed she's different from my boys? The older she gets, the more obvious it is."

Glory bit her bottom lip. His vampire friend, of course, never changed, never aged. She was the same curvy blonde he'd met years ago. Centuries old, she'd had to move and update her look every decade or so. Owning a vintage clothing shop meant she had to dress right and she made the most of a never-ending supply of the clothes she loved. Now she brushed back her long blond hair and sighed.

"Of course, I've noticed. Your boys are all boy,

playing with cars, throwing balls around. *Macho*. Pretty Daniela loves to dress up and lets me play doing her hair. All girl. But, if something doesn't go her way, her eyes start to glow red like I've seen yours do when we've been in tight spots. How could I not see that?" Glory shook her head. "Demon blood. Not in the boys though. you should be glad of that."

"Yes, I am. As werecats they won't begin showing evidence of their powers and ability to shape-shift until puberty, years away. But little demons like Daniela? They can make mischief from birth." Rafe stopped at a red light, drumming his fingers on the steering wheel. "Dani's been getting into trouble lately, impatient with her friends. I was the same. My cousins mocked me, then feared me once they realized I could hurt them if I lost control. Dani…" Rafe cleared his throat. "I've been soft on her. Loved her too much. But not everyone loves her when she sets small fires in inconvenient places or exchanges salt for sugar in the kitchen. Usually her tricks are fairly harmless, but when she gets angry?" He glanced at Glory. "You know what demons can do, even pint-sized six-year-olds."

"Then you'll have to teach her how to rein in those powers enough to be accepted, Rafe. It was something no one bothered to do for you." The light had turned green. Glory leaned forward. "I see a hawk I recognize. That's Jerry circling overhead. Pull over and let him change and ride with us the last few miles. He can tell us what he saw at the cat compound."

Rafe pulled into a driveway where the house was dark. Soon a bird became a man and the back door of the SUV opened.

"Thanks. I figured you'd want to know what you're driving into, Rafe." Jeremy Blade leaned forward and grabbed his wife's hand. "This is going to be an interesting night, my love. Whether you like it or not, you're probably going to have to shift."

"I will. Tell us what's happening up ahead." She glanced at Rafe.

He pulled back out into the highway. "Please. Thanks for backing me up, Jerry. You didn't have to—"

"Sure, I did. You were my wife's bodyguard for years. I owe you for that and we're friends now. I stand by my friends." Jerry settled in his seat. "What you have in front of you are a couple of high-level demons at the gate. There was obviously a fight before we got here. We smelled and saw smoke as we flew in." He pointed. "See? As you know, shooting fire is one of their tricks. But they aren't crazy about water. The cats don't like it either, but they had water cannons. One house burned down but the werecats kept the damage to a minimum."

"Well, shit." Rafe pulled over to the side of the road. He rolled down the window so he could smell the smoke. Could smell the demons, too. The vampires were across the road, still birds and sitting on a fence, waiting for orders, a plan. He wished he had one.

"What about the cat family?" He opened the

car door and walked to the back. He had a duffle
bag with some of his special tools inside. His
scalp crawled as he picked it up and unzipped it.
Ignore it. Easier said than done. His demon half
didn't like touching his anti-demon weapons one
damned bit.

"As your wife said, someone finally got to the
cats and the ones still outside can't move. As far as
I know, only high level demons can do that trick,
freeze people in place, like vampires can." Jerry
shook his head. "We need those special goggles,
the ones that keep you from letting the demon
stare get to you."

"Got anything like that in your bag of tricks,
Rafe?" Glory was out of the car and looking over
his shoulder.

"Yes, I do." He handed Jerry and Glory each a
pair of the special glasses. The tinted lenses had
been invented by one of their enemies. Once
they'd rid themselves of him, they'd talked one of
their vamp friends who was a genius at making
things into manufacturing the lenses. "I wish I
had more." He passed over two more pair. "Pick
out the two vamps you think you want to go in
with us."

"What about some for yourself?" Jerry stopped
before he crossed the street.

"I can do my demon red-eye thing. Useful
enough that I don't want to block it. I stuck those
glasses in here for any backup I might manage to
round up." Rafe found a smile. "I am one lucky
bastard to have powerful friends."

Jerry clamped a hand on his shoulder. "You've

earned my loyalty. Saved my wife on many occasions. No problem here." He took off.

"What else is in there? Anything new you discovered that can hurt a demon? Or kill him?" Glory picked up a Bible. "I know this gives you the creeps."

"Yes, that's why I'm putting on thick leather gloves." Rafe slipped them on. "Also, there's wisteria oil. I've discovered it's like poison to our kind. It made me sick just to buy it. I've loaded a squirt gun with it. A good shot should incapacitate any demon who crosses my path." He picked up the plastic machine gun that was essentially a toy. He'd had to keep this out of sight from his children for sure.

"Would you use that on your mother?" Glory was close again, still holding that Bible.

He backed away. He hated that the book did that to him but he could feel its power making his skin crawl. He bore his mother's evil blood. It would always be part of him. He had proved over the thousand years he'd been alive that his good side could prevail, that he was a good man. So why did this urge to take that black book from his friend and rip it into shreds have him shaking?

You are a demon. You should forget that weak shifter half of yourself and come serve me. The scritch scratch of a voice in his head made him freeze. He gripped the toy gun and fought the need to fly straight up in the air, screaming.

"No! I will never serve you!" He shouted it, startling Glory into dropping the Bible into the dirt on the side of the road.

"Rafe, who are you talking to?" She grabbed his shirt.

"Lucifer's inside my head." Rafe threw the gun back into the duffle and covered his eyes. "I can't listen. He wants me there. In Hell."

"Ignore him. We have to go inside. Save Daniela." Glory pulled his hands from his face. "Come on, I'm with you."

Leave the child and come see me. We can negotiate for your girl's safety. That voice again.

Rafe stared at Glory. "He wants to see me. He might leave Dani alone."

Glory shook him. "Do you believe him? Demons lie, Rafe! I'm sure the Devil does. And what about your mother? She's obviously here for a reason. You need to find out what she wants."

I will handle Lilith. She serves me and must do as I say.

Rafe stared at the ground beneath his feet. "Hah! You just went too far, Lucifer. My mother doing what any man says? I don't believe you. Not even the Devil himself can make my mother obey him." Rafe straightened his shoulders and picked up the toy gun again.

"So what's the plan, Rafe?" Glory grabbed the Bible and dusted it off on her skirt, a short thing that hugged her curves.

"Haven't got a clue. We hit the gates with the Bible, and my squirt gun then go from there. Once the demons are down, we'll see what Lilith has to say. I just hope Lacy forgives me for this."

"Lacy loves you." Glory was biting her lip again. "Let's concentrate on one thing at a time."

Rafe knew bad news when he heard it. If Glory had been the one married to him and her child had been threatened because of his bad blood… Well, forgiveness wouldn't be on her agenda.

He rounded up his vampire army. Once they were all in mortal form, he issued orders, amazed when they actually followed them. Florence was cursing in vivid Italian and her husband had produced his own pocket Bible to add to the misery of the demons. Rafe's head pounded while Lucifer kept up a nonstop stream of cursing as Rafe "*attacked his own kind.*" Too bad. Rafe would do anything to protect his family. Anything.

CHAPTER THREE

RAFE STOPPED IN his tracks when yet another bird, a huge black vulture, flew overhead and landed next to him. The vulture morphed into a man in a blur.

"Cisneros!" Rafe was glad for yet another vampire on hand. But then he got closer. Pain hit him, hard. "What the hell are you carrying?"

The vampire threw open his black jacket to reveal a bandolier. Instead of bullets, it was loaded with glass tubes.

"Holy water, blessed by the Pope himself. Or so I've been told. At least it doesn't stink. What's in your gun? I can smell that shit from here." Cisneros frowned at Rafe's toy gun which looked like an AK47, but was plastic. "Is that supposed to stop them?"

"Your holy water is the real deal. It's already making my head pound. Hit me with it and it'll put a hole in me. Too bad it's so hard to come by." Rafe said it quietly. "This in my gun is wisteria water. I'm handling it carefully. Yeah, I think a blast in the face should put even a full-blooded demon down, at least for a while."

Cisneros nodded. "All right then. You take the one on the right, I'll take the left."

"Don't let the high level ones stare into your eyes. Even I can be frozen if they catch my gaze." Rafe nodded. The two demons guarding the entrance to the cat compound grinned, as if to say "Bring it." They didn't have a clue.

Rafe aimed his gun at the tall demon who sprouted horns when he realized he was being rushed. The demon's eyes blazed red and he leaped into the air, reaching for Rafe with his claws.

"Prepare to die!" The demon screamed.

Rafe aimed and fired, his stream of that sweet wisteria hitting the demon in his open mouth.

What had once been a seven-foot-tall giant slumped into a quivering lizard that curled around its own tail. It choked and twitched, burying its mouth in the dirt and trying desperately to eat then spit, as if to rid itself of the taste and effects of that almost deadly-to-demons poison.

Cisneros threw a vial, splashing his demon with the holy water. Everywhere the water landed, it burned holes in the leathery skin that covered what had been a freakishly tall cyclops. One-Eye screamed as he sizzled, batting at the places where the blessed water scorched his skin and blazed a path up his arms and across his narrow chest.

"Out of our way!" Rafe commanded. He was ready to shoot but he didn't have to use his gun. The creature took off running into the woods and away from the compound.

"So much for the guards at the gate. But what

about them?" Jerry, Glory's husband, wore the tinted glasses and was armed with a broad sword. It would be great for decapitating demons if they faced more inside. But he gestured toward the dozens of werecats who had been frozen where they stood, an army that had been stopped in its tracks. Apparently, they'd tried to make a stand against the demons, but had been unprepared for the special powers their enemy had used.

Flo strutted forward. "Leave them like that." She flicked the leader's chest with a long red fingernail. "This one is thinking he doesn't need a bunch of blood suckers here." She stared into his eyes. "But look at you! Didn't do so great without us, did you?"

"Quit taunting them, darling." Her husband, Richard Mainwaring, pulled her back to his side. "It's a demon spell. I doubt we can break it even if we try."

"I might be able to. Let me see what I can do." Glory moved forward and took off her special glasses. A vampire with Olympus ties, Glory had powers the other vamps didn't.

"We're here to help you," she told the first werecat, who stood in front of the rest.

"Wait. That's Ajax. He'll come out swinging." Rafe stepped in front of the man he knew to be a strong leader of the cat clan. "I know you can hear me, Ajax. She's telling the truth. We're here to help. These are my friends." He put a hand on the werecat's shoulder. "We need them." He nodded. "Go ahead, Glory. Give it a shot."

"I have to touch him." She gestured for Rafe

to move aside then laid her hand on the cat's chest, murmuring words in a strange language. The man came alive, raising his staff as if to swing it. Before he could hit her, Glory froze him again with a look. "Stop! You heard him. We're on your side. You know Rafe is married to one of your own. You want to stay like that, unable to move? Or be reasonable." She stared into his eyes, surely reading his mind. After a long moment, she tried releasing him again.

"Reasonable? Look what you've done, you demon bastard!" The man spit in the dirt at Rafe's feet. "Sheila's daughter may be fool enough to mate with you but that doesn't mean we have to accept you. The very air we breathe is foul with your kind." He snarled and turned into his cat form, a fierce and very large tiger.

"Ajax, you're right. I'm sorry. Lacy called me and I came as soon as I knew what was happening. We will do what we can to rid you of the demon presence." Rafe knew the cat had a right to be angry. But he didn't have time to soothe the man's damaged ego. Ajax was pawing the ground, obviously thinking about leaping for his throat.

Rafe let his eyes glow a warning. "Save it for the enemy. Glory can release all of your people from the demon's spell or not. Right now, I need to see about my family." Rafe looked over the cat crew, ready to push past them.

"Make your choice. Gloriana and I can both take off the demon curse." Cisneros stepped forward. He and Glory had discovered they both had Olympus ties, his from a Mayan background.

"But I warn you all now. We will put you back to statues if you interfere with Rafael and his mission here. Understand?" He gave Ajax a look so hard that even Rafe shivered as a cold wind seemed to blow through the camp. That damned icy thing again.

The cat leader turned back into his mortal form in a moment. "Fine, whatever. But there were a half-dozen demons here. Have you taken all of them out?" Ajax eyed Glory when she began to thaw some of the women behind him, murmuring warnings to them to stay calm and wait for orders. From Rafe. "You don't run this community, Valdez. I do."

Cisneros touched another werecat and said some words in a foreign tongue, not Spanish. He stopped and raised an eyebrow, waiting for orders from Rafe. It was clear he wanted to freeze this arrogant werecat again.

Rafe was tempted but knew he needed the asshole's cooperation. "You can have your crew to command. Six demons? We got the two at the gate. Any idea where the rest of them are now?" Too bad he knew where at least one was. His mother-in-law's house was across the clearing and he knew his wife was there, with his children. He could smell them and Lacy's fear. Along with a demon. Maybe more than one. Damn it, he was wasting time here.

Ajax glanced around the compound. "Sheila and Lacy took your children to Sheila's house. One demon is with them. I don't know if the others are in there or if they left." He inhaled and bent over, coughing. "God, I can't stand the stench of them."

Rafe waved him away and walked toward the house, trying not to panic. He recognized the strongest demonic smell. Lilith. His mother. He gripped his gun. So far, he'd faced minor demons. A strong major demon like his mother would find the wisteria painful but it wouldn't stop her or even slow her down. He could take a vial of Cisneros' holy water but confronting Lilith with something so painful would only make her mad. What would be the consequences of that for his family? He had to handle this carefully.

"Don't worry, Rafe. We'll find the other demons." Florence and Richard started searching houses. He heard Flo exclaim when she came upon the large building that housed the central meeting rooms. "Has no one here read a design magazine? Beige, brown and black. Boring!"

"Darling, we are not here to critique their decorating choices. We are looking for demons, remember?" Richard stayed close to his beloved's side, his Bible in his hand. Rafe noticed that he held a bottle as well. More holy water. Trust Richard, a former priest, to have come prepared.

Rafe forgot about them as he stepped onto Sheila's wide porch. He didn't need to take a deep breath to realize there was more than one demon inside. He turned at the sound of a scuffle behind him.

Glory threw herself in front of a werecat Rafe knew to be a hothead. As soon as she released him, Frank started shifting into his cat, snarling and showing his fangs. He had black fur and yellow eyes. Too bad for him that Glory slapped a palm over his face and caught his gaze, freezing him in mid-change—half man, half cat.

"By God, cat, you'll treat my wife with respect and be grateful or I'll take your head and mount it on the wall in my man cave!" Jerry brandished a knife, something he always carried hidden on his person.

"Jeremiah, please. These cats are upset. My powers scare people. You should remember that." Glory turned to study the man who had the face and shoulders of a cat and the lower body of a mortal. He'd come out swinging his claws when she'd released his paralysis. "Frank, I will leave you standing there like that if you don't calm down." She stared into the cat's eyes.

Rafe knew Frank would be a handsome black panther once he was fully cat. "She will, man. She's not playing."

"You think my husband won't hesitate to lop off your head?" She slid her arm around Jerry's waist. "He's an ancient warrior and he hasn't had a chance to spill blood in a long time. Remember, he's a vampire. We're not crazy about the taste of werecat blood, but it's been a while since we've had fresh from the source." She sniffed and moved in closer to Frank, showing off her fangs. "Seems like you might be pretty tasty, kitty boy. Go ahead, make his night."

Rafe swallowed a laugh. By all that was holy, Glory had Frank's number. Like most cats, he figured vampires were all secretly dying to drink exotic cat blood. He was more than a little scared at the thought of fangs in his neck. If the man hadn't been frozen, he'd be shaking right now.

Jerry was right beside Glory and kissed her cheek. "I have decided his face is too ugly to decorate our walls, my love. Frank, is it? You can stay the hell frozen for all I care. Your choice. She's reading your mind, you mangy feline. Have you calmed down now? We are here to help our friend Rafe. To fight demons. Not cats. But we'll fight you if you force us to. What's it to be?" He looked the man up and down.

Rafe knew Frank to be a hell of a fighter. When the cats did organized training for the young kits, he was the one who wanted to win, every time, and usually did. But now Rafe saw the fight go out of the man. Vampires against werecats? Not unless the cats suddenly brought out wooden stakes.

"He's ready to be sensible." Glory released Frank.

"Find those damned demons. We'll fight Hell together." Frank changed back to a fully formed man with lightning speed and produced a wicked knife from his boot. "I have no quarrel with you, vampire."

Rafe realized he'd been stalling, watching that go down. His children were inside. His wife. He didn't knock, just threw open the door. What he saw made him rush across the room and kneel next to his wife.

Lacy held their two boys in her lap. It wasn't easy because, at six, Lucas and Gabriel were getting too big to both fit there. They were squirming. Neither of them ever wanted to sit still.

"Daddy!" They jumped up, straight at him. "We're playing a game. Look at Grandma."

Rafe staggered under their weight, very aware that Lacy had been stiff when he'd touched her. Now she glared at him.

"Yes, look at Grandma. I wonder how long she can stay like that. What do you think, Rafael?" Lacy's words were clipped, her face flushed. No game this. Her mother, Sheila, stood near the door and was as frozen as the rest of the werecats. She could move her eyes, but that was all.

Rafe gently set the boys on their feet. "*Mis hijos*, I don't think your grandmother likes this game very much. Let me see if I can end it." He walked over to Sheila and grabbed her shoulders, looking into her eyes. He hoped his demon side was strong enough to lift the spell his mother had obviously put on her. To his relief he felt Sheila sag in his arms.

"Mom!" Lacy ran over to her mother. "Are you all right?"

"What do you think?" Sheila grabbed the boys then looked at Rafe. "Fix this," she hissed, her fingers becoming claws as she obviously struggled not to shift to cat in front of the boys. "I'm taking these two out of here." She looked out the open door. "Is it safe?"

"It should be. I brought reinforcements. Glory is out there, with Flo and their husbands. They will make sure you are protected." Rafe kissed each boy on top of his head. "Lacy, will you go with them?"

"Not without Daniela. Boys, go with Grandma." She glared at Rafe. "What have we done, husband?"

"We? Don't you mean me?" Rafe urged the children and Sheila out the door. He didn't want them to hear this.

"No." Lacy bit her lip. "I let it happen too. I could have prevented the pregnancy in the first place. I told you that. But I didn't." Her face crumpled. "I wanted your children. I didn't think . . ." She wiped her damp cheeks with her palms. "Lilith's not interested in the boys, thank God, but Dani! My God, your mother says she is going to take our baby girl."

Rafe swallowed, sick as he held his trembling wife. "Where are they? They can't have gone far. I can smell my mother and others."

"She and the two freaks with her are in Dani's room, packing. You should see the other two, Rafe! Horrible demons. And Dani didn't blink. She was excited to meet her other grandmother and her 'friends.'" Lacy clutched Rafe, sobbing. "We can't let Lilith take our child, Rafe. I don't care what Daniela is becoming. We will handle it. *You* will handle it." She leaned against his chest.

"I'm going to try." Rafe stroked her back. "I'm so sorry. You aren't the only one who knows how to prevent pregnancy. As soon as this is over, I'm having a vasectomy. We can't take a chance this will happen again."

She shoved him away. "Really? You bring that

up now?" She grabbed a tissue and blew her nose.
"Go talk to that woman who gave birth to you.
I refuse to call her your mother. A mother would
not torture her child this way and threaten to
take away her grandchild. Talk to her and make
her see this is wrong."

"Of course, I'll talk to her. If I have to, I'll talk
to Lucifer himself. Whatever it takes." Rafe kissed
her gently. "Go outside and stay with your mother
and the boys. I'll feel better knowing you're as far
away from the demons as you can be."

"I, I love you, Rafe. I don't care what you are.
I hope you know that." She threw herself into
his arms again and kissed him deeply, desperately.
"And I have faith in you. You can work this out.
But don't—" She squeezed his waist then turned
away. "Don't sacrifice yourself for us."

"Not even for Daniela?" He had to say it.
Because at this point, he saw no other way out of
this hell of his mother's making.

Lacy had no words. She ran out of the house,

"Well, that should prove to you what's most
important to that cat you married, my son." Lilith
stood in the doorway to the bedroom wing. "Too
bad."

"Leave my family alone. Where's my daughter?"

"She's fine. Picking out things to take with her
on our little trip." Lilith smiled and held up a
hand when Rafe started to argue. "No, sit. We
need to talk."

Against his will, Rafe fell onto the couch, his
legs suddenly wobbly. He had to make her see
reason and change her mind. He tossed aside the

gun he still held, the reek of wisteria making his head ache. Lilith paced the floor in front of him, finally stopping to gaze down at him. He returned the inspection. He hadn't seen his mother in years but she hadn't changed. Demons were like vampires, never aging and changing only if they chose to change. She could morph into any form she wished. Apparently, she liked the blonde bombshell look or maybe Lucifer liked her that way when she was in human form. Whatever, Rafe wanted his daughter and he wanted her now. Enough of this silence.

"I'm sick of this. I need to see my daughter." He started to get up but Lily pinned him with a look. Shit. He couldn't move.

"Daniela? Such a pretty child. She looks just like her mother. Red hair, green eyes. She will break hearts someday. Of course you were ruled by lust when you married the cat. No surprise there. You made beautiful babies. The boys are very handsome but worthless as far as the blood is concerned. Cats." She waved a dismissive hand.

"I thank God every day that they were spared your hellish blood." Rafe was glad she allowed him to talk.

Lily winced. "Would you not use that name in my presence?"

"God?" Rafe was glad he could at least get her to feel something, though uttering that word stabbed his forehead. "You know I try to be a good man, Lilith. That's why I am determined to keep my daughter out of your clutches."

"Lucifer watches you. This determination to be

a so-called good man enrages him. It is not wise. I blame your grandparents, Emiliano's family. Pious and yet not so good after all. You learned that for yourself, didn't you?" Lily strolled over to a patterned chair and settled into it, crossing her long legs. Her leather miniskirt rose to mid-thigh.

"Your grandfather was a womanizer, a fool for women just like you have been over this werecat." She shook her head. "Your many cousins and brothers never appreciated your special powers either. Fools, all of them."

"You left me there! Clearly you didn't give a damn how I was treated!" Rafe wanted to jump to his feet. Damn, damn, damn. He couldn't move below the neck.

"Would you rather have grown up in Hell's nursery?" She leaned back and studied her manicure. "Daniela is very pretty. The boys will be after her soon."

"The child is six years old. You disgust me. Look at you! Dressing like a hooker. Nothing is too dirty for you to think or try. Is that why you're here? To pimp my daughter out to some pedophile?" Rafe felt his gorge rise. Lucifer's minions would love that. And yet, if Daniela was one of theirs, would they use her? Or train her to use mortals.

"My, your mind does go right to the depths, doesn't it, my child?" Lilith looked amused.

"Don't call me your child! Not when you forgot me for centuries." Rafe was beside himself. Unable to think, plan. The woman who suddenly decided to claim him just watched as if he entertained her. He concentrated and finally was able to break the hold she had on him. Before she could say or do anything he was in front of her, grabbing her shoulders and lifting her from the chair.

"Give me my daughter and get the hell out of here. You will not take her." He shook her until her hair flew around her perfect face. Her head wobbled on her long neck and one of her high heels flew off.

"Stop that. You want Lucifer to notice us?" She whispered that, her mouth brushing his ear. "He loves a good fight. I've already done too much just getting into this place. Then you show up with a herd of vampires!" She managed to get in a good blow to his shin with the pointed toe of her surviving shoe. "I have a plan. Put me down and I'll tell you about it."

"A plan. If it involves taking my daughter, you can forget it." He dropped her, satisfied when she sprawled inelegantly in the chair, a pained look on her face when her hip hit the wooden arm.

"Just listen, Rafael." She brushed at her hair and stared at her missing shoe until it flew across the room and into her hand.

"What are you here for?" Rafe squatted in front of Lilith. If they had to speak quietly, he'd suffer the reek of her strong demon scent and expensive perfume.

"I told you. Daniela. She's in her bedroom, picking out her favorite things to pack. I have two of my most trusted minions with her." She grabbed his hands, holding so tight he felt her nails dig into his flesh. "Rafael! She is wonderful. Even at this young age, her powers! I am thrilled with this child."

"Thrilled. As if I care about that." Rafe jerked away from her. "I must see her for myself." He got up and walked to the bedroom fitted with the bunks and a twin bed where his daughter and sons slept when they visited Sheila. Sure enough, Dani was picking through her dresser, pulling out pajamas and tights.

"Sweetheart."

"Daddy!" She jumped into his arms, no easy feat when they were six feet apart.

Powers. Yes, she had them. His heart sank even as he held her and kissed the top of her head. She did look like her mother with her pretty dark red hair and bright green eyes.

"Did you see that my other grandma is here? She said I can call her Lollie. Isn't that pretty?" Daniela let him go and ran back to her closet. "She's taking me on a trip. Just me. A girl's getaway. The boys are mad about it. They want to go too."

"I'm not sure that's a good idea." Rafe saw her stuff her pink tutu in the rolling suitcase she used for sleepovers with her cousins.

Dani's eyes filled with tears. "But I'll be special, Daddy. Lollie said so. The boys play baseball and soccer. I don't like that stuff. Lollie said we can go see dancers and maybe to a Disney theme park." Dani's eyes flashed red and the suitcase rolled across the room. "Lollie isn't scared when I do one of my tricks like Grandma is. She clapped and told me I was wonderful."

"Yes, Lollie would like your tricks. But we talked about this. Those tricks are powers and your special secret. You are supposed to save them for when you are just with our own little family, remember?" Rafe stroked her hair back from her forehead. She had a pair of purple bows on her braids and naturally they matched her jumper and tennis shoes. The outfit had been a gift from her Auntie Flo. They shared a love of fashion. Dani had inspired a child's section in Glory's clothing shop too. All of his friends loved her and spoiled her. What would happen to this precious child if Lilith got hold of her? No, he couldn't let that happen.

"I only did one trick for Lollie." Dani giggled and pointed. "Oh, there you are. Buster and Bessie hid when you walked in. Aren't they funny, Daddy? Lucas and Gabriel were scared of them."

Rafe turned and saw what passed for a man and woman walk out of the attached bathroom. "Scared? Not surprising. Lollie brought some unusual friends to see you. But you weren't scared?"

"No. They are sworn to protect me. Lollie told me so. I don't care what they look like." She walked over and patted each of them on their leathery arms. "I like lizards and Buster kind of looks like one, don't you think? Bessie is cool too. She can fly. Like a dragon. See her wings? She said she'd take me for a ride later. We'll go up, up into the clouds." Dani beamed, clearly excited at the idea.

Rafe's stomach dropped. Oh, Dani would be safe enough. A dragon like Bessie would see to that. The child was enchanted, who wouldn't be? She'd always loved stories with heroes who rode in to save the day on fantastical creatures. His boys rarely sat still long enough to listen to a book, more interested in racing cars or building with their blocks.

The enchantment went both ways. The demons, who would give most people nightmares, couldn't take their eyes off his daughter. Oh, boy. Whatever Lilith had planned, she'd hit all the right buttons with his pretty Daniela. His daughter was all in on this demon thing and would throw one of her increasingly terrifying temper fits if he tried to keep her here. He realized he was squeezing her hand too hard and eased up.

"You are going to let me go, aren't you, Daddy?" Dani frowned and tugged on his hand. "Please? It'll be okay." She gestured at the twin horrors standing next to her bed. "Buster and Bessie are mine to command, Lollie said so. I'll be perfectly safe. They are my special bodyguards." Her eyes glowed red and Rafe felt the heat, but she was smiling. "No one here likes me anyway." She put her arms around his hips. "They say mean things."

"Oh, Dani." Rafe leaned down to hug her. "I'm sorry. People like you. Auntie Glory and Auntie Flo love you. So do Mommy and I, you know that."

"The cousins call me a weirdo." She stuck out her lower lip. "I *am* a weirdo. I can move stuff around, make fire." She looked over at her suitcase and sent it spinning. "I think it's fun but it scares those stupid cousins."

"Pack. I'm not saying you're going with Lollie, but you have to go somewhere, even if I take you myself. I know where the Disney parks are. You don't need Lollie to go there." He saw her face light up and he turned to give the two demons a warning look. "Guard her with your life? Does that mean against the big guy downstairs?" He didn't want to say Lucifer's name in front of his baby.

"Uh, that depends on what Lilith says to do." Bessie seemed to be the spokeswoman. "I can't imagine…" She glanced at her cohort.

"All we know is the kid is not to be hurt. Not even by you. And you can't take her away. Not unless we go with her." Buster's voice was a high-pitched trill that was strange coming out of his large lizard body. It almost made Rafe smile. Buster's tail twitched but his glare meant business. "Don't test us."

"Good God!" Rafe did smile when he saw both demons cover their ears with pained expressions at the "G" word. "Put in practical clothes, Dani, no tutu. Summer play clothes. Shorts and t-shirts. Now I need to talk to Lollie." Rafe felt like his head was going to explode. The demon energy in the room was almost overwhelming. It wasn't helped by the amount coming from his tiny daughter.

God. Another sharp pain hit his temple and even Dani frowned and rubbed a spot between her eyes. Merely thinking that word always hurt, but he was determined to say and think it over and over again. He was a good man, damn it. And he was going to make sure his daughter grew up in a world that taught her right was might.

Wait, was he even making sense now? Suddenly he wasn't sure what to think, say or do. Lilith was in his head. He had to sit down and find out exactly what his mother was planning. Because if she thought she was going to take his daughter and teach her how to be an evil demon... Well, that couldn't happen. She'd have to go through him first.

CHAPTER FOUR

"SHE'S PACKING BUT I need to hear what you have planned before I can consider letting her go with you." Rafe sat across from his mother. He didn't like her smile, as if she'd won something. "Can you truly protect her from You Know Who? Or is this a ploy and you're thinking to take my child straight to Hell?" Her power filled the room and made it hard for him to breathe. Suddenly afraid he wouldn't be able to stop her if she did take Dani down, he could almost taste his terror. If Lilith made up her mind to act, could even the Devil himself stand in her way?

"Calm yourself, Rafael." Lily moved to the sofa and patted the seat next to her. "Come closer. Someone is very interested in what we say. I can cloak our conversation in a small space, but not across the room. I would never take your treasure down there." She brushed back her hair and let him see a bit of the ravages of time on her face—a wrinkle between her brows, frown lines on either side of her lush lips. She had suffered. For him? He didn't believe it.

Rafe sat. What else could he do? Fight every demon Lucifer sent alone? He didn't doubt the promise of a big reward would bring them out of the woodwork. He'd already seen it happening. But trust Lilith? He had no reason to begin now, after centuries of neglect. A real mother would have… Oh, what did he know of such things?

"Rafael, I'm sorry." She touched his arm. "You sneer. I'm not surprised. Why should you believe me now? All I can say is that I did what I had to do to keep you safe. Yes, I was selfish. You're right. I read your thoughts earlier. I never should have had a child with your father. It was a mistake." She gazed at his face. "You look very like him, you know. So handsome and so all male. Women want you. I have seen it. But your grandparents made sure you did not grow up with the weaknesses that turned Emiliano into the perfect charming companion for a sinner like me. Then there is your insistence on always doing what is right." She wrinkled her nose in distaste. "You keep your demon side hidden."

"I'm sure that maddens you and shames you in front of Lucifer, having a son who hates his demon blood." Rafe shrugged off her touch. It was bad enough that he had to breathe the stench of her evil, but no matter how much he might need her help with Dani, he would not pretend any affection for her. "Get to the point. What are you planning? How can you possibly keep my daughter safe from the Devil? He usually gets what he wants."

"I know that. I have my ways—power of my

own and legions of loyal followers. But, Rafael, you will have to fight off Lucifer's minions when they come here looking for her. The prize he offered is great enough to tempt even some of his high-level cronies."

"I will. My vampire friends helped tonight. The werecats…" He knew they weren't in his corner, even though Daniela carried their blood as well. Even a drop of demon blood spoiled her in their eyes. They avoided her when they could and taught their children to shun her. It pained him to see it. His clever child had certainly noticed. *Weird*. They would call her much worse as she grew older and her beauty tempted their sons.

"Your vampires are useless during the daylight hours. It seems the summer solstice has past mere days ago. That leaves the blood suckers with a very short time to help you each night." Lily studied her nails while he cursed the reality of that.

"Of course." He glanced at the clock he could see on the microwave in Sheila's kitchen. There were only a couple of hours before Glory and her friends would have to take off and settle into their darkened bedrooms before sunrise. Damn it.

"It is a real possibility that your wife and the boys could be taken hostage and used as leverage against you. Lucifer could try to get you to make an exchange, three for one." Lilith crossed her legs. "The werecats here must be persuaded to take the daytime protection detail. Unless you are tempted…?"

"Of course not!" Rafe leaped to his feet but was pulled back down by Lilith's hand on his arm again. That power. He felt it like a lightning bolt as he was thrust back onto the sofa.

"Then you must arrange protection. You cannot do it alone." Lilith let him go and he rubbed his arm.

Trade Lacy? His boys? Rafe was sickened at the thought. He was dealing with monsters and he couldn't forget that. Anyone willing to use children as pawns in their power plays would have no limits when it came to double dealing. He tried to think.

"Sheila is a big influence in the cat clan. She can be very persuasive. Lacy is her daughter, the boys and Dani, her grandchildren. She will beg the cats to help." He glared at his mother. Why was Lucifer acting now? Before he could ask the question, Lilith leaned forward.

"To get the cats' cooperation, a substantial bribe could make a difference." Lily waved her hand and a designer handbag appeared on the coffee table in front of them. "I have a key to a safety deposit box inside this bag. The box contains enough gold coins to persuade even the most reluctant cat to join forces with you to defend your family, my son." She slid out the key and handed it to him, naming a bank in downtown Austin. "You will see. I looked around. The cats may not be as greedy as demons, but this compound can use upgrades. The gold will ensure that your family and their cousins can live well for years to come."

Rafe gripped the key. For the first time he had hope. Did the cats know how to fight demons? He would have to arm them and show them how, but he could do it. There was still the question of his daughter. How in hell could he trust Lilith with Dani?

"You know Lucifer will never quit until he has Daniela if he truly wants her." Rafe leaned back on the sofa, suddenly exhausted. "*Can* you keep her safe?"

"For a while." Lilith bit her lip. "Let me have some time with her, Rafael. A little trip. Hold off the demons while I do this. Then I will have to go to Lucifer and make my own deal. No more trips here among mortals as I have been enjoying for millennia." She looked away. "You don't know it, but I have watched you grow, kept you safe while I've seen how you thrived."

"Thrived?" He shot to his feet. "Are you serious? And do you expect me to believe that you actually watched over me all these centuries? Like a doting mother?" He felt the heat as his eyes flared. "How exactly have you kept me safe, Lilith? Were you caring for me when I was tortured during the Inquisition? Wounded almost to death during more battles than I can count? How about the time I was hanged from a tree and left for dead or staked out on an ant hill by my captors?"

"You survived, did you not?" She didn't move, just stared at him. "All those trials made you the strong man you are today. I could have done more, I suppose, but that would have just convinced the priests that you were possessed and brought you even more pain. No, I saw you draw on all your powers to save yourself each and every time."

She shook her head then smiled. "You cannot imagine how proud I was of your strength."

"Proud? I'm sure watching me suffer also amused you." Rafe heard a sound and looked up to see Daniela in the doorway.

"You and Lollie are yelling. Are you mad?" She clutched her favorite doll, a Barbie that came with a suitcase of her own and a vintage sixties wardrobe her Aunt Glory had managed to find on eBay.

"Yelling but not mad, my love. Just discussing my trip with you. Your papa gets loud when he gets excited." Lollie, aka Lilith, gave Rafe a warning look then held out her arms. "Come here and show me your doll. She is so pretty."

"She has on her uniform. She works on an airplane." Dani gave Rafe a serious look, her own warning to be nice to this new grandmother as she began explaining that TWA was an old airline that no longer flew but had once been popular.

"Yes, Daniela, I am old enough to remember it." Lollie gave Dani a hug then looked at Rafe over her shoulder. "You are such a clever girl and only six years old!" She glanced at her minions, who hovered behind Dani. "Buster, I see you have the suitcase. Bessie, I'm sure Dani would like a snack before we go. Can you find her something in the refrigerator and take it out to the porch while we finish arrangements here?"

"Stay close, baby. Next to the glass doors, where I can see you." Rafe reached for his child and was rewarded with a hug.

Dani ran into the kitchen. "Peanut butter and

jelly sandwich, Bessie. The grape jelly, please. I'll show you where it is."

Rafe turned to Lilith. He scowled at her while his daughter told the dragon how to cut her sandwich into triangles. Why was Lucifer acting now? Before he could ask the question, Lilith leaned forward.

"She is wonderful. I had hoped to keep her a secret a while longer." She closed her eyes and rubbed her forehead.

"You couldn't stop this? Persuade Lucifer to keep his hands off my family?" He waited, wondering if she'd bother answering. Or, if she did, would she tell him the truth?

When she finally looked at him her eyes glowed red.

"I am being punished, Rafael. Taught a lesson." She glanced around Sheila's living room. "He'll destroy Dani to hurt me if he has to."

Rafe was shocked to see pink tears stream down her cheeks. "What did you do? I thought you were the Devil's favorite." He would not feel sorry for her, damn it, especially not when it had endangered his family. *Destroy* Dani? Hell, no!

"Look at this place. So ordinary." She swept her hand toward the leather recliner and another overstuffed chair, then to the jumble of toys in one corner where the boys usually built forts and raced cars. She wiped her cheeks and sniffed.

"Sheila isn't much of a decorator." Rafe didn't get her point and there was no reading her mind, that was for sure. "You can't be fancy with three young children in the house." He waited while

Lilith dragged a lace-trimmed handkerchief out of that leather handbag. She wiped her eyes and blew her nose. "What's that got to do with Lucifer and his problem with you?"

"The King of the Underworld enjoys finding each of our weaknesses and exploiting them." She pulled out a jeweled compact and pressed powder under her eyes, then dabbed some on her nose. "He delights in aiming his tortures where we are most vulnerable. It gives Lucifer great joy to watch us suffer."

"Hurting Dani will do that?" Rafe didn't believe her. Lilith claimed to care, but he'd never seen a sign of her so-called familial devotion.

She snapped the compact shut and glared at him. "You are such a hard sell, Rafael. Much smarter than your father. Not buying my maternal act, are you?"

"Not for a minute. What is it you're really afraid of losing, *Mother*?" He could not have put more scorn into the label if he'd tried.

"Smart ass." She stood and stalked around the room, her high heels stabbing holes into Sheila's new fake wood vinyl flooring. "Lucifer wants me down there with him full time and he thinks threatening you and Daniela will do it."

"What set him off? Why's he putting the hammer down on you now?" Rafe got up. He needed to check on Dani. It had gotten too quiet in the kitchen. When he stepped around the counter, he realized his headstrong daughter had ignored his order to stay close and had taken her demon bodyguards outside through the back door. The threesome clustered under the trees, the two guards watching Dani eat at the picnic table there.

Rafe wanted to yell at her to come closer, but he realized he needed more time alone with his mother. When his little girl stroked the dragon's tail, he could only shake his head. His daughter was fearless. Was he insane to be proud of that? He turned back to where Lilith still sat, looking around the shabby room.

"I've become addicted to comfort, Rafael. This world where you live? It's ridiculously easy here." She picked up a velvet throw pillow and squeezed it. "In Hell? Nothing is soft. There is no comfort, no ease except for the Devil of course. Everything is pain, torture and designed to make Lucifer delight in your suffering. Can you imagine?"

"Of course, I can. I've suffered plenty in the past." He wasn't going to feel sorry for her. She should just go down there and take her punishment.

"Hard, aren't you?" Her tears had dried and she seemed almost disappointed that he wasn't moved by her story.

"Life has made me that way, Lilith. You say you watched me. Then you know why I'm not exactly giving a damn what happens to you." Rafe could feel her trying to compel him with her eyes, using her powers to bring him under her sway. He looked away, walking over to the sliding glass doors to check on his daughter.

"Make no mistake, Rafael. Lucifer will want

Daniela now, no matter what happens to me. She's a prize."

"He can't have her. I will do anything to keep her out of there." Rafe pulled open the sliding glass door. "Dani?" Her empty plate sat on the picnic table but there was no sign of her or her bodyguards. He looked up in case she'd gone for a dragon ride.

"She's gone, Rafael." Lilith stood beside him. "She's safe, for now."

"What have you done?" He grabbed her arms and shook her. Electricity shot through him but he kept gripping her and taking the pain. "Where is my baby?"

"I did what I had to do." She threw off his hands. "My, you are strong. Most men would be unconscious by now from that jolt I just delivered."

"Shut the fuck up." Rafe looked around wildly. Betrayed. By his own mother. She-devil. Bitch. What could he do? He frowned at the picnic table and set it ablaze. Too damned bad. When the fire spread to the tree next to it, he cursed and stalked over to the nearby water hose, turning it on to quickly put out the flames. God damn it!

"Why?" He finally made himself look at her.

"You must help me. Lucifer wants to meet you. It is the price of my freedom. And what you must pay to get your daughter back safely." She was smart enough to step back when he raised a fist. "I wouldn't do that if I were you."

"I don't believe you." He wanted to kill her. Make her think that her visits to Hell were joy rides compared to what her son could do to her.

"Believe me or not, you'll never see your daughter again if you don't meet Lucifer as I ask." Her face became a mask of hard determination. "I know you don't care about me, my son. Do it for Daniela."

Rafe kicked the smoldering wood near his feet. He supposed he'd expected this. Face the Devil. What did Lucifer want? His soul?

He'd give anything to keep his family safe. But could he trust that any deal he made with the Devil would be kept? He turned to ask Lilith just that but she was gone.

CHAPTER FIVE

RAFE WANTED TO shift and go after his mother, tear into her until she told him where she'd taken his daughter. But he'd have to pick up her trail first. Smoke hung in the air along with the scent that was uniquely Lilith's. Then there was the reek of those demon guards. Mixed with it was the achingly familiar aroma of his sweet Daniela. It all had him clutching his head in frustration. Where to start? The door opening behind him made him remember that chasing Lilith wasn't his only concern. He turned to see his wife in the doorway.

"Where is our daughter?" Lacy seemed to know instantly by the despair on his face that he had lost their little girl. "Rafe? What happened?"

He gave her a brief summary. "I have to convince your clan to protect you and the boys. You're not safe. Lilith says Lucifer might take you and try to use you as leverage, a tool to get our baby girl. My mother claims she took Daniela to keep her safe from him."

"Did you believe her? That your mother actually wants to keep Dani from going straight to Hell? Our child could end up serving the

Devil and becoming one of Lucifer's favorite little demons. Or a plaything for Lilith!" Lacy was pale and shaking. "Admit it, Rafe. The fact is, you're not sure if we can save our baby. Isn't that where we stand now?"

Rafe reached for her. He didn't want to admit how helpless he felt when he could see his wife was close to breaking down completely. "Where are the boys now?"

"They're with my mother, surrounded by the Council. The cats may hate demons and that blood you carry, but they will protect my family with their lives." She gulped back a sob. "You can imagine how crazed they were by what they're calling 'The Siege.' Humiliated too." She leaned against him, her arms clinging to his waist. "First, they were set upon by demons, frozen in place and left helpless. Then your vampire friends arrived to save the day. My clan isn't crazy about vampires but Mama vouched for Glory and the rest. Some here say my mother has gotten too close to vampires. She's taken one to her bed, you know." Lacy sniffled. "I don't dare judge her choices when I married a man who is what he is." She pressed her cheek to his shoulder. "Others are not so understanding."

"Baby, I've lived long enough to keep my opinion to myself, especially when it comes to your mother. At least now she's doing what she can to protect our kids." Rafe had to admit he wasn't sure he understood Sheila's current dating situation but he didn't have time to think about it now. He tightened his hold on Lacy when he felt her trembling. "I promise I will get Dani back. No matter what it takes."

"Don't say that!" She pulled back and looked up at him. "You're scaring me, Rafe. I can't lose both of you. Please don't make a promise like that. We're dealing with the Devil here. He's more powerful than anything, anyone." She shuddered and pressed her hand over his heart. "Except God. I know you have a hard time with religion but I'm pretty sure asking for help from Him is your only hope."

"I get that. You think I'm not praying right now? I'm sure God is laughing his ass off, hearing from someone like me." He kissed her forehead. "It doesn't come easy but I've been asking God, a higher power, whatever you want to call Him or Her, for help. I've had a thousand years of dealing with the two sides of my soul." It was all he could do not to grab his head when pain split his skull, a thousand needles driving deep and making him want to scream.

Yeah, his prayers came at a price. Lucifer hated his calls toward Heaven. Too damned bad. At times he did feel like talking to God was his only hope. He sure wasn't stopping. He was used to pain and would bear it like a man.

"Oh, Rafe." Tears ran down Lacy's cheeks. She was beautiful, even when she sobbed and her nose turned red. She wiped her cheeks with her palms. "Please be careful. I need you. Our children need you."

"As careful as I can be, *querida*. We'll see what happens when I go down to Hell." He gently

put her away from him. "Now I must talk to the
Council and explain what I need from them. The
clan has to step up. They've got to fight off any
demons who come after you and the boys during
the daylight hours while the vampires are in their
death sleep. I can offer some tools to your clan
that will help stop the demons in their tracks or
at least keep them at bay. Lilith even left me funds.
A bribe if you want to call it that."

"You're going to insult them." She frowned.

"No, the clan needs money and this will make
it easier for those who are reluctant to fight for a
demon's family to step up." Rafe told her about
the bank and the safety deposit box.

"Let me handle that for you. I can deal with
the cats while you get on with your negotiations
with Lucifer." The voice came from behind him.

Rafe whipped around to face the man. He
didn't like the fact that he'd become so distracted,
he'd let a vampire sneak up on him.

"Ian MacDonald. Looking for Sheila? She's not
here."

"I know. She called me." Ian was Sheila's lover,
a powerful vampire, a doctor and inventor. He'd
actually been the scientist who had produced
more copies of the glasses they'd used to protect
their eyes from the mesmerizing gaze of the
demons. "I came to see if I could help."

"Thanks, man." Rafe slid his arm around Lacy.
His mother-in-law with Ian. It was an unlikely
pairing but the vampire had helped Lacy when
she'd gone into early labor with their triplets.

Rafe had been across the Atlantic at his own clan's island then.

Sheila had pressured her daughter to use the old ways, the cat ways, to give birth. Lacy had refused. A good thing, too. There had been complications, but Ian had helped both mother and babies come through a difficult birth safely. Sheila had apparently been so impressed with the vampire, she'd forgotten her prejudice against "bloodsuckers" and allowed Ian to court her.

"I can train the cats to fight the demons who will come here." Ian's gaze was sharp. With his white blond hair and bright blue eyes, the Scottish vampire had a Viking look that made him intimidating. He'd never lost his Scottish accent and still had a warrior's sturdy build. That had obviously been attractive to Sheila Devereau. "I brought extra pairs of those special glasses and more of that wisteria solution I can load into spray guns like you have."

"Sounds good." Rafe extended his hand for a shake. "I appreciate it, MacDonald."

"I'm doing it for Sheila." Ian gripped his hand then smiled at Lacy. "Her family is everything to her."

"I know that." Rafe looked into his wife's eyes. "You will stay here and let me see what I can do to keep our daughter safe?"

"I will. But not because you are ordering me to do it. I know it's for the best." She threw back her wild mane of red hair and put her hand on Rafe's shoulder. She still trembled but she seemed determined to stay strong. "I will also help fight any demons that threaten us here."

Ian nodded approvingly. "What's your next move, Valdez?" He glanced toward the house. "Where's the little girl?"

"My mother and her demon soldiers have taken her. I'm not happy about it but Lilith promised to keep Daniela safe from Lucifer. She claims she's strong enough to manage that." Rafe looked up at the night sky. He'd be damned if he had a clue which way they had gone. Dani had mentioned a Disney resort and that seemed a likely destination. First, he had to put a stop to this bounty hunt Lucifer had started. He had visions of an endless stream of greedy demons coming after anyone who could give them access to his child.

"Clearly you do need to go straight to Lucifer and see what it will take to get this settled. Find out what you can do to stop this insanity." Ian was also searching the sky. "I only have a few hours before daylight but I'll call a shifter I know in Florida who can keep a watch at the Disney complex for demon activity and your mother."

"Stop reading my mind, vampire." Rafe glared at him before he remembered this was a big favor he couldn't afford to turn down. "But, thanks. Do that. Lilith will find that Daniela demands entertainment or becomes hard to handle. A theme park with people around might actually be a safe place to hide in plain sight for them." He rubbed the back of his neck. "Yeah, I know I need to confront the Devil. Any ideas where the nearest portal to Hell might be?" Rafe tried to ignore the way Lacy clutched his arm.

"Rafe, I hate this!" Her claws were out and she dug them painfully into his bicep. "If you go down to Hell, how do you know Lucifer will let you leave?"

"Rafe has to take that chance, Lacy. He needs to confront the Devil and see what it'll take to call off this bounty hunt. We can't hold off legions of demons here forever." Ian put his hand on Lacy's shoulder. "I came here to tell you that your mother needs you. She's barely holding it together. You know the boys are a handful at the best of times. Maybe you can help her get them to bed in one of the other houses. With a favorite cousin or two?"

Rafe wanted to reassure his wife but knew she'd see through a lie. Instead, he chose to distract her with a growl. "Hands off my wife, MacDonald."

"Relax, shifter. I'm involved with Lacy's mother. I would never make a move on her daughter." Ian did remove his hand. "Though they are both beautiful women." He just couldn't seem to resist goading Rafe. "Lacy?"

"Ian's right. I should go help with the boys." Lacy leaned against her husband. "Please promise to be careful."

"Always, sweetheart." Rafe kissed her then walked her toward the place where she'd find her mother. "Your children need you. Stay safe. I have to know you will be well-protected here so I can concentrate on negotiating for our daughter's future."

"I want our family to be together. *All* of us." She grabbed his shoulders and kissed him desperately. "Come back to me, Rafael."

"I intend to." Not a promise but the best he could do. As soon as she was out of sight, he turned to Ian. "Now tell me where this portal is. Do you know of it?"

"Do you think you are the only one who has noticed the sudden influx of demons in the area? It wasn't hard to pinpoint where they were coming from. Especially since it was from an unlikely place." Ian looked up to where a pair of dragons flew far above them before they settled in a treetop. "Lucifer has an army at his disposal, Valdez. You have no hope of defeating it *mano à mano*."

"You think I don't know that?" Rafe wanted to shove his fist into the vampire's knowing face. But he needed him and respected his skills. Damn it. "That's why I'm willing to go to his lair and confront him. He has always wanted *me*, my mother has told me that. I'm hoping I can reason with him."

Ian's bark of laughter almost undid Rafe's very thin hold on his control. "Reason? With Lucifer? Good luck with that." He pulled a vial out of his pocket. "Here's a new serum I've been working on. I doubt it will get past the man's guards, but if it does, you might try shoving it in the Devil's face."

"And make him mad?" Rafe took the small bottle. It shone with a strange golden light. "He'd turn me to ash on the spot."

"No, no, this is something else. It is an elixir that will make him mellow. Happy. You can imagine what a novelty that will be for a man with his tastes. He is used to violence, anger, hatred. How will it be if he tastes euphoria?" Ian chuckled. "I would like to see the Devil in raptures."

"I'm sure he is in raptures when he peels the skin off a murderer." Rafe slipped the tiny bottle deep into the pocket of his cargo pants. "Now where is this portal to Hell? I'm surprised I haven't run across it."

"It's a business very different from yours on Sixth Street. This one is in the University area and caters to students. Believe it or not, it's across the street from the campus." Ian pulled a business card from his pocket. "I knew you would need this so I came prepared. I find the choice of location and the name and type of business amusing. Not what you'd expect when looking for a portal to Hell."

"I find none of this amusing." Rafe read the card. "Isaac Newton's Donuts, Coffee and Internet Café." He shook his head. "You've got to be kidding. It's a freaking coffee shop?"

"With fast Wi-Fi and free coffee refills. It's got a basement and that's where the demons are coming through. The place is very popular, especially with students. You'll see." Ian gave him a look that was actually sympathetic. "If I don't see you again, Valdez, you know I will watch out for your family. I have become quite fond of Sheila."

"That's a real vote of confidence." Rafe gave Ian the key to the safety deposit box and reviewed arrangements there. He didn't doubt the vampire would figure out how to access the funds. Trusting this man seemed insane, yet what choice did he have? Time was rushing past and his choices were limited. He stuck his hands in his pockets to keep Ian from seeing how they were shaking. Clearly Ian doubted Rafe would ever be able to leave Hell once he went down there. The vampire might be right.

"I will do what I can here, Valdez." Ian tucked the key away. "I don't pretend to know what you will face in Hell but I do know that you have plenty of friends here who think highly of you. You have proved yourself to be a good man, loyal to those who trust you. Many seem to do just that. That is not something a man who rules Hell will like. He will try to destroy you." Ian was very serious. "Hold firm in your surety that you are not evil and you may yet prevail. Isn't that what various religious teachings tell us? Think of the martyrs through the centuries. Angels, saints and such. They relied on their faith and it sustained them."

"All the way to the grave." Rafe took a breath, the stench of his mother's evil barely noticeable in the night air. Where had she taken Dani?

Faith. He tried to think about the concept. "MacDonald, I've read enough over the years while I've battled the dark side of my soul to know the coming confrontation won't be easy." Rafe didn't like talking about this to a man he hardly knew. But then he'd never talked about it to anyone. He lived his life as best he could and had determined early on to never give in to his dark side. Yes, he'd killed and done other things that would condemn him in some eyes. And yet... He'd always seen a reason to choose the right thing He waited for the pain that would come when he contemplated right and good. He wasn't disappointed. It hit him so hard, this time in his gut, that he almost fell to his knees.

Ian caught him and steadied him with a frown. "He's listening, isn't he?"

"Of course. I can't get away from him." Rafe wiped sweat from his brow. "He knows I've got your little bottle. If I'm allowed to keep it, it will be because he's curious and wants to see what it does."

Ian nodded. "Interesting. I've made a study of the world's religions. Good over evil. The theme is a common one, my man." Ian slapped him on the back. "Some say vampires are doomed to the fiery pit. I don't believe that, never have. No, we can be redeemed and so can you." He scanned the night sky. "There are demons watching us even now. You will be followed when you leave here."

"Of course. And redeemed? I hope so, for the sake of my family." Rafe said it softly and for once didn't get punished with a new pain.

"Lucifer himself is a fallen angel. Perhaps he is curious to see if you can defeat him. He may give you a fair chance to try. Use his curiosity to your advantage." Ian scanned the night sky, flinching when one of the dragons watching them screeched. "Evil cannot be allowed to rule,

Valdez. Stay firm and we may yet meet again. Now go. I have work to do and less than an hour to train a bunch of surly cats. If Sheila weren't such a fiery bitch, I'd abandon this cause." Ian laughed at Rafe's raised eyebrow. "It's too bad that I find that kind of woman irresistible. Take off, lad. Good luck to ye and watch your back." He stalked off toward the cats' meeting house.

Rafe gathered his nerve and shifted into a dark bird, soaring over the trees toward downtown Austin. The tower at the University of Texas was easy to spot, even though the city had grown and there were other tall buildings downtown now. Tonight, the tower was bathed in orange light from top to bottom. It was a sign that a sports game of some kind had been won by the home team. Baseball? It was the season for it.

Rafe landed behind a tree near the street that faced the campus. The building across from him was one of the old stone three-stories that looked to have been built about the time of the Alamo. It was sandwiched between a seventies high-rise dorm and a bookstore. He heard noise in the branches above his head. He was being watched but left alone. For now.

"The Drag," as the street was nicknamed, was almost deserted this late but a few cars moved along the thoroughfare. A neon sign flickered in the window. Isaac Newton's Donuts, Coffee and Internet Café occupied the ground floor of that stone building and was open 24 hours. It boasted a few customers even though most nearby businesses were closed. Rafe shifted into his human form and strolled across the street. Pushing inside the glass door, he was hit by the delicious smells of fresh coffee and donuts. He saw three tables were occupied. Two men and a woman each peered at a laptop. They looked like ordinary mortals but at least one, the woman with long blond hair, had the stink of demon.

The man behind the counter was an Einstein clone with the same wild bushy hair as that famous genius. There were posters of other geniuses on the walls around the large room in what was obviously a theme. When the clerk spotted Rafe, he inhaled then let his eyes glow red.

"Good evening, friend. What can I get you?" He wiped the counter with a clean white rag.

"Black coffee and two glazed donuts." Rafe dug out a twenty. "Keep the change."

"Gladly." He snatched up the money then filled a go cup before pulling two donuts from the case and sliding them onto a napkin. "Here or taking them with you?"

"Depends. I'd like an appointment to see the big guy downstairs." Rafe sipped his coffee, humming his appreciation at the strong fresh brew.

"Big guy?" Einstein kept wiping. "Can't imagine what you're talking about."

"I heard this was a…" Rafe leaned in, "portal. I need to have a conversation with You-Know-Who."

"You're demented." Einstein shoved the napkin toward him. "No one gets in to see Him. Try the donuts, they're still warm."

Rafe took a bite then finished it quickly. He gulped coffee and realized he was stalling. He pulled another napkin from a dispenser and wiped sugary glaze from his fingers. The clerk, his eyes now a mild brown, watched him closely, as if he was waiting for something.

"Seriously, dude. I'm not leaving. Just send him a message. He'll want to see me. Tell him Rafael Valdez is here."

A chair scraped back behind him and Rafe turned to see the blond on her feet, a sword in her hand. "Valdez." She took the steps needed to be too close. "Where's the child?"

"How the fuck should I know?" He snatched her sword before she knew what hit her. "Don't come at me with a weapon unless you know how to use it." He glanced at the men on their laptops. "Witnesses?"

"They can't see a thing. I put up a shield." She shook her head, her shiny hair flying. "Taking my sword like that was a slick move. Guess what I've heard about you is true. You *are* a warrior." She pulled a knife from the waist of her snug jeans. "You come to claim the prize for yourself?" Her tank top clung to her curves. At almost six feet and toned, she clearly meant business. "I think you know where your kid, this Daniela, is but you're not saying." She gave him an admiring once over. "Willing to sell out your own child for a big payday. Should have expected that. You *are* a demon, despite the rumors that you're a goody two-shoes."

"Back off, Sharise." Einstein jumped over the

counter and landed between them. "You're right, Valdez. He'll see you." His hand shook as he pointed toward a doorway marked "Employees Only." "Take the stairs down. Someone will meet you at the bottom to guide you the rest of the way."

"Wait a minute, Dennis. There's a bounty. Are you just going to let him go by himself?" Sharise wasn't ready to put her knife away. Now she aimed it at the clerk. "Maybe you and me could work a deal, get a piece of the action. Torture the kid's location out of this father of the year."

"He's here to see the Master. You going to step between this guy and that meeting?" Dennis was truly shaking now. "I'm sure as hell not."

"You're serious? Luc really agreed to see him?" The knife disappeared into her waistband. She gave Rafe a tentative smile. "Nice meeting you, Valdez. If you survive this get together with your balls intact, call me." She slithered closer, suddenly part lizard, and let him see a flicker of her forked tongue. Pressing her breasts against his chest, she tucked a card into his pants pocket while giving his zipper a pat. "We could have some fun." She winked one of her glowing red eyes then sat down in front of her laptop again.

Rafe swallowed. Nothing like putting it all out there. "No, thanks, I'm married."

That made her laugh. "I'm up for a threesome. But whatever." She poked at her keyboard. "Dennis, the Wi-Fi needs a boost. I'm having trouble getting into the dark web tonight."

"You bring us one of your viruses and I'll

ban you, baby." Dennis pointed to the doorway again. "Move it, Valdez. He doesn't like to be kept waiting."

Rafe walked to the entrance. Behind the door he found a metal spiral staircase that seemed to go down a long, long way. Was there a glow at the bottom? It was probably just a light, but it seemed to flash. Red, yellow, white. Like fire. His imagination? He swallowed and wished he hadn't stuffed that donut in his mouth and washed it down with coffee. Now it churned in his gut, acid threatening to rise to his throat.

Meeting with Lucifer. The tiny bottle Ian had given him was in the very bottom of his pants pocket. Could it help? What's the worst that could happen? He remembered Sharise's comment. Oh, he could lose his balls. He started down the stairs, his boots clanging on the metal treads. Whoever waited at the bottom would definitely hear him coming.

He still held Sharise's sword. He knew he wouldn't be allowed to keep it. But holding it made him feel a little better, like the ancient warrior he'd once been. Fight the Devil? The problem was, he couldn't afford to lose. *Daniela* couldn't afford for him to lose. He'd never been so scared in his long, long life.

CHAPTER SIX

A MAN WAITED AT the bottom of the stairs. "Call me Gordon. Follow me." He gestured and they walked down a corridor that could have been in any office building. Closed doors were on either side. Unmarked doors. The floor was a plain white tile that had been polished to a high shine. Rafe had the stupid thought that maybe someone's idea of Hell might be having to scrub floors endlessly.

It was quiet, eerily quiet. Rafe didn't know what he'd expected, screams, maybe. Heat for sure. He realized they had stopped in front of a steel door with an electronic key pad.

"Lucifer uses modern technology?"

"Why not?" The guy punched in a code he was careful to block from Rafe's gaze. "Mortals could wander down here. No sense in wasting resources on guards when a little tech can take care of things." Gordon smiled when the door clicked open. "Of course, uninvited guests would get a hell of a surprise if they tried to break in. The Master does like to freak out anyone stupid enough to invade his space."

"Like anyone actually wants to get in here."

Rafe realized he was more than a little freaked out himself. Gordon was an ordinary-looking man in black pants and a white button-down. Not memorable in any way. He didn't even have a demon vibe. Or a threatening one.

"Obviously you do want in." Gordon looked Rafe over. "Good luck. If you're going to ask for a favor, you'll need it." The man stepped aside. "Straight ahead. You can't miss the throne room." Then he vanished. Just like that.

Throne room? And poof? Rafe looked around, even up at the ceiling. Tricks. He should have expected them. He took a breath and nearly gagged as the door swung inward. He didn't want to identify the stench. All he knew was that the punishment for sinning started at the door.

Heat hit him hard, then he heard his first screams, high-pitched ones that made his hands tighten into fists and his balls shrink. Yeah, this was the gate to Hell all right. He straightened his shoulders and stepped inside. The door swung shut with a decisive clang that made him look behind him. He wanted to try the handle but somehow knew that would be futile. Locked in and he wasn't getting out unless the Devil allowed it. Holy shit. What had he done? What he'd had to do.

Sweat trickled down his forehead as the light dimmed, making him aware of a reddish glow ahead of him. The screams echoed from every side, then reached a crescendo before being cut off so abruptly Rafe jumped. Did someone die over and over again? He forced himself to keep going when all he wanted to do was try that damned exit door. Daniela. He had to remember why he was here.

These side doors were marked with graphics. Some clever artist had imagined scenes from horror movies. Or maybe they weren't imaginings. Door after door was decorated with pictures of horrors—murder, rape, depravities that made Rafe jerk his face away, disgusted and sickened. God.

"You dare bring that word here!" The voice thundered down the corridor and flames licked at Rafe's boots. He almost lost his grip on the sword, his hand slick with sweat.

"You don't want me to say God?" If he was to have any chance against Lucifer, he had to stand up to him.

"You must have a death wish." The sword was ripped from Rafe's hand and melted into a puddle of metal at his feet.

"I'm here to talk. Are you willing to be reasonable and discuss things? Or am I wasting my time?" Rafe stepped over the molten steel and kept going. "At least let me see you. How about a face to face?"

"My, you are a bold one. Your mother's son. It has been years since I've been challenged like this." Laughter rang through what was now a large chamber carved out of stone. Golden stalactites hung from a jagged ceiling that seemed miles above his head. The throne room.

Rafe blinked. He had no idea how he'd gotten there. A man lounged on a golden chair, elevated on a dais. Lucifer. Had to be. He was beautiful, from his blond hair with a pair of golden horns spiked through it to his sculpted chin. He wore an expensive black suit that hugged broad shoulders, a white silk shirt open at the neck. His eyes were the color of the sea off a Greek island. Rafe found his own eyes trapped in that gaze and couldn't look away. The Devil smiled with white, white teeth as he probed Rafe's every dark secret. He seemed amused that this minor, mere half-a-demon, had dared approach him.

Rafe shuddered and tore his gaze away. They were no longer alone in the room. Another man stood beside "the Master." He was slim, another beauty, wearing only a loin cloth and holding a golden goblet. A woman leaned against the Devil's other side, her sheer gown hiding nothing of her perfect figure. She stroked Lucifer's arm with her breast and smiled at Rafe.

"You wanted to see me. Now discuss." Lucifer's bright eyes gleamed, as if he couldn't wait to take advantage of Rafe's desperation. He snapped elegant fingers and the young man handed him the goblet. The Devil took a long drink then licked his lips.

"The finest vintage from a mountain in Italy. I took every bottle then destroyed the village where it was made. Burned the vines. There will be no more of this wine, ever. I like having only the best and I refuse to share." He smiled and handed back the goblet, then picked up the woman's gown and dabbed at his lips. "When I want something, I take it. Remember that."

Rafe swallowed, his throat dry. What could he say?

The Devil grinned, obviously enjoying Rafe's unease. "Isn't Daphne lovely? She has whored for me for centuries." He waved his hand. "Entertain him, woman."

"Yes, Master." She walked up to Rafe and dropped her gown. "Hello, Rafael. Welcome to Hell. I will do whatever you wish."

"Not interested." Rafe let his disgust for Lucifer's order show on his face.

"He thinks he can resist you. Come now, Daphne. Stir the man." Lucifer leaned back, waiting.

The woman looked Rafe up and down then reached for his zipper. He grabbed her hand before she could touch him.

"Don't." He kept his eyes on her face. "I refuse to play his games."

"He will punish me if you won't let me…" Her eyes filled. "Please." Her lips trembled.

Rafe believed her. Then he remembered where he was and who the woman worked for. Yes, she might be punished. How many men had she led astray in the name of stealing their souls for her "Master"?

"Perhaps you crave his punishments. I'm sorry, but I didn't put you in Hell. You earned your place here." Rafe stepped back, slinging her arm away from him. He looked up at the throne, but Lucifer wasn't there. Pulling a knife from his boot, Rafe gazed around the room. Futile, but he'd been a warrior too long to just stand there.

What next? Had he displeased the Devil for refusing to play? The woman disappeared first, then the pretty young man who'd stood next to the throne.

Rafe's stomach knotted as he waited. Would there be another effort to make him sin? Had Daphne tempted him? Not even with her perfect body. What a joke. Sex was the furthest thing from his mind here in the bowels of Hell.

"Lucifer! You know why I'm here. Tell me what I must do to keep my daughter…" Rafe felt his throat close but he choked out the words, "safe from you." He spun when he heard footsteps behind him. His hand was damp as he gripped his knife, ready to defend himself.

The same nondescript man who'd let him into Hell, Gordon, smiled at him. "He heard you. Come this way. It seems you've passed his first test. He'll see you in his office."

Rafe kept his knife at the ready as he followed the man down a new corridor. The screams had stopped again. Perhaps even the Devil got tired of the incessant noise.

"It was a test?" Rafe was sweating. Still hot down here. He would have given a lot for a blast of air conditioning.

The man tapped what appeared to be an earbud. "Yes. He liked your strong will. Daphne would have fucked most men to death in five minutes. You proved you could resist her."

"I'm married and I love my wife."

Gordon shook his head. "So what? You're a demon. Marriage vows, vows of any kind, are a joke down here. And most demons don't understand the concept of love and fidelity." He stopped in front of an elaborate metal door. It was decorated with jewels in a pattern Rafe recognized. Ancient symbols spelled out the many names for Devil— Beelzebub, Mephistopheles, there were dozens.

"I'm only half demon. And I take my vows seriously. What did you do to deserve Hell? You look like an accountant," Rafe asked while they waited for the man's knock to be answered.

"I *was* a very successful accountant. How very astute of you." Gordon smiled. "But I was bored crunching numbers so I became an even more successful serial killer in New Jersey." He nodded when the door opened in front of them. "I've served the Master for only forty years, a relative newcomer around here. Play your cards right and, when it's your turn to serve, you might find it not a bad afterlife. If the Master is pleased with you, the rewards are generous."

He stepped back when Daphne staggered past them. "Oh, dear. The price of failure, I see. Don't worry, dear. He'll repair it when he needs you beautiful again."

"Ass." She slapped Gordon's arm as she wobbled carefully down the hall. Half her face was shredded, bloody and unrecognizable. She wore a shapeless gown made of thorny branches. Every movement ripped her skin, making her hiss.

She glared at Rafe as she staggered past him. "I won't forget this, Valdez."

"You've made an enemy there." Gordon smiled.

"That will make for a fun time down here once you become a permanent resident."

Rafe had no words. God, he hoped that wasn't his future.

"Guard your thoughts, demon. Calling on that higher power is likely to get you sent to the roasting pit." Gordon pressed a hand to his heart. "Trust me, you don't want that. Once was certainly enough for me."

Rafe shivered, letting his imagination fill in some horrific blanks.

"Now don't keep the Master waiting. I'm sure he has a proposition for you. This may be an answer to your, excuse me," Gordon gagged, "prayers." He shoved Rafe inside then shut the door.

Rafe took a moment, overwhelmed. He was in Hell all right. A proposition? He figured he'd be doomed, but, if it spared Daniela, he could only hope for one. He looked around the Devil's office. It featured a massive desk that would have looked right at home on the set of an evening news show. Made of glass and chrome, it held a laptop and stacks of files. Lucifer sat in a red velvet desk chair that he now leaned back so he could watch Rafe when he walked across the room to stand in front of him.

"Your eyes are wide. Don't waste your pity on Daphne. You were right, she loves the bite of the whip. I know Gordon told you why he was here. Did that shock you?"

"Daphne did look bad. But Gordon. He doesn't look . . ." Rafe shook his head. God knew what a serial killer was supposed to look like. "How many did he kill?"

Lucifer frowned. Oh, yeah. Rafe had thought the "G" word again. He had to stop that.

"That very tame looking little man took out twenty-three women then killed the two policemen who tried to capture him. He didn't want to die in prison so he chose suicide by cop." Lucifer nodded. "A glorious way to end a fine career. No one has a way with a chainsaw like the Jersey Turnpike killer."

Rafe grimaced. "I read about him. He left body parts up and down the roadway."

"Yes, very creative." Lucifer leaned forward. "I know why you're here, of course. Obviously, you want to free your daughter from my plan to bring her down to this cesspool of the damned, some call it." He polished his manicured nails on his lapel. "Poor Rafael. You just can't stand the idea of her fulfilling the potential of her demon heritage."

"You're right. I love her, but I knew the first time I saw her that she had inherited the worst part of my blood. I'm going to teach her how to fight her demon urges. Like I've done for myself all these years." Rafe watched Lucifer frown then set a stack of papers on his desk on fire with a glance.

"You've wasted your talents, Valdez. We could have done great things together if you'd been smart about it." He raked his sharp gaze over Rafe.

Rafe's knees turned to jelly but he stiffened

them. No, he *had* fought the evil in himself and won.

Lucifer's intent scrutiny made Rafe sweat. "Be careful, my man. What is it they say? Pride goes before a fall?"

"I'm not too proud to beg you to spare my daughter, Lucifer. You want me on my knees? To kiss your Gucci loafers? Please forget her. Like you have forgotten me for centuries." Rafe staggered when a thousand knife cuts hit him.

"That could have been a mistake. And I never forget anything. Or *anyone*." Lucifer stood. His smile was a twist of satisfaction. Was he enjoying watching Rafe grovel? Whatever it took.

Rafe threw himself face down on the cold tile floor. "Please, please leave my child alone. Give her the freedom to find her own way, like you did for me." His vision blurred and he let his eyes close. When he heard steps coming toward him, he braced himself. What now? More pain? A trip to the roasting pit? How dare he ask for Dani's life.

A shoe nudged his side. "I spared you because your mother made it worth my while. Yes, you had freedom."

He felt Lucifer standing over him, his proximity its own kind of torture. Freedom. With fear always looming that someday he'd have to pay for it. Rafe wanted to laugh, say something, but he didn't have it in him to thank the Devil for sparing him. So he stayed silent.

"And what did you do with your freedom? Played the knight, protecting vampires, fighting evil as if you were a fucking avenging angel." The shoe landed this time, the blow sending Rafe rolling onto his back, his head bouncing on the hard floor.

"God…" Rafe murmured.

"Shut up!" Lucifer was enraged, striding around the office in a circle, his gaze sending bookcases toppling and setting file cabinets ablaze.

Rafe knew he could be dead with a whisper, a touch, a glance. The power coming at him stopped his breath and his heart. He closed his eyes again, trying to find a rhythm, a way back to life. He finally opened his eyes to gaze at the ceiling. Except there was no ceiling, only endless darkness. He was going to be sick, his gorge rising.

"Don't you dare!" Lucifer's order made him swallow and Rafe was suddenly cold and calm again. "You wanted to talk. So listen to me."

Rafe managed to push into a sitting position. Was Lucifer going to be reasonable? Of course not. But maybe there would be a way out of this. He was afraid to hope.

"Your mother protected you and spared you the duties of a demon in my realm. You should have been down here, serving me all these years. Instead, Lilith took your place." He stared at Rafe for a long moment. "I know you don't believe that. But now? Lilith betrayed me. She kept this child of yours a secret. Then, once I found out about her, your mother had the nerve to try to make a deal with me for Daniela and freedom." Lucifer laughed. "Can you imagine? Foolish woman. She should have remembered that I can only be pushed so far."

Lucifer pulled his beard into twin points, to match his horns. "Lilith has always been a little too proud of her powers and the following she has collected." He snorted. "A bunch of ragtag do-nothings she has to pay to worship her."

"She never should have had children." Rafe managed to choke out.

Lucifer leaped and threw his hands into the air. "Exactly!" His eyes blazed red. "Especially if she is going to keep them from me. So much potential power. I can't stand the waste of it. You should have been at my right hand all this time!" He pointed a finger at Rafe and it was as if a knife had been plunged into his chest.

Rafe sank into a chair that hadn't been there a moment before. He looked down. Was he bleeding? No sign of a wound, just a feeling like he'd been burned with a hot iron. He wouldn't have been surprised to see later that he'd been branded, a permanent souvenir of this visit.

Lucifer laughed. "What a wonderful idea! I will use that next time. Like they did to prisoners or heretics centuries ago. A burn right on the forehead or cheek. So you couldn't miss the mark if they escaped. I absolutely love the idea." He pointed his finger at Rafe again, as if thinking about it. "A letter? A symbol? Oh, this will entertain me for days!"

Rafe kept still though he shuddered, inside. He knew history and had had close calls of his own with branding.

"Relax, Rafael." Lucifer kicked back in his chair again. "What I require of you demands a certain amount of," he waved a hand suddenly bedecked with glittering jewels, "anonymity in the mortal world."

"What you require?" Rafe sat up straight, his pain forgotten. "You have something you need me to do? A task to perform that, once completed, will get you to leave my daughter alone?"

"Make no mistake, Valdez, I want your daughter." Lucifer was suddenly right in front of him, so close that Rafe could smell the eau de brimstone he wore like cologne. It was a nauseating mixture of burnt flesh and disease. "You are familiar with sin, are you not? Not the trivial sins like petty theft and idle fucking, but those grave sins that mark a man or a woman for Hell and eternal damnation."

"Yes, of course. I've lived a long, long time." Rafe wished Lucifer would step back. He couldn't breathe so close to the man. Lucifer was all power and intimidation.

"I can smell your fear." Lucifer smiled as he ran a fingernail across Rafe's cheek, drawing blood. "I have in my hand a list for you of my favorite sins, those that get my heart started, you might say." He picked through a pile of papers. "You are going to bring me a few sinners. There were so many choices!" He waved the stack. "But these will do. You are going to end their lives and drag them to Hell where I will welcome them appropriately." Lucifer's smile was the stuff of nightmares. "They've already sold their souls.

No worries there. But they refuse to die, greedily holding onto life instead coming here and taking their 'reward' as they deserve."

"Can't you get them yourself?" Rafe wondered why he bothered to ask. Of course, this was some kind of test for *him*. One of Lucifer's games.

Lucifer threw the pages onto his desk. "I could, but what's the fun in that? No, you'll do it. I want you to prove how serious you are. That you really, really want your daughter safe from me. I can assure you, your pious conscience will not bother you when you take out these sinners. Every one of them deserves their fate. Delicious evil doers, heavy hitters, my boy. Most of them have lived much too long already."

"Modern medicine!" Lucifer raved, listing some of the miracles doctors had performed in the last centuries as if they were personal affronts. "Transplants! Vaccines! Illnesses that used to end lives with such exquisite pain are now cured! Can you believe it?" He glanced at the wall and several sections collapsed in a heap of bricks. "The world is becoming too soft, too tame!" His eyes were bright red. "Even the latest pandemic only took out a few million! The vilest sinner seems scared to use a real weapon of mass destruction. Wimps! Why not open a tank of nerve gas? Go ahead and drop a nuke on a hospital or day care center. That's how a real bad ass shows what he's made of. Don't you think?"

Rafe swallowed. He tried to keep his horror hidden and not think at all.

"You need to spend time down here, Valdez.

You're looking like you want to puke." Lucifer laughed. "Well, we'll see if you are up to a challenge. I've got here five deliciously evil creatures for you to send home. I hope they put up enough fight to entertain me because I've been horribly bored lately." He thrust papers at Rafe.

Rafe caught them before they hit the floor. "Send them home? Here in Hell?"

"What else? This is your task. You have five days to bring them to me. They're the worst of the worst, ones that will please me and keep me amused for a while at least. You can bet they'll try to avoid and evade you. That's part of the entertainment value. But I'm sure you can find them and then take them out." Lucifer grinned. "None of them think they're ready. At least one of them might be what you call 'immortal.'" He smirked. "I hate to destroy your illusion, but *no one* lives forever."

"Vampire? Shifter? Even a demon?" Rafe had always known forever wasn't a guarantee. He'd seen immortals die before. Now it was on him to take out people who deserved to die. He didn't have a problem with it. He'd killed before, usually during war. But five days? He didn't dare take his eyes off Lucifer long enough to read the pages in his hand. There had to be a catch.

"I'll let you figure out the details for yourself." Lucifer strolled back to his desk and settled into his chair. "Five days for five kills. It won't be easy or what would be the fun in that? I'll be watching and so will Gordon. A few of my more interesting helpers might be along for the ride. You won't be able to see them, but they'll see you and send me reports." He laughed, clearly delighted by the entire thing.

"Now I'm in the mood to try that treat you have in your pocket. Of course, I heard about it." He picked up a cell phone and pushed a button. "Gordon, get in here." He glanced at Rafe. "I hope you know, Rafael, that if anything you do causes me distress, my handy serial killer will make sure to end you." He grinned, white teeth gleaming. "What would become of dear Daniela then?"

Rafe clutched those papers, his stomach rolling. "Wait. Before I embark on this mission, test, or whatever you want to call it, I need a promise from you." He wondered if he was a fool for pushing this, but it had to be done.

"I promise if you fail to kill all five in five days, I get both of you—you and your precious Daniela." Lucifer rubbed his hands together and sparks flew. "Oh, there will be a hot time down here celebrating that. And the best part? Your mother will be so unhappy." His laughter echoed through the room as the door opened. "Now give me that golden goo."

Rafe hated to pass it over but realized he had no choice. Gordon had come in with a chain saw slung over his shoulder. "If you heard me with the maker of this stuff, Lucifer, you know I have no idea what it'll do."

"It's supposed to make me happy. Give it to me." Lucifer took the vial and studied it. "You can go, the clock is ticking. Gordo can catch up with you if this stuff causes a problem. That's why he brought his trusty chain saw." He drank it down and smacked his lips. "Ooo. Pretty delicious."

"Stop. I'm not leaving until I have your promise that, if I complete these tasks in the allotted time, you'll leave Daniela and me alone. You will withdraw the bounty you've put on Dani's head and stop all efforts to bring my daughter or me into Hell or the demon realm." Rafe stood his ground, even when Lucifer's brows went up and his eyes glowed again, sending heat across the room.

"You *are* your mother's son, aren't you? You demand my promise? Do you think I'll keep my word?" Lucifer looked Rafe up and down. "Demons usually don't."

"Even the Devil has to have some kind of code. You have devoted followers. It's common knowledge a disappointed Devil is to be feared. But your demons must trust you to keep *your* word. Even if it is only that your rewards will be paid in full. And you will raise them in status when you say you will. Or do you make fools of them?"

"Careful, Rafael. You sound like you are laying down terms here." The room seemed to lose air and Rafe fought for breath. Now who was the fool? But he had to know passing this test was worth it. That it would truly save his daughter.

"I know you are calling the shots. I also know every demon in your realm will be watching me closely. If I jump through your hoops and you don't follow through afterwards? How will you be able to control them going forward?" Rafe's head pounded but he couldn't stop now. He could see Lucifer thinking. He'd made a point.

"There's nothing my mother would like better than to gather your disenchanted followers over to her side. Can you afford a demon rebellion?" Rafe forced a smile. "Frankly, it sounds exhausting."

"You're right about that. And boring." Lucifer laughed again and shook a finger at Rafe. That golden goo was obviously working. "You're a clever son of a bitch, I'll give you that. And that jolly juice has me flying too high to worry about my demon hordes getting their panties in a twist right now. Tell me again. What do you want?"

Rafe stared at Lucifer, at the silly smile on his face. Damn, Ian's golden potion needed a patent. "Promise me completing this task will make my family safe from your machinations. You will leave Dani and me alone forevermore. What say you, Lucifer? Is your word good?"

"Oh, the balls on you. I hope you fail and I can train you to be my aide, vice president, whatever we decide to call it. Such times we will have!" Lucifer was suddenly close and held out his hand. "But I give you my word, and I won't break it. Yes, do these tasks in the appointed time and I will free your family from any further efforts to get you to join *my* demon family." He glanced behind Rafe. "I said it in front of a witness, too, didn't I, Gordo?"

"Yes, Master." The serial killer nodded as he

fingered his chain saw. "And I'm sure Valdez knows the penalty for failure as well."

Lucifer smiled. "Of course, he does. You can play with him for a while. Though I'll want him back in one piece. He has talents I can use." He glanced down to where he waited for Rafe to shake his hand.

Touch the Devil? He'd rather not, but Rafe shook Lucifer's hand anyway, feeling an electric shock down to his toes. "So be it." He took a steadying breath while watching the Devil fling off his jacket and shirt. Then the man began to dance around the room.

"I feel wonderful! Your friend's juice is magic. I may have to pay him a visit and get more." Lucifer laughed when Rafe frowned at him. "Come now, you have to know Ian MacDonald is some kind of scientific genius. I must check the soul registry to see if I already own his. How old is he, I wonder?"

Rafe knew Ian was ancient but didn't volunteer that information. He'd feel damned guilty if this favor from the vampire got Ian on the Devil's watch list.

"Yes, I must see where he stands as far as sins go. Maybe I'll get lucky and he'll land in Hell soon anyway. Immortal? Don't believe it." Lucifer kept talking as he shucked the rest of his clothes. Naked, the Devil had the body of a Greek god.

Rafe eased toward the door where Gordon stood. Could he leave now?

"Gordo, send for those new sluts that just came down after that fire in Amsterdam. The fresh undamaged ones. Smoke inhalation, such a tidy ending." His desk disappeared and a huge bed stood in its place. "Rafael, you look horrified. Don't worry, the girls deserved Hell and whatever punishment I see fit. You have no idea how many customers those clever females ended before a lucky lightning strike took out their brothel and *them*." Lucifer stretched like a languid cat.

"I want breakfast too, Gordo. Pancakes and maple syrup. Lots of butter." He threw himself on the bed. He glanced at Rafe. "Out of here. I am not about to put on a show for the likes of you. I did you a favor though. A reward for those outsized *cojones* you had, daring to make me give you my word." He waved his hand. "I put the profile for the sinner I want first on top. Too bad she's so far away but she'll be easy. Get her first and quickly. The other four will be more of a challenge but don't forget that pesky deadline." He snapped his fingers, obviously a habit of his. "What's the holdup, Gordo? Women and food. Now!"

Rafe was suddenly in the corridor again with Gordon by his side. His stomach twisted and he was drenched in sweat. A surge of air conditioning chilled him as he reached the foot of the stairs going up to the coffee shop.

"I'd wish you luck, but that would just piss off the Master." Gordon slapped Rafe on the back. "I'll be watching. Happy hunting. I can't resist saying that. I always did enjoy the hunt more than the kill." He vanished again as Rafe sprinted up the stairs.

Five days, five kills. A quick glance at the pages showed him names, cities and a brief description of the sins that had marked each one for Hell. Not much to go on. No way would Rafe just take out each target without further research. The Devil and demons lied. He would get on the Internet and double check everything. Lucifer was bound to have made this trickier than it looked. Not that killing strangers was a walk in the park.

Rafe reminded himself these were bad people, sinners who had sold their souls for their own reasons. And *he* had a strong reason for becoming the Devil's hit man. He could do this to keep Daniela safe. Then a glance at the first name on the page made Rafe curse until he ran out of words. No wonder Lucifer had been laughing, almost giddy, when he'd sent Rafe on his way. It hadn't been MacDonald's happy juice. Hell, no. The Devil had been delighted by the way he'd put this arrogant half-demon in an impossible position. Because, God help him, not only would Rafe have to travel all the way to Argentina, but his first target was an elderly nun.

CHAPTER SEVEN

RAFE COULD FINALLY breathe once he was out on the sidewalk again. He looked around to see if he was being followed. When a hand landed on his back, he whirled and pulled his knife, ready to fight.

"Relax, bro, I'm here to help." His brother Tomas jumped back and held up his hands in surrender.

"Sorry. If you'd just been where I have, you'd be edgy too." Rafe saw dawn had come and gone. Damn it, he'd lost a couple of hours. A nearby church bell tolled. Eight o'clock. "Thanks for coming. How did you know where to find me?"

"Ian MacDonald called before he settled for the day. He told me where you'd gone. He and his vampire pals want to give you whatever you'll need if you did manage to work out some kind of deal with the Devil." Tomas crossed himself and looked over his shoulder. "Guess it's a good thing you've made those kind of friends, even though they still freak me out. Anyway, I have a list of what they've got available. Let's get out of here and you can tell me what happened with you know who." He gestured toward his black SUV, parked at the curb. "Come on, I'll drive."

"Okay, let me think. I've got a list of my own here." Rafe pulled the papers out of his pocket. He'd stuffed them there so he'd have both hands free in case of a fight when he left the coffee shop. Students were rushing about on their way to class and into the shop behind him. They came out with coffee and pastries. The students were mere mortals, clueless about what was beneath their feet. But he could smell demon in the air.

Then he noticed the blonde, her eyes gleaming as she watched him through the plate glass window. She was after that bounty Lucifer was offering and, damn him, Rafe realized it was still on until his five days, five kills were accomplished. The demon would probably follow him, hoping for a lead to Daniela.

"Hurry, we're being watched." Rafe shoved Tom ahead of him and they were soon in the car, pulling away into the early morning traffic. It was bumper to bumper as they passed the Capitol building and headed for Sixth Street. Tomas drove carefully, too carefully, moving so slowly in the heavy traffic that Rafe wanted to scream at him to hurry.

He had five days to do the impossible. He bet the sinners he was after weren't going down easily. Who knew if they were even still where Lucifer had said they'd be? Lucifer's grin as he'd handed Rafe the printouts promised twists and turns. All he had were names and locations. Rafe needed to know more before he blindly did Lucifer's bidding. He had to get to a computer and fast.

Lucifer was all about suffering. What if these were good people who didn't deserve to die? He wouldn't put it past the Prince of Darkness to pull a fast one like that. Tests. Rafe hated them. His body clenched in frustration and he felt a headache bloom. His eyes watered, while the sunlight blinded him. Dangerous. He had to focus, stay alert every moment.

"You look wiped out, bro. Can you tell me what happened? Did you really meet the Devil in a freaking coffee shop?" Tomas finally pulled into the lot behind the club. N-V was dark, closed until five o'clock at night when it and the other bars along Sixth Street opened for happy hour. Rafe looked around, sniffed the air then pulled his keys from his pocket and let them in. No demons yet but he bet they wouldn't be far behind him.

"I don't want to talk about it and I really don't want to get you involved. To save my baby, I have to complete some tasks for Lucifer. Bad things. With a five-day time limit. Trust me, *hermano*, the less you know about this shit, the better." Rafe turned and put his hand on Tomas's shoulder. "If something happens to me, I'm counting on you to keep this club going. Its income provides for my family."

"And mine. But, Rafe. Only five days? I don't like the sound of this. Forget about N-V. We can always find work. Stay here, make a plan for us to fight him. You have powerful friends who want to help you. You think the Devil wants you to fail?" Tomas grasped him and pulled him into a hug. "*Hermano*, don't let him do it." His voice broke. "Don't shut me out. I want to be by your side in this fight."

Rafe pounded his back then pushed him away. "I know. But I need you here, like I said. Lucifer is testing me. I have to pass on my own to save Daniela. The Devil will have it no other way. Sacrificing yourself would not help. Understand?"

"Damn it, but I do." Tomas wiped his eyes. "Now let me tell you what your vampires told me. There is a private jet ready for you if you need it. At Bergstrom. Money? As much as you need. Use this, they said." He handed Rafe a debit card with his name on it and a piece of paper with a name and phone number. "That's the pilot's number. The plane belongs to Jeremy Blade and his wife, Gloriana. If you ever doubted they love you, this should prove it. The money? It was dropped off by one of the cats. She said it arranged by Ian MacDonald. She said not to worry, the cat compound is secure. Your boys and Lacy will be safe from any demons trying to take them."

Now it was Rafe's turn to wipe his eyes. "I don't know what I did to deserve such loyal friends." He hoped Ian had accessed Lilith's safety deposit box. Rafe didn't want to think too closely about where Lilith had gotten *her* money. At least it had made the cats cooperative in protecting his family.

"Just come back alive so you prove their generosity was not in vain." Tomas cleared his throat. "In case you do need to fly out today, they said they loaded the plane with what you might need. Weapons, I guess. The pilot will file a flight plan as soon as you tell him where you need to go. If you stay here, the vampires will be ready tonight when they wake to back you up. Or fly to meet you if you call." Tomas shook his head. "It seems they thought of everything. Your vampires really came through for you. Me? *Los vampiros* still make me want to hide in the office here and guard my vein."

"They would never touch you, Tom. Out of loyalty to me." Rafe stared at the debit card. "This is overwhelming. But not surprising. I've known Glory and her husband a long time. She is a good friend. The best. She accepted me despite my demon side. Not many can overlook it." He felt the warmth of Tomas's hand on his back. "My brother, I know it has not been easy for you to ignore it."

"I see only good in you, Rafael."

Rafe couldn't look at his brother or he'd break down. He also ignored the urge to give in to the rage and helplessness that threatened to send him to his knees. No time for that. He opened the safe in his office and pulled out his passport and a gun he was familiar with, ammo too. He took out the cash he kept for emergencies. This certainly qualified. Ten thousand. It would have to be enough. Slipping in and out of a country without being noticed was something he'd done before and cash came in handy.

"The only way I can ever repay you or any

of my friends is to make sure I get Daniela to safety and settle this with Lucifer once and for all." Rafe sat at his computer. "I've got five names, people I will have to drag to Hell." He stared at his brother. "Which means Lucifer thinks they've lived long enough. I'm his hit man, *hermano*. I just hope they really deserve this because I'm here to tell you Hell is a place I pray I never have to see again."

"Rafael!" Tomas watched him spread out his papers. "He wants you to kill these people? I thought you weren't going to tell me…"

"So did I. I guess I have to tell someone." Rafe turned on the laptop and cursed his slow Wi-Fi. "The first one he wants me to seize is in a mountainous area of Argentina, the rest scattered around Texas and Louisiana. I must take the plane and do the Argentinian first. Five days to capture and kill five sinners. It sounds impossible." He finally had the search engine ready to go. "Leave me now. It's better if you don't know any more. Concentrate on liquor deliveries and the band that will be coming to perform in a couple of days. I'm not sure where I'll be then. It's all on you, little brother."

"I will handle your business." Tomas ran his hand over his face. "I have faith in you. You've proven yourself as a warrior, then as a bodyguard. I have no worries that you'll be able to take out these people who I'm sure do deserve to die." Tomas frowned. "Just promise to take care of yourself. Save Daniela then come back to us, all of us. Your children need their *papa*. I need my brother. You can believe I am praying for you."

"Thanks. Keep doing that." Rafe said that to himself as Tomas finally left the room, closing the door behind him.

He checked out the first name on the list. A woman. A nun in a convent in a remote part of Argentina. This was crazy. Not that he didn't believe a woman could be evil, he'd been up against evil women before. He shivered and began to read about Sister Maria Katherine Zitzberg.

"I filed the flight plan for that mountainous area in Argentina. It'll be a long flight. We need a co-pilot, unless you'll be able to spell me from time to time at the controls. You fly?" The pilot, whose name was Buck, was mortal. He didn't seem bothered by either the fact that he worked for vampires or by his orders to fly a stranger out of the country at a moment's notice.

"Yeah, I've done some flying from time to time." Rafe didn't bother to explain that he usually flew as a bird. Hey, he'd learned to pilot planes a few decades ago, surely the basics were still the same.

"Good to know. Of course, I've got autopilot as well when I need a break." The man frowned and waved a hand in front of his face. "Hey, dude, no insult, but can you change clothes before you get on board? Jerry has a nice plane and, frankly, you smell like you've been rolling in garbage." Buck kept his distance. "I notice you didn't bring any luggage. I can get you a change of clothes. Jerry keeps some in the front closet here if you don't mind stepping into the airport office and washing up while I finish my pre-check."

Rafe forced a laugh. He knew he reeked. "Sorry about the smell. Yeah, get me those clothes. I had an unfortunate accident on the way here. Then let's hit the skies as soon as we can. I know enough about flying to spell you from time to time on the way to Argentina. Don't worry about that." He wasn't about to explain how he'd shifted to the airfield after he'd found N-V surrounded by eager demons ready to follow him as soon as he left the bar. That bounty must be a really big one.

It wasn't the first time he'd ended up a cockroach. He hadn't had much choice and the garbage truck that emptied his Dumpster arrived just in time to save him. He'd hitched a ride in the truck until he was far enough away from Sixth Street to do his bird thing and fly out to where the plane was waiting. Luckily the pilot was used to strange. Now he tossed out a clean shirt and jeans that should fit. Rafe and Glory's husband wore about the same sizes. Then the pilot went about his business, getting ready to fly south. He didn't ask questions other than wanting to know if Rafe knew how long they might be staying in Argentina. Blade must pay him really well.

"It should be a quick trip. In and out." Rafe was glad to see there were no demons lurking at the airport. Not that he could smell above his own reek anyway.

In the office nearby, Rafe pulled off his black

shirt and threw it in the trash. His jeans were next after he was sure to put that list and his weapons where he needed them. He washed up, then was soon back in the plane, eager to get going. The pilot gave him a quick tour of the cockpit and seemed relieved when Rafe proved he knew his way around a flight deck.

Buck nodded. "We can leave whenever you're ready. You've got Wi-Fi on board, no password needed." He was a man in his prime, fit and eager to fly. "You have a passport? We'll be met by security when we land. They'll want to see papers and there will be fees involved." He smiled wryly. "Negotiable, if you know what I mean."

"Sure. Money always greases the wheels. Let's go. The sooner the better." Rafe looked around the plane. It was luxurious, could comfortably take a dozen passengers and had a sleeping compartment in the back. The door to that was closed. He washed his face again in the galley sink and ran water over his hair. He felt he could finally breathe again.

"I'm ready." He nodded at Buck.

"Then buckle up." The pilot nodded at the cockpit. "We've been cleared for takeoff." Buck slammed the cockpit door and revved the engines before the plane started moving.

Rafe would have liked to have checked what cargo had been put on board—weapons in particular—but he wasn't about to slow things down. He just strapped in. As soon as the seatbelt light overhead went out, he would do just that. Someone had stocked the built-in bar in front of him and he reached for a wrapped sandwich as they took off. Damn, he hadn't realized how hungry he was. He would certainly need his strength for what was coming. He tore off the plastic and bit into a hearty roast beef on wheat while he opened the laptop that had been left for him. Research. The convent he would have to enter was built like an ancient stronghold. From what he read, Sister Maria had lived there since the 1940s. A fleeing Nazi?

There were plenty of stories that claimed Argentina had been a safe haven for the Nazis who'd managed to leave Germany at the end of World War II. He twisted off the top of a bottle of water, pausing it at his lips when he found an allegation that Hitler himself, with his mistress Eva Braun, might have escaped and made a home for himself there. Rumor or true? He remembered the war, had fought with the Allies and had believed Hitler had committed suicide rather than surrender. Had they all been duped? The more conspiracy theories he read, the more he wondered if it were possible. His fists clenched at the thought. So many people had died because of Hitler's obsession with ruling the world and his hatred of Jews.

Rafe slammed the laptop closed. Hell. Was Hitler even now roasting there for his sins? Or did Lucifer admire the scope of the dictator's evil? Consider him a good buddy? If there was a reward down there for depravity, Rafe didn't know what he would do. Could he take Lucifer down? End him?

"Keep thinking that way, my son, and you will go mad. You may lose your daughter on top of it." A figure appeared in the seat next to him. It shimmered then gradually gained form. It was a man. He was a monk actually, who had the saddest eyes Rafe had ever seen.

Rafe reached for the knife in his boot. "Who are you and where did you come from?"

"You need help." The man looked up at the ceiling, "Someone decided to send me. My name is Abraham. Call me Abe. You can't kill Lucifer. And you can't change Hell. What you can do is what Luc has asked of you. Which is well-nigh impossible." He shrugged. "Typical Devil dealings. He delights in making people suffer."

"Yes, I know." Rafe leaned back and studied the man. "Are you an angel? A ghost? What?" He put away his knife. It had been a kneejerk reaction and probably useless. He sure wasn't going to antagonize this guy since he'd take whatever help he could get. That a higher power had sent him to assist a demon was encouraging. That meant Rafe must be on the right side of things here.

"Don't worry about labels. And don't worry about appearances." Abe smiled. "I know I look like a peace-loving cleric. But I can get down and dirty when it comes to righting wrongs."

"Good to know." Rafe had to admit the man's appearance wasn't reassuring. The monk was short, plump and had soft hands. His face was young, like he was barely out of his teens. What did he know about fighting? "How old are you, anyway?"

"Thousands of years, certainly older than you, Rafael." Abe grinned. "I have powers you won't believe until you see me at work. The seat belt sign is off now but I wouldn't advise you to check out that back bedroom. There are vampires back there, dead during the daylight hours. They don't like to be observed when they are like that, do they?"

"Seriously? Some of my vampire friends are asleep back there?" Rafe was tempted to take a peek. He'd been Glory's bodyguard for years and had certainly seen her dead during the day. It was creepy to be sure, but reassuring to know he'd been keeping her safe. Was she there with her husband? To provide backup in Argentina? Or had MacDonald come because Sheila had asked him to protect her son-in-law? Didn't matter. He was grateful that he wouldn't be alone for this impossible mission. He took a drink of his water, wondering how a monk would feel about taking down a nun.

"You command tremendous loyalty from the people you know. That says a lot about your character. And don't worry about me when the time comes to face this nun you are hunting. If I sense she is evil, I will do what must be done." Abe reached for a sandwich. "Mortal food. I wonder if I dare." He looked up and smiled. "Only one way to find out."

CHAPTER EIGHT

THEY LANDED AT a private airport outside Mendosa, Argentina as the sun began to set. Rafe handed the pilot some cash and sent him out to talk to uniformed officials. One eventually boarded the plane and there was a pleasant conversation in Spanish and English while Rafe showed his American passport. A glance around the spacious interior seemed to satisfy the officer that Rafe's story of a quick business trip was legitimate. Rafe's offer of a donation to a fund for Argentinian orphans was graciously accepted. He doubted any orphans would benefit as the money was tucked out of sight into a uniform pocket.

To Rafe's amusement, Abraham stayed visible, introducing himself in flawless Spanish as Rafe's spiritual advisor. That gained Rafe some respect and certainly hurried things along. When the *"Padre"* asked about the convent they were planning to visit, the customs officer crossed himself.

"I must warn you, they do not welcome visitors there. If you do not have an invitation…" He frowned. "You might be turned away."

"I am never turned away. I am an emissary from a very important person." Abe smiled and the man suddenly dropped to his knees.

"Will you bless me, *Padre*?" The officer bowed his head.

"Of course." Abe mumbled some Latin then touched the man's head. He pulled the officer to his feet and stared into his eyes. The man began to tremble, his knees shaking. "I recommend you go to church, my son, and say your prayers. Then see that the money in your pocket helps those orphans my friend mentioned. It will do much to cleanse your soul." Abe escorted him to the plane's doorway. "But that is up to you. Perhaps your soul is of no concern to you."

The officer crossed himself. "No, I mean yes. My soul. I care. Very much. I will go at once. The orphans. There are many here in Mendosa and in Buenos Aires. Good luck at the convent, *Padre*. But I warn you, things are not right there. People go and don't come back." He glanced at Rafe. "It is God's will. We do not interfere." He hurried down the steps and jumped into the jeep waiting on the tarmac. He gestured to the driver and they roared away as the sky darkened and the sun set.

"Impressive." Rafe turned as the door to the back cabin opened. "Our passengers are awake." He expected to see Glory St. Clair and her husband. Then his wife rushed through the door and threw herself into his arms.

"Don't be mad! I had to come." Lacy buried her face against his chest.

Rafe held her and breathed in her unique scent

of cat and the wild strawberry shampoo she always used. Her red hair was loose and flowing down her back, her arms wound around his neck. Mad? Hell, yes, he was furious, and yet stupidly happy to have her here.

"You're supposed to be at home, taking care of our sons." He pushed her away, so he could look into her eyes, her beautiful green eyes. Damn, he loved her, especially her fiery spirit that wouldn't let her stay meekly in the cat compound while he was off defending his family and trying to save their daughter.

"My mother, my cat clan and a handful of your vampire friends are there. I wasn't about to let you face this alone." She raised her chin, challenging him to rail at her. "I can fight. I *will* fight. At your side, Rafe. Don't try to shut me out of this."

"Baby, this isn't just a fight, we're doing the Devil's handiwork here. It's nasty, filthy business. I don't want it to touch you." He couldn't resist. He stroked her smooth cheek with a fingertip. "You knew I'd turn this plane around and send you back if I saw you here, didn't you? Is that why you hid until we landed?"

"Yes. And I was exhausted. I hadn't slept since Daniela was taken. So I finally fell asleep. With your vampire friends." She tried to hide a shudder. "Glory and Jerry were in one bunk and I was in the other."

"With someone else on the floor between us so Lacy was trapped." Glory stood in the aisle, her husband right behind her. "Your wife now knows how a vampire looks dead during the day.

Not pretty, but you know that, Rafe. Sorry about that, Lacy."

"Hey, you don't look that different once you get used to the fact that you're not breathing." Rafe hugged Lacy. "She survived, didn't you, babe?"

"Yes, and, you're right. It wasn't that bad." Lacy smiled. "I'm just so grateful for the plane and your support, guys."

"As am I." Rafe put Lacy behind him. He hugged Glory then shook Blade's hand. "Thanks for coming. And Miguel Cisneros! You were the one on the floor?"

"Yes. I can die anywhere, no problem. I'm fluent in the language and thought I might be able to help." He reached around Jeremy Blade to shake Rafe's hand. "It is not often we have a worthy task. Saving your daughter from the Devil's clutches! I would like nothing more than to make Lucifer rue the day he came up against you and your army of vampires."

Rafe felt Lacy's arms slide around his waist as he swallowed. An army of vampires. How had he rated such support?

"Cisneros is right. Sure, Glory was all for helping you." Blade kept his arm around his wife. "I have learned not to be jealous of how much she loves you. Fighting the Devil *is* a worthy cause. Let's kick the bastard's butt." He stared at Abe, who was studying the new arrivals with bright eyes. "Going to introduce us to your new friend?"

Rafe cleared his throat. "This is Abraham. It seems even the Big Guy upstairs wanted to help us keep my baby out of Hell." Rafe gripped Lacy's hands as he let Abe take over his own introduction. The vampires were clearly impressed that God was on his side. Rafe still couldn't believe it.

Glory sat in one of the seats and stared at Rafe. "I guess now we head to the convent. I heard the customs agent say the nuns didn't like visitors. Do you have a plan to get around that?"

Rafe looked at Abe. "My new friend says no one turns him away. That should help."

Abe locked eyes with Miguel. "I doubt anyone would dare turn this one away either. Right, *amigo*?"

Miguel nodded. "They can try, but then they will regret it." The two men had a brief staring contest that made the air crackle inside the small cabin until Miguel shrugged. "What are we waiting for? The only plan we need is a map to where we're going. Then we figure out who is going to fly and who is going to use regular transportation."

Lacy let go of her husband. "You know I can't fly. Rafe has told me Glory doesn't like to shift so that means she's riding with me. Who else, Rafe?"

"I guess there's no point in trying to get you and Glory to stay here in the plane." Rafe walked over to look through the bag of hardware Miguel had pulled out of the back cabin. Weapons. Good ones.

Lacy shook her head. "We're going. Either drive us or we'll arrange for our own car and meet you there." Her claws dug into his shoulder as she leaned in to see what was in the bag. "Seriously?

That's an arsenal. Smoke bombs. Rapid fire guns?
I can't imagine using those things on a group of
nuns."

"One nun. And we'll use whatever we have to
in order to get our target. I told the pilot to call
ahead to arrange transportation equipped with a
GPS. Lucifer didn't make clear what we should
do with the woman once we capture her. But he
does want her dead." That bald statement made
everyone in the plane react. The vampire men
were stone-faced. Glory and Lacy shuddered.
Abe? Surprisingly, he smiled. Rafe realized his
target must be really evil.

"Play it by ear, my son. I'm sure we'll encounter
surprises at the convent. We may have to chase
the woman down before all is said and done."
Abe looked eager to begin.

"She's over one hundred years old, Abe, and
mortal. I can't imagine there will be a 'chase.' But
I guess she could have hired guns around her."
Rafe glanced out the open door and saw a black
SUV arrive. "Here's our transportation. Lacy,
Glory, I hope you brought coats." It was winter in
Argentina and the air was cold and crisp. It would
be colder in the mountains.

"Don't worry about us." Lacy had put on a
black hoodie. He knew she could always shift into
her cat, which would give her a fur coat. Glory
had on a jacket with more style than warmth. But
vampires usually didn't feel the cold anyway.

Blade put a serious looking gun under his
jacket. "Miguel and I can fly and check out the
place in advance. Glory will ride with you, Abe,

and Lacy. I can call if I see any issues or guards you need to watch for on the road." He looked around the cabin. "That work for you, Rafe? Abe? Or do you fly too, *Padre*?"

"I'll be happy to take the car with Rafael. Riding in a car will be a new experience for me." Abe smiled. "I like your plan."

"I have the address and can show you a map on the computer." Rafe took a minute to huddle with the two men over the map while Lacy and Glory picked through the pile of weapons Blade had brought on board. When they offered Abe a gun, he shook his head.

"I have my own weapons, ladies. But thank you."

"I have my own as well, *Padre*, but something like this can come in handy when dealing with mortals. We can use them to make noise. Even waving them around can scare them into surrendering." Glory put a small gun in the pocket of her camouflage print jacket. Her pink camouflage jacket. It might have come from her vintage clothing shop along with the matching jeans.

"Shooting at nuns? I can't imagine it." Lacy complimented Glory's sparkly tennis shoes.

Glory frowned at Rafe when he snorted. "Don't make fun of me. I can make a style statement and still take this very seriously. Of course, they're cute, but I wore them because I can run in them, Rafe." She patted Lacy's back. "We will make sure your little girl comes through this safely, I promise. You know I love her."

Lacy's eyes filled with tears. "Thanks, Glory. Thank all of you. The idea that my baby could end up…"

"She won't. She can't." Rafe pulled her into his arms. "Now let's hit the road. First, though, I have to tell you what I've learned about the woman we're going to capture. She's a Nazi. Or at least her husband was. He ran one of the worst concentration camps in Germany and she was right there with him. You can't tell me she didn't know what was going on. She was his secretary. Kept records of who went to the gas chambers." He hesitated to share what he'd read on the Internet, but knew it would make the coming confrontation easier to take.

"Listen, I found stories from survivors of those camps that I believe to be true. This woman who is now a nun would pick out women to cook and clean her house, all while starving them. She would beat them if she caught them trying to eat what they cooked. On top of that, she sent them to their deaths if they got too weak to clean to her high standards."

"No!" Lacy looked sick. "She *is* a monster."

"Evil. She and her husband escaped to Argentina when the war was ending. He died several decades ago. She came to hide in this convent and has apparently been there all this time. Lucifer has let her live there for decades, but now thinks she's lived long enough. He's ready for her to come down to him."

"She deserves Hell and whatever punishment is waiting for her there." Glory slipped her arm around Blade's waist. "She's over a hundred years old?"

"One hundred and one. What is it they say? Only the good die young?" Abe gazed at the group around him. "But then I'm surrounded by ancients here and I sense you are all good people. We will forget that old saying." He walked to the doorway. "Let's be off. I'm anxious to see this convent. Will we have a fight on our hands?" He wiggled his fingers and lightning crackled around the small space. "I admit I'm ready and eager for it."

Rafe exchanged looks with the rest of his so-called army. Lightning? He could smell the ozone and feel the heat, though it had disappeared as fast as it had flashed around them. This was going to be interesting. They all filed out of the plane. The pilot stood next to the SUV, awaiting orders.

"Buck, I don't know when we're going to be returning to Texas. But we can't take too long. I'm in a serious time crunch. Please make sure we're fueled up and ready for takeoff, then take a nap. You'll need the rest." Rafe tossed the duffle full of weapons into the back of the car.

"Yes, sir." The pilot stopped to have a word with Blade, then headed back to the main building to arrange for fuel.

Rafe was relieved to see they were alone. Only a single spotlight lit the area where the car was parked, making it hard to see details in the dark. At least the night sky was clear with a million stars above them and a three-quarter moon. Lights outlined the runway yards away but no other planes were taking off or landing as the group got ready to go. The lights of the town glowed in the distance and the dark shape of mountains loomed nearby.

"We'll meet you there." Blade kissed Glory good-bye then morphed into a black bird and took off. Miguel was right behind him.

"Birds. Why did I expect bats?" Abe climbed into the front passenger seat while the women piled into the back.

"Cliché, Abe. Vampires try to do the unexpected." Glory fastened her seatbelt. "How long do you think it will take to get there, Rafe?"

He fed the address into the navigation system. It announced it would take them forty-five minutes to their destination. Damn it. Flying, he could be there in less than fifteen.

"You heard the nav system's voice. It's going to take a while. Any ideas how we can get them to let us in, Abraham?" Rafe couldn't imagine they'd just open the door to his crew.

"I look like a priest. Why wouldn't they invite me inside to see to their spiritual health?" Abe turned around to stare at Lacy. "Don't I look harmless to you, my dear?"

"Hah! Not after I saw you shoot lightning bolts. You scared me." She reached forward and patted his shoulder. "I'm glad you're on my side." She narrowed her gaze at the driver's side. "But my husband is part demon. That doesn't bother you?"

"We know he has never let that part of himself

rule his actions. Do you believe he is a good man, Lacy?" Abe studied her. "In your heart?"

She blinked until a tear ran down her cheek. "I do. He's the father of my children. But then one of them..." She sobbed and put her hands over her eyes.

"Yes, one of them inherited my evil blood. That precious little girl has the demon in her. I knew it the minute she opened her eyes and saw the red glow in them. I'm afraid she's cursed because of me." Rafe hit the steering wheel, sending the car toward the curb as he drove them out of the airport. "I'm sorry, Lacy. Sorrier than you can imagine. I never should have fathered children. I meant it when I said I'll have a vasectomy as soon as this is over. Don't worry, I swear you won't have to worry about having any more of my demon children." Did he sound bitter? Of course, he did. He was.

"Shut up, Rafe. You're a wonderful father and the way you've lived is proof that Daniela's demon blood won't make her a bad person. Not with you to guide her." Glory patted Lacy's shoulder. "What's done is done. Who could have predicted this? Now Rafe is determined to make things right. Bear with him, Lacy. We're all here to make sure Daniela gets through this safely. The Devil is not getting his claws into her. Believe that."

"Thanks for saying that, Glory. I hope you're right." Rafe concentrated on his driving after that. They left the airport and climbed steadily into the mountainous area. He could hear Lacy sniffling then talking quietly to Glory. His wife didn't deserve what he was putting her through. He felt Abraham's hand on his arm.

"Son, don't be so hard on yourself. This battle has been brewing for a while. That's why *I* am here. The Devil is greedy and always wants more than he deserves. He thrives on torment. What you're feeling now—your pain—is filling him with glee. Don't give him the satisfaction!" Abe glanced back at Lacy. "We will see you through this, my child, I promise." The priest's quiet voice made Rafe's hands briefly relax on the steering wheel.

He'd like to believe the monk. But had Abe met Lucifer? Had he seen the place where serial killers were heroes and torture was part of play time? Rafe swallowed, pretty sure he was going to be sick. He imagined his little girl at Lucifer's right hand, exposed to the debauchery and pain that amused the Devil. No! That couldn't happen. The narrow road blurred and he felt his foot press down hard, sending them swerving again, dangerously close to the road's edge that could send them plummeting down the mountainside.

"Rafe! Look out!" Lacy screamed from the back seat. "Are you trying to kill us all?"

He blinked and managed to steer them back to safety in the nick of time. "I hope not." He hit the brakes and leaned his head against the wheel. "I'm sorry. Give me a moment."

Glory jumped out of the car, then wrenched open his door. "Let me drive. Get in the back seat with your wife before you *do* kill us. How will that help Daniela?"

Rafe didn't resist when she jerked him out of the car. Hell, he hadn't even buckled his seat belt. He was losing it.

"I'm sorry. I don't know what happened. I can't seem to concentrate." He slumped into the back seat and leaned against Lacy. Her arms went around him and she pressed his face to her warm breasts. He inhaled, closed his eyes and felt himself sinking into oblivion. All he wanted to do was stay pressed against his wife. He loved her. How could he hurt her again? The children. He didn't dare make love to her until he was sure he wouldn't plant more demon seed. His eyes burned with unshed tears.

Glory slammed the back door, then jumped into the driver's seat. The sound jolted him but he still couldn't seem to sit up or open his eyes. The car didn't move. He should care. Instead, when Lacy rubbed his back, he sighed.

"Rafe, honey, what's wrong with you?" Lacy whispered. "Are you sick?" she lifted his chin. "Answer me! You don't look right."

He wanted to say something but couldn't form words. He just shook his head and sank back against her, desperate to stay safe in her arms. This must be how his children felt when their mother held them. So warm, so loved. He'd never had a mother's love. Lilith had abandoned him early and left him with his well-meaning grandparents who had never wanted him. No one had ever cosseted him, cradled him in their arms. He had always been pushed aside, in the way, very different from the other grandchildren with his glowing eyes and strange demon powers. He moaned.

"Rafe, for God's sake!" Lacy pushed at him. "We've got to go now. To save Daniela." Lacy's voice rose. "You're worrying me. Wake up! Look at me." She shook his shoulders.

Rafe opened his eyes. "I love you. I'm so sorry I've disappointed you. Please forgive me." He kissed the spot where her shirt was open at her neck.

"Rafael!" Abe reached between the seats to touch his back. "Lacy, make him sit up. I think I know what's wrong here."

"Something is definitely off, Abe." Glory's voice sounded strained. "We need to get moving and Rafe sounds like a different man, like he's been drugged. Certainly not like the tough bodyguard I know."

Rafe groaned when Lacy shoved until he was forced to sit up. "Hey, I don't feel well. Food poisoning? Altitude sickness? I don't know." He stared at his wife. "Baby, give me a minute. Air, I need air." He punched the controls and rolled down his window. Cold mountain air rushed in but he couldn't seem to breathe.

"That won't help. Look at me, Rafael." Abe leaned between the seats. "Did you really think Lucifer would play fair?"

"What?" Rafe's vision blurred. He choked and couldn't focus on the priest. Lacy stroked his hair, as if *he* were the cat in this car. It felt so good he wanted to purr, and leaned toward her again. A few more minutes in her arms…

"The Devil has you under some kind of spell, Rafael." Abe muttered something then grabbed Rafe's arm. "Give me your hand. Hold tight."

"A spell? I don't…" Rafe couldn't concentrate. He tried to lift his arm. Heavy. Lacy finally grabbed it and thrust his hand into Abe's palm.

"Rafe, he's right. Something's wrong. Your eyes are dull and your skin feels cool. You know you usually run hot. This is crazy." Lacy kissed his cheek. "Baby, look at Abe. He's going to try to fix this, aren't you, Father?"

"I hope I can." Abe squeezed Rafe's hand. "Look here, son! Eye to eye." The monk focused on him. "Don't close your eyes or look away, no matter what happens. I mean it!" Abe stared at him, his eyes flaring with blue light.

Pain hit Rafe hard then, as if a thousand volts of electricity were shooting into his palm. He screamed and tried to jerk free. "Oh, God!" It was as if he held a live wire, his body thrumming with all the energy Abe sent into him. His hand was on fire, his arm sizzling while his legs twitched and his heels drummed on the floorboard. If he could just look away, close his eyes.

"Steady. Stay with me. We're almost there." Abe refused to let him break free.

"Shit! Are you curing me or killing me?" Rafe wanted to fight, to look anywhere but at the monk who kept filling him with liquid fire. Pain rolled through him, worse than anything he'd felt before, as bad as the Devil's tricks. Escape. He needed to close his eyes and sink into darkness.

But Abe wouldn't let him have that blessed release, willing him to focus and take the pain.

Rafe wondered if this might be the worst trick of all. Maybe Abe wasn't from God but sent by Lucifer. He went mad then, jerking desperately to free himself from this strange and painful spell. Nothing worked. Tears filled his eyes. He had no choice but to beg.

"Okay, okay, you win. I feel it. Let me go, man! Please. You're killing me!"

Abe finally closed his eyes then blinked and studied Rafe. He must have been satisfied with what he saw because he finally dropped Rafe's hand. "There, I think you're back."

"Back? Where the hell have I been?" Rafe stared down at his blackened palm. Miracle of miracles, it didn't hurt. Not now anyway. He glanced at Lacy when she brushed his cheek.

"You're warm again. You scared us, Rafe." She held him close, breathing in his scent like she usually did. "The Devil had you under some kind of evil spell."

Rafe stared at Abe. "Maybe the Devil still does."

"Have faith, my son." Abe glowed and it wasn't with satisfaction but as if God had blessed him from above. "That was bad, a struggle, but we won." He smiled. "Feel better?"

Rafe took a breath, the chill mountain air finally doing its thing, helping him feel clean. Yes, he did feel better, himself again. Almost.

"Yeah, I guess I do. Lucifer is a cheating bastard. I should have expected something like that." Rafe rubbed his palm on his jeans. "Damn it. I couldn't focus, think." Truth be told, he still needed some time to get his thoughts together. This was wrong. But what had he expected? A smooth and easy trip? He saw Glory in the driver's seat where she looked ready to go. "You going to take over?"

"When Abe gives me the signal. The GPS shows we are about ten minutes out." She put the car in gear when Abe gave her the all clear.

"We need to hurry. This spell thing already wasted too much of our time." Rafe leaned forward. He didn't like being in the back seat. Glory wasn't such a great driver at the best of times. Now she was poking along the dark road until he finally snapped.

"Speed up, woman. There's no other traffic. You know I don't have much time. This is just the first of five sinners I have to scoop up for Lucifer. That flight down here took most of today." Rafe leaned forward, practically breathing down her neck.

"I can't go too fast. These roads are horrible and way too narrow. I don't think there's been any maintenance done here in centuries. We're only feet from the edge of a cliff and a drop that will send us to our deaths." She did speed up a little.

"We're immortal, Glory. But, yeah, a wreck would slow us down." Rafe realized he was being unfair, especially when Lacy gripped his arm.

"Okay, I'm sorry. The road is bad because the customs officer was right. My research says there aren't many visitors up here." Rafe wondered what the nuns thought of Sister Maria. Had they embraced her evil ways? He wouldn't have time to find out. He was only there to take the one woman. He rubbed his aching head.

"Rafe, are you really okay now?" Lacy leaned against him.

"Just thinking about how this is more complicated than I realized. There are others in the convent. They have been living under this woman's influence. I wonder how they will feel once I take her." Rafe leaned back in the seat. "Abe, do you know if the other nuns in this convent are good or bad?"

"Don't worry about them, Rafael. I will make sure they are taken care of once we are gone. They will get what they deserve." Abe smiled. "Just handle your own problem."

"What kind of convent is this? Abe, what do you know?" Lacy held onto Rafe's arm.

"It used to be a good one, helping the locals, the poor, and teaching children. That all changed when your Nazi moved in. It quit serving the community. I'm surprised the Church didn't investigate." Abe frowned. "But perhaps it did. Clever people can fool others if no one looks too closely. I will send someone in after we leave to correct the situation."

Rafe's phone rang. "Blade. What do you see?"

"The place is huge and is built like a fortress. There are no guards though and I don't smell any demons around it. It seems like a quiet place but is equipped with a heavy door. We should be able to surprise them and take the woman, no problem. How dangerous can a convent full of nuns be?"

Rafe felt his stomach squeeze. Overconfidence. If that wasn't a recipe for disaster, he didn't know what was.

CHAPTER NINE

T HE PLACE DID look like an ancient stone fort with high walls and no windows that he could see. It was surrounded by forest, a few miles from the nearest village. It seemed a perfect hiding place for a former Nazi.

Naturally, his wife wasn't going to sit quietly in the car while Rafe went about his business. For the freaking Devil. He didn't bother being quiet as he slammed the car door. He felt Lacy's presence by his side. Hell, no.

"Stay behind me. Please." He turned to give her a warning look. "I mean it, babe. I have no idea what I'll be dealing with. Let me do what I have to. I know you hate my demon, but it comes with powers that I may have to drag out and use here. Understand?"

"Be careful." Her eyes were wide, but she nodded and gave him the space he needed. Not Abe. He was rubbing his hands together, obviously eager to see this woman who was number one on Lucifer's sinner hit parade.

Blade and Cisneros stepped out of the shadows.

"No reaction from the convent since we arrived. If there are guards, I've seen no signs of them and I did a couple of flyovers. There's a back door but I can't imagine an ancient nun making a run for it into the woods there." Cisneros was pretty amped himself. "Shall we just knock and see what happens?"

"Might as well." Rafe stepped up to the massive wooden door bound in iron. There was a rope bell pull. He gave it a tug and heard a distant clang.

"There's movement inside. Someone's coming." Blade pulled his gun.

"Put that thing away. These *are* nuns. If you can't take one down with your bare hands, then what kind of man are you?" Rafe realized his so-called army was way too eager for a showdown.

Forget the nuns. Blade sent him a mental message that he would be glad to show Rafe just what he could do with his bare hands if the demon didn't watch his damned mouth.

Rafe shook his head. "Okay, I'm sorry. Obviously, we all need to take a beat and think about this. I have no idea if the nuns in this convent know who they've been harboring all these years. We ask for her, see what happens. Got it?"

"Sure. You're in charge." Blade still didn't look happy, especially when his wife grabbed his arm and whispered a warning in his ear to chill.

The vampire gave his wife a look, but didn't shrug her off. "But hear this, Valdez. I've tangled with nuns before. There was a time, centuries ago, when hiding out in a nunnery was a favorite dodge for some of the worst women I've ever met." He gently removed Glory's hand from his arm. "Let me finish, love. The very fact that we're here means they gave this woman sanctuary. If she did what you say she did, she didn't deserve to be protected for decades. Hell, they should have slammed the door in her face when she arrived."

"You're right, my son." Abe smiled at Blade. "Your anger is well-placed. But I'm sure you also know that the evil among us can be clever liars. Let's wait before we condemn the rest of the nuns, shall we? They could have been fooled into taking this viper to their bosoms." He turned as the door handle rattled. "Ah, here we are. Calm now, everyone. Let Rafael lead the way."

Rafe forced a smile when a sweet-faced nun, garbed in a traditional black and white habit pulled open the heavy door. He greeted her in Spanish.

She shook her head. "*Lo siento, señor,* but we do not admit visitors. There is *una iglesia* in the village a few kilometers away if you have need of prayers. They also have *un restaurante* and *un hotel* if you are looking for a place to spend the night." She pointed the way as she shivered in the cold mountain air. "If you had car trouble, I'm sure there is someone in the village who can help you. It is close enough for you to walk there from here."

"You speak English!" Rafe glanced back at his friends. "American English."

"Yes, I joined this convent years ago when I was young. I'm originally from Detroit. Michigan." She smiled. "I'm sorry I can't help you. But we are a cloistered order." Her eyes widened when

Abe stepped out from behind Rafe. "Father! I did not see you there. I'm sorry to turn away even you." She glanced behind her. "We have rules, you see."

"Sister, what is your name?" Abe took her hand. "I am Father Abraham. I cannot imagine that any convent would not allow a priest entry. Look. It has started to snow. Surely you would not leave me and my fellow travelers out in this freezing weather."

"I must! I told you, there are rules." She jerked away from him and slammed the door in his face. They heard a heavy lock engage.

Rafe moved Abraham out of the way. "Apparently the convent does have something to hide." He raised his hands, concentrated on the door and shouted. "Step back, sister, or you will be hurt! I'm blowing open the door!"

"Rafe!" Lacy screamed his name just as he let his power surge. The door shook, the hinges cracked and stones flew with a noise that sounded like Rafe had set off dynamite. There was a mighty crash. When the dust and debris settled, he could see the huge door had broken free of its hardware and fallen to the stone floor.

"Well done, Valdez." Cisneros and Blade strode forward to wrestle the door out of the way.

"Father, I think the nun is in shock." Rafe motioned to the sister who cowered behind an antique chair that stood a dozen feet down a cavernous entry hall. He was sorry that he'd scared her, but he didn't have time to beg or negotiate. Drastic measures had been called for.

The stone-lined hallway held little furniture though a colorful statue of the Virgin Mary stood in a niche and an iron cross hung on the wall. As usual, the cross made the demon inside him twitch.

"Yes, I can see your trick frightened her. Thank you for not burning the place down." Abe hurried to the nun. "I'm sorry, sister, but we have an important mission here. Will you tell me your name and why this convent is cloistered? Your order is supposed to be serving the community near here and helping the poor."

The nun pulled a handkerchief from her pocket and wiped tears from her face with a shaky hand. She coughed as cold air blew in from the open doorway.

"Such violence. Surely… Well, I'm sorry I didn't let you in but I told you we have rules, Father. I would be punished if I disobeyed them." She took a shaky breath, glanced at the door now propped against a wall, then crossed herself. "I am Sister Mary Alice, Father. We are cloistered because God spoke to one of our nuns, Sister Maria Katherine, in a dream. Our Lord told her that our convent had a special destiny."

"Really. God spoke directly to her? That is most unusual." Abraham looked at Rafe. "Tell me exactly what God said."

The nun studied her dusty black shoes. "God told her the outside world is corrupt! That we must stay inside and pray for the poor. Pray that they would learn to live without sin."

"And no longer help them?" Abe looked up

toward Heaven. "That is not how this convent was supposed to serve the nearby community."

Her cheeks flushed when she met Abe's gaze. "She was very certain, Father. Then God gave her rules to ensure that we would do His work in the right way. We could no longer go out and mix with the people who would surely bring us disease and impure thoughts. No, God was very clear that we should stay safely inside these walls. Finally, we would not admit men under any circumstances. They would bring us," she flushed, "impure thoughts that lead to sin."

"You could not even admit a priest?" Abe cleared his throat. "Surely that must be an exception."

"Oh, we knew it was wise to be cautious. Sister Mary Grace ran away with one of the gardeners. Broke her vows to be with him." The nun was back to staring at her shoes. "After that we did our own gardening." She sighed. "Sister Mary Grace showed us that we can be weak when faced with temptation. God sees everything, you know. Even our most secret thoughts."

"Yes, He does. But to speak to a nun in a dream? I am surprised to hear that." Abe frowned. "I must examine this nun and hear about this from her own lips. Take me to her at once." Abe didn't bother to sound kind this time. It was a command.

The nun began to shake. She was a small woman, middle aged and plump. Looking around as if for help, she finally answered. "Father, I don't think that's possible. Sister Maria Katherine is very, very old, you see, and confined to her room." The nun's eyes widened when Rafe and the rest of his group moved inside the hall. "Please, you are not allowed here! I told you. No men allowed." She fluttered her hands as if to shoo them away.

"My friends mean you no harm, sister." Abe guided the nun to the antique chair and helped her sit. "Claiming to hear the voice of God is a serious matter. This nun must be examined."

"I, I don't know what to do." She twisted her hands in her white apron. "Please, Father. All these men, so close. God told us. It is one of our rules." She covered her face with her apron.

Rafe hid a smile. He gave Cisneros and Jerry a look and the three of them did step back a few feet. The fact was, the nun should have noticed they were dangerous. At least none of them had shown his gun or his fangs yet. But he'd blown open the door. Why hadn't anyone come running? Another rule? Ignore loud noises?

Rafe forced a smile when he wanted to tell her to get a grip. "Please excuse our intrusion on your peace. Surely you must admit it is about time a priest has come to look into the changes here. Father Abraham should be allowed to investigate this convent, starting with Sister Maria Katherine."

"I must ask the others." The nun jumped up and ran to the rope outside the door. She jerked it and loud clanging from a bell inside could surely be heard all over the convent. She stood next to it, her bosom heaving with her obvious distress. "I keep telling you, you must honor our

rules. No men are allowed inside the convent. It
has been this way since I joined the convent over
thirty years ago." She nodded at Abe. "Not even a
priest has been here."

Abe stopped pacing the floor impatiently.
"Then how do you celebrate mass?"

"We used to go to the church in the village.
Finally, after the incident with the gardener, God
forbid even that." She bowed her head. "We pray
for forgiveness but do without." Sister Mary Alice
turned at the sound of hurrying footsteps. "Ah,
here are the others."

Rafe counted twelve women of varying ages
who gathered in the drafty foyer. The youngest
was Sister Mary Alice who was around fifty. The
oldest looked well into her eighties. They all
wore long formal black and white habits. Their
hair was hidden by their wimples and they had
serene faces, clear of cosmetics, that shone with a
calm confidence that they did God's work. Until
they saw the group inside their damaged front
door. They stopped short, looked horrified, then
began whispering among themselves.

"What is this, sister?" A very old nun stepped
forward, frowning. "You let them in?"

"Your pardon, sister. Look at the door. It, it
exploded! I couldn't stop them. There is a priest
with them, you see. How could I turn him away?"
Her face flushed, Sister Mary Alice quickly
introduced the rest of the nuns. There were Sister
Maria Elizabeth, Sister Mary Carol, Sister Maria
Louisa, Sister Mary Carmen, Sister Mary Joan,
Sister Mary Denise, Sister Maria Anna, Sister

Maria Paulina… Rafe lost track. It was clear they
were all Sister Marys or Marias. What a pain that
was. Obviously, another convent rule.

"The priest, Father Abraham, wants to see Sister
Maria Katherine." The nun reported. "I told him
she doesn't leave her room." The group of nuns
began whispering again.

"If you wish us to go no further, perhaps you
can bring the sister to us." Abraham interrupted
what was clearly an endless argument. "We will
wait here. Unless she is unable to walk and you
need one of us to carry her."

Glory and Lacy had come into the hall. Glory
spoke up. "If you don't want one of the men to
go inside, I will help. I am stronger than I look. I
could carry any one of you." As a vampire, Rafe
knew she certainly could.

"She can walk, but is not well," the old nun,
Sister Maria Anna, said. "We don't like her to
leave her room. But, if you insist on speaking to
her, Father Abraham …" When he nodded, she
frowned and gestured to two of the nuns. "Bring
her here but watch her. You know she can be
difficult."

"What do you mean?" Glory had obviously
been busy reading minds. "Is she locked in her
room? Is she dangerous to others?"

Sister Maria Anna threw back her shoulders.
"The older the sister gets, the harder she is to
handle. Dementia, I guess you would call it. We
do our best with the situation and make sure she
gets her meals and prayer time. She is treated as
she deserves."

Rafe felt a chill in the air even more than from the open door. This nun might look like the kindest woman in the room, but he sensed steel in her. Treated as she deserves? What did that mean? Had these nuns figured out who they'd been living with all these years? Then he heard shouting. In German. They had all been conversing in English.

He decided to find out why. "You speak English here."

"Yes, we have nuns from ten different countries who speak as many different languages. Our numbers used to be more but we've lost many sisters to illness and old age." Sister Mary Alice, the one who'd answered the door, told him. "They decided on English before I got here. I thanked God for that. It was one reason I joined this order and not another one. I was stranded in Argentina by a boyfriend. Then when I realized I had a calling..." She winced when one of the other nuns pinched her arm. "Ancient history. I need to shut up."

"Yes, you do. And put a few feet between yourself and these *men*." One of the sisters jerked her into the crowd. The nuns moved out of the way when the two who had been sent to get Sister Maria Katherine appeared with the complaining nun between them.

"*Ach. Ich habe darum gebettelt, da rausgelassen zu warden. Warum jetzt? Giv mir eine Antwort!*" The tall spare woman, her pale face a mass of wrinkles, shoved at the nuns who held her arms.

"If you want an answer, ask in English, sister,"
Sister Maria Anna ordered.

"Your blasted rules! I said I have begged to
be let out of that cage. Why now? Answer me!"
Maria Katherine stopped when she saw Abe,
Rafe and his crew. "Who is this? You have *men*
inside my convent?" That last was a shriek.

"*Your* blasted rules!" A nun shouted, then
crossed herself when she was hushed by those
around her. "*Our* convent."

"She is almost right. It is not *your* convent,
sister, it is God's house. Though you made the
rules, didn't you?" One of the other sisters dared
speak up. "Look, here is a priest, come to hear
your confession, I think. Your knees will really
hurt you then."

Sister Maria Katherine whirled and slapped
the woman who'd said that. "Insolent! Respect
your elders!" The two nuns who had escorted her
grabbed her again and pushed her away from the
weeping nun who clutched her red cheek.

"Maria Katherine Zitzberg?" Rafe moved in.

"Who wants to know?" The nun glared at him
and raised her chin.

"I was sent here to take you away from this
convent." Rafe could feel the evil coming from
her like a venomous cloud. She wasn't a demon.
No, this was just a mortal female who had chosen
her own dark path. He was glad he couldn't read
her mind. That slap had told him enough. She
had hurt the sobbing woman for the pleasure of
it. He felt a shiver go up his spine. Her pale eyes
raked over him, assessing him. She hated men

unless she had a use for them. She was trying to decide if this was her escape from what had become her prison or something worse.

"It's about time. These bitches have been mistreating me. I am a pious woman who God chose to speak to in a dream. It was a miracle and yet the other nuns have been cruel to me. Jealous that He favored me in such a way." Her sneer showed sharp yellow teeth that had decayed from lack of care. "Oh, God will punish them now, I am sure of it."

When Abraham made a sound of distress, she turned toward him. "Father. You should close this convent and put these sinners out into the streets. They don't deserve the sanctuary this building once was before it became my prison." She tried to look pious, but it didn't work with her permanent frown etched around thin lips and between her white brows. She was a malevolent creature, someone even Rafe wouldn't want to meet in a dark alley.

"No, sister, you are the only one leaving here today." Crossing himself, Abraham backed out of reach. Her long nails reminded Rafe of the talons he'd seen on some of the ancient werecats he'd met in Lacy's clan. "You don't belong here."

"You are so right. That one," She pointed at the oldest nun, "started persecuting me for no reason. She locked me away and treated me like her prisoner. Forced me to pray for hours, on knees that cannot stand the pain of the stone floor in the chapel. Torture!" She waved a gnarled hand at the group of nuns. "I bet one of the cooks from the village heard how shamefully you were treating me and called for my rescue."

Abraham nodded toward Rafe. "This man will escort you from here."

"Where are you taking me? Not another convent, I hope." Sister Maria Katherine studied Rafe.

It seemed the nuns had punished the ancient nun in their own way. It was fitting that she'd suffered, though it was nothing compared to what she'd done to others in German concentration camps. Rafe was ready to move this along as she kept listing her complaints.

"Not another convent." Rafe interrupted her grievances.

"Then my prayers have been answered! I will gladly go with you. Just take me away." She drew off her wimple and threw it on the floor. Thin long white hair trailed down the back of her loose black robe. She spat at the feet of the oldest nun. "I renounce my vows. Anywhere will be better than here."

"I wouldn't be so sure about that." Rafe was glad to see Lacy and Glory were standing safely near the group of nuns. Who knew how this woman would react to the truth?

"What do you mean? Where are we going?" The ancient nun shivered as they stepped outside. She took a breath of the cold air and coughed. "I need a coat. It's snowing."

"You'll be warm soon enough." Rafe noticed Gordon standing next to their SUV. The nuns followed him outside and huddled in the doorway.

They were obviously curious about his plans for Maria Katherine. "You are finally going to Hell."

Maria Katherine stumbled and her eyes widened. "Is this a joke? Surely you don't plan to kill me here and now." She turned to the priest. "Father! Stop this! You've made a mistake. Zitzberg, did you say? No, no! I am Maria Katherine Zidlebergen. You are looking for someone else." She pointed at the eldest nun who had stopped a few feet away. "If anyone here deserves Hell it's that one. Kill her. She deserves to roast for what she's done to me."

"Don't listen to her!" Sister Maria Anna stepped closer to Rafe, a rosary dangling from one fist. "Are you Nazi hunters? I have prayed you would come!"

Rafe nodded. "You could call us that. We know this woman helped exterminate hundreds of Jews while she assisted her husband at a Nazi prison camp decades ago."

"Thanks be to God. Yes, you have the right woman." The nun looked back at the nuns behind her and nodded. "Maria Katherine, to my shame, we know who you really are. I heard you shouting in your sleep. I studied German just so I could understand what you were saying. I hope Hell is waiting for you with a gas chamber like the one you used on those the poor helpless Jews." Tears ran down the woman's face. The other sisters murmured and crowded around her.

"She's lying!" Maria Katherine looked around wildly.

"Please take her away. I am so ashamed that

we welcomed her when she came here to hide." Sister Maria Anna bowed her head. "If only I had been wise enough to see through her sooner. But she was clever, claiming her husband had hurt her and wearing a bruise on her face when she arrived here. She said he forced her to come from Germany to Argentina. She would not admit to ties to the camps or the Nazis."

"Max *was* cruel to me. I never wanted to come here where I couldn't even speak the language. He promised we'd be rich and have a wonderful life. Instead, he gave all our gold to the ship's captain who brought us here. Why? So we could live in poverty? He should have made a better plan! No wonder I hate men. They are worthless." Maria Katherine jerked when Rafe clamped his hand on her arm. "Get your foul hands off of me."

"What happened to your husband, Frau Zitzberg?" Abraham stared at her.

"What do you think? I got rid of him. A little something in his dinner one night and he never woke up." She tried to rake her nails across Rafe's arm, but he caught her hands before she could hurt him. She was very old and easily held.

"I thought this convent would be peaceful. And the mountains are pretty enough." She kicked Rafe's shin with her heavy black shoe.

"Enough of that." Cisneros looked into her eyes and she was frozen.

"No, let her go. I want to hear more." Abraham held up a hand. "I know your tricks, sir. Release her."

"Very well. But it wasn't *you* she kicked, was it,

Padre?" Cisneros waited for Rafe's nod before he let the nun go free.

"What are you doing? I couldn't…" She jerked. "I admit, the convent was a disappointment. Too much praying. And work. They wanted me to serve those filthy poor people. I wanted no part of it. So I had a 'dream.'" She cackled. "They fell for it. Believed God himself spoke to me. What a joke! I have never believed in anyone but myself."

"Sinner! You should be ashamed!" Abraham threw up his hands and what had been a light snowfall became a blizzard.

"Father, control yourself!" Rafe nodded toward the cluster of nuns watching from the doorway. Lightning danced around them. Eyes wide, Glory and Lacy ran to the car and jumped inside.

Maria Katherine wiped snow off her face, shivering in the cold. As quickly as the blizzard had come, it stopped and the sky cleared. Moonlight shone on the fresh snow.

"I don't care who you are, please just take her away quickly. Whatever you plan to do with her, do it elsewhere." The elderly nun, Sister Maria Anna, clearly the leader now, stopped in the broken doorway. "She deserves the same kind of torture she did to those poor Jews."

"Yes, I'm sure she'll suffer." Rafe remembered what he'd seen in Hell. At least Lucifer did some things right.

The nun choked in the cold air and one of the other nuns supported her when she swayed. "Thank God you have finally come. I wrote a letter to Rome as soon as I was sure she'd lied to us. But our mail here…" She waved her hand. "I did the best I could, locking her up. She was a poison in this convent. Now I hope we can begin to serve the poor again."

"You old fool, whining about your precious convent and wasting your time on the poor. I wasn't going into a village and risk being seen. There are Nazi hunters everywhere in Argentina. So I made up the rules." Maria Katherine slapped at Rafe's hand. "Which one of you bitches turned me in? You, Maria Anna? You'll be sorry. I'll haunt your drafty convent, I swear it. You'll never get another peaceful night's sleep once I'm gone."

Rafe had heard enough. "No one here had to turn you in. Your own evil deeds got you on the Devil's radar." He pulled her toward the car.

"Let me go! You're hurting me! I'm old. Where's your respect for the elderly?" The nun dragged her heels.

"I have no respect for the likes of you." Rafe let her see his eyes glow red.

She gasped and her knees failed her. Rafe smiled and picked her up. She didn't weigh much. Had the nuns starved her for her sins? He glanced at the lead nun and thought she was just angry enough to have tried it. But Maria Anna had tears rolling down her wrinkled cheeks.

Abe stepped forward. "I'm sorry you suffered, sister. I will send help so you can get back to charitable work. Don't worry, Rafael is right. There will be no ghost here to disturb your peace. That woman will be too busy in Hell to bother any of you ever again." Abe blessed the nuns while Rafe headed to the car with a screaming Maria Zitzberg beating on his chest.

When Blade and Cisneros noticed Gordon, they drew their weapons.

"Relax, he's from Lucifer. I hope he's here to take this sinner away." Rafe set Maria on her feet next to the car. She made a run for it, stumbling and falling on the ground.

"Ow! I think I broke my hip!" She struggled to sit up. "Mercy!"

"Hah! How foolish of you to run at your age, old girl." Gordon smiled when Maria Katherine staggered to her feet, her long habit tripping her again. "Yes, Rafael, I'll be making the pick up when you capture anyone on your list." He laughed when the old woman got up and staggered forward. "She moves well for her age. She'll be a novelty for Luc to break in."

"Good to know. About the pickup anyway." Rafe had to remind himself of all the things the woman had done when Gordon grabbed Maria Katherine's long hair and began dragging her by it across the snow toward the woods. Her screams made Rafe's skin crawl.

When Gordon stopped to look around, sniffing the air, Maria Katherine whimpered. "Will I see my husband in Hell?"

"Do you want to see him, your beloved husband?" He nodded and changed directions. "Ah, there's the portal beyond those trees."

"Max Zitzberg? Arrogant bastard. He never appreciated my genius. I helped him double the number of those we exterminated in the camp.

Did he ever mention me in his reports? Of course not!" She began babbling something in German. "Some people call them sins. I'll bet the Devil will admire me for what I did. I'm not sorry for anything." She hit at Gordon's hand on her hair. "Must you be so rough? Let me up. I will walk if you give me a chance."

"I don't think so." Gordon jerked at her again, dragging her over rocks and brush. "This is just the beginning of your pain. As for your husband? Since you hated him, you'll see him every day. Torture is an art, Frau Zitzberg. Lucifer saw how you put the screws to those nuns back there. So you understand."

"I *was* clever." She cursed, showing a fine command of profanity in several languages.

Gordon sneered. "Forgive me if I'm not impressed. You killed starving prisoners and old women in their sleep. Too easy. I had to work to find and end my victims. Well, there will be nothing easy where you're going." He picked her up and threw her over his shoulder. "You're slowing me down. I can't wait to see what Lucifer has in store for you." He set off, disappearing into the woods.

Rafe heard her scream once more after she and Gordon were out of sight.

"At least you don't have to take your catches back to the portal in Austin each time." Abraham looked calm as he walked up beside Rafe. "Speaking of easy, that was surprisingly so. Let's go back to the plane and look at that list of yours."

"You call that easy?" A shivering Lacy was out

of the car, holding onto Rafe. "It was horrible. Those poor nuns! Then that old woman dragged out of here…" She looked at the forest. "Rafe, who was that man?"

"Gordon works for Lucifer. I was glad to see him. It meant I didn't have to kill a nun." Rafe opened the car door. "That old woman was evil, babe. Remember, she got to live decades longer than her victims. Now she'll finally suffer for her sins."

"Right. I hope she'll get what she deserves in Hell. Can we forget her now?" Glory stood next to the car. "Jerry, you and Miguel are flying back to the plane, aren't you?"

"Of course. Right after we put that door back on its hinges. Can't leave the nuns exposed to the elements like that." Jerry wrapped his arms around his wife. "I can see that scene upset you, my love. We don't have to participate in any more of these captures if you hated it."

"No, it's for a good cause. We're getting justice for the victims of these 'sinners.'" She kissed his cheek. "I was going to suggest you and Miguel look over Rafe's list when you get to the plane and see where we need to go next. Work out a plan. By the time we get back down the mountain, you two should have our next destination figured out."

Blade glanced at Rafe. "That okay with you? Miguel and I work out logistics for our next move? Tell the pilot to file a plan?"

"I'd be grateful, man." Rafe realized Abe looked troubled. "What's wrong, Abe?"

"This convent. They suffered under that woman's dominance for too long. It makes me wonder how many others who serve God need more care than we've been giving them." He glanced back at the solid door that Cisneros and Blade were propping into place.

"They constantly prayed for relief and they did finally get it. Just took a long time." Rafe helped Lacy into the back seat. He was ready to drive again. "Lots of people feel like their prayers aren't answered. Did you know that?"

"It's not so simple, Rafael. You don't just pray for what you want and all is well. Sometimes God must weigh His options. Helping one person could very well destroy another."

Rafe started the car. "Yeah, we're all aware that life isn't fair. But when you see kindly nuns made to suffer or a sweet child like my Daniela struggling to understand her demon powers…" He put the SUV in gear. "That's why it can be hard to believe there's a benevolent God up there." He rubbed his forehead. "I'm damned sick of this pain in my head every time I think or say G-O-D."

"I get it, my son. I'm really close to Him and I struggle myself with what I see happening in the world." Abe sighed as they drove down the mountain. "At least I'm helping you round up sinners that deserve to be punished. I'm sure of that."

"I heard Sister Maria Katherine brag about sending Jews to the gas chamber." Lacy laid her hand on Rafe's shoulder. "What a horrible woman."

"Glory could read her mind. I'll bet that wasn't all Maria Katherine did." Rafe glanced in the rearview mirror. Glory was staring out the side window, tears running down her face.

"Her mind was a cesspool. She took out several of the older sisters before they locked her up. She would sneak into their rooms at night and smother them with a pillow. Everyone thought they died in their sleep of old age." Glory sniffed and reached out to grip Lacy's hand. "She'd planned to kill Sister Maria Anna next but the nun figured out what the Nazi was up to. They locked the old nun in and blamed her behavior on dementia. Sister Maria Katherine was obviously thinking clearly just really evil."

"That settles it then. No more regrets about that takedown." Lacy handed Glory a tissue from her pocket. "You did good, Rafe. I'm proud of you. You say the rest of your targets are in Texas and Louisiana? I hope they are as simple."

Rafe hoped so too but he'd read the files. He bet Jerry and Miguel decided a serial killer was next. In The Big Easy. There was that word again. Easy. New Orleans was a fun place unless you were hunting a killer. The swampy area around the city provided way too many places to hide. This killer had eluded police for years. According to Rafe's research, the killer bragged on social media and yet couldn't be caught. Lucifer expected Rafe to find him and bring him in, in less than five days, no, make that four now.

"A serial killer next, Lacy. Imagine that." Rafe kept his eyes on the road, but his mind was on the man who had kidnapped thirteen women, tortured them and then dropped them like so much trash in a bayou outside of New Orleans. By the time the alligators got through with them, they had been hard to identify. The police found the women had one thing in common—they'd been working girls who plied their trade in the French Quarter, prostitutes who had tourists as their customers.

Ironic, wasn't it? This hunt had gone from nuns to hookers. Lucifer had an interesting sense of humor.

CHAPTER TEN

THE FLIGHT TO New Orleans gave Rafe plenty of time to read about his next target. He was becoming a profiler, like he'd seen on TV shows. This guy was obviously obsessed with women of a certain type. He liked blondes with curvy figures and seemed tech savvy, bragging about his kills on social media. He'd frustrated the police because his posts were untraceable. He must know the area around New Orleans well because he slipped in and out of the city undetected. And he was vicious. The bodies he'd dumped showed signs the women had been raped and tortured before he'd dumped them in a swamp. Rafe hoped he'd kept souvenirs and those keepsakes would be his downfall. So far, the killer had been too damned clever to be caught.

"Baby, you look like you're ready to kill someone." Lacy slid into his lap. "Put that laptop away and take a break. I appreciate that you're doing this to save our child, but it's coming at a cost, isn't it?"

"Yeah, the Devil's clock is ticking and this next one seems impossible." Rafe held her slim body against his. The real cost? He felt too filthy to even touch this amazing woman. They were alone. The vampires were in the back bedroom again since dawn had hit an hour ago. The pilot had assured him he'd had a decent nap and was okay to take them all the way to Louisiana, but Rafe had promised to give him a break in a couple of hours.

Abraham had vanished, saying he had concerns that he needed to discuss with his boss upstairs. The monk had been quiet since he'd seen the convent and the damage Maria Katherine had done there. Obviously working for God wasn't easy. Abe had promised to meet them in New Orleans.

"No cost is too high to save Daniela from Lucifer's clutches." Rafe leaned the seat back, letting himself enjoy Lacy next to him. He wasn't going to make love to his wife, not even when she was clearly trying to seduce him. She kept touching him in the ways she knew he liked. As if he needed coaxing. He *always* wanted his werecat woman. Lacy was beautiful, inside and out. But he didn't trust condoms, not with his demon seed so powerful. And her own birth control had failed before.

"Rafe, I need you. Quit thinking and just love me." She kissed his neck, her hands roaming under his shirt and across his chest. "You have no idea how much you mean to me."

"You mean everything to *me*. But I'm not going to risk…" She kissed him quiet. Her mouth was hot on his, taking him out of his mind as only she could.

She opened his jeans, sliding her hand inside to touch him, stroke him. God, he wanted her. There was no place he'd rather be than deep inside her. She sat back and ripped off her top. No bra. Why bother when her breasts were full and firm and right there where he could taste them. She moved in, making sure he would do just that.

Rafe pushed down her jeans and panties and found her damp and eager. No, he couldn't take her. But he could touch her and bring her satisfaction. He found the spot that made her shiver and call his name. She clinched around his fingers and moaned when he drove them deep.

"That's it, baby, come for me." He held her as she trembled, her crest close.

"No!" She bit his lip, then raked his back with her claws. Her cat was taking over and he loved it. She went wild, ripping open his jeans until he was exposed. "I'm making *you* come for *me*." She slid down, stroking him with her tongue. It was raspy, a cat tongue, and he shuddered.

"Stop. I can't take it. I won't—" He held her hair, trying to pull her up and off of him. Even his cum held demon seed. The idea that she might take it inside her made him sick. And he was close, about to lose it.

She went down on him, drawing so hard he spasmed, helpless as she finished him. He was usually strong, powerful. But she made him weak, lost as she left him wrung out. He fell back against the seat, cursing his own weakness even while he stroked her soft red hair and told Lacy how much he loved her.

"I love you, Rafael. All of you. Don't ever forget it." She lay against his chest and closed her eyes, falling asleep quickly with apparently no worries.

Dear God he hoped he hadn't tainted her with what he was. What he was made of. When exhaustion forced him to close his eyes, he dreamed of screams in Hell and a man with horns who laughed at him and his efforts to avoid his fate.

They got hotel rooms in New Orleans when it became obvious it was going to take more than a minute to find the second sinner on Rafe's list. Lucifer hadn't given him a name this time, just a list of his sins and the general location. The clues Rafe would need to find this person were dependent on his research and that was going nowhere.

"The police have a massive manhunt on for this killer, Rafael. They even formed a task force." Cisneros paced the floor of the large two-bedroom suite. "According to you, they don't have squat on this guy. We need to do something special if you're going to track him down as fast as Lucifer expects. He wants you to fail."

"You think I don't know that!" Rafe wanted to throw something across the room. Lacy was in the shower. He wished he could take the time. After Rafe had shared what he'd found on the

Internet about this second sinner, they were all on edge thinking about that tight deadline.

"I'm his type—a curvy blonde. Put me out on the street as bait and see what happens. He's obviously mortal so he won't stand a chance against us." Glory got her husband in an uproar with that idea, and Rafe didn't blame him.

"Obviously mortal? I don't think so." Blade was livid. "He's gotten away with his killing spree for too long to be an ordinary human. Besides, I won't let you do it."

"Won't *let* me?" Glory stomped over to face her husband.

"Hold up, Glory. Before you get into a battle over him telling you what to do, Jerry's right. Let's touch base with the paranormal community here first." Rafe wished Abe would reappear. He'd been handy in Argentina. In a large city with more than its fair share of interesting characters, Rafe saw his time limit slipping away with no progress. "Who has a connection they can tap here?"

Jeremy Blade looked at his wife. "I can't believe you've forgotten, Valdez. The three of us had a run-in with a woman from here, though Glory will hate that idea as much as I hate using my wife as bait. She's my former lover, a voodoo priestess…"

"Melisandra Du Monde." Rafe, Glory and Miguel said it together.

"You have got to be kidding." Glory paced around the room in her sparkly tennis shoes. "It's a miracle she finally let you go, Jerry."

"Not a miracle. A potion made by our scientific friend Ian MacDonald made her hate me. I threw it in her face on Halloween a few years ago. Unfortunately, I have no idea how long that stuff lasted. I sure as hell don't want to test to see if she still loathes the sight of me." Jerry grabbed Glory when she stalked past him. There was a brief wrestling match until she finally let him hold her. "You know I would rather drink Zombie blood than deal with her again, love. But if anyone knows who is killing these women in New Orleans, it's probably Mel."

"Don't call that bitch by a nickname!" Glory yelled.

Jerry was speechless as his wife pushed him so hard he fell into a chair. "What the hell, Gloriana? *She* was obsessed with *me*. I never loved her. You have been my only love for centuries and you know it. Calm down."

Rafe took a steadying breath. "Both of you stop it. I would never ask Jerry to approach that woman. She had some creepy as hell powers and, Jerry's right, her obsession with him was sick. Who's to say seeing him again wouldn't stir up her old feelings? We can't take that chance." Rafe felt Lacy, fresh from her shower, press against his side. Yeah, she'd heard enough to want him to contact the priestess. Jeremy Blade had brought it up, hadn't he? "We might need her but *I'll* go see her. Jerry's not getting within a mile of her."

"She'll recognize you and me, Rafe. But, yes, I'd feel better if my husband avoids her." Glory had calmed down. "He's right though. Mel," She spit out the name like it was toxic, "is dialed into the paranormal community here. If he's not mortal, she's bound to know who this killer is and where to find him. He's probably someone she could summon if she chose to do it."

Jerry was staring at his wife, trying to read her mind and true thoughts. He shook his head, obviously striking out. "Baby, I won't risk what we have. I'm staying away from the bitch. I hope Rafe can see her and take care of this. Once we have what we need to take down this serial killer, I'm all in." He glanced at Rafe. "Sorry, guy."

"Let me go see her." Miguel Cisneros strode to the door. "I'll be able to read her mind, I don't care how powerful she thinks she is. Once I ask the questions we want answered, if she knows, I should be able to get the information we need."

"I'm not sure that will work, Miguel. I never could read her." Glory approached him. "Do you think you're stronger than I am?"

Miguel smiled. "Yes. You may be my sister or cousin or whatever our Olympus tie is, but I was once worshiped like a god by the Mayans. I'm pretty sure I will be able to read her mind."

"I'm going with you." Rafe hoped this arrogant man was right. Miguel did have some awesome powers. "The rest of you need to hang here and be ready to move fast if we get a location." He looked at Lacy. "Melisandra du Monde is unpredictable but she is also interested in making a profit. If nothing else, I can offer to pay for the information."

"Be careful, Rafe. A Voodoo priestess? The very

idea scares me." Lacy gave him a kiss goodbye. "Call or text as soon as you leave her. Let us know you're safe."

"Sure." Busy with his phone, Rafe followed Miguel out the door. "Here, I have the address of her shop. It's not far, on the edge of the French Quarter." He'd picked their hotel for its location. Many of the killer's victims had been taken from this neighborhood.

"All right. As soon as we get outside, let's shift. It's dark and no one will notice." Miguel was clearly fired up. His eyes were shining and he patted his pocket where Rafe knew he carried a weapon. Gun? Knife? Didn't matter. The man's power was like a shiny shield around him. Rafe was glad Miguel was on his side. Was it out of boredom with his ordinary life in Austin? Didn't matter. Rafe would take what help he could get, even from a freakin' Mayan god.

★★★

The shop specialized in the occult and sat on a side street not far from popular Jackson Square. It would be easy for gullible tourists to find. A display of voodoo dolls in the window would lure them in as well as a sign that promised psychic readings. It didn't surprise Rafe that he smelled demon energy in the air, not to mention the stench of zombies. Melisandra had liked to travel with a pair of the noxious creatures as bodyguards. No one approached her when those were nearby. Of course, mortals thought her bodyguards were just people in creepy costumes.

Miguel pushed inside the store first. Candles

illuminated the dim lighting. The incense burning couldn't disguise the reek of death and decay that came from the zombie guarding a back room.

"May I help you?" A shapely blonde in a short dress patterned with zodiac symbols approached them. Her eyes widened when she saw Miguel. Even Rafe had noticed the vampire was a handsome man.

"We're looking for Melisandra du Monde. Is she here tonight? It's important." Miguel picked up a candle and sniffed it. "Interesting. Lavender. Do you think this will protect you?"

The woman smiled. "Of course. You should try it." She glanced at Rafe. "Women like the scent. If that interests you."

"I am always interested in women." Miguel moved closer to her. "Now please tell Madame du Monde that we desire her company. We will pay well for a few moments of her time." He touched the woman's name tag. "Tina. If you are free once our business is done, perhaps you can show me if the lavender will make me, hmm, safe," he winked. "From you."

Tina flushed and hurried to a door with a beaded curtain. She ignored the zombie standing guard and disappeared inside. Rafe and Miguel exchanged glances.

"Seriously? You're making a date for later?" Rafe gave the vampire an elbow.

"Only if we have time. Maybe we'll wrap this up quickly. You must admit Tina is beautiful and her blood? Promises to be delicious." Miguel blew out the candle. "This smells like shit."

"Careful, you're giving away your own evil intent." Rafe couldn't hide his grin.

"Shame on you. I only give pleasure. I won't harm her. And, as a bonus, she won't remember a thing." Miguel turned as the beads rattled again. "Ah, here comes your Mel. You met her before, didn't you?"

Melisandra came gliding into the room, her hand outstretched. "Rafael Valdez. I remember you. You took my seminar in Austin several years ago. How did it work out for you?" She gave Miguel an assessing stare. "Have you brought me a new client?"

Rafe and Glory had taken Mel's course called "Own the World." Mel was a motivational speaker, besides being a voodoo priestess. When she ran those courses, she looked like any successful entrepreneur. Tonight, in her shop, she was dressed in the flowing robe of her priestess profession, a headwrap covering her long dark hair. She wore dramatic makeup and looked beautiful and exotic.

"I would recommend your seminars to anyone, Melisandra. My own bar is thriving, thanks to the risks you encouraged me to take with my business." Rafe shook her hand, admiring the jewels that adorned most of her fingers. "My friend Miguel could certainly benefit from your course, but that's not why we're here."

Mel smiled. Tina had followed her into the shop. "I am intrigued and always interested in handsome men. Come into my private room."

She turned to Tina. "We will not want to be disturbed."

Tina bowed her head, obviously disappointed. "Yes, Mistress."

Rafe and Miguel followed the priestess, soon settling into seats at a round table covered in a red cloth. A zombie stood in the corner of the room.

"Really, Mel, is he necessary? You know I am a shapeshifter and my friend Miguel is a vampire. The smell from your buddy there is enough to make us both gag." Rafe leaned back in his chair. "We are not here to harm you, only to make a business proposition."

Mel studied them. "I know you both carry weapons. Alfred will step outside but can be back within moments if either of you make a wrong move. Understand? I've not forgotten, Rafael, that you were friends with that vampire, Glory, was it? She caused me nothing but grief."

"Of course. I promise I'm here because I have need of your knowledge of New Orleans, that's all." Rafe leaned forward. "I am after the killer who has been preying on the women in the French Quarter."

"Really?" Mel gestured for the zombie to leave them then reached for a box and removed a deck of cards. "How strange. Why concern yourself with such as that?"

"The why is not important." Rafe was not about to let Mel know something so important as his deal with Lucifer. "I will tell you this—I have only a few days to bring this killer to justice or someone I love will suffer for it. If you know where to find this murderer, tell me and I will pay you well. Very well." Rafe tapped the table. "I would think you would be glad to rid New Orleans of this person. His bad acts are bound to be hurting the tourist trade."

Mel shuffled her cards, eyeing Miguel, who watched her intently. "And why is your friend here? Mere curiosity? I can tell he is no ordinary vampire." She smiled and lowered her lashes. "My clerk is already asking to get off early so she can meet him."

"I may be too busy for such a meeting. I am here to help my friend take down a serial killer." Miguel nodded toward the cards that Mel had cut and had started laying out in a pattern on the table. "We are not here to play games. This is very serious."

"I can see that." She gasped when she turned over a card. "The Tower. Things are changing. For the better or worse? I wonder."

"Start talking or it will definitely be for the worse." Miguel slapped a hand over the next card. "Death? I know that is not a bad card. Unless it is upside down. What do you say?"

"I say this killer does need to be stopped. He is out of control. My customers are afraid to come by the shop, though I've been selling a lot of protection spells lately." Mel picked up Miguel's hand. "Let me finish my reading."

"We don't have time for that." Rafe shook his head. "Do you know who we seek and where to find him?"

"So impatient." Mel sighed. "He lives near the

swamp where he dumps the bodies. His name is Pierre Le Croix. At least he goes by that name this century. He is a vampire and will be hard to kill. If that is what you intend to do." She gathered up her cards.

"The swamp is a big place. We need more than that." Miguel stood. "But I see you are reluctant. Are you afraid of Pierre? Is that why you keep rotting corpses near you? Has he threatened you?"

"He doesn't like my zombies, that is true. But Rafael can tell you I travel with the creatures as proof of my powers. I have been doing it for years. Pierre? He is bad for business. Take him down." She stood and tucked her cards away. "Now you promised to pay for my help. I will give you an address when I have a figure from you. What is it worth to you?"

Miguel laughed. "I have read that information in your mind, Madame. You are wasting your time trying to squeeze money out of my friend."

Mel glared at him and began to chant. Rafe didn't doubt a curse was coming. He'd seen her work her magic before and it was no joke.

"Stop." He held up the debit card Ian had sent him and named a figure that made her shut her mouth with a snap. "I'm paying. Miguel needs to mind his own business. I pay when I say I am going to pay. We may well need your good will again, Melisandra."

"Pay this time but I don't like mind reading." Mel frowned but took the card and walked into the outer area of the shop. With quick efficiency, she ran the card, showing Rafe a receipt with the amount she had taken from his account.

"There. Now we can part on good terms. Thanks for helping us." Rafe shook her hand then practically pushed Miguel out the door. For a moment he hesitated. Mel could see the future. He'd seen her predict things and they had come to pass. Did he dare ask her if Daniela...? He shook his head. No, he didn't want Mel to know his daughter's name. He was working on his baby's future and was determined to make it bright not dark.

"Wait!" Tina ran after them, tucking her phone number into Miguel's hand. "I get off in half an hour. I hope to see you then. I will walk to the bar next to…" she named a popular tourist spot in the Quarter. Then she flushed and waved before going back inside.

"You should have told her you won't be done in an hour." Rafe walked toward the alley where they'd shifted before.

"She will meet someone else if I don't show. She is very beautiful. Now why did you waste your money?" Miguel put the number into his pocket.

"I didn't. You have no idea what a powerful enemy that woman can be. And her spells work." Rafe stopped when they got to the alley where they'd shifted before. He faced Miguel.

"What the fuck, man? Why'd you go so hard at the voodoo woman? You were supposed to let me handle things back there." Rafe saw the vampire stare up, as if wanting nothing more than to ignore him and shift out of there.

Finally, Miguel met Rafe's gaze. "I read her mind, like I said I could. You don't want to know the kind of evil shit I saw. She should be on the Devil's list. I cannot understand why she is not." Miguel's fangs were down. "That bitch is lucky I didn't rip out her throat then and there. I'd have been doing the world a favor." He closed his eyes. "Why didn't I? Her blood would be like poison on my tongue."

Rafe put a hand on Miguel's arm. It was hard, solid muscle and almost vibrating with his need to change. "I'm sorry. Thanks for telling me. That had to be rough."

"You have no idea." With that Miguel shifted and flew into the dark sky.

Rafe followed, not surprised to find Miguel still complaining when they arrived in their suite.

"I think I could have handled a voodoo priestess without you buying her off."

"It's done. Let it go. We're dealing with a vampire this time. That's enough to worry about without the possibility of Mel putting one of her curses on you or me or both of us."

Miguel just shook his head and listened as Rafe shared their news with the others. They had five hours until dawn. They had rented a car at the airport and he looked up Le Croix's address on his computer. The house was an hour away by car. They spent some time deciding whether to wait for Abraham and who should shift and who should drive. It was too much to hope that the killer would be sitting there waiting for them. By the time they were ready to leave, Abe still hadn't shown up.

Glory had the television on and they all got quiet when a news bulletin filled the screen. Another woman had been attacked in the French Quarter. This time it wasn't a hooker, it was a local girl. The city was in turmoil. The balcony door was open and they could hear police sirens converging on the area.

Miguel decided to shift and check out the situation. He was back in a few minutes, his face pale.

"You won't believe it. The vampire must have a spy in Mel's shop or have it bugged."

"Why do you say that?" Rafe watched Miguel stagger inside and fall on the couch.

"Because the woman he took was Tina, the clerk in du Monde's shop. Tourists heard screams then called the police. After that Mel found blood on her front door and a note. He's daring us to come after him." Miguel dragged himself up to dig a tiny bottle of tequila out of the mini-bar. He drained it in one long swallow.

"A note?" Rafe hated to ask.

"Shit. He says we have three hours before he throws Tina to the alligators."

CHAPTER ELEVEN

"DID MELISANDRA CALL the cops?" Lacy stopped Miguel as he was reaching for another tiny bottle of booze. "She should tell them what she knows."

"She won't. The selfish bitch is no fan of the police. I'm sure Rafe told you I read her mind. She's been helping the killer find his victims. She's afraid she might be implicated as an accessory to murder." Miguel gently removed Lacy's hand and helped himself to another Tequila. "Besides, it won't be long before that asshole puts something on social media. Open your laptop, Rafe. Bet he's already got Tina up, crying and begging for her life."

Rafe checked the site the killer had used before. Nothing yet, but it had only been minutes. The police didn't know they were dealing with a vampire. He could have carried Tina out of there in his arms, even flying her over the city. Shit.

"Mel rightly blames herself for Tina's abduction. But she figures this team of ours, with other paranormals, has a better chance of catching up with Le Croix than the cops do anyway. They've been on the case for months with no success."

Glory stood next to Miguel. "I'm sorry you had to look into that woman's thoughts. They had to be a swamp."

"No shit." Miguel finished another bottle. He looked at Jerry when he made a noise. "I'm sure you get it. Mel has a nerve, feeling bad now when she deliberately hired Tina, a curvy blonde who fits Le Croix's preferred type. What the hell did she expect? If the woman gave a damn about her, Mel should have told Tina to stay home, away from the French Quarter, until the killer is caught or killed."

"Then you came along and flirted with her, tempting her to go out after work and walk to a bar where she'd be bait." Rafe blocked the mini-bar when Miguel cursed and looked like he was about to go for another bottle. "Relax, Cisneros. We all know the only one to blame here is the out-of-control killer who decided to challenge us. Now let's look at the map and see the best way to approach this asshole."

Jerry sat in front of Rafe's laptop. "Give me the address and let's try to figure out nearby areas where he could have taken the girl. You say there was blood on the door. So she must have put up a fight."

"Her blood... Rare and fresh. I bet he was hungry enough to drink from her right away." Miguel had a haunted look. He turned to Glory. "Find a news channel and see if there's been an update."

"Will do. Seriously, this is not on you, Miguel." She patted him on the shoulder then picked up the TV remote. They all jumped when a figure appeared in the open balcony door. "Abe! Have you heard the latest?"

"Yes. It breaks my heart. This sinner is cruel and is holding a fine young woman." Abe crossed himself. "I can pick up enough to know she is still alive but is suffering. I wish I knew more than that. We must hurry." He walked over to peer at the laptop where Jerry had pulled up a map. "Modern technology can go only so far. You need to take off, get out there and use your senses to track him down."

"Yes, we do." Rafe glanced at Cisneros and Jerry. "The three of us can fly out to his place. Glory, you and Lacy take Abe with you and drive to a gas station/convenience store not far from Le Croix's place. Stop there and wait for us to call."

Glory had found a news station and they all listened as a reporter gave them details. A witness had heard a scream. Police had found a high-heeled shoe and a purse with ID belonging to Tina Benoit, clerk at a shop near the French Quarter. Her phone had been found at the scene as well. Melisandra du Monde, owner of the shop, had been interviewed and had confirmed that her cashier had left work minutes before, on her way to a popular bar nearby.

No mention was made of blood found at the shop or a note. Apparently, Mel was keeping that from the police. But, because Tina fit the description of recent victims, the police were assuming she was indeed the latest captive of the serial killer they'd been hunting. The public was asked to come forward with any information that could help in the manhunt.

A few miles from the city, a mist covered the road to the house in an isolated area near a swamp. Rafe stared at the killer's home and concentrated on any clues there might be a vampire inside. Or an injured woman.

"I don't think he's here. I made a careful circle overhead and can't get a whiff of anyone, vampire or mortal. I don't think he would want to leave the woman yet." Jerry looked up. "Here comes Cisneros. He's still blaming himself for this."

"He shouldn't. Le Croix obviously had his eye on Mel's shop already. Sure as shit, Mel hired Tina to please him." Jerry's fists were clenched. "It's something she would do. Never doubt it. I don't trust that woman."

"Why should you? You have a bitter history with her. But this isn't about you. She doesn't even know you're in New Orleans." Rafe watched Cisneros take one more circle above the house in the distance.

"Thank God. Of course, she's been helping Le Croix. She stood by and let him kill helpless women, Valdez. If she'd gone to the police…" Jerry's fangs were down.

"You think mortal cops would listen to the ravings of a voodoo priestess and her talk of a vampire serial killer?" Rafe shook his head. "I'm glad we're here. Maybe we are just in time to stop this. Mortal cops don't have a chance against him."

"You're right. Let's see what Cisneros found." Jerry watched the vampire land silently.

Miguel shifted and shook his head. "No sign of them. I broke a window and went inside the house." His shoulders sagged. "He's very careful. Of course, he isn't using his own home for this shit. He made one mistake though." The vampire held up a crumpled piece of paper. "I found this in the trash outside. It's a notice. He forgot to pay an electric bill, for a place on the other side of Lake Pontchartrain. That's where we need to go." His smile would have made a mortal scream. "I love it when blood lust clouds a man's thinking."

"Jerry, call Glory. Give her the address and have her meet us near there. Not too close. You know she's just Le Croix's type. They should wait for instructions." Rafe scanned the paper then looked up the address on his phone. A map showed him that this was going to take a while, at least for the people in the car. The three of them could fly over the large lake faster.

"Lead the way, Valdez. That girl is living on borrowed time." Jerry looked grim. "But, first, I want to know if there's more you're not telling us. What else did you learn in your journey through the filth in Mel's mind, Cisneros? Why the note this time?"

"Apparently you're not the only vampire Mel has put through the wringer, Blade." Miguel's fists were clenched again. He had a dark energy that made Rafe take a step back.

"What do you mean?" Working with other paranormals had become a way of life for him, but Rafe had learned to be wary. This vampire was a stranger, tied to his best friend Glory in some inexplicable way. Their Olympus connections meant they could be as powerful in their own way as the Devil himself. That power could be useful or dangerous.

"I saw a lot of things in Mel's mind that I didn't share with you." Miguel looked up at the night sky. "You're right, Blade, that woman isn't to be trusted. She wasn't about to tell us everything. She and Le Croix have had dealings in the past. The greedy bitch could have stopped him sooner, but chose to let him go on this killing spree, for a price. Do you think Tina is the first beautiful blonde Mel has found for him?" Miguel turned and stared at the dark house in the distance. Suddenly it burst into flames, as if a fire bomb had been tossed through a window.

"Damn her to hell!" Jerry gazed at the house, soon fully engulfed. "Why isn't she on the Devil's list, Valdez?"

"I don't know. She should be." Rafe knew the clock was ticking. "But this time Le Croix has drawn attention to the shop. Was that wise? The police will be watching du Monde. There must have been some sort of falling out between these two."

"Yes, Mel had become fond of Tina and decided that the killing spree had gone on long enough.

This started as a way for Le Croix to have blood donors. He wasn't supposed to kill the women. But blood lust took over and he lost control. Now tourists are afraid to come to her shop. Mel finally refused to help him find victims anymore. Or maybe she raised her price for that help. I saw LeCroix is having money problems. The electric bill in the trash wasn't the only overdue bill there. He became obsessed with his killing and forgot to tend to his business." Miguel smiled when the home's roof collapsed in a shower of sparks. "Now he's going to have to find a new place to live."

"What's his business?" Jerry was a successful businessman, naturally he'd want to ruin it or take over whatever the other vampire had started.

Miguel shook his head. "I saw evidence that he runs some kind of investment firm, or used to until he lost interest in it. Imports too. There were some beautiful things in that burned out shell." He smiled. "Too bad."

"We need to move." Rafe didn't care about anything but getting this man to Hell and an innocent woman free before Le Croix killed her.

It started to rain, lightning and thunder making it clear a storm was coming. That put out the fire but the damage was pretty complete now. The house was in ruins.

The three men took to the skies after a quick look at the location of Le Croix's lake house on Rafe's phone. It was a miserable flight, but a matter of minutes before they were near a frame house on the shore of Lake Pontchartrain. The brief squall had blown over and they stood under a dripping tree, looking at the dark building. Apparently, the electricity hadn't been turned on again, but Rafe could see the flicker of candlelight through one of the small windows.

A woman's scream cut short any talk of strategy. Miguel leaped into the air, headed for the house. Rafe and Jerry were right behind him. Miguel blew through the bedroom window. Jerry hit the back door and Rafe the front.

"She's here!" Miguel shouted from the bedroom. "And she's alive."

Rafe and Jerry ran to meet him. He was standing over the naked woman tied to the bed. She wasn't alone. Several snakes were crawling over her legs and around her body.

"Careful, they're poisonous. Water moccasins." Rafe pulled the knife from his boot. He knew they'd be deadly if they bit her.

"Tina, lie very still." Miguel grabbed a snake slithering between her breasts with his bare hand and flung it away, across the room where it hit the wall. Her gasp made her choke. "Steady now."

Jerry threw one of his knives with precision, severing a snake's head as it seemed ready to strike. The body writhed in its death throes against one of her legs. Tina sobbed, her eyes wild.

Rafe's hand twitched when Jerry threw again. The man was a master with a knife and always carried more than one. He impaled this one onto the mattress, jerking out his knife and tossing the dying snake aside. That left one for Rafe and he quickly grabbed the last one on the bed by the tail and threw it down, stomping its head with his boot until it was still.

"That's it." He let out a breath he hadn't realized he was holding. "Let's search the house." It didn't take long to see there was no sign of Le Croix in the small frame shack.

Miguel quickly untied the sobbing woman and picked her up, checking her for snake bites. "We got to her in time. Any sign of Le Croix?" He picked up a blanket from a chair and wrapped her carefully while she clung to him.

"No, not in the front of the house." Rafe realized they'd been fooled. "Jerry?"

"Not in the back either." He nodded toward Tina. "We need to question her."

Miguel nodded. "Little one, please. Tell us. Do you know where the man went?" He stared into her eyes, compelling her.

She clutched his arms, clearly still in shock. "He, he flew. He, he bit me." She touched her neck.

Miguel went very still. "Look at me, Tina." He lifted her chin until her damp eyes were open and focused on his. "You will be all right. I will take care of you. But did he say where he was going?"

Rafe could see the twin marks where the vampire had taken her blood. He found a snake with life in it and stomped it until it was still.

Tina shuddered and sobbed, burying her face against Miguel's chest. She murmured something Rafe couldn't hear.

"What did she say?" Rafe moved closer.

"Mel. He's after Melisandra. For her betrayal."

Miguel walked to the front of the house. "I hear the car. That's got to be the women and Abraham. I'm going to ride with them and take Tina back to town. Can you two head to Mel's shop and take care of this?"

"Yes, of course." Rafe was glad to be out of that house. Snakes. It had to be snakes. He wasn't about to tell Lacy about them. They horrified her.

Miguel stared down at Tina. "I'll make sure she remembers only that a bad man took her." He shook his head as he stepped outside. "And there will be no sign left of what he did to her." He smoothed her tangled hair back from her forehead and stared into her eyes. "No one bit you, *querida*. No one can fly."

"Yeah, we're on our way to that shop now." Rafe saw Lacy headed his way. He didn't have time to tell her his plans. He knew Jerry didn't look forward to seeing Mel again and he sure didn't want Glory to know he was going anywhere near her. "Got to go," he shouted. "Talk to you back at the hotel." He turned to go.

Abe was suddenly in front of him and held up his hand. "Wait a moment." The monk must have seen the look on Rafe's face. "It's important or I wouldn't slow you down. Trust me on this." He paused when Miguel pushed past him.

"I'm headed to the car. Tina needs medical attention." Miguel was eager to get going.

Abe laid a hand on Tina's head and murmured soothing words. "Poor child. Yes, leave her only enough memory to tell the police what they need to know."

"I will, *padre*." Miguel eased Tina into the back seat of the car. Glory was there and made sure the girl was well-covered. "We will stop at Le Croix's house. He had a shed in back with his trophies. It will be proof that he was the serial killer. Tina will remember only that she escaped, got to a phone and called for help. *My* help." He glanced at the car. "I brought my friends, my female friends, to make her feel safe. Then she let me call the police." Miguel slammed the car door, leaning forward to urge Lacy to get moving.

"Rafael, all of you, listen." Abe turned to Rafe. "Now you must catch this man and send him to Hell. It seems you think he is going to be at that voodoo shop." Abe sighed. "Let me say this. My God and the Olympus gods, even the gods the Voodoo priestess serves each have their devotees." He looked at the black SUV when Miguel slammed the door. "I cannot condemn any of them. True believers, as long as they do good and not evil, have the right to their beliefs. But this woman, Melisandra, has crossed a line, helping your vampire killer. She may not be on your list for Hell, but she should be stopped." Abe looked Rafe in the eye.

"I understand you, Father. But understand me. I am running out of time. I have to save my daughter. You want others roasted? You may have to get your own hands dirty. Come yourself. You seem to get where you need to go when you need to."

Abe frowned. "I wish I could but..." He shook

his head. "I have my own orders. Good luck." He disappeared.

Rafe had no more time to worry about the monk. He shifted into his fastest bird and flew toward town. Damn it, he couldn't think about theology or Abe's personal requests. Of course, Mel had done horrible things. He'd seen that back in Austin when she'd used her voodoo magic to treat Jerry like her personal slave. It had taken a serious intervention to get Glory's man free from the priestess.

He felt Jerry's presence nearby as they flew toward New Orleans and the French Quarter. Glory's husband would be risking a lot getting close to Melisandra again. Mel had been obsessed with him and she had powers that had overwhelmed the vampire before. When they got to the shop, Rafe owed it to Glory to insist Jerry stay out of this confrontation, well away from the voodoo priestess. Surely, he could handle Le Croix by himself. He had God on his side, didn't he?

CHAPTER TWELVE

THE SHOP WAS dark when they arrived. The summer heat rose from the brick sidewalk in waves. The area would have seemed charming but for the scattered body parts in front of the door. Rotting body parts. A zombie had obviously bit the dust. The odor was almost enough to mask the tell-tale smell of vampire. And blood.

"You're staying out here." Rafe thrust a chunk of tattered pants and foot aside then tested the door. Locked. No problem, he needed to release some frustration anyway. He was poised to kick it in when Jerry grabbed his arm.

"The hell you say. I recognize that blood. Mel is in there bleeding out. You think I want to miss this?" Jerry tried to push him aside. "If I get a chance to finish her, I'm taking it. She's not on your list, so she's up for grabs. Right?"

"One of you boys go ahead and kick it in. Standing out here waiting makes me want to put a boot up one of your backsides, *capiscimi*?"

Rafe would know that feminine voice anywhere. He looked over his shoulder. "Flo, what the fuck are you doing here?"

"Watch your mouth around my wife, Valdez."

Richard Mainwaring gently slid Florence Da Vinci out of the way. "She's here to help. You think I could stop her?"

"Of course not. Sorry, Flo, but the serial killer is in there. *I've* got to do this. Devil's orders." Rafe quit wasting time and kicked. The door crashed into the shop. Inside, it was clear there'd been a battle. Shelves had been overturned. Broken glass and crystals littered the floor. Many different smells mingled in the air, creating an overpowering stench.

"Aye! *Un disastro*." Flo picked up a decapitated voodoo doll and tossed it aside. "Creepy. But what's this?" She spied a beautiful bottle that had been spared. She lifted the stopper and sniffed the contents. "A love potion, I think." She stuffed it into her black leather bustier. "Where is the voodoo woman? And that vampire who is giving all of us a bad name?"

"Patience, darling. This is Rafe's show, remember? We are just here for backup." Richard had pulled out a stake. "I've got a couple of these if you need them, friend."

"Thanks. I'm just supposed to capture, not end him, but I'll take it." Rafe stuck it in his belt. Then he followed the scent of blood and vampire toward the beads that hid the back room. He could tell he was close to his target. He pushed the beads aside and bumped into the table where he and Miguel had sat with the voodoo priestess earlier. Mel was lying across it, her hair loose and her dress ripped open so her bloody throat was exposed. She was still alive, but her breathing was shallow. A man stood over her, his fangs dripping with fresh blood.

"Here they are, dear Melisandra. Your guests from earlier. You told them my name, didn't you?" He gripped her throat and squeezed, blood streaming from the twin marks there.

"I told them nothing. I swear. . ." Her voice was weak, her eyes flickering from Rafe to the people behind him. "Vampires! One of them... very strong. Must have. . . read my mind."

"Let her go, Le Croix." Rafe moved closer.

"When I'm ready. Who is the man you are staring at, Melisandra? The one with the knife behind the others. A former lover? He certainly has no love for you now. Can't you feel his hatred? He wants to kill you. Shall I let him have the pleasure?" Le Croix squeezed harder.

Mel gasped. "Jeremy!"

"Don't be pathetic. He wants to rip out your throat. You must have been very cruel to him." Le Croix released her and stepped back. "Not surprising. You are a faithless bitch." He ran toward the back of the store and a door there. A pair of Mel's zombies flanked it but didn't move. He must have frozen them when he'd arrived. Le Croix shoved them aside and struggled with the lock.

Rafe leaped over the table and onto the vampire's back. He pulled the stake from his belt and pricked Le Croix enough to show he meant business. The vampire didn't move.

"You're done, Le Croix," Rafe said as the door

in front of them opened and a man appeared.

"Yes, indeed." Gordon grinned happily. "Good job, Valdez. Number two on the hit list, delivered. Don't poke him hard enough to finish him, the Master enjoys that privilege." He stared into the vampire's eyes. Le Croix, a short, slender man dressed in black, stiffened, and suddenly became a statue.

"Who are you? Why can't I move? Master? Not *my* master. I answer to no one." Le Croix was allowed to talk but clearly struggled to understand how this man had control of his body. He blinked, his mouth moved, but nothing else.

Rafe had to admit he was enjoying this. "How do you like the feeling, Le Croix? I heard you toyed with those helpless women before you ended their lives. Did you paralyze them the way Gordon is paralyzing you now?"

"Shut up! Shut up! Who are you people? Where are you taking me?" Le Croix actually had tears in his eyes when Gordon snapped a shackle on his wrist and used a chain to tug him through the door. "No! Stop this. I can't…" The vampire staggered stiffly forward, much like one of Mel's zombies, with no will of his own.

"Such whining. Come along, little vampire. How do you like being at someone else's mercy?" Gordon shook his head. "You never took on a strong adversary, did you? No, you chose women you could control. You were ridiculously predictable." Gordon yanked on the chain until Le Croix fell to his knees.

"They were sluts, whores! Nobody would miss

them." The vampire looked around the room for sympathy.

Rafe and the others stared at him with contempt. "I doubt their loved ones felt that way."

Gordon shook his head. "You had a type, didn't you? No wonder your friend Mel here was able to easily find victims for you." He snorted. "Really, there should be a serial killer's handbook. Now *I* had eclectic tastes. Drove the cops crazy. I liked women too, but dark, light, big, little, didn't matter. Though I did appreciate a decent butt and…" He stepped on Le Croix's wrist and the vampire screamed. "Oh, shut up. I do have an absolute passion for a pretty manicure." He studied Le Croix's hand under his boot. "Your nails are quite lovely, Pierre. Enjoy a manicure yourself, do you? I wish I had my chain saw now. Your right hand would make a nice addition to my trophy case."

Le Croix howled. "What kind of monster are you?"

Gordon looked back at Rafe and winked. "The kind you'll recognize. You'll meet them in Hell, little man. Just wait and see." He jerked Le Croix to his feet again, then led him into the darkness of the alley behind the shop.

"Hell? No, no, I'm going to…"

"Going to what? Fly away? Nope. You can't shift, can't even run now unless Lucifer or I decide watching you try to escape would entertain us." Gordon laughed. "Get used to it. Your version of Hell is just beginning. You will soon be the Devil's new plaything. Think about what you did to those women. Then imagine much worse happening to you."

Le Croix's wail sent chills down Rafe's spine as Gordon and the vampire finally disappeared down a manhole which suddenly opened in front of them.

Rafe slammed the door. "He's gone."

Flo clung to her husband, muttering in Italian. "I'm glad. No wonder he had to capture women. I'm sure his *pene* is the size of my little toe, eh? Now he will get what he deserves."

Rafe nodded. He realized Melisandra stared at him from her place on the table. It was clear from her pale face and lack of movement that the vampire had taken most of her life force. She was near death. "What should we do about *her*?"

Flo and Richard looked at each other. Flo stepped forward. "Let her bleed out. Jeremiah has told us how she helped that vampire take his victims. She might as well have killed them herself." Her eloquent gestures said the rest.

"If we go now, we can leave her fate in God's hands." Richard pulled Flo toward the front door. "That's my vote." He glanced at Jerry who couldn't take his eyes off Mel. "She's lost so much blood, she's too weak to help herself. Someone could call for an ambulance. That's another choice." Richard crossed himself. "We'll see you back at the hotel, Rafe. We're available and want to help with your next take down." They hurried out of the shop.

"Jerry? You heard what Abe said. He'd like to see Mel sent to Hell tonight as well." Rafe stayed clear of the woman. Her lips moved but apparently the effort to speak was beyond her. Her fingers fluttered helplessly against the table.

"I think that was a test. A man like Abe, if he *is* a man.... Maybe he's an angel, I don't know." Jerry ran his hands through his hair. His knife was back in his boot. He'd pulled it out as soon as they'd arrived there.

"Shit, Rafe. I'm not killing her. I won't kill a helpless woman, no matter how evil she is or how much I hate her." He tore his eyes away from her gaze. "Damn her, be glad you can't read her mind. She's still trying to manipulate me and calling it love. I'm out of here. Get help for her if you want. I don't care. I never want to see her again." He turned his back on her and strode away.

Rafe noticed a tear running down Mel's pale cheek. "Are you expecting me to believe you really loved Jerry? I'll call for help if you promise to leave him alone—Jeremy *and* his wife Glory." He realized she was moving her fingers, trying to point at something. He looked around. On the wall was a poster of Loa, the god she worshiped, wearing several rams' horns with a huge snake clinging to his neck. She'd made a little shrine to him. She was probably hoping to pray for a miracle.

Rafe wished he did have the vampire ability to read minds. A voodoo priestess. If he saved her, she'd owe him. But he needed promises. He grabbed what looked like another of her voodoo dolls, but this one was clearly intended to be Loa decorated with the horns and snake. It was worth a shot.

"All right, Mel, I know you have pride. Surely you can see it's time for you to move on from my friend Jeremy. You need to let him go." Did her face change? She closed her eyes, as if acknowledging the truth of that.

"What do you say, Mel? Will you swear to forget him on the life of your god, Loa?" Rafe leaned close, close enough to hear her if she managed a whisper. He waited. Maybe she was ready to die. Her shop was a shambles and the man she had always wanted had just rejected her. Finally, she whispered.

"Please. Help…me." She struggled to reach for the doll.

"Not until you swear it. Say you are no longer going to bother Jeremy Blade or his wife, Glory St. Clair. Swear it!" Rafe waited, holding the doll just out of reach.

Her breathing was labored and blood still seeped from her wounds but she finally stared into Rafe's eyes and managed to say the words. "I will leave…alone. Your friends…safe…from me."

"Forevermore?" Rafe waited until she nodded then laid the Loa figure in her hand and left her. Outside, he punched 9-1-1 and reported a woman seriously injured at the voodoo shop. Then he shifted and flew back to the hotel.

He didn't have time to worry about Mel and whether she would survive her wounds. He had a time limit and needed to figure out his next destination. It would be a while before Lacy, Glory and Miguel would join him at the hotel.

They'd have to deal with the police and make sure Tina was returned to her family or taken to the hospital. Miguel and Glory could at least make sure the policemen had false memories that would make it possible for his group to leave New Orleans without further complications. They could claim Le Croix had been consumed by an alligator. That would close the serial killer case.

Miguel might need some time to get over his guilt about Tina's kidnapping, but the vampire should realize that Melisandra had hired the woman with Le Croix's type in mind long ago. Maybe saving Mel had been the wrong move. But, as Richard had said, her fate was in God's hands now.

Back at the hotel, he heard giggling coming from one of the bedrooms. If he knew Florence, and he had known her for years, she was testing that love potion she'd found in Mel's shop. Richard was a lucky bastard.

Rafe ordered room service and concentrated on picking out his next target. If he wasn't tainted like he was, he'd enjoy playing love games with Lacy. Instead, he worked the computer and wolfed down some delicious Cajun food from the hotel menu. He also ordered her favorite seafood gumbo for his lady to eat when she got back.

He needed a nap. He couldn't keep going on little sleep and too much adrenaline. Three more targets left. It was good that all three of them were back in Texas. Knowing the Devil, there was bound to be a catch.

"You've got to be kidding me. The next two are twins?" Lacy finished her bowl of gumbo and wiped out the bowl with the last of the bread. "That sounds too easy."

"I know." Rafe watched her sigh with contentment and lick her fingers. Everything Lacy did was sexy. She stretched and her shirt rode up, showing her flat stomach. You couldn't tell she'd carried three babies in there. She'd obsessed with getting her figure back and had exercised until only the faintest stretch marks showed where his children had ridden inside her for nine months. He leaned over and kissed her smooth tummy.

"I love you. Thanks for coming. I know I didn't act grateful when I first saw you." He laid his head between her breasts. He could hear her heartbeat through her thin cotton t-shirt.

"Not only were you not grateful, you were pissed." She ran her hands through his hair, pressing him closer. "I understand. You're always trying to protect me. Get over it."

"Not possible. That's how I'm built." He sat up and pulled her across his lap.

The other couples were in the two bedrooms, showering and doing whatever else they liked to do before their death sleep hit them at dawn. He'd let them know that the next destination was Houston. It was a very short plane ride from here. Since the vampires would be useless during daylight hours, Rafe and Lacy would go ahead to the big city. They'd set up in a hotel, then do the research he needed to get started while the vamps slept here. The rest of them would fly into Houston after sunset. Hopefully, by the time they arrived, Rafe would have figured out what needed to happen to take down the two sinners.

"Tell me what you know so far." Lacy snuggled against him. "What have these men done to deserve Hell?"

Rafe reached for his laptop. "They specialize in scamming the elderly. No target is too poor or too old for them to prey on. Between the two of them, Barry and Bonnell Pomeroy have stolen the life savings from hundreds, maybe thousands of old folks. Over a billion dollars has ended up in their off-shore accounts."

"That's a lot different from murder, like Le Croix. Or war crimes like the nun." Lacy leaned over to punch a key. "Their social media seems legit. Barry has such a kindly looking face." She gestured at the computer. "Look at him. His smile reminds me of Santa Claus, a jolly man with a white beard running a legitimate business." She scrolled down the site. "It says they're sending food and clothing to help war victims in Ukraine." She shook her head. "Maybe the Devil is jerking you around this time."

"I tried to follow the money and the shipments." Rafe pushed the laptop away. "It's fake, all of it. They get donations, lots of them, but the food, clothing, whatever people send never gets where it's supposed to go."

"But there are pictures." Lacy rubbed his shoulder. He was sure she could feel the tension in him. "Are you telling me those are fake too?"

"Real, but taken from news stories and other sites. Bonnell is the tech guy. He does all the social media posts and manipulates the sites. Barry is the spokesman. He goes around the country talking up the charities. Tomorrow night they're throwing a gala to raise funds for the homeless. I'll book us into the hotel where they're holding the event. That will put us on the scene where they will be." Rafe fought against a headache throbbing between his eyebrows. He hoped he was right about these two. On the surface they seemed dedicated people, but the deeper he dug, the more evil he uncovered.

"They're making the right moves, but when I keep digging…" He turned to Lacy. "Listen to this. You know how many mass shootings we've had. Children…" He had to swallow when he thought about his own kids going to school without fear. What could happen to them. "Well, these men rush right in after one of those tragedies and set up one of their charities. Start collecting for the victims' families. Make it look like they are taking care of everyone. Pretending to be saints."

Lacy looked frozen. "What are you saying?"

"They funnel every damn dime to their own off-shore accounts. They take advantage of grief

and chaos to line their own pockets." Rafe couldn't

look at the laptop another minute. It hadn't been that hard to find the truth. Why hadn't others looked behind their smiles and empty promises to catch them? Lacy asked that question.

"Oh, they give a little. Unload trucks of water. Pay for the occasional funeral. But that's a drop in the bucket compared to what they keep." Rafe paced the room, unable to stay still as he thought about it. Hell was too good for these guys. He imagined Lucifer putting them to work in his own accounting department, thrilled with their cunning. How was that a punishment?

"Then there are the scams for the senior citizens. Apparently, they have dozens of people working for them who call, text or email their targets pretending to be grandchildren in trouble or men looking for love who pretend to court a widow then ask for her money."

"Well, that's just sick. My own mom might have fallen for that if she hadn't met Ian and gotten involved with him." Lacy picked up her phone. "I'm calling her right now. Checking on the boys."

"You do know it's four o'clock in the morning. If she's awake, she might be with Ian and… you know." Rafe raised an eyebrow. "Honestly, it was Ian who helped me do this deep dive on the Pomeroys. I'm not the computer genius he is. And that's what it took to find out all this shit. It takes serious hacking skills to look behind the twins' business dealings to dig up the evil underneath. Ian spent hours working on this for me. His reward is that he's probably with Sheila right now."

"Okay, okay. I'm glad he's helpful. But don't even go there with talk about rewards. I know my mom is a passionate woman, but please…" Lacy flushed. "All right, I'll wait until morning." She threw her phone on the table. "I'm a passionate woman too. When are you going to get over this thing you have about being too evil to let me love you?"

"Damn. Why not just come right out with it?" Rafe sat next to her and picked up her hands. "You know how I feel. I've got a lot on my mind right now and just had a fresh reminder of where half of me comes from when I watched Le Croix dragged off to Hell."

"You are not like Le Croix or Gordon or people like that." Lacy squeezed his hand.

"I know that, but you want to talk to your mother, well, I need to talk to mine. What is she doing with Daniela? Is our baby safe? Lucifer wants Lilith with him and this is all about getting her down there in Hell with him full time. That should tell you just how filthy my mother is." Rafe leaned back and closed his eyes. The shit he'd seen in Hell suddenly overwhelmed him and he couldn't seem to draw a breath. He felt Lacy's hands on his chest, soothing him, trying to help him breathe.

"My precious man. Stop this. You're doing good. Every day and night. Let go of everything else. I wouldn't love anyone who's as bad as you say you must be. I couldn't." She wrapped her arms around him, her cheek against his.

Rafe felt her warmth seep into him. Her faith was so strong he couldn't deny it. That a good woman loved him so deeply, so completely, had to mean something.

"She's right, Rafael." Abe spoke from the doorway.

"Father!" They should learn to close the balcony doors. Not that it would make a difference with a celestial being. Rafe sat up. Maybe this angel, this whatever he was, had an answer for him.

"You are doing God's work. Two sinners who were hurting decent people can no longer walk the Earth thanks to you. Take heart." Abe strolled to the room service cart and picked up a piece of lemon tart. "Mortal food. I'm learning I have a weakness for it. You, Rafael, should indulge yourself more. Stop beating yourself up and enjoy the blessings God has given you." He winked. "Including a beautiful wife."

"You hear that, my love. We have holy approval." Lacy kissed Rafe, not shy about it. "There's a flight to Houston at six this morning. If we hurry, we can make it. What do you say? Then we can check into a hotel and have some alone time before we get to work on bringing down the twins."

"Listen to her, Rafael. I have it on good authority that your little girl is safe for now. Your mother is no prize, but she does seem to love her granddaughter in her own way. She wants her to enjoy a normal life on Earth. Do your part to satisfy Lucifer and all should be well." Abe took a bite of the tart and shivered. "Oh, my! Heaven has nothing like this."

Rafe couldn't believe the man was encouraging them to take off and enjoy a little break. But then why not? He and Lacy were married, Abe seemed to have received some kind of assurance about their daughter, and there were hourly commercial flights between New Orleans and Houston. The vampires could bring their weapons in the private plane when they came at sunset. He and Lacy had little to pack except for a few clothes and his laptop.

"All right. I'll leave a note and we can go." He stood and reached for Lacy's hand. "Or you can tell them what's up, Abe."

"No, you write out your instructions. I've been checking on Cisneros. He's taking this business with Tina hard. He wants to harm Melisandra, but I actually approve of the way you've handled her fate, Rafael. I will make sure Miguel joins you in Houston." Abe picked up a chocolate cookie from the cart. "He should come here before sunrise for his death sleep. If he doesn't, I'll find him. Go on, take your little break and enjoy a few hours to refresh. After you get the Pomeroys, you'll only have one more to go. Barring interference from Lucifer, you should make your deadline."

"Thanks, Abe, for taking care of Miguel. I knew he was upset about Tina, but didn't know what to say to make him feel better." Rafe shook the monk's hand.

"That's why I'm here. Your Miguel is very powerful, but he's been a loner too long. He doesn't know how to interact with a group comfortably. I'm hoping that at the end of this, he will see all of you as the family he needs."

Lacy smiled. "I don't know, Father, he's a little scary. You know the cats in my clan are all about family, but that vampire? Well, he has an edge that makes my fur stand up, if you know what I mean."

"Not exactly, my dear, but you do paint a picture." Abe laughed. "Cookies. Oh, I'd better pray for restraint. When I was a lad, there was nothing like these. Go now, catch that plane. I will see you in Houston. It's hot there. I hope you packed swimsuits."

Lacy laughed. "Knowing my man, he packed knives, but not a swimsuit. I did pack a credit card. I like the idea of swimming. What do you say, Rafe?"

"I say you are both crazy if you think I have time for something like that." Rafe realized he was actually thinking about it. "I'm calling for a reservation now." It took a few moments with a search engine, but he had plane tickets and a hotel suite waiting for them before he sat down to write out a note to the vampires. Dawn was only an hour away. No sign of Miguel yet but Abe didn't seem to be worried.

Rafe wrote down the name of the hotel he'd chosen. It was in the part of Houston where the Pomeroys had their headquarters. For some reason Rafe felt optimistic about this pair. Was *he* the one who was crazy? The men had a sophisticated operation but it was white collar crime. As far as he knew, they hadn't killed anyone, just taken billions of dollars with their scams. How dangerous could these two guys be? Maybe not dangerous, but they must have very hard hearts to take advantage of situations like they had. They were both men without a conscience.

Rafe felt a shiver run up his spine at the thought. No conscience, no guilt. He would have to be very, very careful.

CHAPTER THIRTEEN

"ARE YOU SURE we're at the right place?
I thought these guys were rich." Lacy
tugged on Rafe's sleeve. They both stared at the
forlorn-looking strip center that had windows
covered from the inside by sheets of brown paper.
The parking lot was full of sad cars and battered
pickup trucks.

"Obviously this isn't where they spend their
money. If they have corporate headquarters, I
couldn't find out where they are."

At least it had been easy for Rafe to find
an address for the Pomeroys' telemarketing
headquarters. There had been an ad in the local
throwaway newspaper for people to work at the
call center. With the promise of a decent hourly
wage and no experience necessary, the ad would
be irresistible for people who needed quick cash
and didn't care how they earned it.

Rafe couldn't just sit and wait for the rest of his
crew after he and Lacy had enjoyed a shower and
a long nap. It was mid-afternoon and they still
had hours before the vampires would arrive in
Houston. Damned long summer days.

So here they were at the only location that

might give them a clue. As they sat in their rented car, a man came out and walked to the street. He slumped on the curb and lit up. Smoke break. Rafe opened the car door. "Stay here. Let me see if I can pick his brain."

"Are you sure he has one?" Lacy rolled her eyes. "Unfiltered cigarette and his clothes are filthy. He'd be better off spending his money on doing a load of laundry than paying for that pack in his shirt pocket."

"He has his priorities, we have ours. Right now, it's information." Rafe pulled out a ten-dollar bill. "Let's see what this buys us." He walked over and sat down next to the guy. Not too close, he didn't appreciate second hand smoke. The man gave him a narrow-eyed look.

"If you're looking to bum a cig, fuck off."

"No, man, just wondered if you'd tell me what's up in there. Name's Joe. Saw their ad in the local throwaway paper and was thinkin' about checking into a job. What's it like? Worth my time?" Rafe kept his money hidden. The bribe was a last resort.

"I'm Carl. They ride you pretty hard. Listen in on every call. Expect results. And it's noisy as hell." He took a deep drag. "I can't stay out here long. We get ten minutes, every three hours. Good luck if you've gotta take a leak."

"Harsh. Ad in the paper says fifteen an hour. That right?" Rafe knew it wasn't bad for telemarketing.

"Depends. We got quotas. You find a live one and talk 'em into sending in some cash or a gift card, you earn that. You get a bunch of hang ups, you're lucky to make five." Carl had managed to suck that cigarette down to the end, almost burning his fingers. "Got to go, man. You don't mind scammin' little old ladies, it's okay."

"Scamming?" Rafe glanced back at the store front. "What do you mean?"

"Oh, they don't call it that. But you call folks, and they always seem to be older than hell, then you pretend you're collecting for a charity or maybe you're from the government." He got up and glanced around. "I'm not supposed to talk about it. At first it was kinda fun, scaring the shit out of them, you know?"

"I don't get it." Rafe pulled out that ten. "Fill me in. What do you say that scares them? I don't mind running a con if that's what it is. Details, man."

Carl snatched the bill, stuffing it into his pocket. He lit up again. "You're not a cop, are you?"

"Oh, hell no." Rafe tried to look insulted. He even showed the guy the gun he had tucked in his waistband, under his t-shirt. "We just moved here to get away from trouble up north. I want the scoop. If there's money to be made, I want to know about it, that's all.

"Yeah, well, they won't let you bring that piece in there. But a hustler can make pretty good bank. Put the fear of God into those old folks and the head honcho, Bonnell Pomeroy, will reward you. He's got lots of scams going." He looked around.

"There's a back room where, if you know computers, you can really rake it in. I thought about it, but I opened my big mouth and my lady don't like what I'm doing. Now she's after me to quit." He shrugged. "What can I say? I'm willing to do whatever that little gal wants to get what I want, know what I mean?"

Rafe glanced across the street. "Sure. My woman has me whipped and that's a fact." The two men shared knowing looks.

Carl kept his eye on the door into the call center. "I've pretended to be the IRS, Social Security, from places like that. We put on an act so the old people will send in gift cards because they think they'll lose their house or their checks will stop if they don't."

He started walking toward the building, smoking as fast as he could. "I admit, it's getting to me, too. I keep thinkin' about my gran. A lot of the marks can't hear shit either. That's why it's noisy in there. You have to yell so they can hear ya." He stopped and ground out his cigarette butt under his worn boot. "Megan gave me a deadline. As soon as I have enough for a deposit on an apartment, I'm out of here. My girl and me are movin' in together. Hey, you don't mind conning people, come on in and apply." He nodded to a girl who was coming out, then disappeared inside.

Rafe watched the young woman get into an aging pickup truck and struggle to get it going. After the engine ground a few times, it finally clicked.

He saw her bang on the steering wheel and walked over.

"Dead battery?"

She hit the steering wheel one more time. "Dead and probably won't take a charge. This has been coming on for a while." Tears rolled down her cheeks. "Shit. And I just got fired."

"I'm sorry. Can my wife and I give you a ride somewhere? Or do you need to make a call?" Rafe gestured for Lacy to come over, figuring the girl was late teens, maybe twenty tops. She'd probably be more comfortable knowing he wasn't alone.

"A ride. Yeah, that would be great. My phone is out of minutes so I can't call and it wouldn't do any good anyway." She hopped out of the truck and slammed the door. "My boyfriend might be able to bring me a new battery after he gets off work. Maybe he can get this piece of shit going."

"I hope so. I'm Joe and this is Laurie. We're over there." He pointed to the car parked across the street. "Come on. You'll have to give us directions. We're new in town." New and he wasn't about to throw around his real name. If things went to plan, he'd be making the Pomeroy brothers disappear.

"Thanks, Joe. It's not far." Once they were in the car, she leaned between the seats. "I'm Kelly. Kelly Booker. What were you doing hanging around the job? You don't look like most of the people who work there. This car is too nice. Most of us have hit hard times." She glanced down at her faded blue jean shorts and t-shirt. "It's a shit job. Bullying old people. I didn't have the stomach for it."

Lacy gave her a sympathetic smile. "Really?

That's what they do in there? Like Joe said, we're new in town and saw the ad in the paper. We rented the car for now, but we need cash. I'm sorry you were fired. What happened, Kelly?"

"I just couldn't do it. They give you a script. You're supposed to call the number they give you and pretend to be a relative, like a granddaughter or niece, someone who needs help, cash for an emergency. They do background checks on these old folks and they know who lives alone and who has money. It's pitiful, really." She told Rafe where to turn.

They were in a part of Houston with row after row of rundown apartment buildings. Many of them had kids running around outside, between cars and into the street.

Rafe had to watch where he was going and drive slowly. He jerked to a stop when a basketball rolled in front of the car, a boy and a barking dog chasing it.

"What exactly were you supposed to say to these old people?" Lacy looked back to talk to the girl.

"Pretend you were in trouble. Cry, put on a full show when you beg them for bail money or for cash to help get out of a jam." Kelly pointed to a building at the end of a row. "There, building C, I can get out here. No sign of Jimmy's truck so he's not home yet. I'll just wait for him and we'll figure something out."

"But you got fired. Why?" Rafe stopped the car while Kelly picked up her purse and struggled to open the door. She'd also grabbed a bag which must have contained her lunch or dinner.

"They wanted me to put more pressure on the old folks. Say someone was goin' to kill me or *them* if I didn't get the money fast. Can you believe it? I wouldn't do it. Threaten some granny on social security." Kelly frowned at Rafe. "Is this door locked or something?"

"Oh, sorry." Rafe hit the door lock "Tell me. Did you ever meet either of the Pomeroys?"

"Yeah, a time or two. Why? You reporters?" She gave them a searching look. "The bosses were in yesterday, both of them. I overheard them talking about the big gala they're throwing tonight. Raising money for the homeless."

She shoved the back door open. "Shit. Like Bonnell Pomeroy cares about any of that. Some of the folks who work there have to sleep in their cars. Would he let them do it in his parking lot? Hell, no. He had a security guard run them off at gunpoint."

"That's terrible!" Lacy glanced at Rafe. "He sure doesn't care about the homeless then. What about his brother? Barry? Isn't that his name?"

"He always has his picture in the papers, talking about his charity work. Bonnell stays close to the call center, checking the time sheets, docking pay if you don't get enough calls through in a day." She sniffed. "You think I got paid for the three hours I put in today since lunch?"

"He wouldn't pay you?" Rafe saw Lacy open her purse. "Yeah, we're investigative reporters, sort of. We'll pay for more information. Sit back down and I'll turn up the AC. It's hot out there." He nodded when Lacy pulled out some twenties. "I'd like to know more about this gala the Pomeroys are throwing."

"You'll pay me for that? It's been in the newspaper. But if you just got to town…" Kelly slid into the back seat again. "Yeah, it's cool in here. We can't afford to run the AC during the day, the light bill is horrible. It'll be hot as hell in the apartment." She sighed.

"Relax, cool off, and tell us when and where this gala is going to take place. Is this homeless charity run by the Pomeroys? Or someone else?" Rafe realized this might be where he could get both men together. He pulled into the parking lot, careful to avoid potholes, and found a spot under a drooping tree that looked starved for water.

"They started it, believe it or not. It's in a fancy hotel at the Galleria. Have you been there?" Kelly settled back, ready to talk.

Lacy glanced at Rafe. "We're from Dallas. I haven't been but I've heard of it. Lots of fancy shops there. Too rich for my blood."

"Me too." Kelly exhaled. "But the rich folks in Houston just love a chance to get dressed up and hit the social scene for a good cause. A party for a homeless charity is right up their alley." She got a dreamy look. "Someday, that'll be me and Jimmy, lookin' smart and dinin' and dancin' with the rich and famous. We have plans."

Lacy reached between the seats and took Kelly's hand. "Good for you. Do you know anything more about this gala the Pomeroys are throwing tonight?"

Kelly was only too eager to tell what she knew, including how the twins had wormed their way into Houston's fashionable social scene. When Houston's mayor had decided to clean up the tent cities that had grown under the many freeways in the area, the Pomeroys had proposed raising money to build homes for the people who would be evicted from those tents and displaced.

This gala was expected to raise millions for the project that would make sure the poor people who needed affordable housing would get it. The tables for the event had sold out quickly and a few famous faces among Hollywood stars who were native Houstonians were expected to attend. There was even a Grammy-winning entertainer who was going to perform for the audience and a popular band for dancing.

"It was all anyone could talk about at the call center. Very fancy. The Pomeroys have custom made tuxedoes. Can you imagine?" Kelly pulled a sandwich out of her rumpled paper bag. "Do you mind? I ran out of time and didn't get to eat my lunch."

"No, go ahead." Rafe remembered there hadn't been any personal information on the Pomeroys' website. "Are either of the men married?"

"No, not now. They're both divorced. There was a scandal a while back. Barry got caught with the wife of one of his big donors. He and Bonnell had a big fight about that right there in the office at the call center. After that, Barry broke it off with the lady. Bonnell is all about the dollar. His marriage didn't last because I've heard he pinches a penny so hard, it hollers." She laughed. "Imagine. Raking in all that money and then don't never enjoy it. If I had plenty, you wouldn't see me acting the tightwad." She finished her peanut butter sandwich and carefully folded her baggie and put it in the paper bag.

Kelly looked up when a truck drove into the lot. "Heard he screwed over his ex. She'd signed a pre-nup and he caught her cheating. No surprise there, he's such a bastard. Anyway, she didn't get so much as a dime after that. He even made her give back her engagement ring. He must have a hell of a lawyer."

"I appreciate the information, Kelly." Lacy must have noticed something in the woman's body language. "Was that your boyfriend's truck that just pulled in?"

"Yes, that's him. Anything else you want to know?" The girl's eyes were on the money in Lacy's hand.

Rafe had been busy trying to figure out how they could get into a sold-out gala. "I can't think of anything right now." He dug into his pocket to pull out some more cash. "Good luck with your truck. If we come up with any more questions, how can we reach you?"

"I'll give you my cell number. We'll buy more minutes when Jimmy gets paid on Friday." She gave Lacy the number, who punched it into her phone.

"Great. And good luck finding a better job. I

have a feeling that call center won't be around much longer." Rafe handed her a couple more twenties. He knew what it felt like to live paycheck to paycheck.

"Thanks a lot. This will sure help pay for a battery." Kelly opened the back door. "I hope you turn them into the cops, or the feds, like I've seen on TV. I felt dirty every time I managed to get some old lady to send in money. If you do turn in those Pomeroys to the cops, maybe I can testify. I'd love to see them behind bars."

"Don't worry. I think they're going to get what's coming to them." Lacy smiled.

"I sure hope so." Kelly slammed the car door and hurried over to the man getting out of his battered pickup.

"Cute couple and so young." Lacy slid her hand over Rafe's knee. "I can see your mind working. Do we need to go shopping? The Galleria is calling my name. I'd love to catch the Pomeroy twins at their gala."

"I'll just bet you would." Rafe leaned over to kiss her smile. "I was thinking it would be easier to sneak in as servers than socialites."

"Remember, we have help coming. I can't imagine Flo carrying champagne flutes on a tray around a dining room." Lacy laughed as Rafe put the car in gear. "Admit it, lover. If anyone can talk her way into an elite gathering of the rich and famous, Florence da Vinci can."

CHAPTER FOURTEEN

"I DON'T KNOW ABOUT this takedown." Rafe drove back to the hotel.

"What do you mean? The scams are horrible. They target the elderly." Lacy stared out the window as the got close to the hotel. "But then the last sinner was a serial killer. This seems bloodless, mild compared to that."

"You'd think so, wouldn't you?" The voice from the back seat made Rafe hit the brakes. That earned him a horn honk.

"Father, you shouldn't startle me like that when I'm driving." Rafe waved at the man behind him and sped up. Houston traffic was a bitch. Luckily, he hadn't been followed closely or there might have been a road rage incident to deal with. As it was, he got a one finger salute.

"Sorry, my son." Abe leaned back. "This can wait until we're back in the hotel. But I heard your reservations about the Pomeroys. You need to know the whole story about the men."

"Now you've got us curious." Lacy turned around in her seat. "Whatever they are up to, their sins are well-hidden. Rafe has spent hours on the computer. All he could find was the call center and the charity scams."

"This gala tonight is connected to one of their worst sins." Abe stared out the window. "Houston has a mild climate. It attracts its fair share of homeless. And the poor. The Pomeroys own a lot of property that will be suitable for the low-income housing the funds raised at the gala will finance."

"They must have shell corporations under different names. Ian and I could find no records of property they own." Rafe had been frustrated at the lack of information they'd found. Of course, he was no computer genius either. The difference between the rundown apartment buildings and the luxurious digs where he and his crew were staying couldn't have been more obvious.

Once at the hotel, he let the valet take the car and steered Lacy into the lobby, Abe trailing behind them. Crystal chandeliers loomed overhead and there was a pleasant hum from the bar to their right. The three of them were silent until they were safely inside the two-bedroom suite he and Lacy had used earlier.

"What else don't I know?" Rafe grabbed a bottle of water from the minibar, tossing it to Lacy. Then he got one for himself. Abe was inspecting the tray left from the lunch they had enjoyed before they'd gone out for the day. Rafe had put a "Do Not Disturb" sign on the door and housekeeping had left the suite alone. "Father?"

Abe picked up a pickle, smelled it then threw it back on the plate. "All right, here's what I found out. The men were what they used to call slum lords. They own rundown apartment buildings they don't bother to properly maintain. The rents are low enough that the people who live there have no choice but to deal with the rodents and leaky roofs." He dipped a finger into a bowl of melted ice cream and tasted. "Ah."

"All right, that's horrible, but still not on a par with a killer." Rafe wondered if he should order the monk a dessert from room service. Obviously, the cleric lived a spartan life in Heaven. Abe spooned up the melted chocolate until he scraped the bowl clean.

"Abe." Rafe touched the monk's back. "What's the deal? I always figured Heaven would be full of whatever you'd want, whenever you wanted it. You act desperate for treats."

Abe laid down the spoon with a sigh. "Your Heaven would be like that. Mine?" He stared at the ceiling. "Let's just say I have an important job that keeps me too busy to enjoy the rewards available to most who arrive there." He smiled. "When I'm on a job, I'm afraid I can get distracted." He gestured for Rafe and Lacy to sit. They settled on the couch.

"Now about the Pomeroys. When the brothers hatched this scheme to build homes for the homeless, they needed cleared land near where the tent cities had been. They started evicting the tenants in the apartments where they proposed building. It was going too slowly for them, so they did something that would speed things along." He bowed his head and murmured what sounded like a prayer and then crossed himself.

"What did they do, Father?" Lacy got up to put a hand on his shoulder.

"They set those rickety wooden piles on fire. Timed it to when there were thunder storms in the area so the authorities would blame the fire on lightning strikes." Abe had tears in his eyes. "Ten adults and five children, some babies, were killed, unable to get out in time. Those that did escape lost everything they owned."

"You sure about this?" Rafe gripped his water bottle.

"Of course. My boss sees everything." Abe wiped his eyes. "The reason so many adults were killed is because they included the elderly and the disabled. If you can't get out of bed, you have a devil of a time moving fast when a fire is consuming your home." He frowned, shaking his head. "Yes, I said devil. I'm glad Lucifer is taking action. About time, I say." He went back to studying the tray again.

Lacy settled on the couch next to Rafe again. "Those assholes burned down their own apartments."

"Yes, now the land is cleared and ready to build on. Perfect for the Mayor's new homeless project." Abe picked up the pickle, took a bite and made a face. "The city is paying a premium for the property. Because the Pomeroys are being so helpful in hosting this fundraiser to finance the construction. Isn't that kind of them?" He tossed the pickle back on the plate.

"They *are* murderers." Lacy leaned against Rafe. "I feel better about sending them to Hell. Thanks for telling us, Abe."

"Yes." Rafe slid his arm around his wife. "The rest of the crew will be here an hour after sunset. I wish we could do something about this situation before then."

Abe smiled. "I have a plan." He looked up again. "Why wait for the Pomeroys to disappear to take down their telephone and Internet business?"

"What are you going to do?" Rafe leaned forward as Abe walked over to the doors to the balcony. Rafe had requested rooms with a balcony on a high floor. The vampires could fly in and out without being noticed after dark. Now Abe could walk out and do his thing. Rafe and Lacy got up and followed him out into the heat and wind.

Abe smiled. "I know that the people who work in the center are mostly good folks who are down on their luck, like your friend Kelly. This will affect them, I'm afraid."

"You were listening in?" Rafe didn't know how he felt about that. Had the monk been paying attention when he and Lacy had been enjoying each other in bed before lunch? He'd given up trying to keep her hands off of him and vice versa. He'd hit the gift shop downstairs for a box of extra-strength condoms and figured that would have to do.

"Relax, Rafael. I know better than to invade your privacy. I only look in when you are at work doing what the Devil asked you to do." Abe flushed. "As tempting as it would be to take a peek. I've been celibate all my life, you see."

"Sorry about that, Father." Lacy grinned and nudged Rafe. "Tell us your plan."

"You've seen me create lightning, right? I think it might be a useful tool here." He smiled when Rafe exclaimed. "Yes, I'm going to take out the electrical system in that call center for starters. Completely fry it. Bonnell and Barry will be busy getting ready for tonight so they will have no time to fix things. That should shut it down." Abe stared out at the view of the Houston skyline in the distance then down at the busy freeway much closer. "I don't know much about computers but surely they need electricity too."

"Brilliant! Yes, the Wi-Fi, routers, cooling equipment, all that stuff, needs it. Do a general annihilation of their power grid and phone lines in that building and you should take care of it. Fry it all!" Rafe laughed. "With Bonnell and Barry gone to Hell, no one will be able to start it up again. It's a really expensive proposition."

"I wonder if you could figure out a way to pay those folks who are working there. Bonnell won't do it." Lacy leaned against the railing then shuddered. She wasn't a fan of heights. "People like Kelly deserve to be paid, even if they were doing horrible things. You heard her, she was desperate or she never would have taken the job in the first place. She seems like a good person."

"Let me think about it." Abe clapped his hands. "I'm enjoying this project. It's a challenge." He smiled. "See you later." Then he disappeared.

"Abe certainly has a sweet tooth. I'm going to order some desserts for him from room service." Rafe walked inside to pick up the house phone. "Taking out their power. So damn clever. I wish I'd thought of that."

Rafe also wished he'd remembered that not only was he being helped by vampires, but he was traveling with rich vampires. It certainly made things easier. Three beautiful ladies had made good use of their credit cards in the Galleria and were ready in time to stroll into the lavishly decorated ballroom on the arms of their men. Rafe knew better than to complain at the hit to his own plastic. He had a new tux he didn't need but it was a decent fit.

Why had he worried about getting into the gala? Those mesmerizing vampires paved the way past security and the ticket takers at the door. The fact that the seven of them looked the part of wealthy donors didn't hurt. They didn't need a dinner table, though Rafe and Lacy hit hard the canapes that were being passed by waiters. He guessed the vamps had dined on each other or hapless mortals where they could find them.

"Dining and dancing. Too bad we can't enjoy it in the usual way." Glory gripped Jerry's arm. "Can you hear that music? The band makes me want to slow dance with you."

"I'd like nothing better, my love. But Rafe has a job to do. We need to spot our targets first."

He kissed his wife's cheek then turned her toward the stage. "Look who's here for the main entertainment."

"Ray! I must go say hello." She hurried into the crowd.

Rafe stifled a groan. Wouldn't you know it? Vampires everywhere. Israel Caine was the Grammy-winning singer who would be in the spotlight tonight. He had been involved with Glory for years and knew all of the Austin vampires. Lucky for her marriage, she'd never actually hooked up with the handsome singer, but they'd be forever linked because she was Caine's sire. She had turned him vampire to save his life. Rafe saw them chatting across the crowded ballroom. Then Ray, as he was called, headed their way.

"Well, well, well, what is this?" The very famous Israel Caine kissed the ladies and shook hands all around. "Don't tell me you came to donate money to Houston's homeless situation. Last I heard, Austin has the same problem."

"That's true. But we're here for something else." Rafe knew he might as well get the singer in on their plan. He'd already looked around to make sure they couldn't be overheard. Fortunately, Ray's own security, shifters he paid to take care of him, had them boxed in from eager fans. Even rich socialites weren't immune to Ray's fame and sex appeal. His own wife played Caine's CDs enough to make him crazy. He put himself between Lacy and the singer. Yeah, he was stupid jealous.

"Oh, yeah? What is it?" Caine moved closer.

"I'm in a jam, Ray. You know I've got demon blood. It's complicated but I'm here for the Pomeroy brothers. The Devil sent me. So I can send them down to Hell." Rafe saw the singer's eyes widen. Blurting it out like that made him sound crazy. If he wasn't desperate, he never would have said a word about it to someone he hadn't seen in a while.

"That's quite a story. The Devil and Hell. I want to hear more but this isn't the place." Ray signaled his men. "I've got a dressing room backstage. Come with me. Anyone who wants to. Though maybe some of you should stay out here and figure out where the Pomeroys are hiding. I expected one or both to greet me, but, so far, I haven't seen either one. Which is strange, come to think of it. They were eager enough to hire me. Acted like they were big fans."

"Miguel and I will come with you." Rafe glanced around the group. "Is that all right with everyone else? You want to circulate and see if you can spot our targets?" He'd shown them pictures of the men from their website before they'd left the rooms. It had been a short walk to this ballroom which was part of their hotel.

"Yes, we will look. I wonder if that Bonnell might be lurking by the silent auction tables. There are some very valuable things there." Florence turned that direction. "You did say he is obsessed with money."

"Saving it, not spending it, darling." Her husband, Richard Mainwaring, put his arm around her.

"Haven't you had your fill of shopping tonight? You look beautiful and very expensive."

"Thank you, *amante*." Flo smiled as she dragged him away. "That is exactly the look I was going for. You watch for the Pomeroy, I watch for the bargain."

Glory tugged on Jerry's arm. "I think we should head for the bar. I looked up the city leaders and the mayor of Houston is there. I'd think Barry would stick near him. He had pictures with powerful men on that website. And usually with a drink in his hand."

"Good plans. Thanks." Rafe followed Miguel and Ray to the stage area and then around the back of it. "Ray, you're booked into my bar after this, aren't you?"

"Yes, that's why taking this gig made sense. And it *is* a good cause." He nodded, posting his guards at the door when they got to his dressing room. "Now fill me in on what's happening here. I'll help if I can."

Rafe quickly told him about his deal with the Devil and what he'd managed to accomplish so far.

"This is unreal. That bastard wants your little girl?" Ray opened a bottle of synthetic blood and offered Miguel some of the premium he seemed to keep by the case. The vampire didn't hesitate to take it. "No wonder you have quite a crew helping you. I'm in. Whatever you need."

"Thanks, man." Rafe touched his heart. It was more than a gesture. He didn't dare give in to the emotion that could send him to his knees if he let it. He cleared his throat. "Yeah, I've been lucky. My friends have really stepped up. It's all about saving my child." Rafe couldn't meet Ray's sympathetic gaze, so he helped himself to a sandwich from food set out on a table against one wall. The spread had been provided by the hotel and Ray's shifters probably enjoyed it. He'd learned to fuel up when he had a chance. He hoped Lacy did the same in the ballroom.

Ray stepped in front of him. "It's about more than that, Rafe. I've known you a while." He glanced at Miguel. "Hell, since you were forced to guard Glory shifted into a dog body 24/7. I don't know how you stood it. That was a shit show." He rested a hand on Rafe's shoulder. "You've spent your life protecting others, haven't you? No matter what it cost you personally."

"He's right about that, *amigo*. Glory told me your story." Miguel stood on his other side. "You're always doing it. Protecting people. Yeah, you were paid, but you did more than a job. You took it to heart." Miguel nodded. "Why wouldn't we aid you when you needed us?"

Rafe was speechless. "I…"

"Say no more." Ray must have realized Rafe was about to lose it. "Let's talk strategy. When I'm performing might be a good time to hustle the Pomeroys out of here. The band is loud and I'll make sure to arrange a distraction if you need one." He finished his drink then tossed the bottle into a bin marked for recycling. "I can even call the Pomeroys up to the front if you need me to. For a special thank you."

"That would be great. If we can't get them out by then, I'll signal you to do just that." Rafe tossed his sandwich into the trash. Strategy. Yeah, planning was much better than talking about stuff that made his eyes burn and his throat close. Emotions. Macho men didn't share stuff like that. He could almost hear Lucifer laughing at him for such feelings.

"I'd better get out there. Unless we missed it, I'm sure there will be some sort of ceremony. Hype for the silent auction maybe. The mayor will speak and I would expect at least Barry Pomeroy to say a few words." Rafe moved to the door. "Thanks, both of you. I mean it."

"Hey, good luck. Where do you go from here? After you get these two?" Ray picked up some sheet music.

"If we get these guys tonight, then it's back to Austin for my final grab." Rafe paused with his hand on the doorknob. "I need to do more research. Knowing Lucifer, this last one will be the worst. I have a deadline, Ray. If I don't make it…" Rafe ran a hand over his eyes. "That can't happen. I have to get this done in time. Daniela's future depends on it."

Miguel threw his own empty bottle away. "You will make it, Rafael. Stay strong." He pushed Rafe out of the way, jerked open the door and stepped out.

Ray moved next to Rafe. "That is one scary dude. Power out the yin-yang."

"Yep. That power has come in handy. He's been a big help." Rafe shook his hand. "Break a leg tonight. Watch for me in the audience. If I give you a sign, call up those bastards and then send them right to me next to the closest exit after that. They are the type of sinners that need to burn in hell." He shared with Ray what the Pomeroys had been doing to make their money, including what Abe had just told him.

"Shit. You're doing a public service, man. I see now why your friends have rallied around you." Ray's face was grim. "It will be my pleasure to help make those assholes pay." They slapped hands, then Rafe stepped into the ballroom.

Finally, he saw one of the Pomeroy brothers. Barry Pomeroy himself, with his deceptively benign face and his Santa beard perfectly groomed, was peering down the low-cut dress of the most beautiful woman in the room.

Rafe felt the heat of rage flash through him as he forced himself to stay where he was. If he didn't calm the fuck down, he'd kill the man with his bare hands. Right there in front of a crowd of well-heeled party-goers. When Barry actually moved closer to the woman, Rafe couldn't stay still another moment. He stepped forward.

"Why there he is now. Joe, darling, you have to meet Barry Pomeroy." Lacy's smile didn't reach her eyes as she held out her hand. "He's one of the forces behind this wonderful event." Her freshly manicured nails landed on Rafe's chest as if to warn him that they had to be careful not to scare Barry into hiding before they found his brother.

"This is your husband, little lady?" Barry held out his hand as if he expected Rafe to shake it.

"Now that's a shame. I was hoping to find you available." He winked and laughed, his belly shaking in his expensive custom-tailored tuxedo.

Rafe stared at the outstretched hand as if it were one of those poisonous snakes he'd left behind in the Louisiana swamp.

Lacy giggled and gave Rafe a warning look, before she grabbed Barry's hand. "Who said I wasn't? Someone had better dance with me right now or I might scream this place down."

"Can't have that now, can we, honey?" Barry was licking his fleshy lips as he led her onto the dance floor, throwing a look of triumph over his shoulder at Rafe. "You snooze, you lose, fella." He pulled her close and started what he must have thought was a cha-cha. "Let's show them how it's done."

Lacy threw back her red hair and did a twirl right out of his arms. "Oh, I don't know about that!" She danced around him then fanned her cheeks with her fingers. "Ooo. Maybe I had too much champagne."

Barry made a grab for her waist but missed. "Is there such as thing as too much of a good thing?"

Rafe started toward them, about to lose his shit. He stopped when a heavy hand landed on his shoulder.

"She's got him handled, *amigo*." Miguel had a drink in his hand.

"You think?" Rafe could smell the tequila. He had no idea how this vampire could drink alcohol when none of the other vamps he knew could. Didn't matter. "I want to twist his head off his neck and use it like a bowling ball."

Miguel laughed. "I like the image. But this is good. We know where he is. Now we need to find the other brother. Keep watching this one and your woman. I will search for Bonnell. Be patient. You trust her, no?"

"Of course. She is doing this to save our daughter." Rafe could barely speak. Barry had managed to brush Lacy's butt with one of his roving hands. Damn, she looked incredible in a green silk dress that hugged her curves and barely covered her breasts. When it looked like one of those breasts was about to escape the silk as she shimmied to the Latin music, Barry stumbled and almost landed on his butt in the middle of the dance floor.

"She is a good dancer." Miguel laughed again when Rafe growled. "Relax. She is playing him. I can see in her eyes how much she hates him. Let this go. It gives her a chance to use her power. Why not allow her to do what she can to help?"

Rafe made his hands unclench one finger at a time. He nodded and Miguel melted into the crowd. He sometimes forgot how important it was to let his strong wife do her part in this mission. But he didn't want her out of his sight. Barry Pomeroy was a man without a conscience. Rafe didn't doubt that if Barry had a chance to get a drunk woman alone, he'd take advantage of her, by force if necessary.

When the music changed from fast to slow, Barry reached for Lacy, eager to pull her close.

But Rafe's wife was having none of it. She staggered toward the bar, making sure Barry was right behind her with a wiggle of her hips. Rafe followed at a distance.

Let Pomeroy think he was a submissive husband with a wife who was eager to cheat on him. Rafe knew better. If Barry put one slimy hand on Lacy, Rafe wasn't sure he would wait for Gordon to escort the man to Hell. He was simmering with the urge to do the killing himself. The sooner, the better.

CHAPTER FIFTEEN

"I'VE FOUND BONNELL." Jeremy Blade approached Rafe where he stood watching Lacy. She stood too damned close to Barry Pomeroy at the bar.

"Bonnell?" That was enough to snap Rafe out of his hate-filled fog. "Where is he?"

"Out in the lobby, on his phone." Jerry followed Rafe's gaze. "I see Lacy's got Barry occupied. You want me to stay here and keep an eye on them while you go check out Bonnell? I heard him ranting to someone about an electrical problem at their call center."

Rafe nodded. "That means Abe got the job done. Thanks. Just make sure Barry doesn't try to get my wife alone somewhere or slip something into her drink. I don't trust the son of a bitch."

"Don't blame you." Jerry frowned when Glory joined Lacy. "Now my wife is getting within reach of the creep. Good thing you can't read his mind. He's started to think threesome."

Rafe heard himself growl again. People nearby looked around, trying to figure out how a wild animal got into the elegant ballroom. Little did they know, he was inches away from shifting and giving them a show they'd never forget. He pulled out his phone, like the growling lion was his ringtone. One more from the depths of his hatred and he pretended to shut it off. He shook his head in apology as he started to make his way around the crowded room by way of the bar. He'd show Barry—

Jerry grabbed his arm. "Get hold of yourself, man. I'll go over there. He won't have a chance to touch either one of our ladies." Jerry's grin showed a hint of fang that no one else would even notice. "I doubt the Devil will care if Barry comes a few quarts low. What do you think?"

"Have at it, Blade. You want to drag him out of here and drain him? Be my guest." Rafe felt better. "If I get lucky with Bonnell, I'll meet you backstage."

"Shit. I would, but the mayor of Houston just walked up to him and warned him that they were going on stage in a few minutes to pump up bids for the silent auction." Jerry nudged Rafe with his shoulder. "Find Miguel. He can help you with Bonnell. I'll stay close to this asshole. As soon as he's through with the mayor, he's all mine."

Rafe nodded and strode toward the entrance to the ballroom. He kept his eye out for Miguel. The vampire's ability to freeze mortals in place was a real asset. This wasn't the first time he'd thought how lucky he was that his friends had decided to come to his aid. No sign of Miguel, but he spotted Richard Mainwaring standing next to the silent auction tables. His wife, a wild look in her eyes, was hip to hip with a woman

in purple satin hovering over an expensive purse.
Rafe gestured. Soon Richard and a protesting Flo
were by his side near the ballroom doors.

"I swear that *strega* in the Versace ballgown is
going to beat me to the Louis bag." Flo frowned
back at the table.

"Darling, you have a dozen Louis bags in your
closet already." Richard kept a grip on her tiny
waist. "Remember why we are here."

"Of course. So sorry, Rafael." Flo pinched
Richard's arm hard enough for him to flinch.
"You can let me go now, *darling*. I like to win and
I got carried away. But there is no reason to drag
me across the room like you are a Machiavelli
enforcer."

"Sorry, love." Richard managed a grin. "It was
either drag you or pour champagne on your head
to cool you off. You were in the zone."

Flo flushed. "You're right. If you had ruined
this beautiful dress... Well, I could have made
you regret it. *Capiscime*?" She turned to Rafe.
"You need us? What is happening? I am sorry, I
really am. Did you find one of the *peccatori*?"

"Sinners? Jerry said he found Bonnell in the
lobby. On the phone. Abe managed to shut down
the call center electricity. Bonnell is furious and is
trying to get it fixed." Rafe looked out and didn't
see the man they were after. "Let's split up and see
if we can find him. There are too many people
out here. He's bound to have looked for a quiet
corner to make his calls. He's desperate to get
the lights back on." Rafe smiled. "Not happening.
Abe has a way with high voltage."

"We're on it. I will go to the restrooms." Flo held up a tiny clutch bag. "I can accidentally go into the men's room. There is always a line in the ladies' room and I must check my lipstick."

The men divided the rest of the lobby. They all agreed to text each other if they found Bonnell.

Rafe had pushed into the kitchen area when his phone buzzed. Flo had cornered Bonnell outside the restrooms. Rafe headed that way and was just in time to see her having some fun with the man.

"I heard you are one of the two Pomeroys who organized this gala, no?" She leaned in, flashing enough cleavage to make Bonnell fumble his phone.

"Why, yes. We're raising funds to build several apartment buildings on a site near where the tent city used to be. Uh, affordable housing." Bonnell couldn't take his eyes off the enormous diamond drop that dangled on a chain between Flo's breasts. He looked like he'd found a treasure trove. Flo's form-fitting gown in her favorite red plunged low in front and back.

"It is terrible to be homeless. Can you imagine? No, mmm, privacy." Flo ran a fingertip down Bonnell's lapel. He swallowed then jumped when his phone rang.

"Oh!" He frowned down at it. "Sorry. I'm having a business problem tonight. It's costing me a lot of money."

"Money is important to you, am I right?" Flo stared into his eyes when he nodded. She held out her hand. "You will give me your phone now."

Bonnell had a glazed look in his eyes that

Rafe recognized. The man handed Flo his phone without a word. She answered it.

"Yes, Mr. Pomeroy is right here. He is going to have to close the call center. Permanently." She gripped the phone, obviously getting an earful. "You heard me correctly. I'll let him talk to you in a minute." Flo grinned when Richard walked up and put his arm around her. "Here is what you will do. Can you open the safe? Good. He wants you to take out the cash on hand." She sighed. "Yes, all of it. Then you are to pay the people working there. Double what you owe them. This is like, what you call, severance pay." She listened with a frown. "Quit arguing with me. That's what I said. Double. Don't worry, I will put him on the phone in a minute to confirm this. If you don't have enough cash, give them gift cards to make up the difference. I know you have them there."

She bared her teeth. "*Mi scusi*! What kind of language is that when speaking to a lady, *signore*. Now do what I say. Here is Bonnell. He will tell you this is his order. He is feeling very charitable tonight. The gala is a huge success."

She handed the phone to Bonnell and told him what to say. He repeated her words carefully. Apparently, the man on the other end of the call was struck dumb. When Bonnell gave the phone back to Flo, she smiled and patted his cheek.

She spoke into the phone which she put on speaker for Rafe and Richard's benefit. "Did you hear Bonnell's orders?"

"Yes, ma'am. I know Bonnie's voice. It was him

all right. It's just, um, strange. He's not usually so, um, generous."

"I told you. We are at his gala. They are raising so much money, he is feeling like he can afford to do this. He has an image problem, you see. Someone called him stingy. That ex-wife of his is telling everyone bad stories about him."

"I believe it. She told the tabloids he made her buy cheap toilet paper, wore socks and underwear with holes in it. She's a bitter woman."

"Then you understand Bonnie wants to prove she is a liar. You must quit arguing with me and get busy. Or do I have to put Bonnie back on the phone?" Her voice rose. "Bonnie, this man is not doing what you want him to do."

"No, ma'am. Don't make him mad. I'm doing it. Cash, then cards. Everyone is out in the parking lot because it's dark in here. No lights and the AC isn't working. I told them to stay out there cause it's hot as hell in here, beggin' yer pardon. I kept thinkin' the lights would be back on any minute. Checked the breaker myself but it's strange. It's like the box is plumb melted down. A real mess. Never seen anythin' like it." There was the sound of a crash.

"What is happening there?" Flo looked around. Luckily, the mayor was speaking inside and the lobby was deserted.

"I'm trying to find the payroll list. Got to get this right. Can't just hand out cash willy nilly. Bonnie always says to be careful down to the last dime."

"I'm sure he does." Flo rolled her eyes. "Uh-oh,

Bonnie's face is getting red. I hope you don't get fired for wasting his time. This is an important night for him. The mayor is so happy with the Pomeroy brothers. He may be giving them an award." Flo winked at Rafe and Richard.

When a woman came out of the restroom, Flo covered the phone and waved her toward the ballroom. "Listen to the mayor, getting more donations! Isn't it exciting? Have you pledged? Such a worthy cause, no?" The woman clutched her tiny purse and hurried away.

Flo spoke into the phone. "Are you giving away money yet?"

The man on the phone sounded upset. "I'm trying, lady. I am. But I'm working with a flashlight here. It will take a while." His voice was shaking. "Who are you?"

"I am Bonnell's new lady. We are going away together and you should not expect us to be back any time soon." Flo bit her lip to keep from laughing.

"What?"

"His brother is joining us. The Pomeroys have had a few disturbing phone calls lately. From the FBI." She gave a big sigh when the man on the phone exclaimed in disbelief.

"What did you say your name was, sir?"

"George, lady. The FBI? This sounds serious. I need to talk to Bonnie. He wouldn't—"

"Listen closely, George. Take care of this for Bonnie and do it fast. Then, if I were you, I would take a little trip myself. Know what I mean? The FBI has been such a pain in Bonnie's backside.

It started with calls. But I wouldn't be surprised if they come knocking on the door next. That's why the jet is fueled and ready to go. We are going to disappear."

"Disappear? And leave me with the FBI? Oh, my God." George choked.

"It's possible. So you should make those workers happy if you don't want them testifying against you." Flo held the phone away from her ear.

"Testifying?" George screeched, clearly terrified. "I'll pay everyone then I'm out of here. But I'm the only one here who treats these people decent. They should know it too."

"Good for you. Now take whatever is left for yourself after they are paid then pack your bags. Do you speak Spanish, George? I hear Ecuador doesn't extradite. Or try Iceland if you don't mind the cold. *Buona fortuna*." With that she ended the call. She dropped the phone on the floor, gestured for Richard to stomp it with his black dress shoe before he tossed it in the trash can behind her.

"Magnificent, my dear." Richard kissed her lips. "Where do you want this man to go, Rafe? I can put him anywhere you want and we can wait there for his brother."

Rafe grabbed Flo and gave her a hug. "You *were* magnificent. I'm glad those workers will be taken care of. We should figure out how to transfer the Pomeroy millions to worthy charities. Before we let him go, we need to get some information about his off-shore accounts. You know how to move that kind of money around, don't you, Richard?"

"Yes, I do. While we're waiting for Barry, I'll get account information and passwords from Bonnie here and put them in my phone." Richard smiled. "Darling, go back and bid again on that Louis. You just earned it. We'll figure out where we want to stash Bonnell and then Rafe can concentrate on getting his brother."

"Another Louis?" Flo's eyes were bright. "Why not? You're right, I did earn it. I read this man's mind. All he thinks about is either getting more money or ripping my dress off my body. He doesn't have a kind thought in his head." She sniffed. "When I read your mind, Ricardo, I see you believe I am clever and beautiful. You, too, Rafael. You see a woman is more than a sex object." She pointed at Bonnell, who still stood unmoving. "This man has no heart, no love for anything but himself. Pah! Go to Hell, Bonnie, and see what you get there."

"I'm sure the Devil has big plans for him." Rafe pictured Bonnell on his knees endlessly pinching pennies until his fingers bled. "Now where can we put him? As soon as the mayor is through talking, I'll meet Jerry and we can go after Barry. Fortunately, no one expects Bonnell to be a public speaker so he won't be missed now. Barry is the one who always takes the spotlight."

"Let me check what's through that exit door." Richard pushed it. "It's the parking garage. There's an elevator. I'll take him to the top level. That should be deserted this time of night. I'm sure this well-heeled crowd used valet parking." He grabbed Bonnie's arm. "Text me if you want

him moved. Otherwise, I'll see you up there."
Mesmerized, Bonnell had no choice but to
walk stiffly along at Richard's side, a zombie in
a custom tux.

Rafe followed Flo into the ballroom. It didn't
take long to find Lacy near the front of the crowd
staring up at the speakers. If Barry was concerned
about his brother's absence, it didn't show. He was
praising the crowd for their generosity and urging
everyone there to open their wallets and hit the
silent auction tables. After wild applause, the band
started up again and some couples hit the dance
floor. Rafe was about to go for Barry when he
saw Miguel greet Pomeroy as he stepped off the
podium. The vampire took the man's elbow and
led him away toward the dressing rooms.

"Thank God for the vampires." Lacy slid her
arm around Rafe's waist. "Bloodthirsty Miguel
is going to take advantage of Barry behind the
bandstand. Can you believe it? He and Jerry were
practically fighting over who got his blood but
Glory wanted to show her husband something
at the auction tables so Miguel won that battle."

"I'm glad one of them has him. Does that mean
we have time for a dance?" Rafe pulled her into
his arms.

"I guess it does." Lacy leaned against Rafe's
chest. "God, I need to get the stench of that
creep out of my nose. Whatever kind of cologne
Barry uses, it will forever remind me of greed and
lechery. That slimy bastard. He was always trying
to put his hands on me."

"I'm sorry. I'd like to put a hurt on him for

that." Rafe pulled her close while moving to the music. It was a slow song, an old favorite from a few years ago. It would be nice if they could stay for Israel Caine's concert after they delivered the Pomeroys to Gordon. If only they had more time. But they didn't. They'd have to leave town on Jerry's jet as soon as the sinners were out of their hands. Then there was the worry about whether Lucifer would honor his deal.

"Try to relax and enjoy this, sweetheart." Lacy reached up and traced the lines he knew were between his brows. "Or is that possible?"

Rafe pulled her closer, breathing in her sweet, familiar scent. "If we ever get free of this curse, I'll relax. This catch has almost been too easy." He saw Barry Pomeroy, looking pale, stagger out from behind the stage. Before he could collapse, Miguel looped an arm across his shoulders and escorted him around the perimeter of the ballroom.

"Take the win and don't look for trouble." Lacy rested her head against his shoulder.

"I'll try. Now let's go." Rafe pulled Lacy over to the auction tables where Flo was adding one more bid for the purse she wanted. A drum roll, a clash of cymbals, then the band leader made an announcement.

"Sorry, ladies, but the bidding on the women's accessories is now closed. To see if you won, check with the cashier. If yours was the final bid, you can pay up and collect your merchandise." The leader grinned. "I hear we broke a new record for fundraising tonight. Between the bidding for the trips and those on the donations from the many boutiques in the Galleria Mall, we've raised over ten million dollars!"

There was wild applause and a few squeals. Flo was waving the bidding sheet next to the purse she'd wanted. "I won!"

"Really?" Miguel stopped next to her. "You were shopping?"

"She can do more than one thing at a time, Miguel." Glory with Jerry joined them at the table. Glory snatched up her own paper. "I found a vintage leather piece that will look great in Jerry's man cave. And it was for a good cause. Am I right, Flo?"

"We are always right, *amica*." Flo tapped Miguel on his shoulder. "I see you got our other Pomeroy. I helped get Bonnie. Now Richard has him waiting for us. My man texted me. They are on the top floor of the parking garage. Very quiet there, he says." She stopped. "I'll pay for my Louis bag and be right there."

The rest of them moved toward the lobby, Barry in tow.

"Where are you going? The entertainment will start in a few minutes." The mayor and his entourage were also waving papers they'd collected at the table. "Barry, you told me you were a big Israel Caine fan."

Glory took the mayor's arm. "Barry loves Israel Caine but he's suddenly not feeling well, sir." She leaned closer. "Too much champagne." She grabbed the mayor's elbow. "Did he tell you he and Bonnell have business taking them out of the country later tonight? Urgent business. Too bad he has to catch a plane when he's under the weather."

"What? No. I thought we were meeting tomorrow to go over the figures from tonight." The mayor looked surprised as Glory led him away into the crowd.

"He'll have to cancel. But here's someone who will be happy to meet with you. She was the chairwoman of the silent auction and loves to dance. I know you want to tell her what a fantastic job she did." Before he could protest, Glory put the two together in the middle of the dance floor and hurried back to the rest of the vampire crew.

Rafe followed Miguel out of the ballroom. He was eager to get the two Pomeroys together and ready for collection in the parking garage. Surely Gordon would be waiting. It seemed like the Devil's minion knew how and where to find him when he was ready to deliver his catches.

He showed Miguel, with the silent, obviously mesmerized, Barry in tow, where to find the restroom area and that same exit door. There was the elevator and they pushed Barry inside.

"Wait for me." Flo hurried to catch up, her high heels clicking on the rough concrete. She carried her prized bag.

"I'm coming too." Glory was right behind her. "Just had to tie up a few loose ends." Jerry followed her, carrying a beautiful leather saddle.

"Can you believe she bought this for me? It's

like one I had decades ago." Jerry stroked the leather.

"We're going to get back into riding. You bought a ranch recently, didn't you? Now we need horses." Glory slipped into the elevator, which was getting crowded.

Rafe hit the button for the top floor. He shook his head. He couldn't complain that his friends had mixed pleasure with business for the Devil. At least they'd made it possible for their donations to go to a good cause and not into the Pomeroys' offshore accounts.

Barry was like a statue, though he was leaning to the right, so pale he could be a ghost.

"Pah, how could you drink from him, Miguel?" Flo shook her finger in the vampire's face. "I had Bonnie in my power but I was not tempted. He is a nasty man, caring only for money and using women. His blood would taste like *pisciare*."

"Get over it, Florence. Piss is piss. Blood is blood. Though I admit some blood is better than others." Miguel grinned at her, his gaze roving over her breasts. "Yours would be ancient and taste very sweet if you're ever feeling generous, *bella donna*."

"How would you like a taste of my fist in your fangs." Glory punched him in his stomach. "That is my best friend you are disrespecting. I don't care if you are my half-brother. Behave."

"It was a compliment." Miguel glared at her.

"It was a pass and she's married." Glory looked like she was about to take another swing.

"He's your half-brother?" Lacy exclaimed.

The air in the elevator suddenly got very warm and the lights blinked then went out.

Rafe hid a smile. He loved it when Glory got fiery. "Calm down, both of you. I can't deal with you two having a pissing contest right now." The lights flickered back on but Miguel looked made of stone as he stared at Glory. His sister, for God's sake.

"I just found out. Our father is Mars. My mother is Hebe. God only knows who *his* mother was." Glory patted Flo's shoulder. "I'm sorry he is such an oaf. He's been worshipped by too many. It's made his head too big for his own good."

"I ignore him." Flo sniffed. "If Ricardo had heard that? Smack! Miguel would be looking for his fangs in his stomach."

"Please. Enough, you guys. This is serious," Rafe said as the elevator lurched to a stop. "If all goes well, Gordon, Lucifer's minion, will be arriving to take our two to Hell. That's how it's been working. Richard has Bonnell. Miguel will have to take the freeze off Barry when Gordon shows. Both Pomeroys should be fully aware of their fate once it's time for them to go. I think Lucifer likes watching their fear when they realize what's up."

"You mean when what's going down." Jerry stepped out of the elevator first, looking for danger like he always did. He carefully set his saddle aside and pulled a knife. "I don't see Richard or Bonnell."

"Everyone out. Keep looking." Rafe didn't expect any surprises, but there was always a first time. They were at the roof level and Rafe could see the lights of the surrounding buildings. There were hotels and office buildings. High rises. The parking garage was quiet except for sounds from the street below. He could smell car exhaust from busy Westheimer Street that ran in front of the hotel. Even this late there was traffic. The night air was still warm from the heat of the day but he felt a cooling breeze. There were very few cars parked here. They probably belonged to hotel employees on the night shift.

Suddenly he heard a noise from one of the cars. Rafe stopped. "Is somebody there?"

Another noise, whispers, then the back door in a black Mercedes popped open. A teenaged boy jumped out, swiping at his rumpled hair as he pulled on his valet jacket.

"Hey, man, what's going on? This level is closed."

A giggling girl, her skirt barely covering her hips, crawled out of the car. "Kev, is your break over? What are these old people doing here? You said we'd have alone time." She jerked up her sagging tube top.

Glory and Flo exchanged a look.

"Old people?" Flo stomped over to the car. She said a few choice words in Italian.

The boy helped his date out of the car. "I don't know what you said, lady, but you don't belong here either. You and your fancy friends. I bet you're supposed to be at the gala." He pointed at the group in front of the elevator. "Come on, Megan." He pulled the girl to the elevator. "I'm reporting you guys to my manager."

"How are you going to explain being up here?" Rafe punched the down button. The elevator doors opened.

"Uh." The boy looked confused.

"Just go. We're at an impasse." Rafe stood aside as the two got into the elevator.

Megan eased past Lacy. "Love your dress," she whispered. "Come on, Kev. You can't say a thing or they'll fire you." The doors closed.

Rafe felt Barry come to life beside him. Miguel must have decided the time was right.

"What's going on? Where am I? Who are you people?" Barry sank to the floor. "I don't feel right. Shit." He looked up and seemed to realize he was facing three beautiful women. "Oh." He struggled to his feet and stood there swaying. "My place or yours?"

"Scum to the end." Flo kicked his shin, sending him staggering.

Gordon suddenly appeared, smiling. "My, but we're all fancy tonight. Good evening, beautiful ladies."

Flo, Glory and Lacy stood together. Rafe stepped in front of them. His wife hissed and rested a claw on his back.

"We can handle ourselves." Lacy pushed until he felt a prick through his new tux jacket. She might even have drawn blood.

"I'm sure you can handle plenty but this is my deal. You don't want any part of this. Trust me on that." Rafe stared at Gordon. "Here's Barry Pomeroy, Gordon."

"Bring me the other one." Gordon's voice

echoed off the hard surfaces. They all turned as footsteps came from behind the building that housed the stairs.

"Here he is. I had to wait until those kids were gone." Richard looked very solemn. He glanced at Bonnell then shoved him. The man ran to his brother.

"Barry, what's happening?" Bonnell looked terrified.

"I don't know, Bonnie." Barry threw his arms around his brother. "I feel weird. Maybe I had too much to drink."

"Again? Fool. This is an important night for us. It's your job to get the donations rolling in." Bonnell flung off his brother's arms and stepped away. "We got trouble at the call center. Big trouble."

"I can't worry about that now. We need to get back downstairs. The mayor will be looking for me." Barry blinked. "Who *are* these people?"

"You don't know them? We need to think. We're outnumbered." Bonnell waved his hand. "But three of them are women. No problem there."

"Pig." Flo spat on the floor.

Gordon laughed and rubbed his hand down the front of his pants. "Oh, a feisty one. I'd have loved to have had a piece of her back in the day. Though the blonde is my type too. And redheads are fun. You men have excellent taste."

Rafe wanted to wipe the floor with this creep. A serial killer. He was glad Gordon spent most of his time in Hell, suffering, he hoped. Jerry and

Richard both looked ready to pounce on him and tear him apart. He held them back with a look. But he could see it wasn't easy for either of them to restrain themselves. Even Miguel was staring, fangs down, ready to start something if Rafe gave the signal.

"Back off, Gordon. You're here for the sinners." Rafe pushed the twins toward Gordon. "Take the Pomeroys and let's get this over with."

"Don't rush me. I don't get out that often." Gordon laughed when the twins made a dash for the elevator. "Come on, vampires, show me how you do it. Freeze them in place."

"We're not trick ponies." Richard stood in front of the elevator buttons. "Take them now. Lucifer is waiting, isn't he? I doubt you want to make him mad."

"You're a holy one, aren't you?" Gordon sneered. "Former priest. I can't tell you how much I despise your type."

"Yes, he is. A good man. *My* good man." Flo latched onto Richard's arm and pulled him toward Rafe. "Go, we hate the sight of you."

'She's right." Glory stomped over to stand with her. "Do your business and leave, you Devil's pimp. We're sick of jumping through Lucifer's hoops."

"You don't have to be here. This is Rafe's problem." Gordon grinned. "But you are such loyal friends, aren't you?"

"Yes, we are. So fuck off." Jerry moved in, his knife ready. "Maybe you want a little souvenir to take with you. Rafe told me you liked to chop off body parts. I can rid you of an arm or an ear. They'd look good on my mantle."

"You're a mean son of a bitch," Gordon mumbled as he shook his head and approached the Pomeroys who were unmoving after all. Someone had frozen them.

"Come on, boys. You've racked up an impressive list of sins. Mass murder is the worst. Remember the fire you set that killed those people in your apartment buildings? That's enough to get you to Hell right there. Then there's greed and graft and all those other minor little things that make Lucifer feel the sweet urge to punish." Gordon waved his hand and the elevator doors opened.

The shaft loomed but there was no elevator car inside. Barry and Bonnell were able to move again, looking around with wild eyes. When they saw that empty shaft, they jumped back. Barry crawled away from the edge, his face pale. Bonnell was clearly thinking hard, trying to figure out how to escape.

"Is this some kind of joke? Not funny." Barry pulled out a wad of bills. "What will it take to make this go away?" He grunted when his brother made him put his money back in his pocket.

"Help us, people. Are you just going to stand there and watch?" Bonnell cried. "This guy is creeping me out."

Flo shook her head, gestured, then turned her back on him. As one, the rest of the vampires did the same.

"Wait! This isn't right. That fire was an accident. Those victims? No big loss." Bonnell stared at

Rafe and tried to step closer to him but his feet seemed stuck to the concrete. "Come on, listen to me. I don't know who this guy is, but I'm telling you, the fire was nothing. The buildings should have been condemned long ago and needed to come down. We did those people a favor. They had pathetic lives and were living in a slum." He reached out with a shaking hand, finally making eye contact with Gordon when Rafe and Lacy turned their backs on him as well.

Bonnell whined. "We can pay. A hundred bucks to let us walk away."

"Cheap till the end." Gordon sneered then, with a gesture, sent the men tumbling back into the elevator shaft. They screamed all the way down until there was a sudden silence. With a final salute, Gordon disappeared.

The friends looked at each other. Lacy leaped into Rafe's arms, Glory pressed her face against Jerry's chest and Flo held onto Richard, muttering in Italian while she covered her eyes. Miguel settled for violently punching the elevator button until the empty car came rumbling up to them. There was no sign of the brothers.

"That's done." Jerry patted Glory's back then picked up his saddle. "Seems like we've got time to fly to Austin tonight. Only one more sinner to go." He stepped into the elevator. "You all coming?"

No one had anything to say. The rest of the group crowded in. Rafe was the last to enter, hitting the button for the lobby. When the doors opened, they could hear Israel Caine singing in the ballroom. They all stopped to listen to one of his famous love songs. It was soothing. Or at least Rafe thought so, since the Pomeroys' screams were still echoing inside his head. He had to remember that he was doing a good thing. Ridding the world of evil.

Jerry was right. One more to go. They'd head upstairs, pack and the jet would take them on the thirty-minute flight home. Home. If only Daniela would be waiting for them there. He was going to make it happen. Soon.

Glory and Miguel were whispering together, obviously arguing. Another elevator ride got them to the suite where they packed. It was a silent group that met in the living room. Miguel hit the mini-bar for one more tequila then stood in front of the door, his solemn face daring anyone to make a move to leave.

"I have a couple of things to say."

CHAPTER SIXTEEN

RAFE NODDED. EVERYONE else waited. What choice did they have? No one was willing to go through the most powerful entity in the room. Abe appeared from the balcony and moved closer.

"We're all here, my son. What do you have to say?" Abe folded his hands in front of his stomach. It was a little rounder than it had been when they'd first met him. Rafe had noticed the dessert selection he'd ordered had been well sampled. He should remember that Abe loved chocolate and lemon but seemed to avoid anything with peanuts. Did spirits have allergies?

Miguel cleared his throat. His gaze traveled around the room until he must have decided he had everyone's full attention.

"Two things. This hotel bill is on me. I've been hitting the mini-bar hard. I will pay. The drinking has made me have a short fuse. I will stop it." He glanced at Flo. "I'm sorry if I offended you, Mrs. Mainwaring."

"I take no man's name. Call me Florence." She sniffed. "Clearly you have a problem, Miguel. Too much power, not much control. I can relate. I

have had my own bad years when I was a little…
out of control." She glanced at her husband. "We
forget it."

"Thank you." Miguel shifted his gaze to Glory.
"We have the same father, Gloriana. Please do
not disrespect my mother. I am still searching for
the truth about her. It does not help my efforts at
self-control when you goad me."

"I admit, it was a low blow." Glory nodded.
"But Flo is my best friend. Please don't disrespect
her again."

"I will do my best." His mouth was firm, no
promise there.

Richard stepped forward. "What did I miss?
Florence? Gloriana?"

"We are moving on, Ricardo. We must work as
a team, am I right?" Flo gripped Richard's hand,
holding him by her side.

"She's right, Richard. I am sorry if I made her
uncomfortable. I called her beautiful. It is hard not
to notice." Miguel made the mistake of smiling.

Richard flew at him, his fangs down, his hands
around Miguel's neck before any of them could
move. Obviously, he'd read something in the
vampire's mind he didn't like. "Notice, but if you
touch a single hair on her beautiful head, you are
a dead man."

Miguel was clearly working to keep from
using his power and throwing the man across
the room. Instead, he gently put his hands over
Richard's and removed them from his throat.
Even leashed, his power obviously made Richard
no match for him. "Understood. She is yours. I

will find my own woman. I should do it soon. My dissatisfaction with my current situation has made me careless around people I would like to call friends."

"All right, that's enough." Rafe knew better than to get between them but someone had to be the voice of reason here.

"Easy for you to say, you weren't reading his mind." Richard's fangs were still down but he did step back.

Rafe shook his head. "I get it. He's said he'll back off. Now we need to get moving." Danger simmered in the air like a hot wind from a desert, or maybe from a jungle full of predators. Flo reached for him and jerked Richard back to her side, hissing that if she needed defending, she'd damn well do it herself.

Rafe knew better than to smile. "Anything else to say, Miguel?"

"Just that I have spoken with Father Abraham. I am old enough to recognize a wise man when I meet one. He has told me to work with this team. That I need you all. He says it is the only way I will ever find who and what I'm looking for." He shot Abraham a hard look. "Cryptic son of a bitch, but for some reason, I trust him. So you are stuck with me. I want to help you and I hope, when the time comes, you will help me."

"Well said, my son." Abraham stepped forward. "I'm sorry if my message seems a little confusing. Time will make everything clearer." He glanced at the ceiling. "At least I hope it will. The jet is waiting and so is Austin. I will meet you in the city, I have business upstairs."

Rafe sighed. "Fine. Miguel, call downstairs and give them your card number." He wasn't about to turn down a generous offer. "I assume you'll shift and fly from here. We'll meet you at the airport." He shook his hand. "I'm glad to have you on the team. You have proved to be a valuable member."

"Thanks." Miguel nodded then stepped to the house phone. The rest of them picked up their bags. Jerry cradled his new saddle and duffle. Glory carried her new ballgown, a daring black number that had made the most of her curvy figure.

Rafe touched Miguel's shoulder and gestured toward the vampire's own duffle and the garment bag containing his new tuxedo, indicating he and Lacy would take them to the airport. They were all leaving with a lot more than they'd arrived with. Maybe he should have called down for a bellman but it was four in the morning, a strange and inconvenient time to be checking out. He managed to get his and Lacy's stuff together and the suite emptied.

It was a tense ride down the elevator with Flo on one side and Richard on the other. Finally, Flo's husband threw down the luggage he carried and punched the stop button. The elevator started buzzing immediately.

"Damn it, Florence, I can't let this go."

Glory shoved Flo toward Richard. "Maybe you two need privacy for this." She hit the button for the lobby and the buzzing stopped. "Or at least wait till we get to the car."

Flo had gone pale. "Let him speak."

Rafe blocked her move to stop the elevator again. "Parking garage. You want to wake the whole hotel?" He wasn't a mind reader, but he knew pissed when he saw it. Richard Mainwaring had been a priest before he'd been turned vampire centuries ago. It had also been long before he'd met and fallen for the volatile Florence da Vinci. Usually calm and collected, now he was obviously about to lose it. "Ten minutes. Tops. You can hold it till then."

Flo and Richard glared at each other but nodded. It was a tense and silent group that made it to their rental car. Luggage with their new finery was carefully loaded into the trunk then, one look at the crowded car, and Jerry offered to go ahead and shift to the airport. Glory wasn't about to miss this. Rafe was the designated driver and had to turn in the rental. Lacy sagged against him, exhausted, but didn't want to miss the coming show either.

"Speak, Ricardo. What is your problem?" Flo squared her shoulders. She put up a hand. "Oh, I know. You don't like for me to say I can defend myself. Is that it?"

"Of course, it is!" He ignored that hand, her stop sign, and moved closer to her. "Don't you know that your fire only whets a man's appetite? No wonder Cisneros could hardly contain his desire for you." He turned to Rafe. "Am I wrong?"

Rafe glanced at Lacy. "I have to admit my own

woman's ferocity turns me on. Nothing hotter than a wildcat."

Glory snorted. "Men."

Flo flushed. "*I* have to admit, Ricardo, that when you attacked Miguel, you looked very *formidabile*. I liked it."

"What was that remark about taking no man's name?" Richard pulled her into his arms. "You sure as hell don't mind my last name on your credit cards." He kissed her until Rafe cleared his throat.

"Time to go if this fight is over."

Flo shoved Richard away. "It will be over after I have a new bracelet." She turned to Glory. "Did you see the emeralds on the auction table?"

Rafe ushered them into the car, ladies in the back seat, Richard in front with him. Yes, Florence always made her men pay for aggravating her. Glory had told him about Flo's early years in desperate poverty. It made the vampire seem grasping, but he knew better. There was a deep well of pain behind her need for proof that she was worth emeralds to the man in her life.

When they got to the airport, the jet was ready and Jerry's pilot was alert, clearly used to night flights. They all piled in and Rafe opened his laptop. Jerry sat beside him.

"Who are we going after this time? You've been quiet so far. This must be the worst." Jerry read over Rafe's shoulder as a website came up. "You've got to be fucking kidding me. That's our last sinner?"

"Buckle up, guys. The pilot is ready for takeoff."

Glory stopped in the aisle. The women had announced they were going to sit together in the back and gossip about the clothes they'd seen at the gala.

"Take a look, baby. We know this guy. He's Rafe's final target." Jerry aimed the laptop at his wife.

"No way." She rested her hand on Rafe's shoulder. "It's got to be a mistake. He's a nice man. His wife shops at Vintage Vamps. They have kids, dogs. They're an All-American family. Picture perfect." Tears filled her eyes. "Rafe, no!"

"This is a case of what you see may not be what you get. Mr. Wonderful could have a dark side. I'm starting my due diligence, but this guy is next on Lucifer's list." Rafe heard the jet engines rev. "You'd better sit down, Blondie. I'm sorry, but I'm charged with getting this guy and I only have two days to do it."

"I don't read the minds of the mortals who come into my shop on general principle. TMI, if you know what I mean." She looked around and got nods from the other vampires nearby. "But, on the surface, the Finks are good people. I'm telling you, Rafe, this is wrong, just wrong." Glory staggered down the aisle.

She shared her news and he heard exclamations coming from the back of the plane. Lacy, as manager of Glory's store, also knew the family. Across from him, he felt Miguel's stare. Richard sat behind Miguel, keeping his eye on the powerful vampire while he worked on his own computer. He was moving the Pomeroy money to worthy charities. Rafe had given him Kelly's phone number and he was arranging to send her a generous severance package.

It would be a long time, if ever, before those two vampires would get along easily. That was too bad. Rafe went back to Fink's website. There was plenty of information on Dr. Howard Fink, a medical doctor and also holder of several PhDs in scientific areas so specialized Rafe didn't pretend to understand them. He'd won a Nobel Prize, along with another researcher, for discovering a gene that promised to lead to curing several kinds of cancers.

Not only was he the kind of genius that other brainiacs looked up to, but a link to his Facebook page showed he was a cool guy. He and his wife liked the music in the bars on Sixth Street. Hell, he'd been to Rafe's N-V bar for a couple of shows. Fink was into craft beers and vintage band t-shirts and, yeah, even Glory showed up as a friend of his. He was a popular professor at the University of Texas when he wasn't in his lab discovering radical cures.

Jerry nudged him. "I told you, he's a regular guy, but super smart. I think he hangs out with Ian from time to time, doctor to doctor. They discuss science, stuff like that. Call MacDonald and ask him. If there are any dark secrets about this guy, Ian might have read his mind enough to know them. MacDonald has a pretty dark side himself."

"I remember. Yeah, that's a good idea." Rafe realized they were already about to land in

Austin. He expected the vampire to still be at the werecat compound, overseeing the cats guarding his children. He sent a text to check and got a quick answer. They could meet there when he and Lacy went to see his sons. Ian would wait for him at Sheila's house.

"If Dr. Fink is who he appears to be, about to cure cancer, then I wonder if Lucifer is pulling a fast one." Rafe realized that would be just the kind of thing the Devil would enjoy doing to him. The horned one would laugh his ass off at the dilemma he'd created for Rafe.

"That would be the worst." Jerry's hands were in his hair. "We need Abe. He'd know if this guy is doomed for Hell or Heaven, wouldn't he?"

"I'm afraid it doesn't matter." Rafe slammed the laptop shut. "This is the name I've got. Those are Lucifer's orders. That means I'm supposed to deliver Fink to Gordon. The Devil's henchman will take great delight in killing the doctor, no matter where he is supposed to go after he's dead. Heaven or Hell, won't matter to Gordo. That would be the end to all the potential good the doctor could do, unless..."

"What? What can you do?" Jerry stared at him on one side, Miguel was out of his seat, looming over Rafe on the other.

"You honestly think you can go back down there and negotiate with the Devil, Rafael?" Miguel stared at him, his hands fisted. "Do you have the *cojones* for that?"

"Quit reading my mind and don't worry about my *cojones*." Rafe unbuckled his seat belt. He couldn't sit still another minute. Negotiate with the Devil. As if that were possible. The only way Lucifer would go for a deal was if Rafe offered to drag his own mother down to Hell instead of Fink.

Persuade Lilith to spend eternity there? Rafe stalked to the bar at the front of the plane and poured himself a stiff drink. He could feel Miguel breathing down his neck. Yeah, he was testing the vampire's new vow to lay off the booze. Rafe tossed back the drink and then turned.

"You still in my head?" He met Miguel's hard gaze.

"*Sí.*" The vampire returned to his seat.

Rafe followed him and fell into his own seat. "Then you know I'm thinking about it. When we hit Austin, I'm going back to that coffee shop. Lucifer is asking too much. Unless between now and when we land, I find something in Howard Fink's background that justifies his extinction, then I can't just take him out." He looked up at the ceiling. "Hopefully Abe is going to show up to clarify things before I have to do that."

Rafe buckled up as he felt the jet making its descent toward the runway.

"I wouldn't put anything past the Devil." Jerry glanced at the women in the back of the plane. "Forget the coffee shop for now. You're going straight to the cat compound. Glory needs to check on her shop anyway after being gone a few days. Let us know what Ian says and we can all meet up at your bar later."

Rafe realized his friends did have their own

lives to take care of. "Hey, if you have other obligations, I understand." He felt eyes on him. "Richard, Miguel, same goes for you two. Jerry's right. I'm meeting Ian at the cat compound first to see what he knows about this doctor. If he confirms the guy is decent and doesn't deserve Hell, then I guess I'm going to have to confront Lucifer about this one."

"Will that do any good?" Richard slammed his laptop shut. "It seems like what the Devil wants, the Devil gets."

"Yes." Rafe hated to acknowledge the truth of that. "But he must answer to *someone*. Can he kill anybody he wants before their time? Father Abraham will know about that."

Miguel clutched the arm rest as the plane bumped along the runway, the engines whining as the pilot closed them down. Clearly, the powerful vamp didn't like planes. Rafe hid a smile while Miguel gave him a stony look.

"I like to be in control. I could have flown here on my own, but I ride in the plane to be part of this team." He almost growled that. "Smile at your own risk."

Rafe held up his hand. "I get it. You're very old. So am I. It's unnatural to fly in a metal tube. Soaring free under your own steam is much better. But shifting takes a lot out of you. We need to conserve our strength in case there's a fight coming." He did smile though. Couldn't help it. Richard laughed and risked a beat down.

"Fuck teamwork." Miguel unbuckled his seatbelt, up and at the door as soon the pilot walked out of the cockpit to let them know they could disembark. Miguel glared at Richard. "I'll be at Rafe's bar if you need me." He was out of the plane as soon as the pilot unlatched the door. It obviously didn't bother him that the steps weren't down yet. It was only a twelve-foot drop, nothing for a large black bird.

"He's missing his tequila." Richard got up and stretched. "And he'll be missing his bags unless one of us takes care of them for him."

"I'll get them." Jerry unbuckled his seatbelt. "He's my brother-in-law or something like that. Can you imagine? Glory has the strangest family, but mine is no prize either. You know my mother has tried to kill my wife more than once. So I guess I can deal with her touchy half-brother. His powers could certainly be useful in a fight." He glanced at Richard. "He handled you easily enough."

Richard swore. "Thanks for reminding me."

"Be glad he's on our side." Rafe moved out of the way, waiting for Lacy to come down the aisle. They gathered their luggage then figured out who needed a car and who was going where. It took some time and a few phone calls, but finally everyone agreed to meet at Rafe's bar later to discuss the next steps.

Once Rafe got to the cat compound, he had obligations of his own. His sons were thrilled to see him, though they were rubbing their eyes at the early hour. Sheila kept them on a regular schedule because school would be starting soon. Of course, they'd heard the commotion when their parents arrived and had jumped out of bed to greet them. It took some doing to get time with Ian. Then the vampire was facing daylight and his death sleep.

"You're kidding. Lucifer wants to take out Howard Fink and drag him down to Hell?" Ian paced Sheila's living room while Lacy kept the boys in their bedroom, showing them some souvenirs she'd picked up in New Orleans.

"He's on my list. The last one. If you convince me he doesn't belong on that list, then I'll have to go talk to Lucifer about making a change." Rafe felt dread eating a hole in his stomach like acid. Where was Abe? Surely there was a godly solution for this.

"He's only forty years old, Rafe. The discoveries this guy has made so far could save millions of people. Hell, he's already on track to cure at least one type of pancreatic cancer. If he dies before he finishes what he's started..." Ian showed fang. "You can't let this happen. He's bright. A great mind. And, yes, I've been around him enough to know he's a good guy. As far as I have seen, he's hiding no dark secrets in that brilliant mind of his." He frowned. "But then I haven't really looked. I don't, as a general rule. Mortals tend to be boring as hell, thinking about sex, money, sex, work, sex, kids. You get it." Ian shrugged. "And the sex isn't even that interesting."

"You need more time with him. To look deeper." Rafe had an idea. "I'll see what I can do to get you together."

"Yeah, take care of that. We have to save Fink."

Ian looked out the window. "Fuck. I've got to go if I don't want to be caught by the sun. I can't bed down here. It's too busy during the day. Love your kids, but I can't trust them not to find me dead and play 'poke the vampire', if you know what I mean."

"Yeah, I do. Sorry. They are too smart and curious for their own good." Rafe couldn't believe he'd forgotten about vampires and daylight.

Ian frowned. "You can forget meeting your team at the bar until tonight. If you plan to talk to Lucifer, go ahead. But I don't see how you can get the Devil to give in on this. Screwing over humanity seems right up his alley." With that, he opened the back door and flew off into the sky that had a hint of gray in it.

Rafe collapsed on the couch and dropped his head into his hands. Vampires and their damned death sleep. That left him with a long, long summer day to figure out what to do about a doctor who could save millions of lives if he was allowed to live.

When he felt a hand on his back, Rafe hoped it was Abe's. He needed an answer from above. Because he couldn't imagine persuading the Devil to cut him or Howard Fink a break.

CHAPTER SEVENTEEN

"I'M NOT ALLOWED to interfere, Rafael." Abe sat in Sheila's favorite chair, a plate of cookies in his lap. "There's something of a power struggle going on here. I hate to say it, but you may have to go down there and try to negotiate with Lucifer if you decide Fink must be spared."

Rafe jerked the plate from Abe's hand. Sheila's chocolate chip cookies were too good for the monk. He sat there all pious and glowing with righteousness but what good was he? Had he been to the bowels of Hell? Had he? Of course not.

Rafe could hear his sons giggling as they walked outside with Lacy. She was going to drive them to the mall. They'd outgrown everything. They would put up with shopping for school clothes because she'd promised them a stop at a toy store. It was all so normal, that was the hope anyway. For the boys' sake.

Not like his time was running out and he had no idea what his daughter was doing. He decided to find out. He punched in the number his mother had given him, after he took a bite of cookie, ignoring Abe's baleful look.

"Rafael, darling. How goes your mission for Lucifer?" His mother sounded happy, as if she was sure everything was going her way.

"I'm sure you know, Mother. Don't you have spies everywhere? I saw a bee buzzing past the open window a moment ago. Bet that was one of your demons, doing a fly by." Rafe took another bite, making a point of crunching loudly.

"Yes, I'm keeping tabs on you. One more sinner to go. I'm so proud of you." She laughed. "Would you like to speak to Daniela? We're having a wonderful time."

"Yes, please put her on." Rafe set aside the cookies. "Facetime. I have to see her."

"Of course, darling." And there she was, his little girl.

"Daddy! Lollie bought me a pretty new dress." His daughter held out the phone. He saw a fluffy pink thing with matching flats and those little white socks with lace trim that made his heart turn over.

"Very pretty, sweetheart. Tell me what you've been doing." Rafe felt his throat closing. His precious child. She did look happy. Her hair was combed back and she had butterfly clips holding her ponytail up high. She talked fast, telling him about the rides at the Disney resort. She was also excited about the shopping she and her grandmother had done.

"Is Mommy there?"

"She's taking the boys to the mall. I'll have her call you later. Let me talk to your grandmother now. I love you."

"Love you too." And she was gone.

Lilith's face was there for only a moment, then it was voice only. "Are you satisfied? She's having a wonderful time."

"School is starting soon. She needs to come home and get ready for first grade." Rafe knew what Lilith was going to say and he hated it.

"She's not safe there. Finish what you must, son. One more sinner. I hear there's a catch. Trust Luc to play dirty."

"You sound like you expected it." Rafe stood, knocking the plate of cookies to the floor. Abe actually moaned.

"Of course, I did. Didn't you? Honesty is a foreign concept to that man. Are you going back down there and beg for that mortal's life? Tell me you're not so stupid. It's a waste of time." Her voice had gone cold. Yes, the real Lilith was on the phone now.

Rafe heard her tell Dani to take her new dolls into the suite's bedroom and play there.

"Listen to me, Rafael. You will not exchange me for this little girl. Try to make that kind of bargain with the Devil involving me and I guarantee you will never see your precious child again." The phone went dead in his hands.

Rafe cursed and threw the phone across the room. Lucky for his bank account, it hit a throw pillow and didn't break. Sheila had dozens of pillows, one in every chair and a half-dozen on the sofa. He threw one of those next but it didn't help his mood.

"I'm sorry, my son. What did you expect from

a powerful demon like your mother? Tender feelings? Sympathy?" Abe began to collect the scattered cookies from the rug. He set them back on the plate and put it on the coffee table. "Any idea what you can do?"

"First, I want to get Howard Fink in front of one or more of the vampires. Let them read his mind. Maybe he's not the good guy everyone thinks he is. That would solve my problem. Then I could happily deliver him to Gordon on time and release Daniela from Lilith's clutches. Assuming Lucifer follows through with the deal we made." He'd sent Fink some messages, computer and text, and hoped they were enough to lure the doctor to N-V later.

"I can't tell you about Fink. As I said, I'm not allowed to interfere in this one. I'm here for moral support. It took some fast talking to get that much out of Him. This is a test of some sort. For Lucifer? For you? He wouldn't say. I'll do what I can, I promise you that." Abe sighed. "Anyway, how are you getting Dr. Fink in front of the vampires? You know that has to wait for darkness, doesn't it?"

"Yes, it does. I have a plan. Right now, I'm going to finally get some rest. I think I need it. I have to be sharp tonight." Rafe looked outside.

He could tell there were still demons in the trees, watching and waiting in case his daughter did show up. They weren't sent by his mother. No, these were after that damned reward. He was sure several of them had trailed Lacy and the boys when they'd left. His wife had arranged to take two burly cousins, armed with that wisteria, along as bodyguards. Rafe was afraid there was an idea floating around that kidnapping his boys or even his wife could be a play that might help them get to Dani.

That reward for Dani's recovery was a problem. If Lucifer would drop it, that would take some pressure off here. Maybe he did need to go down to Hell after all. The very idea made Rafe shudder. But he'd do anything to save his little girl, innocent and pretty in her pink dress and butterfly hair clips. God, how he loved her.

Rafe realized the bee was gone and he didn't think he could be overheard. He lowered his voice anyway. "I want to see if it would do any good to track down my mother and try to get Dani back myself."

Abe's eyes widened but he didn't discourage the idea. Good.

Rafe was so tired he couldn't see straight. He nodded toward the plate of cookies. "Enjoy. We have a thing called a five-second rule around here. Sheila keeps a clean house so it doesn't matter if a cookie hits *her* floor. Guess you don't have to worry about germs anyway, *Padre*."

Abe sat next to him on the couch and put a comforting hand on his shoulder. "My son. You are a good man. I hope you remember that when you do go down to see Lucifer. He was once an angel, until he fell. We have always prayed that he would one day remember where he came from and soften." He picked up a cookie and sniffed it. "Some prayers get answered, some don't. It is not for us who are less than God to figure out why those decisions are made."

"I've lived a long time." Rafe let the comfort from that hand soak into him. It felt warm, soothing. "I've seen things that made me want to lose what faith I had. But, for some reason, I always stayed determined to fight the dark side of my soul. When I was down there in Hell before, I felt the pull. Lucifer is beautiful, charismatic and so damned powerful. It would be easy to give in and let my freak flag fly." He looked into Abe's eyes. "Do you know what I mean?"

"Yes. And you may have to do that, fully embrace your demon side, to get your daughter back." Abe stuffed a cookie into his mouth, the whole thing. He chewed and swallowed, almost looking sick, as if he couldn't help himself.

"Remember this, Rafael. No matter how far you go to protect the one you love, it is for a good reason. It does not make *you* evil or a lost cause. You can come back from this. To your family."

Rafe heard Abe's stomach gurgle. It seemed like maybe the monk was suffering for his indulgence. He thought about what Abe was telling him. Not a lost cause. He'd let his demon side out before, when he'd been up against a wall and felt like he had no choice. So far, he'd always managed to come back from the edge when darkness had taken over. His demon side was powerful, he'd always known that. How powerful? He'd never fully unleashed it to find out.

He'd had centuries to nourish his good side. That was worth something. He must remember that. Abe had a reason for reminding him. Rafe looked up at the white ceiling as if he could figure out what to do, how to proceed. Nothing. Unanswered prayers. Boy, did he know about those.

His eyes grew heavy and he fell back against the sofa cushions. Tired, so tired. Lacy would be gone for hours and it was quiet in the house. Sheila had gone to visit a friend to give Rafe privacy. He stretched out his legs and finally allowed himself to relax. He needed to sleep and recharge. Because he had a plan and the hours after dark were not going to be easy. That was his last thought before he let go.

"Are you sure you don't mind?" Rafe was glad to see Miguel already at the bar as soon as darkness fell. The vampire wasn't drinking, obviously just waiting for the others. "It's a long flight. Hours by plane."

"You know I'm not getting into one of those death traps again any time soon. I'll shift and fly. I can make it quick." Miguel stared at the variety of top shelf tequilas behind the bar. "It will be good to have something to do. I've never been to Orlando before. I will study a map and get going immediately. I can buy anything I need when I get there. Weather might be a factor."

"I checked. It's good all the way to Florida. I need to know exactly where Lilith is. I'm guessing one of the hotels attached to the theme park. Sniff around for demon activity. That will help you zero in on her location. No idea what name she might be traveling under, not her own, that's for sure." Rafe signaled the bartender for a bottle of water.

"Yeah. Luckily, I've got a nose for demons. Your scent is not very strong because you're not a pure blood, but there's an asshole standing near the bandstand right now that I'd like to break in half before I go." Miguel glared in that direction. "Do you know him? He seems to have arrived with the crew for your friend Israel Caine."

"Shit. No. He must be a new hire. A roadie." Rafe took a quick drink of water. "I'll handle it. Thanks for making this trip for me. Call when you have any information. We may all show up out there sooner than you think."

Miguel smiled. "Confronting the bitch and getting your daughter back ourselves. I like it. It's bound to involve a battle. But I won't make a move without your say-so. Is that right?"

"Yes. She has legions of demons on call. It won't be easy if that's the way we have to go. I'll try negotiations first but I don't hold out much hope for a peaceful resolution." Rafe shook hands with Miguel. The vampire was gone so quickly, Rafe wondered if the mortals around them had noticed the vampire's supernatural speed.

The bar was already busy and they'd had to speak quietly. Israel Caine was performing tonight and he was very popular. The gig had sold out. Rafe had two men on the door, confirming reservations. Rafe headed toward the bandstand.

He stopped before he made it when he saw Glory and Jerry arriving. They had special seats in the balcony and knew he stocked synthetic blood for his vampire customers. Flo and Richard were right behind them.

"Are the Finks coming?" Glory glanced around the room. Almost every seat was already filled. A disc jockey was playing music for dancing until Caine's performance, scheduled to start much later.

"I sent them special invitations. Said they'd won a contest and had free tickets including drinks. I haven't heard back." Rafe pointed to the man helping set up the drums on the stage. "Miguel says that guy is a demon. One of you want to handle that?"

"I'll do it." Richard smiled. "I have holy water in my pocket for just this kind of situation. If you hear a squeal, it's his pain talking."

"My man." Flo followed him across the room to watch.

"There they are. The doctor and Carly Fink." Glory pulled on Jerry's arm. "Come with me. We can invite them to sit with us in the balcony. We'll both look into the doctor's mind and see if there are any dark secrets he is hiding."

Rafe breathed a sigh of relief. He saw Ian MacDonald come in behind the Finks and the couple was quickly surrounded by three vampires determined to examine the doctor's thoughts.

He felt strangely detached as he watched his bar fill up with happy customers. It had once been all he'd dreamed about—having a successful business. Now he was almost irritated when his brother approached him, a clipboard in hand and clearly eager to discuss more business.

Tomas slapped him on the back. "Good crowd, eh?"

"You did a fantastic job, *hermano*." Rafe gave him a hug. "Thanks for taking the reins."

"Where is your beautiful wife tonight?" Tomas turned to greet a longtime customer.

"She was tired from our trip and needed to be with the boys. They missed us. I told her to stay home and get some rest." Rafe nodded toward the bandstand when there was a squeal and a slight commotion as a man fell off the side of the stage. "We actually saw Ray perform in Houston last night." A lie but believable. If they'd stayed a while longer...

"Really? You had quite a trip then." Tomas frowned. "I thought you were in New Orleans."

Rafe smiled. "We went where Jerry and Glory wanted to go. Luxury jet. Who was I to object when they suggested a side trip?" Rafe looked around at the full house. "Hey, it *is* a great crowd. You really got the word out, didn't you?"

"No need. Caine has a loyal following. I wish we could book high-dollar entertainment like him every night. And he never charges us a small percentage of the gate. I don't understand it." Another question in Tomas's eyes.

"He and Glory go way back. He wants this place to be successful, so he puts us on his tour when he's on the road. He knows it's a small venue, but doesn't care. He likes an excuse to come to Austin and visit with her."

"And her husband doesn't mind it?" Tomas laughed. "That singer is too handsome to let my wife close to him."

"Sorry you don't trust her." Rafe dodged a punch. "Excuse me, I need to check on the balcony. I invited a special guest: Dr. Fink and his wife—drinks on the house tonight."

"Never heard of them." Tomas jotted the name on his clipboard.

"Won the Nobel Prize, bro. You should read a newspaper sometime." Rafe glanced at the balcony. "Anyway, thanks again, brother, for running things here. I hope I don't have to leave town again soon, but I might. I'm warning you now." Rafe headed for the stairs, Tomas grumbling as he left.

He was anxious to meet the Finks and get the verdict. Was the good doctor really good? If so, he was going to have to fight Gordon to keep Fink out of Hell tonight.

CHAPTER EIGHTEEN

RAFE MADE HIMSELF known to the Finks. They looked a little bemused, surrounded by powerful vampires. Not that they had a clue the five people at the table were anything but the well-dressed business owners they claimed to be. Even Ian MacDonald, *Dr.* Ian MacDonald, claimed to run a consulting business and laboratory. Rafe knew he had invented a daylight drug for vampires that allowed them an hour or two awake to see the sunrise. It was so costly only the very rich could afford it. Israel Caine bought it frequently. What Ian told Dr. Howard Fink he sold was anyone's guess.

"I still can't figure out what contest we won." Howard, he insisted they call him that, gestured at his glass of top shelf bourbon. "But I'm not complaining."

"Did you drop a business card into a bowl at the bar? We draw one twice a month." Rafe settled into a chair at the table. He actually did have that contest but he certainly didn't give away high-priced tickets to an Israel Caine show and unlimited drinks.

Carly Fink laughed and touched Howard's

sleeve. "Honey, I bet you did and forgot. Or maybe one of your grad students did it. No matter how it happened, I'm thrilled." She looked around the table. "I love Israel Caine." She flushed. "Well, you know what I mean, don't you, Glory? We've talked about his music enough."

"Oh, I do." Glory kissed Jerry's cheek. "My husband used to be jealous of Ray, but he got over it. Ray and I have been friends for years. We've even sung duets together. Jer knows I picked *him*, right, love?" She looked into Jerry's eyes.

"Right." He had his arm around Glory. "And Caine finally quit flirting with you. He used to enjoy pulling my chain. Now we've come to an understanding and he's backed off."

Howard sipped his drink. "You're a better man than I am. Carly's raved about Caine too many times. He's her free pass. But I'm not so sure I could let it go if she ever followed through." He gripped Carly's hand. "I can be the jealous type."

"So can I, man, so can I." Jerry stared into Fink's eyes. "But acting on it? I see you as a lover, not a fighter. Right?"

Fink flushed and picked up his glass. "Yep. If she wants the man, she can have him."

Rafe studied the couple. The doctor was decent looking but had a nerdy vibe—Clark Kent with black rimmed glasses, vintage t-shirt and sport coat. His wife was attractive, in her thirties, blond and in great shape. Rafe could imagine Caine going for her.

"Hey, I'm right here." Carly poked Howard on his arm. "That free pass business is just talk. You're all I want or need and you know it." She looked around the table. "I'm sorry, how did we get on this?"

Flo laughed and pushed back her chair. "I don't know. But I hear a song that makes me want to dance." She wiggled her hips. "Come, Ricardo. Let's show them how it's done. Look down there. It's pitiful how those couples are hopping around like bunnies on a hot skillet." She grinned at the rest of the couples. "Anyone else want to move to this music?"

"Yes. Howard, up we go. I'll bet Mr. Valdez will make sure you have a fresh drink by the time we get back." Carly dragged her husband to his feet.

"It's Rafe. And I certainly will. One for you too, Carly. Margarita?"

She grinned. "Yes, thanks." She turned to Glory. "Are you two coming?"

"Not yet, we need to talk to Rafe about something. Give us a minute but go ahead. Flo is already tearing up the dance floor." Glory laughed. "Is that a cha cha or the macarena?"

"Uh oh. We are seriously outclassed, honey." Carly dragged Howard toward the stairs.

"Help." Howard glanced back. "I consented to six weeks of dance lessons and my wife thinks I can keep up with her. She's a pro."

"I am. A ballroom champion once upon a time and I have the trophies to prove it." She did a twirl that showed off her toned legs and black panties. "That was back in college with an old boyfriend. Once Howie stole my heart, Danny was history. I'll take Einstein here over Patrick

Swayze any day of the week." She did a hip bump that made Howard stagger.

"Easy, baby." Howard took off his glasses and laid them on the table. The sport coat was next, on the back of his chair. He was grinning as he looked around the table. "This is what love gets you." He held out his hand.

"That's right. Now try not to crash into other couples, Howie. I'll dance around you and make you look good, just like I always do." She shook her hips and gracefully boogied down the stairs, tugging Howard in her wake.

As soon as they were out of earshot, Rafe leaned forward. "Tell me they're okay. I *like* that couple."

Ian slapped the table. "You will not take Howard Fink down to Hell. He has too much to offer humanity. He should live for decades more. I'm even thinking of offering to turn him so he will live for centuries. His mind is incredible."

Rafe wanted to bang his head on the table. Turn Fink vampire. Wouldn't that be a fine outcome. "Cool it, Ian. Let him stay mortal." He saw Ian didn't like Rafe seeming to give him an order. "For now."

Ian nodded. "I won't be hasty. Working only during the darkness of night is limiting, to say the least. I've had to do it for centuries."

"Yes. Now about the mind reading. I don't want to, but I heard him seem to threaten Ray. He obviously *is* the jealous type." Rafe focused on Jerry and Glory. "Was that a hint at a deeper issue?"

"He's no more jealous than I am. I don't blame

him. He married up when he got Carly. Just like I did when I finally persuaded Gloriana to have *me*." Jerry squeezed Glory's hand. "I hope my jealousy doesn't mean I'm destined for Hell. It does make me crazy to see other men lusting after my wife. Howard feels the same about his woman."

"I think you're okay there unless it leads to murder. But what else did you see in his mind? Any mortal sins worth eternal damnation?" Rafe held his breath. What did he want the answer to be? There were complications either way.

A chair scraped back and suddenly Gordon was sitting at the head of the table.

"Oh, shit." Jerry threw back his chair, on his feet with a knife in his hand.

Ian was up too. "Who is this? I can smell the stench of demon on him."

"I'm not a fucking demon." Gordon frowned. "But I'm here to tell you, when you're around those hell-apes twenty-four/seven, it's impossible to get that smell out of your clothes and hair." He glared at Rafe. "The Master hears you're having doubts about sinner number five. You want me to do the pickup once those two get through dancing with the stars?" He looked over the railing. "The man has absolutely no rhythm. His wife, though, can sure shake her groove thing. She's a fine piece."

Rafe had stayed seated. He was thinking fast. "I need to talk to Lucifer. Don't touch the Finks until I get back."

"You don't give me orders." Gordon smiled.

"But don't worry about Mrs. Fink. She's not on my list. As for Dr. Fink? I can wait. I'm looking forward to Israel Caine's performance. Live music that might actually be in tune? Not something we enjoy downstairs. Our usual entertainment makes my ears bleed."

"He can't wait here." Jerry's eyes were wild. "Find him a seat at the bar. A drink. Anything to get him away from the rest of our team."

"Oh, you have a *team*. How delightful." Gordon got up and strolled to the top of the stairs. He glanced at Ian. "Some of you have been very, very bad in your long lives. You have come close to eligibility for our deluxe services." His smile was cold. "Then you do something remarkable and Upstairs intervenes. Amazing really." He turned his focus to Jerry.

"Murder during battle seems to be allowed. What a pity. You have quite a head count, don't you, Campbell, Blade, or whatever you call yourself this century." Gordon smirked. "It's amazing what gets a pass from The Man Upstairs."

"Slaying your enemies is not a mortal sin. At least that's what priests have told me." Jerry still gripped his knife. Glory kept her hand on his arm.

"He's a good man, protective." She glared at Gordon. "Go back to Hell where you belong, creep."

Gordon made a gagging sound. "Protective and loyalty from his woman. Pardon me if I'm not impressed." He started down the stairs. "Rafe, I'll take that seat at the bar and Scotch, the best in the house. You be sure to tell Lucifer it was your idea. I don't want to be punished for enjoying myself."

"Fine." Rafe followed him, aware of the eyes on his back. If he could slip in a hint to Lucifer that Gordon had insisted on staying for the show, he would. Gordon needed a time out in Hell. A long visit to the roasting pit. Bastard. Ian stopped him with a hand on his shoulder.

"Can this man be killed?" His voice was low.

"No, he's already dead." Rafe shivered. "Believe me, I'd love to do the deed myself."

"Too bad. Be careful down there. You want company?" Ian watched Gordon settle at the bar and give his order.

"I'd love company, but Lucifer wouldn't allow it. Thanks for the offer." Rafe stopped at the bar and told the bartender Gordon was to have whatever he wanted, on the house. He also told him to send refills to the balcony. Then he left quickly by the back door.

He shifted and was soon across the street from the Devil's coffee shop, in the tree again. It was dark and he changed into his mortal body, dressed in black and ready to go inside. His stomach churned when the smell of fresh donuts and coffee hit him as soon as he opened the door.

"You're back." The Einstein look-a-like was working the counter again.

"Hey, cutie, you're looking a little ragged. That's what happens when you fight your fate." The same blond demon was at her laptop, sitting at the same table. She smiled. Lucifer's guards apparently never got a break.

Einstein nodded. "He's expecting you. Guess Gordon let him know you were coming. Go on down. Someone will be there to open the portal."

Rafe walked through the door and saw those spiral stairs that went down endlessly. His footsteps echoed as he hit each metal tread. When he finally got to that heavy iron door with the electronic keypad, there was a man standing there. He was someone Rafe recognized with a jolt, an old enemy he'd killed centuries ago.

"Rafael. It *is* you. Been a while."

Rafe didn't know what to say. Did he expect someone he'd known in the nineteenth century to still dress like he was on his way to see the queen? Instead, Byron Stanhope, one of the worst purveyors of human flesh in the London stews during Elizabethan times, now wore jeans and a t-shirt. With tennis shoes. The shirt said "Shit Show Supervisor."

"Good to see you landed where you deserved." Rafe waited while Byron punched in the secret code, carefully hidden by Byron's bulk. The man had always been huge, well over six feet and wide at his shoulders. He'd started life as a dock worker and had the brawny muscles to prove it.

"Hell ain't so bad if you know how to work the angles. I got a position with power." Byron pointed the way as the door swung open.

"I see, if the shirt and your smell is to be believed. Guess showers are optional." Rafe felt the heat as soon as he entered. And there were the screams, louder than the last time if that were possible. "You'd know the angles. I bet none of your victims are down here."

"No, but Ma Brady made the trip. You know her house burned up with her in it. A sad accident." Byron eyed him. "Or was it an accident?"

"She had plenty of enemies. It wasn't me who set that fire. Whoever managed to take her out is probably enjoying the good life in Heaven right now." Rafe smiled when Byron had nothing to say about that.

"Yeah, well, Lucifer has her runnin' the doxies down here who did people dirty during their lives. Ma thinks it's a fine life," Byron looked around furtively, "until the Master reminds her that there's punishment to be had if she shows too much enjoyment, if you know what I mean."

"Yes, I'm sure Lucifer knows how to keep anyone in line when there's any sign of pleasure here." Rafe stared at Byron. "I imagine running a shit show is a, um, dirty business."

"Don't you worry about it." Byron sped up the pace. "Quit dallying. He's waiting in the throne room. In a mood, he is. Says the clock is ticking on you, whatever that means." Byron grabbed Rafe's arm. His hand was covered in sores, oozing with rot.

"Let go of me. I'm here to see him, not you." Rafe jerked away from him and his reek that made him nauseous.

"You always were too good for the rest of us. Protectin' the girls, stealin' them away so they couldn't earn me a decent wage." His grimace showed a mouth full of black teeth. "You're still alive? After all this time? What year is it anyway?"

Rafe told him with quite a bit of satisfaction.

"No! Fuckin' immortal bastard!" Byron swung his arm but was suddenly paralyzed. Then he slumped to the ground.

"Get in here, Valdez. Homer, clean up the trash." Lucifer appeared in front of Rafe. He was sitting on his golden throne. "Can't stand a freak who doesn't understand his place. *I* take care of the punishment here."

A man appeared with a spear. He stabbed it into Byron's backside and then dragged him away, leaving a streak of blood on the gleaming floor. Then Homer rushed back with a mop and bucket to make sure the evidence of that removal was cleaned away.

"Did you hear me? Come closer and state your case, Valdez. I can't wait." Lucifer waved a hand to urge Rafe closer. He had a woman on her knees in front of him, servicing him. "Don't mind Ma. I thought it would be amusing to see your reaction when I brought in some of your old enemies. A reunion of sorts."

Rafe moved into the throne room. Yes, that was Ma Brady giving Lucifer a blow job. Her head never stopped moving, even when the Devil ran a hand over her tangled gray hair and jerked, taking a clump of it with him. He tossed it aside with a frown.

"When you're done, Ma, you will have a bath. A hot bath."

Rafe heard her moan. He could imagine how hot that bath would be. The old madame had never been one for cleanliness anyway. He wanted to cheer. She'd been cruel and merciless and many young girls had died either by her hand or because of her neglect.

Lucifer nodded. "Yes, I can see you appreciate the advantages there are in having a Hell. This is where the truly evil meet their proper punishments. Brady and Stanhope are getting what they deserved and have for hundreds of years. It will never end." This must have hit Ma hard because she did something with her mouth that made Lucifer kick her away. She tumbled down the stairs to land near Rafe's feet.

"Homer! Put this creature in the hole and keep her there for fifty years." Lucifer straightened his clothing. "Maggots and snakes. It's quite a disgusting pit." He waved a hand. "Hurry, Homer, I promised her a bath first."

Rafe fought the urge to throw up as Ma was dragged past him. Her stench was disgusting but her wails of pain and horror went right through him. When a door slammed and her cries were suddenly cut off, he could finally breathe.

Lucifer smiled. "Now let us begin. Valdez, I understand you have a problem with sinner number five?"

"Yes. Dr. Howard Fink is an award-winning researcher who is finding cures for human diseases. My vampire friends have read his mind and can find no deep dark sins on his soul." Rafe straightened his shoulders. "I don't think he deserves Hell. It would be a huge loss for humanity."

"What do I care about humanity? You know how I feel about cures. They prolong lives that should belong down here." Lucifer got down from his throne and strolled closer. "Dear me, the reek of that woman is still in the air. Follow me to my office. I sense you want to make a deal. This is all about saving Daniela from a life here, is it not?"

"Yes." Rafe could barely choke out the word. "I will do anything to keep her from this place. What will it take to make that happen and save Howard Fink?"

Lucifer smiled again and it chilled Rafe to his bones. "I assume you'd rather not be here either." He threw open the door to his office and stalked to his desk.

Rafe followed, determined to stay the course, though his legs were having trouble remembering how to work. He knew Lucifer could read his every thought. No point in keeping up a brave front.

"You want Lilith, don't you? I will bring her to you in exchange for our freedom, mine and Dani's." Rafe stopped in front of the massive desk. Lucifer picked up an elegant pen, as if he was prepared to have them sign an agreement, a formal contract.

"It seems you have read *my* mind." He picked up an old-fashioned telephone and spoke into it. "Send in Elizabeth with the contract." He hung up and raised an eyebrow. "Yes, that's my plan.

You seem to want it all formalized. For some reason you don't trust me."

"Why should I? This place is full of liars, murderers and thieves. Why wouldn't you be the biggest one of them all?" Rafe found a chair behind him and abruptly sat. Good. His knees were jelly. And there needed to be negotiations. "First, call off the reward for Daniela's capture. The demons are everywhere, surrounding my family, and hoping for a chance to capture her. There's even talk of an exchange, my sons or wife for her."

"Clever demons. Not a bad plan. Sure, I can do that. Call off the reward. If I think you have a dog's chance of succeeding in bringing Lilith to me, permanently." He glanced at the door as a woman entered. "Ah, I don't think you have met Elizabeth, my scribe."

Rafe nodded, shocked when he recognized the woman. She'd been on the news a decade ago for embezzling funds and bankrupting a major bank. She had taken down the pension funds for teachers, firefighters and policemen's unions. She'd murdered her partner then committed suicide before she could be tried for her crimes.

"I really should have thought before I ended my life and Melanie's," she said as she stood behind Lucifer's chair. Her lips quivered. "Mel isn't here. She was good and decent. My selfish victim. Then I ended up here as a glorified secretary. I didn't work my way up in corporate America all those years to end up doing endless days of dictation and typing." She held out her hands. Her fingers were bleeding. "I've learned every person here has a different kind of Hell."

"Shut up. I didn't call you in here to listen to complaints. Would you like a trip to the spa?" Lucifer tapped his desk impatiently.

Elizabeth shuddered and glanced at Rafe. "Believe me, that's not what it sounds like. No, sir. Let me know what terms I need to put in this contract and I'll type it up right away. In triplicate."

"I told you the terms, Elizabeth. Didn't you listen to me?" Lucifer picked up the telephone again. "Homer, clean up in the office."

"No, please. It's just as you requested. But, since you have the supplicant here, I thought it may have changed. Look it over. I assumed…"

"Assume nothing." Lucifer studied the contract. "Hand it to Mr. Valdez, the supplicant, then come back to my side. Supplicant. I do like that term. Using it may have saved you."

Rafe read the agreement, once she'd given it to him with shaking hands. It was straightforward. In exchange for bringing Lilith to Hell, Rafe and his daughter Daniela would be free from any further obligation to Lucifer and Hell, in perpetuity. The mortal Dr. Howard Fink was no longer under threat of capture unless he became guilty of a worthy sin in the future. There was a place for both Lucifer and Rafael Valdez to sign.

"I have a question or two before I sign this." Rafe got up to stand in front of the desk.

"Oh?" Lucifer had used the time Rafe had been reading to open Elizabeth's dress and fondle her breasts. Her eyes were closed and she bit her lip, as if this were a new kind of torture. Rafe remembered reading that she had been in a loving relationship with a woman, the one she'd killed. She grimaced as if she hated Lucifer's touch. The Devil was a master at punishing his victims.

"First, is this just another of your games?" Rafe held out the contract. "Who's to say you will honor this?"

Lucifer smiled, a baring of teeth that made Rafe shudder. "Excellent question." His eyes glowed red and the temperature in the room rose until Rafe began to sweat. "You're going to have to take that chance, Rafael. Bring me Lilith. I guarantee I will be so happy, I'll give no more thought to you and yours." He pulled Elizabeth closer.

"You expect me to believe that?" Rafe braced himself for the same kind of pain he'd endured when he'd been down here before. Where had he found the nerve to question the Devil himself?

Lucifer snarled, his horns quivering. "That's all you're going to get, boy. Take it or leave it." He bit the woman's neck, drawing blood. He licked his lips, eyes gleaming.

Rafe looked away, sickened. He had no real choice here. He suddenly found a pen in his hand. It trembled as he signed, then threw the contract on the desk.

"One more question." Rafe took a breath of brimstone and his own fear. "How am I supposed to capture Lilith? She *is* the most powerful demon in your realm."

CHAPTER NINETEEN

"REALLY? YOU EXPECT me to give you advice?" Lucifer laughed, squeezing Elizabeth's nipple until she dropped to her knees, whimpering. He finally let the woman go and kicked her aside. "Get out of here. I hate whiny bitches."

She pulled her dress together and scurried out of the room.

"You want Lilith badly enough, I think you'll do whatever it takes to help me." Rafe sat again. He couldn't afford to be distracted, though he hated what Lucifer had done to that poor woman. Hated what he'd have to do to his own mother. He had to remember his daughter's future was at stake and that Lilith had never been a true mother to him. She'd abandoned him at birth to be raised by his strict grandparents.

As far as he knew, she'd been all about her own pleasures. The son she'd borne had been an accident and one she'd only remembered when it suited her purposes. And those purposes...? He shuddered. He'd been relieved when it seemed she'd forgotten he existed.

Lucifer had been staring at him, thinking, and

undoubtedly reading his thoughts. "You're right. We must work together to end this thing. Lilith belongs to me and I am sick of her rebellion. Her rightful place is by my side." He was up and pacing. "She's very powerful, you know."

"She reminds me of that every time we speak to each other." Rafe couldn't stay seated. He walked beside Lucifer, keeping pace. It was exhausting. "I think I need to get in touch with my own demon side."

Luc whirled, grabbing Rafe's arm. "Yes! It's about time. Do you have any idea how many legions of demons are at your command?"

"What? No." Rafe felt that hand on his arm like a vise. He knew better than to try to pull free. "What do you mean?"

"Do you know your middle name?" Lucifer's eyes were red again now, gleaming with his own demon power.

"I have one? A special secret name? That's news to me." Rafe felt the heat of the Devil's power as it bored into his brain. *Seir.* Now he knew it.

"Don't say it out loud. Your mother gave it to you, every demon has one, but not as powerful as yours. Look it up if you want to know more. It comes with the authority to call legions of demons to aid you. That decision may well be her downfall." Luc finally released him and walked to his desk.

He picked up the phone again. "I want the Book. You know the one. Now." He hung up. "We will see how many you can call. I may be able to augment that number. Countless here are jealous of Lilith's freedom to roam the Earth. Bringing her in will please them. You'll have allies in forcing her to Hell."

Rafe felt unsteady from that blast into his brain. Usually, his demon side was like a mild buzz, underlying his shifter being. Now he felt his demonic urges ramping up, trying to take over. He wanted to blast apart the chair he'd been sitting in. Before he could stop himself, he lifted a hand and the piece was nothing but kindling and feathers, flying through the air and landing against the door.

"Bravo! You're feeling it, aren't you?" Lucifer was clearly delighted.

The office door slowly opened and a man peeked inside. "Is it safe to come in?" He clutched a huge leather-bound book with metal bindings. It looked ancient. "I brought the Book."

"Yes, let me see it." Lucifer gestured for the man to place it on the desk. "Leave us." He didn't bother to introduce this latest underling. He began flipping through pages. "Here it is. You are entitled to twenty-six legions of demons. Using the Roman method of counting, let's estimate that's five thousand per legion."

Rafe wished he hadn't destroyed his chair as the room seemed to spin around him. "Five thousand demons times twenty-six. I'll have that many demons to command?" Could he even control that many? He'd never known a demon to meekly follow orders. They were wild cards.

"That's a hundred and thirty thousand." Lucifer preened. "I was always good at math."

"How many does Lilith command?" Rafe leaned against the desk.

"You don't want to know." Lucifer sighed. "The bitch has twice that at least, plus she has charmed some of the major demons with their own legions to support her. Can you believe it? The bastards show no loyalty to me. She has amassed a fortune and uses it wisely to reward those who pledge to her. I could try to buy them back but that would take time. You can't use force alone to get her down here. There has to be something she wants that will lure her to my side."

"I suppose it's too much to hope that she loves you and might secretly want to come back." Rafe couldn't believe he'd dared say it. Love? The King of Darkness? But Lucifer had been an angel once. Abe had reminded Rafe of that. Even through his fear, Rafe felt how Lucifer oozed charisma and had the beauty and power Lilith admired.

It was a struggle not to be mesmerized by him and Rafe had to constantly remind himself that this man was EVIL. He would do anything to get what he wanted. Certainly, he would not be above stealing Rafe's own child if it would help him have his way. Just as Lilith had done. That thought was like a splash of cold water in his face, sobering Rafe to the point that he glared at the Devil.

"So tell me what this is really about." Rafe demanded. "Why is she so important to you?"

"I won't call it love. That's a tame mortal word for what Lilith and I had. Can have again." Lucifer leaned back, his eyes on the ornate ceiling, a bemused smile on his face.

Rafe hadn't noticed it before but there were paintings on the ceiling, as if Michelangelo himself had done some of his best work there, but with the erotic touches of the Kama Sutra set on fire. It was beautifully disturbing. And set *him* on fire wishing he had Lacy here so he could take her to bed and ravage her. Damn.

"Love. Hah! Lilith and I were mad for each other. Your mother is a woman beyond compare." Lucifer glanced at Rafe. "And I would know. I've had thousands, hundreds of thousands." He sighed. "Then she had to take that Spaniard into her bed. And let him plant his seed!" No smile this time.

"I've wondered why. She never acted the mother. When she remembered me, it was to test me. She told me once she had to bring my father down here but always erased his memories of the tortures he'd suffered once they left." Rafe grimaced. "To spare him. I wish she'd done that for me." As a child, Rafe had endured nightmares of his visits with Lilith. No amnesia for him. His mother had picked him up to witness some of her atrocities, then hurried him back to his grandfather when he'd cried instead of being thrilled by her clever tortures and torments.

Lucifer laughed. "Oh, yes. I took great pleasure in making her watch her lover put through his paces here. The screams! The begging for mercy! Emiliano was a weak shell of a man after I got through with him. Now you tell me Lilith made sure he didn't remember any of it as soon as they left here? That vixen."

"Spare me details of the sick games you two played. All I know is that she hated I didn't share her pleasure for causing pain. I had no taste for evil so I felt her wrath. When she stopped coming to see me, it was a relief." Was Dani even now being subjected to Lilith's displeasure? To her harsh judgments and cold punishments? His child had always known only love and approval. His mother's volatile temper would devastate his little girl.

Pressure built behind his eyes. A scream crawled up his throat. Time was passing and he was no closer to getting his baby back than he'd been when he'd come down here. He had to do something. But what? The desperation to rescue his child made him feel helpless, like that child again, whose mother left him because he was too soft, too weak, a disappointment.

He breathed in that hellish air, remembering that he was a man now, with demon powers. He'd faced Lucifer and was still alive. He had hope, damn it. Or did he? Suddenly Rafe's knees gave out and he sat on the floor. God help him. Thinking that "G" word sent an arrow through his brain. He felt weak and strong all at once.

"Don't call for Him! Get up. Come to my bedchamber." Lucifer jumped up.

Rafe struggled to his feet. He had no choice but to obey. He had to know more and he needed to get away from those disturbing images on the ceiling. He'd stared at them long enough to realize the men were all Lucifer. And the women? His mother of course. Lucifer's fantasy of a happily ever after.

He followed Luc down a corridor lined with many doors. It was deathly silent. No screams. But unnerving just the same. Rafe felt raw, exposed, and braced for something, as if at any time someone or a *thing* would burst out of one of those doors and attack or perhaps the screams would start again.

Finally, they came to a golden entrance. It opened at Lucifer's touch. Inside he saw a waterfall and a pond at one end, the sound of running water soothing. There were leafy green trees and colorful birds singing. It was as if the Devil had created an idyllic outdoor setting here far under the Earth. A luxuriously appointed bed was set up next to that tranquil pond with goldfish swimming in it. Flowers bloomed on lily pads floating on its surface. Luc's version of Heaven?

Rafe couldn't resist looking up. This high domed ceiling had been painted a celestial blue. A few fake clouds seemed to drift across the false sky.

"You may well stare. I like to feel like I am outside. Because I so rarely go there." Luc threw himself on the bed. "Sit. You look overwhelmed." He gestured at a chaise placed next to the rocks and the waterfall. They were cooled by the water's spray but seemed dry. "There are refreshments if you are hungry or thirsty."

As if Rafe would dare eat or drink here. "No,

thank you. You were telling me about Lilith and her decision to have a child. Me. Unless there are others?" What a thought.

Rafe sat on the end of the gilt chaise. The cushions were fluffy and it was tempting to lean back. No, he had to stay alert every second he was down here.

Lucifer smiled. "One was enough for her. As far as I know." He lost that smile. "Damn, I wish you hadn't asked that." He stared at the water for a long moment then shook his head. "We're talking about you, Rafael. To say your birth was a surprise was an understatement." Luc picked up green grapes from a bedside table and began to eat them one by one. "Your father was so inferior!"

He reached for a goblet of golden wine and took a gulp. "If the bitch wanted a child, think what a cub she and I would have made." He looked Rafe over. "She was damned lucky you turned out as well as you did. Emiliano was weak, but at least from strong blood lines."

Rafe realized he'd just received a high compliment. He licked dry lips. Wine. He could use a drink about now. No, too dangerous. Though there was some of that golden wine right next to him on a small table.

"She hung onto my father for years. Centuries." He had to say it.

"Foolish pride. Do you think Lilith would ever admit she'd made a mistake?" Lucifer finished his wine and refilled his goblet from a carafe. "I can see your thirst from here. Come now, do you think I'd stoop to drugging you? I have you where I want you. Surely you realize that by now. Drink. We need to discuss strategy."

Rafe gave in. He needed a clear head but he also realized his own foolish pride and fear were obvious. He picked up his goblet and tasted the wine. It was so delicious that he'd drained the glass before he could stop himself. He waited, in case he'd been drugged. But, no, he just felt a pleasant buzz from a fine wine.

"Mother obviously regretted her little experiment. I didn't turn out to be the evil little offspring she'd hoped for. She abandoned me almost immediately. My grandparents tried to beat the demon out of me." Rafe realized the wine had loosened his tongue.

Lucifer laughed. "Beat out the demon! As if that were possible. Lilith is one of the strongest fiends there is, second only to me. You have no idea of your potential, Rafael. She gave up too early. Has underestimated you. That is how you will defeat her. And bring her back to me." He held up his cup. "A toast. To success. You will soon have your daughter safe from my Hellscape and I will have my favorite lover back in my bed."

Rafe had to drink to that. He refilled his goblet and raised it. Then he drank. That was the last thing he remembered until he woke up in the alley behind N-V. His phone was buzzing in his pocket.

"I've found her." Miguel didn't wait for Rafe to say hello.

"That's good news." Rafe looked around. He had no idea what time it was but the position of the moon told him he had some time before dawn.

"Good and bad. She's in one of the Disney hotels here. A suite. The place is overrun by demons. Hordes. I lost count." Miguel sounded frustrated. "I had to book a suite for us at a hotel down the road."

"That *is* bad news but I'm not surprised. I had a talk with Lucifer. I have command of a few demons myself. If it comes to war, I will call them out." Rafe leaned against Israel Caine's tour bus. He could hear familiar music coming from inside the club. He hadn't lost much time after all. "You really flew, man. Supersonic speed."

"I can do it when motivated. And I *was* motivated." Miguel sighed. "I saw your little girl having dinner in the dining room with her grandmama and demon bodyguards. I would have tried to take her myself but I knew it would scare Daniela. I recognized her from pictures, but she doesn't know me. And, like I said, she was surrounded by demons, fuck, even demon Donald Ducks."

"Lilith has pulled out all the stops." Rafe pushed away from the bus. "Don't do anything until we get there. Lucifer is helping me. He wants Lilith back more than he wants Dani. That's in our favor. I got Dr. Fink off the hook, too."

"That's good news. So you went down there?" Miguel sounded sympathetic. "Must have been a trip."

"It was. I hope I never have to go again. But

I'm afraid…" Rafe rubbed his forehead. There was something he couldn't quite remember.

"Shit, man. I hope you didn't sell your soul for your little girl. You promised your wife you wouldn't go that far. She told Glory about it. The whole thing has Lacy torn up. You don't have to be a mind reader to know that."

Rafe heard the back door open. "Yeah, we both are. Torn up. I don't think I did, Miguel. It was strange down there. Surreal." He wished he knew for sure what he had promised Lucifer. "Let's just say one problem at a time. Got to go. Thanks for taking point on this. I'll touch base when I know more. *Adios.*" He ended the call.

"There you are!" Tomas stepped out of the club. "I've been looking everywhere for you. Caine's set is almost over. I know you want to say a few words to the crowd. They'll expect it."

Rafe put his phone away and followed his brother inside. Obviously, he'd been gone less than two hours. It felt like days. His forehead throbbed and Miguel's question haunted him. Had he sold his soul? The whole visit down below was fuzzy. He'd signed a contract. Yeah. But how could he trust the Devil to honor it? Rafe pushed his way carefully past customers who were having a good time and moved toward the bandstand.

Tomas touched his shoulder and whispered, "He's already done two encores. Get up there and put a stop to this. He looks exhausted and is scheduled to hit Dallas tomorrow."

Rafe nodded and took up a position next to the stage. The song, one of Caine's greatest hits, came to a close and Rafe bounded up to take the microphone as the crowd roared.

"How about that, folks? The amazing Israel Caine!" He embraced Ray and stood back while the singer took a bow then ran off the stage, wiping sweat from his brow as he disappeared into his dressing room. The band followed and the applause soared.

"I know you want more but you can always head to Dallas if you're willing to make the drive. He'll be performing there tomorrow night. Check his website for details." More wild applause and a few "Hell, yeahs!"

"But tonight's not over. Here's Johnny D with more tunes, if you still want to dance, and the bar's open. Keep having fun and come back next week for the incredible…" His mind went blank. Who the hell was scheduled to perform next week? An audience member yelled out the name of the popular female singer and he laughed. "There you go! Just checking to see if you were paying attention. You can make reservations here and on our website. See you next week." He gestured to the disc jockey and a popular rock song blasted from the sound system.

Tomas grabbed his arm as soon as he got off the stage. "Are you okay? You forgot our next headliner?"

"Tired. It's been a long day. Excuse me, I have guests on the balcony, remember?" He shrugged away and walked off. It was rude and he felt bad, but he wanted his friends to know Fink was in the clear. He stopped by the bar but Gordon was gone. That was a relief and meant Lucifer had followed through and called off his henchman. Or had he?

Rafe took the stairs two at a time. To his relief Dr. Fink and his wife were at the table, talking excitedly to the rest of the crew about Israel Caine's performance.

"There he is. Rafe! Thank you so much for this incredible treat." Carly Fink jumped up to give him a hug. "Glory just got a text. We're going down to meet the star in his dressing room and get an autograph. I can't believe it."

"That's right." Glory walked around the table. "Rafe? You okay? You look tired."

"I'm fine. Please take the Finks down to see Ray. I'll stay here and fill in the guys on where I've been. Jerry can tell you later." Rafe shook hands with the doctor. "I'm glad you enjoyed it. Hope that will make you a regular customer. That's why we run these contests."

"Don't worry. We're now customers for life. We've already made reservations for next week. Carly likes Caine but that hot singer next week? She's *my* crush." Howard grinned when Carly socked him on the arm. "Thanks a million."

"No problem." Rafe watched the Finks disappear down the stairs behind Glory then he collapsed in a chair. Jerry, Richard, Flo and Ian stared at him, probably reading his mind. He wished like hell he could block his thoughts like they could.

"You want a drink?" Ian was ready to flag down a waiter.

"No, I had a drink in Hell and I'm pretty sure it was laced with something. I blacked out."

"Rafael." Flo moaned. "I'm so sorry you had to go there." She gripped Richard's hand. "But you got the doctor free. We are so proud of you."

"Yes, well done." Richard looked worried. "But at what cost?"

"Nothing I can't handle. Lucifer is all about getting Lilith down to Hell. If you can believe it, I think he's in love with her. Or obsessed. However you want to categorize it." Rafe did need a drink. Water. He leaned over the railing and caught one of his waiters' eyes. "I need water, Stan. Please toss a bottle up here for me."

"Yes, sir." A cold bottle was soon thrown upstairs and Rafe took a deep drink.

"Good idea, water will help flush out the toxins from whatever you imbibed down there." Ian was studying him like Rafe was in the doctor's office.

Rafe nodded. "Miguel called. He's in Orlando and has spotted Lilith and Dani. She's got a mass of her own demons helping her protect Daniela. The reward for my baby's capture has supposedly been called off. I hope the word is out about that." He took another drink.

"Do we need the jet to fly out there? I can call the pilot right now." Jerry looked at his watch. "Four hours until sunrise and it's a two-hour flight to Orlando. That's too tight to make it and get settled out there. But as long as we get on board before then, the vamps can sleep on the plane, stay there during the day and get going at sunset."

"Yes, let's do that. Miguel has already booked us a suite. Not at Lilith's hotel. She's filled it with her own loyal demons. But nearby."

"This seems hopeless, Rafael." Flo made a face. "How are we going to fight so many?"

"There's something I need to tell you." Rafe drained his water bottle and crushed it in his fist. All eyes were on him. He deliberately let his eyes go red. "I'm a demon, remember?"

"How could we forget? Are you ready to take advantage of that fact? I see it as an asset in this situation." Jerry was always a warrior first. He put both fists on the table. "What weapons do you have at hand? We need to know what will work against Lilith's army."

"What I have are legions of demons at my command." Rafe stood, feeling his body swell with power. He fought it down. He was in public, even if the balcony was fairly private. "Lucifer is adding to that from his own arsenal. Each demon can be lethal. I'm afraid of what this war, and that's what it is, will do to Dani." He turned to Flo. "I know it's sexist, but I want the women with us to try to get to my daughter and protect her from the fighting. Dani will feel safer surrounded by them. Are you okay with that, Flo?"

"I can protect *and* fight, c*apiscime*? But I see what you are saying. Remember, our kind can help your little girl forget what she sees once the battle is won. It will be a kindness." Flo kept gripping Richard's hand. "This is why I never had children. In our world, you never know what dangers you will face. A child at risk like this…"

She waved a hand bedecked with jeweled rings. "I was turned very young and then no longer had the chance… Well, to worry about having my own." She sniffled. "We cannot let anything bad happen to your *bambina*, Rafael."

"Thank you, Flo." Rafe smiled at her. Flo rarely let anyone glimpse her tender heart.

"Contact your pilot, Jerry. I have to call Lacy. She'd never forgive me if I left her out of this. Much as I'd like to. Let's head to the airport. Once we land, Lacy and I can go from the plane to the hotel. I'm sure there will be demons to greet us, but Lucifer has shown me how to raise my own demon army." He walked to the stairs. He'd have to tell his brother to mind the business again.

"We have no time to waste." Ian patted his pockets. "I brought along some of my demon poison and I have more in the car. While you were gone, I created a weapon that should help. It disburses the wisteria oil better than what we had at the cat compound. Something else too." He smiled. "I'm anxious to see it in action."

Rafe smiled. "Excellent. Just don't aim any of it my way."

Ian nodded. "Flo and Richard, need a ride to the airport? Or must you stop and pack?"

"We never unpacked from the last trip. We'll ride with you." Richard was obviously more than ready to go.

"I have to get Glory free of Caine and the Finks. We'll meet you at the airport. Never unpacked either." Jerry smiled. "We're getting your child, Rafe. Don't doubt it."

Rafe put a hand over his eyes, his *red* eyes. He had to calm down before he talked to his brother. Tomas knew it but didn't need a fresh reminder that his brother was a demon.

Rafe took a steadying breath. "Thanks, everyone. I can't say everything that is in my heart or I might bawl like a baby." He felt tears in his eyes anyway. "Shit. You know how I appreciate this, don't you? This could literally be the death of us."

"We've known that from the beginning, Rafe." Richard had his arm around Flo. "Say no more. We've talked it over. Supporting you is the right thing to do. Now let's go. You cry and we're leaving you to shift to Orlando. Pull your shit together and get moving."

Jerry cleared his throat and even Ian punched him on the arm.

Rafe found a smile. "You got it, brother. Okay, I'll make my call then see where I stand with my wife. Meeting everyone at the airport."

"See you on the plane. With food. We tend to forget you and Lacy actually eat." Jerry shoved past him. "Glory is taking too long with that rock star. Bet he's flirting with her again. Asshole."

Rafe grinned and called his wife. God, how he hated to do it. Lacy fighting against demons. It was one of his worst nightmares. But then he had plenty of them. He'd just lived through one down those stairs below a coffee shop.

He felt things were coming to a head. The final battle. If only he could survive that and bring his daughter out safely. He tried to picture it and just couldn't. Lacy's phone was ringing and ringing and ringing. Why wasn't his wife answering?

CHAPTER TWENTY

RAFE HAD NO choice but to go by the house. He had to know why Lacy wasn't answering her phone. He drove like a madman, lucky he didn't get a ticket. It was late, four in the morning, and the cat compound was out of town. The isolation was necessary for the cats to have the freedom to feel comfortable when they shifted. Too bad that, even driving over the speed limit, the drive took precious time Rafe didn't have.

When he got to the gate, it was quiet. Too quiet. No sign of demons hovering. He hoped that meant Lucifer had kept his word and called off the reward. Rafe punched in the security code, not happy there was no guard posted. Maybe that meant the demons had left hours ago and the cats had relaxed, sure the threat was over and their usual security system was adequate. There were few lights on in the compound. One of them was at Sheila's house. He parked in front and opened the door quietly. His boys were bound to be asleep inside, unless something was wrong.

Sheila sat on the couch, a drink in her hand. He could smell from the doorway that it was alcohol, the top shelf Scotch she preferred. She watched him walk in, her gaze not telling him anything.

"Where's my wife? Why isn't she answering her phone?" Rafe stopped himself before he charged toward the bedroom where he and Lacy slept when they visited. He needed answers first.

"She's sleeping. You have any idea how stressed out and exhausted she is?" Sheila gestured. "Sit. You're running on fumes yourself. What good are you going to do her like this?" She finished her drink and set the glass on the table. "When was the last time you had a decent meal, Rafe?"

"I don't have time for this." Rafe stood rigid. He assumed this was Sheila's version of mothering. He'd never had it, didn't need it now.

"Don't be foolish!" Sheila jumped up and grabbed his arm. "You're staggering." She pushed him into her recliner. The very fact that she could do it proved her point. "I'm bringing you a plate and you're going to eat every bite. Do you hear me?"

"Yes. Loud and clear. Now tell me where my wife is." Rafe ran a hand over his eyes. They burned. Yes, with exhaustion. He'd been through Hell, literally, and it had taken a toll. Food would help. He smelled something savory and looked down to see a plate in his lap—roast beef, potatoes, greens of some kind. He picked up a fork and dove in, suddenly starving.

"I just did. She's curled up in your bed, a boy on each side of her. She ate first and demanded I wake her as soon as you called." Sheila picked up a phone off the bar. "I'm sorry I freaked you out.

I admit, I stole her phone from the bedside table in there and shut off the ringer. I wanted her to rest. I needed to talk to you before you dragged her off again."

"You know what I have to do. Dani…" Rafe didn't need to finish his statement. Sheila's eyes had filled. Yes, she knew and hated it. Hated what he was and what it had brought down on them all. "I'm sorry Lacy is part of this. I can go without her. There's a battle coming. She could be hurt."

"I realize that. But she'd never forgive either one of us if you left her here." Sheila took his empty plate away. "You want more?"

"No, but it was delicious, as always. You were right. I needed that. Fuel for what's to come." Rafe leaned forward. "Thanks for taking care of my sons. I know they're safe here, with you. When did the demons leave?"

"A few hours ago. Very suddenly. As if they received a message. Do you know what that was about?" She stared at him.

"I went to see Lucifer. Asked him to take away the reward for Dani's capture. He must have followed through."

"Oh, God, Rafe, what did you do?" Lacy stood in the doorway. She must have heard them talking. She'd always been a light sleeper.

Rafe got up and went to her. He pulled her close and held her then kissed her trembling lips.

"Answer me, Rafe." She stepped back and brushed her hair back from her forehead. She still looked tired, her hair wild. She had on a sleep shirt and was barefoot. She'd never looked more beautiful to him.

"I went down to see if Lucifer would help me get Dani back, baby. I was getting desperate." He jerked her to him again and breathed in her scent, wild and strawberry sweet.

"You didn't give him your soul, did you?" She gave in, holding onto him tightly, as if afraid of his answer.

"I don't think so. But we agreed I'd have to summon all of my demon powers to fight Lilith for our baby girl." He put Lacy away from him and shook his head. "You won't like seeing it. It'll be rough. The vampires are already headed to the airport. I don't suppose you'd agree to stay here."

"I don't suppose I would." She looked at her mother. "Mom, you know I'm going. You'll guard the boys with your life?"

"Of course. I won't waste my breath trying to persuade you to stay. At least the demons trying to get in here left right after you went to bed. Rafe got the Devil to call off the reward for Dani. That should mean we'll be all right here." Sheila took Rafe's empty plate and her glass to the kitchen.

"Good." Lacy still wasn't moving, studying her husband as if worried he was keeping secrets.

"Lucifer wants Lilith, not Dani. That works in our favor. If you're going with me, you need to hurry. Get dressed. My car is outside. You haven't unpacked yet, have you?"

"No, I was too tired." Lacy turned toward the bedroom.

"You still are, honey." Sheila spoke up. "You're flying again, Rafe? Where are you going?"

"We're headed to Orlando in Jerry's private plane. Miguel Cisneros is already there. He saw Dani with Lilith and our daughter looked well. She seemed to be having a great time at a Disney resort." Rafe followed Lacy into the bedroom. His boys were asleep in the king-sized bed. He lowered his voice to a whisper while Lacy stripped off her sleepshirt and ran into the bathroom to brush her teeth and wash her face. Their bags were still near the door and he picked them up. It seemed none of them had bothered to unpack since Houston. They'd all known a showdown was coming and assumed it would be with Lilith in Orlando. She'd made no secret of where she'd taken her granddaughter. Her confidence in her power was that strong.

"I'll put these in the car. Jerry already called the pilot. We're meeting the team at the airport." Rafe strode out with the bags.

Sheila followed him. "Do you need me to send some of the clan with you? I can do that."

Rafe threw the bags in the trunk. He still had wisteria there and a few other things that might upset demons. He turned to face Sheila. It touched him that she was willing to risk some of the werecats for the cause. But then Dani was her grandchild. He thought about it. There wasn't much room in the plane and the vampires weren't crazy about werecats, truth be told.

"Thanks, Sheila. I appreciate the offer, but let them stay here. I don't know what the outcome will be and I'd feel better knowing my boys and you are well protected here." He hugged her. "I promise to do everything I can to bring Dani back safely and settle this once and for all." He forced a smile. "Believe it or not, Lucifer even signed a contract. If I can get Lilith down to Hell for him, Dani will be safe from what he called his Hellscape forever."

Sheila hugged him back then gave him a narrow look. "What else was in this contract, Rafael? Lacy's greatest fear is that you would sacrifice yourself for this."

"I don't think I did." Rafe rubbed his forehead, the buzz of his demon side still there, getting stronger. But his trip to Hell was a little fuzzy. "He drugged me. Not surprising, when you think about it. The Devil and his tricks. But I went down there determined not to sell my soul so I believe I'm in the clear." He looked up to see Lacy staring at him with concern. "I swear, baby, I didn't offer up my soul in exchange for our child. Now let's go."

"I wouldn't be surprised if you did." Lacy climbed into the car after she hugged her mother. "But you promised you wouldn't. If he did drug you, then he can't hold you to anything you might have signed under the influence." She fastened her seatbelt then crossed her arms over her stomach. "I watch a lot of those lawyer shows. I know things."

Rafe surprised himself with a laugh. "Yes, you do. I think you should go to law school when this is over. You're a natural. Totally wasted in a clothing store."

"Well maybe I will. The kind of trouble you and your friends get into, you need a good lawyer on the team." She grinned at him. "I could be it." She brushed her thumb over his lips. "That smile looks good on you. Let's get our girl back and then I want to see much more of it." She stretched to lean over and kiss him. "I love you desperately, you know."

"I love you more." Rafe started the car. "I'll prove it when we get back. You wouldn't believe what I saw in Hell earlier. The Kama Sutra painted on a ceiling. It gave me some ideas…"

"Save them." She rubbed his thigh. "I'll have something to look forward to after the fight." She sighed and leaned back. "Flying again. You know, Miguel isn't the only one who isn't crazy about planes. You should have heard Flo muttering about it." She glanced at Rafe. "Vampires really prefer to shift and take their own wings places. Especially ancient vampires. I think if Flo had had a rosary, she'd have been saying it during the flight from Houston. When we hit that air pocket, she came unglued."

Rafe smiled again. But his amusement was on the surface. Inside, he was trying to figure out how he was going to fight legions of demons. And wondering what his beautiful wife was going to think when he let her see his ugly side, full demon, calling up his own hideous legions. Would she still want to make love to a man who could grow horns and a tail?

When Rafe and Lacy arrived at the plane, Ian was waiting at the bottom of the steps. He had a look on his face that warned Rafe things weren't right. It was tempting to send Lacy inside and spare her, but, after years of marriage, he knew better.

"What's up?" Rafe scanned the tarmac and took a whiff. "Demons on our trail. Lilith has spies. She knows we're on our way to confront her."

"Yeah. I'm tempted to put my new weapon to work. As a test. What do you think?" Ian reached for a duffle bag at his feet. He drew out a weapon that looked like something from a sci-fi movie. It was the size of a tablet but had been fitted with four small speakers on brackets that could rotate. Ian got busy adjusting them. He was aiming at an area in front of him.

"What does it do?" Rafe held out his hand. He'd expected some kind of water cannon. This wasn't it. It was actually awkward to hold and he quickly handed it back. It had a small keyboard that Ian began punching numbers into.

"This sucker will emit a high-pitched sound that will bring those assholes to their knees. It's not a new concept. But it will temporarily immobilize them so you can finish them with holy water or wisteria. What do you think? I've got extra-strength earplugs for all of us." Ian handed Lacy and Rafe ear plugs and waited to put a pair in his own ears. "This is a crude version. I promise I will eventually get it into a more sophisticated case but we were in a hurry. Shall we give it a try?"

"Let me get out my water gun." Rafe pulled out two of the pistols and handed one to his wife. Her satisfied grin helped soothe the knot in his stomach. Yeah, she'd come to fight and he had to get used to the idea. "Give me a moment to pinpoint our spies. Earlier, I saw some of Lilith's demons at Sheila's house. Insects, very tiny. Even bees." Rafe glanced at the plane. "Should we warn the others?"

"The sound won't reach them. It's directional." Ian frowned "I'm working on it. Trying to get the frequency just right as well. Demons are… well, they're not human." He shrugged. "The army has been using shit like this for years in combat to immobilize the enemy, but making this fit our circumstances was a challenge."

"Hey, I appreciate it." Rafe hid his gun under his shirt as he strolled around the plane, like he was checking the wheels, the undercarriage. As if he knew beans about planes. He finally spotted a small swarm of gnats hovering behind the trash can in front of the building that housed the waiting room. Gnats? Not when the odor of demon was a hell of a lot stronger there. Had her spies already reported that Rafe was on his way to Orlando? Maybe so, but he wasn't going to miss this chance to take out some of Lilith's followers.

"I see them. Let's move." Ian stuck in his ear plugs, then ran toward the can. Rafe and Lacy plugged their own ears, ready for whatever came next.

As soon as Rafe pulled his gun, the gnats began to change, morphing into monsters and flying in a dozen different directions. They were hideous, with claws, fangs and scales in different shapes and colors. It would be impossible to hit all of them with the wisteria as they disbursed. But one blast from Ian's ray gun—and that's what Rafe was calling it—and they suddenly dropped to the ground, every one of them, helpless and unmoving.

Screams came from the people inside the building. Lacy frowned but didn't stop spraying those revolting bodies where they'd fallen. Rafe was there, too, making sure they didn't miss any of the creatures.

A man staggered out of the building. He held his hands over his ears, blood trickling from them. "My God! What was that sound?"

"Field test of an early warning system. Did you know it's hurricane season?" Ian took the man's arm and led him back inside. "I'm a doctor. Let me take a look at your ears."

Lacy was breathing fast as she stomped closer to the pile of pests, pulling out her ear plugs. "Think these monsters can come back from this?"

"Doubt it." Rafe kicked at the shriveled remains, tucking his own ear plugs into his pocket. No movement. In her zeal, his wife had saturated them. Poor bastards. "I think you drowned them, baby." He slung his arm over her shoulder. "You definitely annihilated them. Excellent work."

"Good." She turned toward the building. "I hope no one inside was seriously hurt. Or was looking out the window when we did our thing. I guess bleeding ears is what you call collateral damage."

"Yes. It's something to think about." Rafe walked her to the plane. "We need to go."

Ian exited the building, talking fast to another man who had tissues stuck in his ears. "A few drops of aloe or lidocaine should do the trick. Or sleep on a heating pad. Sorry about that. I'll mention you in my report. Your country thanks you." He shook the man's hand then walked toward them.

"How'd we do?" He glanced at the pile of black debris lying in a pool of liquid. "I hope we don't run out of wisteria. I'm guessing the sound waves might have been enough to kill them, but now I'll never know."

"Sorry, Ian, I got a little carried away." Lacy flushed. "I'll do better next time."

"You got them, that's all that counts." Ian grinned. "It worked. Sorry about the mortals. Luckily there were only two inside waiting for a pilot. I erased their memories in case they saw anything then I did some fast talking. They think they were in a NASA experiment." He chuckled then frowned down at his weapon. "Give me more time and I can put this in a case like a cell phone. Definitely make it appear more high tech. I hate how crude this looks."

"No, it's brilliant. Thanks for dreaming it up." Rafe helped Lacy up the steps. "I'll let the pilot know we're all aboard now."

It was almost sunrise by the time the plane finally took off for Orlando. The two vampire couples retired to the double beds in back of the plane while Ian MacDonald volunteered to sleep on the floor between the two beds.

"I've certainly spent many a day in worse circumstances. Beats burying myself in the earth." He made a big deal out of locking the door, reminding Rafe to wait for them before taking on Lilith.

Lacy stretched out on the couch near the bathroom, still trying to catch up on her own sleep.

When Abe suddenly appeared in the seat next to him, Rafe shut his laptop. He'd studied the layout at the theme park and the hotel where Lilith was staying. There wasn't much more he could do until they landed in a couple of hours. He had a long day ahead of him before his vampire team would be awake and ready to help. He hadn't needed Ian's warning to wait. He wasn't about to start something until they were all together in top form.

"Back to offer some moral support?"

"I wish I could offer more than that." Abe stared at the food arrayed on a tray in the galley.

"Please, eat. Lacy and I had something at her mother's house." Rafe smiled when Abe snagged a brownie. "Tell me about yourself. You look young. What's your story?"

"I *was* young when I met my end." Abe looked blissful as he took a bite. "Brownies. Delicious. Anyway, I was but seventeen when I took my vows. I always had a calling and my family was poor. It was a blessing that the church could provide for me."

"Where are you from? You don't seem to have an accent." Rafe gave in and took a brownie for himself. They *were* delicious.

"Why thank you, I worked hard to lose it." He cleared his throat and then spoke in a thick brogue.

"What did you just say?" Rafe hadn't understood a word.

"That was the old language. Gaelic. I was from the north of Scotland. We were raided by Vikings and I was killed not long after I entered the monastery. I'd barely reached the age of ten and eight, eighteen you'd say." Abe looked sad. "Our entire village was slaughtered. My mother, father, brothers. The Vikings carried my sisters and other young women off to their land. At the time, I could only imagine their fates. I was sure Lucifer had a place in Hell for those heathens." He muttered a prayer and crossed himself.

"I'm sure he does." Rafe shook his head. "I'm sorry. But you landed in Heaven and took a vow of service?"

"Yes. I was filled with rage, hungry for revenge. I wanted to see every Viking wiped from the face of the earth." He took a big bite of the brownie and chewed fast. "It took me a long while to realize that was a waste of energy. I could do good instead." He sighed. "Our Father let me see what happened to my sisters. They found husbands who loved them and had many children. Their fates were not so bad."

"So the Vikings weren't all monsters." Rafe thought about that. It was so easy to paint villains as totally evil. Just as thinking all demons were surely irredeemable. He shuddered. He hoped not.

"A plague had taken most of their women and they were desperate to replace them." Abe stared at his lap, covered in crumbs. "But how they did it was wrong!" He covered his eyes. "I will never understand His ways, never."

"Nor will I." Rafe put his hand on Abe's shoulder. "To wipe out entire villages…"

"After all these centuries, I am still learning forgiveness." Abe took another brownie. He finally met Rafe's gaze. "But Heaven can be a wondrous place, Rafael. I know you have seen and walked through Hell. God willing, perhaps someday you will see Heaven. I can call upon my dear mother and father there. My brothers. My sisters too when it was their time. They never age and they live full and happy lives. After all these many years." Abe's eyes were shining. "So you see? I never lost them at all."

"I wish I had that kind of faith." Rafe looked back at his wife. She'd fallen asleep again. Lacy looked so peaceful. She had faith. Whether Abe would approve of the kind of worship the werecats did, he didn't know. It included pagan rituals, holdovers from an earlier time. He felt the warmth of Abe's hand on his shoulder again.

"God doesn't care how you worship, only that you are a good and loving man. He doesn't even care what you call him. Buddha, Krishna, oh, there are many names for the Light upstairs who watches over us all." Abe seemed surrounded by light now, as he sat in that leather seat, covered in chocolate crumbs. "Trust that you are doing the right thing, my son. Fight evil with your own decency and you will win."

Rafe shook his head then realized he was alone. Had he dreamed that visit? Was Abe a ghost, an angel or something more? He leaned back and closed his eyes. Heaven. Who would he like to meet there? His stern grandfather who had tried to beat the demon out of him? Matias had only done his best for the boy he'd never understood. There had been others in his life who had come and gone. Mentors, lovers, dear friends. He'd even had a dog who had been a good and loyal companion for more than a decade. Would he see him again someday? He let himself drift into a dream state until the pilot came over the intercom and announced they were approaching Orlando.

Rafe had spent so many years protecting others, it was second nature to him. Now he was already thinking ahead, figuring out how he could get to Dani and protect her. From her own grandmother. How sad was that?

CHAPTER TWENTY-ONE

"YOUR FRIEND WAS lucky to get the rooms." The clerk handed over two keys with a smile.

"Guess so." Rafe had already noticed the Disney complex was crawling with tourists…and demons. He wasn't even at the park. It was down the road a few miles.

"Mr. Cisneros took over the entire top floor. He said you have a group of friends coming." The clerk leaned over the counter, like he had a secret. "We had a last-minute cancellation. Wedding party. Groom got caught in bed with the maid of honor. What a mess. There were a few things broken in there, but your friend didn't seem to care that we have some missing lamps and mismatched tables in the living room. I'm afraid you might smell fresh paint and carpet shampoo. But we tried to make things look good and offered a discount."

"Sounds fine. We're not picky. Put it on my credit card, not the one Cisneros gave you." Rafe passed it over then slung an arm around Lacy. He improvised a story on the spot. "We invited a few other couples to celebrate our anniversary. We were married here ourselves, ten years ago this weekend." He felt Lacy lean into him. He looked down at his love. It *had* been ten years since he'd met her. A lucky day when she'd decided to put up with him and his baggage. He dropped a kiss on her parted lips.

"This celebration was a last-minute thing. Left the kids home with Grandma and they're pouting, but they'll get their own trip later. We wanted some adult fun and to let our inner child out." He winked as he tucked his card back in his wallet. "Know what I mean?"

The clerk nodded. "See it all the time. Bring the kiddos back at Christmas. Weather's cool and they'll have a ball. Rates are good then too."

"I like it. We couldn't believe it when Miguel texted us the details about these rooms. This will be perfect." Lacy was purring as she rubbed against Rafe. "Our friends will be here tonight. Send them right up, please." She glanced at the clerk's name tag. "Paul. I'm really sorry to hear about that cancellation, though. I'd call that a near miss for the bride." She gazed up at Rafe. "If her man was fooling around with her best friend…" Her smile was feral. "I hope he lives to regret that."

"I'm sure he already does. I think there was a lot of alcohol involved. He looked pretty hung over when he checked out and you should have seen the black eye he was sporting." Paul shook his head. "The sap had left his credit card for the bill and the hotel stuck it to him good for the damage. The repairs had just been finished when Mr. Cisneros showed up looking for rooms."

Rafe slapped the counter. "You won't have to worry about us. We're spending most of our time at the park. My lady loves a good ride." He winked and Lacy flushed when the clerk snickered.

"I'll have a bellman bring up your luggage right away." Paul pointed toward the concierge desk. "You can get discount passes for the park over there. A shuttle leaves the front door every fifteen minutes. Summer hours so the park is open until midnight. Have fun!" He turned toward the next customer in line.

"Wow! I don't believe we have the entire top floor!" Lacy laughed and threw her tote on top of all the luggage that had been unloaded from an Uber van they'd taken from the private airport.

"Yes, ma'am. It includes the honeymoon suite." A bellman in uniform, pushing that luggage cart, escorted them to the elevator and got them to their floor, chatting all the way about the amenities in the hotel.

Lacy clung to Rafe, acting like this *would* be a second honeymoon. When they got to the suite, there was a "Do Not Disturb" sign hanging on the door.

"Um, what should we do?" The bellman waited for instructions.

Rafe used his key and threw open the door. "You said there are several bedrooms included. Our friend got here first and is a night owl. I'm sure he is sleeping late. We'll be quiet and try not to disturb him. I'll bet he saved us the honeymoon suite. For now, put everything in the living room and we'll sort out the luggage when he wakes up." Yes, the rooms had that honeymoon vibe, with red roses in a vase on a glass coffee table, champagne chilling in a silver cooler and chocolates in a heart-shaped bowl. There was a big screen TV at one end next to a wet bar and mini bar that wasn't so mini. The faint scent of fresh paint and carpet cleaner made Rafe wrinkle his nose. He walked over to slide open the doors to the balcony that ran the length of the massive room.

"I guess the desk clerk explained that we just did some repairs in here. Sorry about the smell." The bellman began unloading the luggage. They'd brought everyone's things in case the vampires decided to shift from the airport. "It should be fine after you air it out a few hours." He pointed out several amenities, including a small kitchen behind the bar.

"Here we go, baby. Honeymoon heaven." Rose petals were strewn on the pale pink carpet leading to double doors of what was obviously intended for the newlyweds. Rafe pulled Lacy closer for the bellman's benefit and opened the doors as the man piled the luggage in the center of the living room. The king-sized bed was empty and unused. No way would a single man have staked a claim to this layout. There were several other closed doors leading from the massive living room. He figured Miguel was dead in one of those.

Soon, the bellman was gone, happy with

a generous tip. Rafe put their bags in the honeymoon suite.

"Oh my God, look at this!" Lacy walked into a decadent bathroom. "And all I can think about is our little girl in that woman's clutches, surrounded by demons."

Rafe put his arms around her. "I know, baby. Think positive. If all goes right, we'll get Lilith down to Hell then return here to celebrate." He gave Lacy a kiss that was a promise of things to come. It was a waste of effort. She was stiff in his arms, as if she knew his heart wasn't in it.

Lacy pushed him away and sighed. "Yeah, right. Honeymoon? With Dani in the bed with us? That's the *best* case scenario. God, Rafe, I'm terrified we'll lose this fight."

"So am I. Let's get on that shuttle and see if we can spot my mother and Dani. Miguel texted me the name of their hotel." Rafe stuck the keycard in his pocket and pulled his wife out of the room. They had hours before the vampires would wake up. Might as well do some reconnaissance.

They bought their discount park tickets then caught that shuttle. His credit card was getting a workout. It was a good thing the Caine concert had been such a success. He needed to give Tomas a bonus for handling the bar so well in his absence. If he didn't survive this confrontation with Lilith… Well, he couldn't think that way, he just couldn't.

Rafe realized how lucky Miguel had been to find rooms available so close to the theme park. There were crowds everywhere. It was the end of

summer vacation and hot as hell. Well, not really.
Rafe now knew just how hot Hell could be. He
hoped he never had to experience *that* again.

There were long lines at the rides, demons
mixed in with mortals and their children. The
sight of happy demons screaming and laughing as
they rode thrill rides, got drenched riding water
slides or flew overhead in a gondola reminded
Rafe that even those creatures who served Lucifer
or Lilith had feelings of fear, surprise or even joy.
Something to think about.

They got off the shuttle in front of the hotel
where he knew Lilith and Dani were staying. It
was five star and exactly what he'd have expected
of his picky mother. What wasn't expected was
the pervasive scent of demons thick in the air
as they walked into the lobby. A restaurant with
waiters and waitresses dressed as Disney characters
was right off the entrance. At least those workers
were mortal. Since it was lunch time, he and Lacy
stepped inside to look around.

"Mama! Daddy!" The shriek of joy turned
diners' heads. Daniela had been enjoying a meal
and had spotted them in the doorway.

Rafe bumped into Lacy when two small arms
wrapped around his legs. He lifted his daughter
and kissed her cheeks, breathing in her unique
scent of kitten, demon and sweet child. His eyes
filled and he blinked them clear. Dani leaned over
to grab Lacy's shoulder and got a kiss from her
mother too. He looked up. A man and a woman
stepped close behind Dani.

"Who's this?" Demons, he knew that instantly.

"Buster and Bessie." Dani giggled. "I know you don't recognize them, Daddy." She wiggled to get down. "They can *change*."

Rafe wasn't about to let go of her. What would happen if he made a run for it? A hand gripped his arm, warning him to forget it.

"Stay here, Dani. I've missed you." He hugged her close. "Yes, I can see that now. Buster and Bessie. You're right. They don't look the same as the last time I saw them." Lizard and dragon. Shifters. Son of a bitch. "Where's your grandmother?"

"She's in a meeting." Buster still held his arm. He now stood about seven feet tall and had dark hair and rough, almost scaly, skin, He had a lean look and yellow eyes. His split tongue flickered from thin lips. "Put her down. We're taking care of her for Lilith." "Lilith" came out as a hiss.

"I'm her father. I can take care of her." Rafe took a chance and tried to jerk free. That earned him a grip so crushing he was sure he'd wear bruises on his arm.

"Right now she's *our* responsibility." Bessie's eyes went red and Rafe felt a blast of electricity run from his hair to his toes. Damn if she hadn't given him a jolt. She was a stocky woman, solid but attractive in a bright colorful print dress that swished around her muscular legs. He didn't doubt she could hurt him with more than a blast of her demon energy.

"Dani, you didn't feel a shock, did you?" He handed her off to Lacy. Two could play that game. He let his own eyes heat.

"No, Daddy. Bessie won't hurt me. She and

Buster are my friends! Please don't make them mad. Or Lollie. They love me." Dani pushed at Lacy and finally slid down to the ground. "I have to be a good girl, though, if I want to go to Cinderella's Castle tonight."

"Mama and I will take you anywhere you want to go." Rafe was suddenly aware of the people surrounding them. People? If only. There wasn't a mortal among the crowd of half a dozen creatures moving in close. The two had backup.

"Lilith will be here in a moment. Step into the dining room, Mr. Valdez. I'm sure you would enjoy the chef's special." Buster gestured toward a table in the corner, away from the other diners. "Your wife will love it. Grilled halibut. I hear her kind is very fond of fish." Another hiss.

Rafe wanted to deck the lizard. *Her kind?* Asshole. But they were surrounded. Not only by demons, but there were families of mortals everywhere, with lots of children chattering happily. Damn it. Innocent bystanders. Dani took his hand and led him toward the table. He could see that she had her own fish sandwich wrapped in colorful paper and a cone of fries being set down at her place by a waitress dressed as Daisy Duck. Balloons made the table festive.

"Mama, please have lunch with us. The fish here is yummy." Dani's eyes pleaded with them to behave and play along. "Look. Daisy Duck is our waitress. Quack." The waitress happily quacked back and brought two more menus. She recited the specials, staying in character, with her duck talk and a waddle that would have been charming if Rafe hadn't wanted to throw fire balls at the two demons who settled at the table across from them, bracketing his daughter.

He and Lacy quickly ordered then focused on their child. "Tell us what you've been doing here, sweetheart. Have you had fun?" Rafe sat back, watching Dani's glowing face while still trying to figure out if there was a way to spirit her out of here before Lilith appeared.

Dani began telling them all about the rides she'd been on and the souvenirs her grandmother had bought for her. It seemed she was being spoiled rotten.

"I have mouse ears in three colors and the t-shirts to match." Dani hopped out of her chair. "Here comes Lollie." She ran to grab her grandmother's hand to tug her to the table. "Look, Lollie. Mama and Daddy came to Orlando. Can they go with us to Cinderella's Castle tonight?" She gazed up at Lilith adoringly.

Rafe felt like he'd been punched in the stomach. His daughter was totally under his mother's spell. As he watched, Lilith bent down to straighten the bows on Dani's pigtails. They were pink polka dot ribbon and matched her tennis shoes. Then his mother cast a glance in his direction.

"I don't know, Daniela. We have reservations. Front row seats. They were very hard to come by. The event is sold out." Lilith straightened and took the chair Buster had been in. He stood behind her, the picture of an alert bodyguard. He kept his hands behind his back. His dark suit was fine Italian, with a telltale bulge where he must keep a gun.

"Maybe Bessie and Buster can stay here and Mama and Daddy can take their seats." Dani gave Lilith a pleading look. "What do you think?"

"And miss seeing Cinderella dance with the handsome prince?" Bessie looked horrified. "Dani, I told you how much I love that story. I read it to you last night. I've been looking forward to seeing it."

"But I want Mama and Daddy to come!" Dani's eyes flashed red.

"Daniela!" Lacy was now the one to look horrified. "I don't like your behavior. We don't treat people this way."

Dani's eyes welled. "I'm sorry, Bessie."

"Nonsense. Bessie and Buster work for me. They do as they are told. Dani understands that, don't you, sweetheart?" Lilith's smile could cause a snow storm in the Sahara. "If I want to give their tickets away, I will."

Dani's eyes lit up. "Really? So Mama and Daddy can come with us?"

Lilith turned that icy smile on Rafe. "That depends. Your father and I have to talk first. He's not happy with me and my arrangements for your future. If we can come to an agreement, then of course we can have a lovely family outing tonight."

"Daniela, you're not being fair to Bessie and Buster." Lacy ignored Lilith. "I don't like the way you're treating them. It doesn't matter if they are working for your grandmother or not. A promise is a promise. You are being rude."

Bessie was shaking her head. "Don't give it another thought, Mrs. Valdez. Lilith is our boss and we are here to serve her. She's told us that our first concern is always to keep Dani safe." She smiled at Buster. "I'm sure she'll be safe with her parents, isn't that right, Buster?"

"Is it? Lilith?" Buster waited until Lilith turned to stare at him. "That's what you said. Keep the kid safe. Are you satisfied with this arrangement? There will be two of them, one of you."

"So?" She gave Buster a look that made him move closer to Bessie. "I didn't bring you two along to enjoy Disney entertainment. You're my granddaughter's bodyguards. Of course, I can take care of Daniela." She waved a manicured finger and the air crackled. "Tonight, I won't need you. If I change my mind after my visit with Rafael, I'll let you know."

"Got it." Buster nodded. "I guess if anyone can keep her safe, you can, boss lady."

"Exactly. The play starts at eight. A little late for Dani, but she can take a nap this afternoon."

"I'm too big for naps." Dani whined.

"No, you're not." Lacy and Rafe both said it.

"Eat your lunch." Rafe wasn't happy with his daughter's attitude. She was showing signs of having been so indulged she was turning into a brat. He wasn't having it.

His own lunch arrived and he ate every bite, knowing his mother was paying for it. If it wouldn't have made the meal last too long, he would have ordered dessert. The food proved to be delicious. Points for a Disney hotel. After all, he would need his strength for what was coming. Not only was he going to have to figure out how to get his daughter home safely, but he was going to have to outsmart Lilith.

After they finished, a protesting Dani was taken away by Bessie and Buster. To Rafe's disgust, she was promised a trip to the gift shop before her nap. Bessie whispered that she'd seen pink princess shoes to match Dani's dress for tonight. His daughter barely spared her parents a wave as she danced away, her hand in the dragon's.

Lilith signaled that Rafe and Lacy were to follow her to a nearby meeting room. It boggled his mind how much this trip was costing her. Everywhere he looked, he saw demons that almost bowed when they saw his mother coming. She barely acknowledged them. The demons didn't love Lilith. It was obvious they feared her.

The conference room was a generic meeting room with a long table and chairs around it. A hulking man appeared to guard the door as Lilith led them into it.

"We don't want to be disturbed," Lilith commanded. "Sit, you two. Rafael, I want to know what you and Lucifer have cooked up between you."

Rafe helped Lacy into a chair. Did his mother really think he was going to tell her his plans? He decided to give her just enough information to satisfy her.

"I think Luc is in love with you."

Lilith laughed so hard she almost fell off her chair. "Love? I didn't know you were so delusional. Lucifer has no idea what love is. Unless it is love for an object he wishes to own. Or his love for the pursuit of something he wants. Yes, he loves games. Lust? Oh, I don't doubt he is very much in lust with me." She blotted her tears of mirth with a handkerchief that had materialized from her bodice. She wore a slim fitted dress of blue silk. It made the most of her figure and had a relatively modest neckline. Suitable for a grandmother, Rafe supposed.

"He has a room with scenes from the Kama Sutra painted on the ceiling. You are pictured as the woman, he is the man. They are very erotic."

"I'm sure they are." She got up and began to pace the room. "Luc always knew how to stir me. Bastard. I would like to see that room." She stopped and gazed at Rafe. "I'm sure it embarrassed you. Seeing your mother naked. I *was* naked, wasn't I?"

"Oh, yes. So was he. Quite a stallion, isn't he?"

Lacy gasped and pinched Rafe's leg.

Lilith laughed then sighed. "Yes, indeed. I've never had a better lover. But the downside of consorting with the Devil…" She looked down at her expensive designer shoes. "I'm sure you got a taste of that when you met with him."

"Mother, he is determined to have you. He's obsessed." Rafe stood and walked over to her. "Are you really going to make me lose my daughter to avoid him?"

She stared at him for a long moment. Finally,

she shook her head. "I can not go down there again, Rafael. If there is no other way to avoid living in Hell again, then so be it."

"And I can not sacrifice my daughter." He pulled Lacy to her feet. "So it will be war between us."

"War." She nodded and threw open the door. "Come back in time for the Cinderella play. It may well be the last time you see your daughter."

"Or the last time *you* see your granddaughter." Rafe led Lacy out of the hotel and hopped on a shuttle to their own rooms. War. He shuddered. He still had a few hours until sunset. What could he do to prepare? Was this hopeless? Even if he called up his legions of demons, he knew they were no match for the numbers he had seen already.

"Rafe, I can't stand this. War?" Lacy held his hand as they rode the tram. "Now we're on our way to the Honeymoon Suite. Damn it, I want our kitten back and to make love, not war."

Rafe now had that phrase in his head. *Make love not war.* Was there any way to make that happen? Demons had feelings, strong feelings. At least he did. He'd seen Buster and Bessie exchange looks. They were clearly a couple. Love? Maybe. They'd also been hurt by Lilith's attitude, their feelings so easily dismissed. He could see they cared for Dani. She wasn't just a job for them. An idea began to tickle his mind.

When they arrived back in their rooms, Rafe rummaged through Flo's Louis Vuitton suitcases piled together.

"What are you doing, Rafe?" Lacy watched him zip open Flo's tote.

"I'm looking for something. I don't think Flo has had a chance to unpack since New Orleans." He found the small vial he was looking for and held it up. "Here. Put just a drop of this on your throat."

"Is that what I think it is? Are you crazy? I'm not in the mood…" Lacy just shook her head. Once Rafe pulled out the stopper, she dabbed her fingertip on it, sniffed then put a tiny dot on her throat. "Oh, it does smell nice. And…" She gave Rafe a heavy-lidded look. "You are looking really good to me, lover."

Rafe leaned in to inhale that scent. "Oh, yeah, baby." He picked her up and threw her over his shoulder. Damn but the potion worked, He didn't have time for this, but he couldn't help himself. He'd been talking about that painted ceiling. All those sexual positions… Shit, he had one in mind that he and Lacy had never tried. He threw her on the bed, turned her away from him, on her side, and jerked down her panties. Her short skirt was already above her waist. He kicked away his jeans next.

"Please, I need you." She moaned and raised one knee, giving him room to slide between her thighs. She was already wet, eager, and helped him find his way home. "Rafe!" Her scream could have waked up dead Miguel if that were possible. "Oh, yes!"

Rafe started moving, almost manic as he breathed in the aroma of that love potion, heated by her damp neck. Lacy reached back for him, squeezing his balls until he was the one crying out. They took each other, letting the wild animals inside them loose, desperate to mate. He hoped like hell they weren't making another baby. Not another demon. He'd already been careless once. But he lost that thought as he pressed against her, wanting, needing to have her. He drove inside her, one hand under her tank top squeezing her breast. He couldn't stop until her shuddering release gripped him and dragged his own from him. No, he shouldn't … but she held him between her legs with all the strength she had and the intensity was too much, irresistible.

"I love you." They both screamed it, in a frenzy, as they kept plunging together. They were lost, out of themselves and this room. Somewhere so private they vowed to never speak of this again. Breathing raggedly, Rafe held her tight, kissing the side of her neck. He worshipped her, his love.

Lacy clutched him wherever she could get purchase and whispered his name like a prayer.

Gods. Yes, they were seeing stars and the heavens. Until they fell back to earth on a pillowtop mattress in the honeymoon suite. Spent. Glad they had found this with each other. The potion… One tiny drop had done this.

When Rafe finally found breath, he knew he had something, an idea that might work. He slipped from her and lay back to stare at the ceiling. "I know what we have to do."

"Yes." Lacy smiled at him. "We need a witch. And I think I know where to find one."

CHAPTER TWENTY-TWO

IT TOOK SOME phone calls, one of them heated, before there was a knock on the door. Rafe couldn't believe it was still daylight outside, though the sun was about to hit the horizon. Summer hours were killer for his vampire friends. He really would have liked to run his plan by the fanged ones before this went any further. Too late now.

He opened the door to a woman who glared at him, then pushed past to embrace Lacy. She kissed his wife on both cheeks in the European manner then set down a huge woven basket with a sigh. She was shapely and dressed like a typical Disney tourist, in shorts and a bright red vee-necked t-shirt. If the shirt hadn't featured a black cat on a broomstick, you'd never know you were looking at a werecat who was also the head of the local coven of witches.

"Auntie Lena, I can't thank you enough for coming so quickly." Lacy flushed and cast furtive glances at Rafe. They were both still feeling that love potion. A shower had just made things worse. They'd ended up entangled and hitting the tile walls hard before they'd finally switched to cold water and forced themselves to get dressed.

Lena Aragon smirked and unwound a colorful scarf from around her hair. That let loose blond curls that crackled around her head with a life of their own. "I see you two tested the potion you already had. I'd say it was a wise idea, but you're obviously still suffering the effects." She waved a beringed hand at them to sit then settled into an arm chair. "Try to breathe through it. You won't be able to relieve that itch that's driving you crazy while I'm here." She shook her head. "You said this was urgent, Lacy."

"Yes, it is!" She pulled Rafe down beside her on the couch then swatted away Rafe's hand on her thigh. "This is my husband, Rafael Valdez."

He hadn't realized he'd started groping her under her dress. "I'm breathing. I hope that helps. Thanks for coming." He stuck his hand between his legs then realized he was already sporting another obvious erection. Damn, that stuff was strong. Lacy frowned and dropped a throw pillow in his lap.

"Please, Auntie, like I told you, we're desperate." Lacy gripped Rafe's hand which had landed on her leg again. "We have to get our daughter back. I know Mama told you our situation."

Lena stared at them, her golden eyes narrowed. "Your situation, kitty girl, is because you married a demon. You cannot know how I regret that for you."

Rafe had no defense against such an obvious truth. "I realize this hasn't done anything to repair the rift between your clans. I'm sorry for that. I'm only half demon, if that helps." Lacy had filled him in on the problems between the Orlando cats and the Austin clan while they'd waited for the results of the phone calls. It was not something she'd talked about before. Lena and Sheila were sisters in a powerful family of werecats. But they'd had different ideas about how to run their families. When Lena had felt called to become a witch, Sheila had left Florida and taken her own loyal followers to Texas. Now that Sheila's daughter had hooked up with a demon, Lacy was afraid Lena was gloating over the fact that Sheila had called for help.

Lena laughed. "Even a drop of demon blood is too much. Isn't what happened with your Daniela proof of that?"

"What's done is done and I love him!" Lacy jumped to her feet. "Are you going to help us or not? I'm prepared to beg if that will make you happy." Her eyes filled with tears.

"No, I'm not that mean, child. Sit back down. Honestly, I was glad Sheila reached out. It's been too long since we've talked." Lena pulled a pair of red rhinestone-studded reading glasses from her basket. "Now let me see what you have from New Orleans. I can smell it on you. Faintly." She frowned and nodded at Lacy's damp hair. "I know you tried to wash it off but it's still there so it must be very potent."

"Yes, we did try to scrub it off." Lacy glanced at Rafe.

"We're meeting my mother and Daniela in an

hour. We sure didn't want to show up reeking of that stuff." Rafe felt compelled to explain to a woman he'd just met. It was damned embarrassing.

"Sheila claimed your mother is Lilith, a very powerful demon." When Rafe nodded, Lena's eyes widened. But there was no look of horror. Instead, she tapped her chin. "Well, I can see why you're so worried. Let me look at that vial."

Rafe dug it out of his pocket. He hated the way his wife was having to beg for help, but what choice did they have? If there was any chance this could work, they had to try it.

Lena's nose wrinkled. "There are many different ways to stir the appetites. I've made love potions for a few desperate individuals. But none that smell like yours." She clicked her fingers. "Come. Hand it over. What are you waiting for?"

Rafe gave it to Lena then got up when he heard a sudden noise from the balcony. They'd kept the doors open because of the lingering paint smell. Yes, the sun had finally set and he saw four of his friends land on the long concrete balcony. He had texted them the arrangements and they'd apparently had no problem finding the rooms.

"What is this? You are giving that woman my love potion?" Flo stomped into the room, reaching out for the vial Lena was carefully inspecting. Then Flo stopped, frowned and turned on Lacy and Rafe. "I smell it on you! I can't believe you went through my luggage while I was dead to the world. You helped yourself?" She sniffed Rafe, then Lacy, like a dog on the hunt. "Oh, you have been making love all afternoon!" She stomped her foot so hard her heel broke. A spate of Italian swear words filled the air.

"Darling, calm yourself. I'm sure Rafe had a good reason…" Richard tried to take Flo's hand but she swatted at him.

"I was saving it for later. Ricardo and I tried a bit once and found it *divertente*. Am I right?" She turned to her husband, taking off the broken shoe and actually throwing it across the room. More Italian. The other shoe followed.

Rafe was glad she hadn't aimed the stilettos at his head. "Richard is right. Lacy and I weren't just playing, Flo." Rafe put himself between Lena and the Italian firecracker when it looked like Flo was going to lunge for the vial. "We were doing research."

"Is that what we're calling it now?" Richard laughed and finally managed to put his arm around his wife. "When you've been married a few years, it's not a bad idea to shake things up once in a while."

Now Flo wheeled on him. "Are you saying you are bored with our bed play, Ricardo?"

He looked alarmed. "No, did I say that?" He pressed a hand to his forehead. "It's the heat. Flying in the heat has made me lose my mind. My darling, I could never be bored with you."

Rafe knew that was right. "Relax, you two. Sit and let me tell you what I'm thinking about the love potion. We're weaponizing it. I promise, Flo, you'll get more when we're done, even if I have to go back to New Orleans and find another witch to make you some." He walked over to pick up the broken shoe. "I owe you a pair of shoes too. This brand. I promise." He ignored Lacy's hiss that they were very expensive. "Now I hope you will sit and listen. This was Lacy's idea. Please let me introduce her aunt Lena Aragon from the local werecat clan. She is Sheila's sister."

"Really." Ian had just landed on the balcony. "I can see the resemblance, she has the same beauty." He walked inside and took Lena's hand, bowing and kissing it as if he was back in the king's court. "Charmed to meet you. I am Ian MacDonald, your sister's lover."

Lacy moaned while Lena quickly capped the vial of love potion and stuffed it between her generous breasts. She looked Ian over and smiled.

"Oh, really. How nice to meet you, Ian. Though I have to admit being surrounded by vampires makes me want to work up a protection spell. Rafael, you'd better tell them your plan before the little Italian attacks me. I would like to get started analyzing this potion."

"Analyzing?" Flo moved closer and suddenly snatched the vial from Lena's cleavage before that lady could blink. "Careful or I'll show you this little vampire's big powers." She slid the vial between her own abundant breasts. "I'm quick too. Did you notice?" She smiled in satisfaction. "Now what do you mean? Are you going to try to make more?"

"Yes, Flo, that's why she's here. Please calm down and give it back to her." Rafe got between the women. Lena's claws were out and her hair waved in the air as if she were Medusa and the curls might have a power of their own. "Lena, do you think you can make something like it?" Rafe needed to know that before this discussion went any further.

"I believe so. You know I came here to do my dear niece a favor. Not to be manhandled—" She froze when a bedroom door opened. "Tell me there aren't more of them."

"One more." Rafe introduced everyone who had come in from the balcony. "The new arrival is Miguel Cisneros. He arranged these rooms for us." He saw Lena's eyes widen when Miguel, dressed all in black despite the summer heat, strode across the room to take her hand.

"Madam. I sense magic around you." Miguel gave her one of his rare smiles. "It is a pleasure to meet you." He reached out and captured one of her wild curls on a fingertip. "Beautiful."

"I sense magic around you as well. Are you a sorcerer?" Lena flushed and gripped the vial of potion Rafe had managed to get from Richard. He'd been brave enough to pluck it from Flo's bodice. Rafe had quickly passed it on before Flo launched a counter attack. Luckily, the energy surrounding Miguel and Lena had them all fascinated, even Flo.

"I have been known to dabble in the arts. Some light, some dark. Perhaps I can help you with your analysis." Miguel looked around the room. "There is a kitchen behind the bar. Did you bring ingredients in your basket? We can let the others discuss strategy while we work." He held out his

GERRY BARTLETT

hand to lead her to the kitchen. "Rafael, does that suit you?"

Rafe realized Miguel had already looked into his mind and knew what he planned to discuss with the others. "Sure, go ahead." He nodded toward Lacy. "Lena is Lacy's aunt. Be a gentleman."

Miguel's eyes hardened. "Of course." He turned to Lena as he picked up her basket. "Unless the lady prefers me otherwise."

Lena's laughter trilled across the room. "Oh, my, I think I am in several kinds of danger here."

"Call for help if you need it," Rafe said while he, Jerry and Ian showed their knives. Richard cracked his knuckles.

"Yes, Miguel, call for help if you need it." Lena patted the vampire's lean cheek and sashayed out of sight, into the kitchen.

"I like her," Glory whispered to Lacy. "I think my brother might have just met his match."

"Good luck to them if they inhale that love potion while they're working on it." Lacy grinned then looked down to where she was gripping the pillow she'd placed in Rafe's lap. "When this is over, you need to try it."

"That reminds me. We all need some kind of gas masks while we distribute this stuff or we won't be able to carry on the fight." Rafe had to force himself to stop rubbing Lacy's thigh. "Flo and Richard, you can testify to the fact that it's impossible to think about anything but sex once you've inhaled that shit. It's what I'm counting on to distract the demons so we can get Dani away from them."

Richard had been whispering in Flo's ear. Probably an apology for taking the vial from her. His wife was standing stiffly by his side. If Rafe knew Flo, this was going to cost Richard some jewelry.

"Yes, yes, you're right, Rafe. Powerful stuff. Which is why my darling was so determined to keep it." He tried to put his arm around Flo.

She stepped away. "You are not apologizing for me, are you?"

"No, of course not. I'm sure you just needed to think about Rafe's plan first. Remember, he has promised to get us more." Richard looked at Flo intently. "We came to help him."

"I know. I am sorry, Rafael." Flo gathered her shoes and sat in a chair. "Make your plans. I will behave."

Richard nodded. "Excellent. Rafe, first, we have to get all the mortals out of harm's way. We don't want an orgy going on while we make our effort to get your daughter."

"And we *must* get her. Lacy and I saw her today. She's surrounded by demons and Lilith has her under her spell." It made Rafe sick to remember the scene earlier.

"But how are you going to satisfy Lucifer?" Glory sat in the chair where Lena had been. "Rafe, you said he had to have Lilith in Hell or he would need Daniela to take her place."

"I know." Rafe glanced at his phone for the time. He and Lacy needed to catch the next shuttle or they would be late for the Cinderella performance. He couldn't disappoint his little girl. He told the group about their appointment with Lilith and Dani.

"I looked it up. We'll be there a couple of hours. That hopefully gives Lena and Miguel enough time to duplicate the love potion." He turned to Ian. "First you can immobilize the demons we fight with your sound machine. Then, if you can make the love potion work in our guns, we can spray it on the demons like we'd planned to do with the wisteria oil. That should put them out of commission as soon as they're hit by the love bug."

Jerry nodded. "I'll go out and get us each a gas mask. No way do we want to be put under the influence of this stuff." He glanced at Glory. "Though Richard and Flo have convinced me, I wouldn't mind a sample or two for later." He grinned at his wife.

"Sure, why not? I'll be the first to admit that centuries together can make things, um, predictable." Glory laughed when Jerry snorted and seemed inclined to argue. "From me as well as thee, my love." Then she got serious. "But I'm still very worried about Lilith. She's the strongest demon there is, right, Rafe?"

"Yeah. We can't hope to use the same tactics on her. My best hope is to somehow lure her to where Lucifer might be waiting." Rafe got up and tossed the pillow across the room. He'd calmed down now. They had to leave and he was worried as hell. Sex was the furthest thing from his mind. Well, maybe not the furthest. But at least he had his urges under control.

"Luc hinted he might actually cooperate. Can I trust him? Hell, no. But if all of the demons Lilith is counting on to fight for her are out of commission, I'm hoping I can use the ladies to spirit Dani away to safety." He took Lacy's hand. "We'll talk about it when we get back."

"Good luck, you two." Glory kissed them both on the cheek.

Flo was next. "I'm sorry," she whispered. "No more temper fits, my man calls them. I am so worried about your Dani. We must save her. We will do whatever you tell us to do. Take care, Rafael."

Rafe had no words for how much he appreciated the support. He touched her hand. Then he hurried Lacy to the elevator. He was relieved when they managed to squeeze onto the shuttle right before it was to leave. Soon it stopped in front of Lilith's hotel. His mother and Dani were waiting in the lobby with no sign of the two demon bodyguards.

"Mama, Daddy!" Dani ran up to them. "Look at me. I'm Cinderella."

She was dressed in a sparkly pink gown that must have cost plenty. She had the shoes to match, pretty ballet slippers. She even had a crown on her head.

"You look like a princess!" Rafe tried to pick her up but she wouldn't allow it.

"No, Daddy, you'll wrinkle my dress. I *am* a princess. Cinderella after she married her handsome prince." She did a little twirl. Her hair had been brushed and curled and hit below her shoulders.

Lacy leaned down to rub at her cheek. "Is this makeup? Really, Lilith, I don't think she should be wearing lipstick and blue eye shadow."

"It's a special occasion, Lacy. Relax. We were only having fun. She's such a beautiful doll." Lilith had on a cocktail suit in white with rhinestone trim at the collar and around the hem.

"She's not a doll! She's a six-year-old girl. Starting first grade this year." Lacy pulled a tissue from her purse, as if to wipe away some of the pink rouge or lipstick. Then she was suddenly unable to move, frozen in place.

"Don't touch her, cat. She looks beautiful and is in my charge. Understand?" Lilith's famous cold smile was back.

"Mother! Release her this minute. You're scaring Dani." Rafe touched Lacy's arm, hoping he could do the job. Not happening. "Don't be a bully. Let's go, we'll be late for the performance."

"Lollie, don't hurt Mama. Can we go now?" Dani pulled on her grandmother's sleeve.

Lilith frowned down at a brown stain on her white sleeve. "Child, what have you been eating?"

"A brownie." Dani's eyes filled with tears. "I washed my hands after."

"Not very well." Lilith pulled one of her handkerchiefs from the neckline of her jacket, scrubbed at the stain, then cursed and gave up. She waved a hand at Lacy who came alive. "Take this child to the bathroom and clean her up. Don't bring her back until there is not one drop of chocolate on her grubby hands. If you're not back in five minutes, you will both feel my wrath."

"I thought you were all-powerful. Can't you remove that stain yourself?" Lacy gripped Dani's hand.

"I'm not a witch. Go on, clean her up." Lilith lifted her chin, her tone glacial.

Dani sniffled. "I'm sorry, Lollie. Don't be mad."

"It's too late for that. Now hurry or we'll miss the beginning of the show you were so eager to see." Lilith examined the pretty pink dress. "Do not touch your dress until your mother has cleaned your hands. Understand me?"

"Yes, ma'am." Dani hung her head as Lacy hurried her toward the restroom in the lobby.

"That was nice." Rafe leaned against a column near the front door. "Did you have to be so harsh with the child?"

"That was nothing. She's going to have to get used to tough talk when she ends up living with Lucifer in Hell." Lilith shook her head. "You think I don't know what you are up to, showing up here? You have a time limit and it's running out. He wants me or the child. Since I'm not going, it will be Daniela. Sorry, but that's the breaks, my son." She stared at him as if waiting for him to sink to his knees and beg.

"God, but I hate you." Rafe was glad to see that the "G" word made her wince. He would have begged if he'd thought it would do any good. Or he could have attacked her, tried to put a hurt on her. But a glance around the lobby showed him she had dozens of demons dressed as tourists ready to make sure he'd regret a move like that.

"Of course, you can always sacrifice yourself. Your family would miss you. For a while. But the lovely Lacy would soon find a man to take your place. Don't you think?" She gave him that Arctic blast of a smile. "You believe in sacrifice, don't you?"

"I believe in family, friendship and doing good. None of those fit your value system, I know that. We declared war earlier. Let's see how that turns out before I give up and become Lucifer's latest boy toy." Rafe saw Lacy and Dani come out of the bathroom. In an act of defiance, Lacy had managed to scrub off all of Dani's makeup. Their little girl looked much prettier to his eyes. Natural. Lacy looked pretty too in a short blue dress that skimmed just above her knees and white sandals. She had a nice tan and her hair had dried in a beautiful red cloud that tumbled past her shoulders. Her natural beauty made Lilith's seem hard and artificial. Yes, other men would be happy to take his place. He pushed that thought away, it would only make him lose focus for the fight ahead.

"War, yes. After the Cinderella story. Surely you know that you will lose this so-called war." Lilith frowned when she saw Dani's clean face. "Well, Lacy, I see you had your way. Your six-year-old looks very sweet now. Like every other ordinary child who will be there." Lilith shook her head. "Let's go. I'm afraid we're going to be late."

"Surely the great Lilith has the power to

delay the performance until we get there." Rafe couldn't resist goading her.

"I could. But I'm saving my power for later." His mother sent him a warning look. "I do so love a good battle. I'm just afraid this one will be much too short to be satisfying."

CHAPTER TWENTY-THREE

"DANI'S AFRAID OF her grandmother." Lacy held his hand in the elevator. "Our little girl acted like she was enjoying the play, but I could see how tense she was. Her shoulders were stiff when I touched her."

"Baby, I know." Rafe wanted to hit something, someone. The hours had crept past. They'd been surrounded by both mortal families and demons. Front row seats for a play with Cinderella and her prince. But it had been like their own play as they sat in the audience. Lilith had been the doting grandmother, her evil nature making it impossible for her to be convincing. She'd obviously let enough of her true character show for Dani to flinch away from her whenever her grandmother pressed the little girl's hand, pointing out the costumes and laughing at the pumpkin carriage.

Rafe had come away from the ordeal almost mad with the urge to snatch his child and change in front of everyone. But he'd known he wouldn't have gotten far. Even flying away from the castle was out of the question. This was a place where magic happened. Tricks could be explained away to the crowd. But he'd been so outnumbered, he

knew Dani would have been ripped out of his
arms before he could clear the first turret. If he
lost his chance, where would that leave the child?
Lilith had made it clear that she knew he had
friends with him who might try to get to Dani.

"My spies have pictures of your vampire crew.
They are being circulated now. Any of them step
a foot inside my hotel thinking to snatch Daniela
and they will be sorry." Lilith glared at Lacy.
"Vampires, werecats. They are nothing compared
to a powerful demon, my dear. You would do
well to remember that."

Lacy had left that hotel in tears, all the fight
drained out of her.

Rafe unlocked the door to the suite and found
his friends waiting. They were armed to the teeth
with the special guns Ian had made. They might
look like toys capable of shooting water, but some
of them were now loaded with what smelled
like that very strong love potion. Rafe and Lacy
quickly took the gas masks Jerry handed them
and strapped them on. Everyone else already
wore them.

"How did it go?" Glory took Lacy's hand. "I
know this mask makes it hard to communicate,
but when we started loading the guns, we all got a
bit, um, excited. Miguel and Lena did an amazing
job of replicating the love potion. Boy, does it
work." Her voice was muffled by the mask.

Rafe thought the whole scene would be funny
if he wasn't so upset by what he'd just been
through. Lacy was crying as she told the crew

about the play and how Dani had only pretended to enjoy it.

"Because Lilith has managed to scare her to death!" Lacy collapsed on the couch. "That bitch! As soon as we got back to the hotel she started fussing about the way Dani had wrinkled her princess costume. Then the poor baby started limping because those damned princess slippers made blisters on her heels. You should have heard Lilith carrying on about walking like a princess. Telling Dani to suck it up." Lacy sobbed into a tissue. "The woman has no heart."

"At least she sent her straight to bed." Rafe sat next to his wife. "Bessie and Buster take good care of her. Did you notice Buster pick up Dani and carry her to the elevator? Bessie slipped off those shoes as soon as Lilith was distracted by you, honey."

"Yes, I distracted her. I couldn't hold in what I thought of your mother." Lacy looked around the room. "I told her she needed to try a little kindness if she wanted to be a grandmother. That my own mother could give her lessons."

"Oh, gods." Lena stood beside Ian. "You'd better warn my sister, Ian. Lacy just put a target on her mother's back. How could you say such a thing, girl?"

"I just told her the truth." Lacy turned to Rafe. "That was stupid, wasn't it? Especially after she told us she'll be watching for us to make a move to snatch Dani."

"You spoke your mind. But maybe Lena is right. Lilith can be very vindictive. Call your mom and warn her to watch out. Double her guard." Rafe needed more than ever to get Lilith back into Hell and have her stay there. Hopefully Lucifer would keep her too busy there to seek out personal enemies and make them pay. Because she'd hate Sheila now. For being the "Good Grandmother."

"I'll call her." Ian pulled out his phone then stepped outside so he could pull off his gas mask to make the call.

"Thanks. Now let's discuss our plans. My time is running out. I've always known I have until dawn tomorrow to finish this. I'm sure Lilith knows it too. Lucifer will open a portal then. Exactly where is up to him but I want to pick a place where there is little chance for mortals to be caught up in our fight." Rafe looked around the room. He'd spent hours looking over the area and thought he'd found the place most likely to offer them isolation.

"Where will it be, Rafael?" Miguel probably had already read his mind but was being polite.

"The mountain ride inside the park near Lilith's hotel. It's connected to two other rides by their roofs. The area at the top should offer good space for my demon army to fight without anyone passing by to notice and there's a bunker in the bottom of the mountain, where they keep all the technical equipment. If we can get Dani down there, we can hold her safe while we try to force Lilith close enough to wherever Lucifer opens a portal, and he can take her."

Jerry had his laptop open. "I like it. The park closes at midnight and it's close to that now. That's when all visitors are ushered out and the cleaning and maintenance staff come in to get the park ready for the next day. We'll want those mortals out of there as well before we make our move."

"I thought you'd want to use somewhere in the park." Richard spoke up. "We discussed this while you were gone." He turned to Lena. "You're lucky you have Lena here who knows people in Orlando. They've offered to help us and sent some uniforms, jump suits from one of the utility companies. Now that we know the place you've picked, we can phone in a gas leak. We'll clear out the night workers first and show up as gas company inspectors who will be coming in to find the leak. We'll wear those uniforms and these gas masks and have our guns hidden in our packs."

"I like it. You got a lot done in three hours." Rafe admired their thorough planning. "But we've got to get Dani out of the hotel first. We need a different strategy there. You phone in a gas leak and you'll have chaos. Lilith won't buy it either. We'd never be able to get close to my little girl."

"What about an active shooter drill? I could take over the front desk and alert all the hotel visitors to stay locked in their rooms until they hear the all clear. Unfortunately, they'll believe it. Happens way too often." Jerry produced a police uniform. "This comes with a SWAT helmet with a gas mask attachment."

"I'm afraid that would also make Lilith just send more men to guard Dani." Rafe remembered

Flo's offer to help keep Dani from remembering anything that would scare her. "I wonder if we could get our vampire ladies in there somehow. Lilith's spies know what you look like. They have been passing around your pictures. So you'll have to figure out disguises but look like typical tourists. If the ladies could get Dani out without alerting Lilith and her people, maybe we won't have to have another fight there in the hotel."

"I would be happy to get your *bambina*. We can hide our guns in a big purse." Flo smiled in a way that made Rafe glad he wouldn't have to cross the little vampire. "I am not afraid to take down a demon or two."

Lacy looked at Rafe. "After watching them with our girl, I actually think Bessie and Buster might not put up a fight. I got the feeling they were not happy with how Lilith has been treating Dani."

"But you have to assume there will also be guards outside the door, in the hall. You need backup. I'll go with you." Ian frowned. "But I'll have to shift into something small and hope I can keep from alerting Lilith that we're making a move to take the child."

"The key is to get Dani away from her. That will make Lilith realize she has no choice but to fight and win or I'll be taking her down to Hell in Dani's place. Her pride will demand she confront me and what she will consider my inferior forces." Rafe kept going over the plan, seeing holes everywhere.

"Are you sure your mother will fall for this?

She could let this go for another time, another century." Glory sat next to him and took his hand. "I'll do whatever you wish. Go after your girl, kill a few demons, dress like a tourist from Yoohoo, Michigan. But, Rafe, Lilith is unpredictable. If you get Dani back, who's to say this woman won't just say forget it and take off for parts unknown and try again next century?"

"No. I can't imagine that. She's called in a lot of markers, paid legions of demons to back her. Her pride demands she make a stand. Against me. Against Lucifer. And she's determined to win." Rafe squeezed Glory's hand. She was his best friend. He looked around the room. They were all risking so much. He hoped none of them regretted it. They had to win this.

"It's not too late to bail, guys. I'd understand. This is crazy." Rafe stood and held out his hand to Lacy. "My wife and I will never be able to repay you for what you're doing."

"Quit saying that. Just lead the battle against Lilith. Trust your girls to get Dani out of there." Glory grinned at Flo and they both grabbed Lacy and hugged her. "Girl power. Right?"

Lacy looked at her aunt. "Lena, could you help us with disguises? We can always carry large totes with gas masks inside then put them on before we use the potion."

"Sure, honey. I'm here for the duration. Whatever you need." She wiggled her fingers. "I'd like to try a cloak of invisibility but they've never worked around demons." She focused on Rafe. "Watch me and see if I disappear." She chanted and was obviously trying something but nothing happened. At least for Rafe. The rest of the group exclaimed.

"You did it!" Lacy jumped up. "Where are you?"

Rafe shook his head. "Still there for me so it would be useless against Lilith's demons or Lilith. Sorry, Lena. But you could get past a mortal, no problem."

Jerry turned to Lacy. "Now tell us how you will get Dani out of the hotel."

"Either Glory or Flo can fly Dani out. I'll meet them in the park at the mountain ride. I may have to shift into cat form, depends on if there's an alarm." Lacy held out her hand to Rafe. "What do you think about Dani's demon bodyguards, babe?"

"Even if they don't resist you, you're going to have to spray them or Lilith will kill them for failing to properly guard Dani. She may kill them anyway. That's my dear mother for you. I know they did their best for our child, but this is war. If things go our way, they can get to the cat compound in Texas on their own if they decide their loyalty is to Dani and not to Lilith. After this is over, we can work something out for them." Rafe frowned. He hated that Lacy and her friends would be taking on the rescue mission without him.

Lacy was biting her lip, obviously also worried about how this would go.

Rafe couldn't blame her. "Take it one step at a time. Be careful. You have to call it off if there are too many guards on Dani's floor." He turned to Flo and Glory. "You should shift and check the balcony door. Try to get in that way. Call that plan B. You can always text Lacy if you manage that and she can take off for the park to meet us there."

"I wish we could tell Dani to leave her balcony door open a crack." Glory glanced at Lacy. "Did you raise her to need fresh air at night?"

"Wouldn't that be convenient? But I wouldn't be surprised if the demons liked the balcony door open, now that you mention it. One of them is a dragon. Bet she flies out when she gets the chance." Lacy sighed. "I'm liking plan B a lot."

"So am I." Rafe hugged his wife. "So you scope out the situation on Dani's floor and then decide how to proceed." He looked at Ian. "Once we know Dani's out of the hotel, we can make a call to the hotel and warn of a potential active shooter, putting the hotel in lockdown. Lilith will go straight to Dani's room. You all need to be gone before then. When she sees the room is empty, she'll come looking for me and my crew. That's when the battle for the portal will begin."

"Are you going to call up your own demons?" Jerry was clearly imagining hand to hand combat. "How many can you get for our side?"

"Thousands. I've already seen big numbers of demons working for Lilith. I'll call mine when I know Lilith is sure to challenge me. Demons can be unpredictable at best. Making Lilith's force useless to her is the goal. When she's surrounded by demons making love not war, it will be up to me and Lucifer to get her to Hell."

"Just the two of you?" Jerry clearly didn't like that. "You'll need backup."

"I want you guys to stay on the demons, keeping them under the influence." Rafe fiddled with that damned gas mask. It was making him sweat like crazy. He wondered if he could go out on the balcony and take it off for a while. He got up with that in mind. He did want someone with him but he hated to put his friends in the line of fire. He didn't trust Lucifer to come when he needed him. Though the Devil was highly motivated to get Lilith where he wanted her.

"I see you're going with Lacy's idea of making love not war." Abe opened the balcony door and walked in. "Oh, my! That smell! I'm not sure I should be in here."

"No, Father, you probably shouldn't." Rafe took his arm and escorted him out. Ian had just ended his call. He smiled at both of them.

"Sheila has rallied her own clan and is ready if Lilith thinks to attack there again. If it comes down to Granny versus Granny, the werecats think they have an edge." He nodded at Abe. "*Padre*, all prayers are appreciated."

"You certainly have mine." Abe waited until Ian had shut the door and was inside settling beside Lacy to tell her about his phone call. "Daniela is certainly seeing her other grandmother's true nature. Lilith has no compassion. You endured her neglect but that turned out to be a good thing, wasn't it, Rafe?"

"Yes, I know that now. My grandfather was stern but taught me right from wrong. That lesson has served me well." Rafe leaned against the iron railing. The fresh air was hot and steamy. Summer in Florida. It was not very different from Texas. "Will we win this battle?"

"I don't know." Abe rested his hand on Rafe's shoulder. "But I like the way you're proceeding. Lilith belongs in Hell. If Lucifer comes out to play…" Abe smiled. "How can she resist him? Especially if you manage to douse her with your love potion. Brilliant, lad, absolutely brilliant."

"I hope you're right." Rafe turned to look through the thick glass doors. His friends were arguing about a play list. They had decided romantic music was necessary. It would be blasted over loud speakers. The problem was that Jerry, the warrior, was looking for something with a fast beat. One that an army could march to. The ladies all agreed that romantic music was slow and sensual and no one got it on to symbols and drums. A lively debate ensued with battling phones playing tunes and voting underway. Rafe wanted to shake some sense into them. This potion might not work and then where would they be?

"Rafael, let them have this. It's a good distraction from what is to come. You are part demon and the potion hit you hard. Why not assume it will work on the demons coming?" Abe shook his head. "Don't you think I know you've repressed your own demon side for centuries? If you must fight, bring it out and let it work for you. I know you told Lucifer you would do it. For Daniela. Do it for yourself as well. Prove there can be good demons as well as evil. Start your own army in case there's a need in the future. An army for what's right."

Abe smiled and fanned his face with his hand. "I'd best go. Even that whiff I got when Ian opened the door has me thinking carnal thoughts. Oh! I cannot." He hugged Rafe. "Put on that mask before you go inside or your wife will distract you from your mission, my son. Now good luck." He vanished.

Rafe shook his head then did strap on that heavy gas mask. No, he couldn't afford to be distracted by Lacy, much as he loved her and wanted to comfort her. She'd hated every moment with Lilith. Had been goaded into saying things she should never have said. He didn't doubt that, if his mother had a chance to put a serious hurt on Lacy, she would. She might even kill her. He closed his eyes for a moment and said a prayer. He wasn't much for praying, but this was certainly the time for it.

God, bring them through this safely. All of them. And send Lilith to Hell where she belongs.

CHAPTER TWENTY-FOUR

A HALF-DOZEN WERECATS ARRIVED bearing the packages Lena had ordered. By the time they were done putting on their disguises, Rafe wasn't sure he would have recognized his own wife, much less Flo or Glory. They wore wigs, padding and outfits that made them look like typical tourists from somewhere that favored big hair and unlimited buffets. It would have been funny if the clock hadn't read almost midnight.

"No one will give you a second glance but how are you going to keep them from sniffing out the fact you're paranormals?" Rafe couldn't take his eyes off Lacy's generous butt in flower-print shorts. Her red hair was hidden under a blond wig. Then there was the way her hot pink tee stretched over what had become double Ds. Her exaggerated lips were painted the same color of pink. Extra-long fake lashes completed his wife's transformation. Her two gal pals had obviously been done over at the same "spa" that must have run a special on those lashes.

Glory was having trouble with hers. "I think my eyes are glued shut, Lena. Help!" She suddenly ripped off one lash and waved it around. It was stuck to her fingers, a black many-legged spider.

Lena got busy fixing the situation with expert hands. "Dee, I told you to go easy on the glue. These women aren't used to the fakes." She looked them over and finally nodded her approval. "You'll do."

"Thanks, Lena. When we get home, I'm thinking of finding a lash bar that's open late. With a little trimming these could be sexy. What do you think, Ricardo?" Flo did a seductive walk over to her husband, the slinky move ruined by the sound of her sequined flipflops smacking the tile floor.

"I'm not sure the world is ready for you to be any sexier, my love." He grabbed her in his arms and bent her back for a deep kiss. Then he straightened and made a face. "What the hell is that taste?"

"My lipstick. It is how we disguise our scent." Flo pulled a tube out of her oversized purse covered with fake silk flowers. "Lena made it. Too bad you smeared mine. But it was a very nice kiss." She smiled then opened a compact and concentrated on her lipstick. As they watched, her lips swelled to look pouty. "See? It's magic. I think the smell is not so nice, but it will keep the demons away. What is it, Lena?"

"Not so nice? Pizza with pepperoni?" Lena looked offended. "I thought it was genius. You just proved vampires don't enjoy it. Most mortals and werecats love pizza and it certainly hides any hint of what you are. You'll reek like you just ate one of Gino's belly buster pizza specials. Try to burp your way through the lobby and talk about the popular place down the street." Lena reached out to straighten Lacy's blond wig. "You'd better get going. You got everything you need?"

"Yes." Lacy patted her own tote. "Guns inside loaded with the potion in case we need to subdue anyone. And gas masks." She hugged Lena. "It *was* genius. Thanks."

"Mine has the wisteria oil. That can put down anyone we meet who tries to stop us outside Daniela's door." Glory stood next to Jerry and ran a hand over his cheek. "I don't dare kiss you goodbye but you guys be careful. Don't try to be a hero."

"I could say the same thing to you, darling." Jerry reached out and pulled her tank top up toward her chin. "Was showing all this cleavage necessary?"

"It's a distraction. You know that. Any demon males we run into will take a look and…" Glory laughed and tugged it down again. "Demon or mortal, men are pretty predictable. Wouldn't you agree?"

"Unfortunately, yes. I just wish I could be there with you. I don't like this." Jerry wrinkled his nose. "Pepperoni pizza. I don't mind that smell, but is it driving you crazy, love? Making you hungry?"

"You know me too well." Glory pulled down her shorts. "Hungry and not too happy with these tight shorts crawling up my butt. Too bad I didn't need padding like Lacy did for that to happen. Now we'd better catch that shuttle. In case there are demons watching the hotel, we need to make every move from here on look like we're ordinary mortals going back to our hotel after a night out."

"Yes. Ordinary mortals. I hope you two can remember what that's like." Lacy led the way. "Rafe, I'll text you as soon as we have Dani safely out of there. Then you can call in an active shooter alert to the hotel staff. They'll start the lockdown. That should give Lilith notice that her plan is in trouble. She'll rush to Dani's room and see her hostage is gone. It won't take her long to realize it's time to come to the park and battle if she wants to avoid Hell."

"Don't text me until you are safely out of the hotel and where we agreed our girl will be safe." Rafe never said the exact spot out loud. He might be paranoid, but he was not so sure Lilith didn't have spies even here in their hotel room. A bug? One of Lena's crew? He and Lacy knew where they were stashing Dani. The mind-reading vampires with his wife would find out on the way to Lilith's hotel. Otherwise, the safe place for Dani was his secret, his and Lacy's.

He felt eyes on him. Everything else had been discussed. He ignored the questioning looks. "I'll send Ian in as our SWAT leader." Rafe was suddenly full of doubts. Could this work? It suddenly sounded too easy.

"We've got this, honey." Lacy touched his cheek. "Don't worry. You have the hard part. Be ready for when Lilith comes at you with her legions of demons. Glory's right. Please, please be careful and don't play the hero." Lacy stepped back and licked her lips. "Damn but this lipstick is delicious. Lena, did I tell you you're a genius?"

Rafe followed her to the door, fighting his fears. Pizza. He loved it. His whole family did. Would that smell be enough to get the women safely through the lobby and up to Dani's room? He'd found out her floor and room number by sending a gift to the hotel. Miguel had shifted into a small fly and followed the bellman who delivered the package up to Dani's suite. It had been quiet up there. As if Lilith didn't want to draw attention to her rooms. So this should work. Unless Lilith had moved their daughter since yesterday, they were ready to act.

"You're sure you have the right room number?" He knew he was hovering but couldn't stop himself. If he could be two places at once, he would stay with them. He could shift, like Miguel had. Fly overhead and…

"Yes, we do." Lacy slipped her arms around his waist. "Please try to concentrate on your part and trust us to do ours." She sighed and leaned against him. "Can you do that?"

"I do trust you. It's just—" Rafe ran his hand down her back and squeezed what must be foam padding. "I can't lose you."

"You won't." She pushed back and laid a fingertip on his lips. "I'll see you later after Dani is safe. Once this is over, we're celebrating with a giant pizza. This smell is making me remember how much I love it." With that she turned and pushed Flo and Glory ahead of her and out the door.

"They'll be fine." Miguel stood next to him. "Just in case, do you want me to follow them? I can pick up a pizza and pretend to deliver it to a room on Dani's floor in the hotel. That could work and I'll be available as backup for them."

"You flew in and out yesterday and no one noticed you." Rafe was thinking it over. "Man, I'd like to have video. A way to stay apprised…"

"Your wife wants you to trust her. And I just *hope* no one noticed me. I did get some looks. Had to hide more than once. Luckily the place has plenty of greenery around. I could stop and blend. But doesn't Lilith know your deadline?"

"Yes, she does. Our time is running out and she knows it. We're assuming a portal to Hell will be somewhere inside the park. Lucifer won't let Lilith and me know where he'll open it in advance. All we do know is that we have until tomorrow at sunrise to finish this. My mother thinks she's going to sacrifice Dani to keep her own freedom. But I'm prepared to fight with everything I've got to stop that." Rafe stalked to the balcony and stared at the lights of the entertainment complex. "If we get Dani to safety, my mother will try to send me down there next."

"Seriously? And has Lucifer said he'll accept that? Whoever wins the fight can decide who is going down to Hell?" Miguel was close.

Rafe was very aware of the crowd in the suite. They could hear whatever he said through the open doors. His friends were waiting for his answer. He shook his head. "I'm counting on the fact that it's Lilith he really wants. We even signed a contract. But do I trust it? I'm not that stupid. All I can do is put up a good fight and hope he'll open a portal and force Lilith to go with him. No one but God has more power than Lucifer does."

"Then that's what we do. Get Dani to safety then make a good stand for you. We must take the fight and Lilith all the way to where Lucifer opens a portal." Jerry glanced around and the men nodded.

Rafe didn't dare let doubts cloud his thinking. "Go ahead, Jerry. Call in the gas leak. We've got to get rolling. Lilith will hear about it and laugh. Do you think she cares if there are any mortals still inside the park? Not at all. But she'll understand that I'm ready to call up my army of demons. She'll want to lead whatever is going to happen at the entertainment complex. Without Dani as a bargaining chip, she'll call for her own army to meet mine. The woman is arrogant and sure to think she can defeat me." Rafe took a breath, the gas mask making it no pleasure. "I refuse to believe she's right."

"She'll still be trying to find Dani, Rafe." Jerry glanced around the room. "You're sure your child will be safe?"

"As long as the ladies get her out of the hotel, I'm confident we can keep her away from Lilith." Rafe stared at each vampire in turn. He let them see what he had in mind for his daughter. One after the other nodded. They agreed.

He couldn't stall any longer. It was time to get moving. "Suit up. We'll take off from the balcony."

"What do you want us to do?" Lena had moved next to Miguel, her hand on his arm.

"You should leave. There is a chance the fight could move here." Rafe smiled at her. "You've been a great help. I can't thank you enough for it."

Lena glanced at the rest of the werecats who'd come to help disguise the ladies. They huddled then, after a few moments, broke apart. "We want to help you. The idea that your mother is willing to sacrifice her own granddaughter does not sit well with us. We can fight if you give us weapons. Do you think Lilith will send anyone here to your suite?"

"It's a possibility. I found out where she was keeping Dani easily enough." Rafe saw his force being stretched thin. "Yeah, Miguel can give you some weapons. I'm sure someone has explained what besides the love potion we're using to neutralize the demons."

"Yes, Miguel filled me in. I can use some magic as well." Lena looked solemn. "I'm sorry you're dealing with such a situation. We will hold down this position for you and, if you need us elsewhere, say the word. Daniela is my grandniece. It makes me ache for my sister that she is going through this." She had tears in her eyes. "I will call for more of our people if you give the word."

"I appreciate that, more than you know." Rafe went to Lena and hugged her. "But I have already cost your family too much. I can use your help here, with Miguel. When this is over, I hope you can come visit Sheila and meet the rest of my family. I have two boys who have no demon in them." Rafe shook his head. "Stay safe. And thanks." He hurried to the balcony doors, his gas mask in his hand, his backpack with his weapons strapped on. "We had better go."

Jerry ended his call. "I talked to the facilities manager of the mountain ride and convinced him I was from the gas company. Told him to start evacuating the area, all three rides in that area, immediately. The tourists had already been cleared out at midnight and only the cleaning crews and maintenance staff are inside. He was calling them as soon as he hung up with me." He pulled on a jumpsuit with a gas company inspector patch on it. Richard already wore his. They had their own gas masks and backpacks with weapons inside.

"Seems like we're ready to go." Rafe stepped out into the sultry night air. "As soon as we're in the park, I'm calling up my demons. Lilith won't be able to resist calling hers then."

"How will we be able to tell your demons from Lilith's?" Ian had his new toy, the sound machine that would immobilize anyone in range, in his hand.

"A good question." Jerry stared at Rafe. "No uniforms, I suppose." He pulled his ear plugs from a front pocket. "You will warn us, Ian, before you turn on that bloody machine of yours. I admire the technology, but have to admit, it scares me.

Rafe said it puts whoever hears it right on the ground."

"Aye. But it's temporary, lasts only a few minutes. Just long enough to give them a blast of the potion or the wisteria oil. You decide what you need. If I'm to be at the hotel, I should pass this on to you. Or Richard. I can quickly teach you what to do." Ian pulled it out of his backpack and went through the steps with Richard.

"Got it. Clever gadget." Richard slipped it into his own pack. "Good question about telling your demons from Lilith's. I have to say all demons look evil to me, Rafe, if you want to know the truth."

"I can answer that." Abraham suddenly appeared on the balcony.

"Father!" Rafe gripped the iron railing. "We were about take off. What can you tell us? I'm afraid Richard is right. You never know how a demon is going to behave. They're not known for their loyalty. Lucifer told me my legions must come to me when I call them. As will Lilith's when she demands their presence. She's bought her army with the promise of hard cash but that doesn't mean they won't run at the first sign of a losing proposition. And mine won't necessarily stick with me."

"I made my case upstairs and my prayers were answered." Abe managed a smile. "While I cannot interfere, I was given one power that can help you, my son. It is because an innocent child is being used as a pawn. He is not happy about that." Abe looked up at the starry night sky.

"What can you do?" Rafe didn't hold out much hope. This was a fight that involved Lucifer and evil demons. What could a higher power do to interfere?

"You asked how you could tell the different sides apart. Well, I am going to make it easy for you." Abe laid a hand on Rafe's shoulder.

Rafe felt heat flow down his body. When he looked, it was as if he had a spotlight in the middle of his chest. It didn't hurt, but it was damned annoying. He tried to cover it with his hand.

"Will you look at that!" Jerry elbowed Richard. "That's as good as a uniform, especially at night."

Abraham nodded. "That's what I thought. Rafael, your demons will glow with a white light. Lilith's will not. I have managed that much." He rubbed his hands together. "Wait and see."

"But it's also like a target, Father." Rafe realized he was complaining.

"That's why you have your potions, my son. Use them." Abe looked a little annoyed. "I did my best. Call up your first legion as soon as you get to the park. I'm sure you will see the usual band of creatures." Abe shuddered. "Some of them are quite large and ugly."

"Yes, I know. Have you seen my own demon come out to play?" Rafe resisted the urge to show him. He didn't want to scare off the gentle cleric. "Anyway, demons come in all shapes and sizes and powers."

"Yes, and now your demons will glow like you just did. Kind of like lightning bugs on steroids." Abe glared when Ian chuckled. "Not funny,

I'm afraid. That light is sure to displease them. Many of them like to hide in the shadows. Rafe, you'll have to let them know it's to keep them from being killed by your own trigger-happy vampires." Abe nodded toward the men standing by, waiting to take flight. "No offense, gentlemen, I realize being bloodthirsty is a virtue in this situation."

"It certainly is, Father." Jerry nodded. "I appreciate the help. You've insured we won't take out any of our own people. Very helpful." The vampire crossed himself. "I was raised in the church myself. Never doubt I always intended to try for Heaven in the end."

"Yes, my son, I know. I am praying for all of you." Abe murmured and gave the group his blessing. "Now God speed. I hope to see you all once this is over." He vanished.

"That was unexpected." Rafe stared at the spot where the monk had been. "He's right. The demons will hate that glowing bit. *I* hate it. No hiding with this thing on us."

"Abe *is* right. We use the potions. Tell your troops to become aggressive. It's the only way to survive." Richard nodded. "Time to go." He took off, morphing into bird form and disappearing into the night. Ian and Jerry were right behind him. Ian peeled off to go toward the hotel.

Rafe was about to change when there was a knock on the door to the suite. He glanced at Miguel.

"Go." Miguel reached for a weapon. "If it's some of Lilith's people, we'll handle it. You know the battle has to be at the park. She's going to bring it to you. I have a feeling Lucifer is going to make sure he gets who he really wants."

"He wants Lilith." Rafe hesitated when the banging on the door got louder. "Are you sure? I can—"

Miguel stepped toward the door, his cannon loaded with wisteria, obviously eager to get started. "Take off! I've got this. Lena, it's magic time. Put your girls in position."

Lena began to chant as her armed women scattered around the room and took aim at the door.

Miguel grinned and nodded toward the balcony. "Trust us, Rafael."

Rafe hated that he had to trust anyone but himself. The room was filling with waves of something. A protection spell? He didn't have time to worry about whether it was working. The plan was in motion. He changed into a black bird and leaped into the night.

CHAPTER TWENTY-FIVE

THE THEME PARK was eerily quiet except for his own footsteps as Rafe climbed over rocks and rubble inside the huge mountain. He was relieved to see the paths were wide and the map he'd studied had been accurate. A dozen more feet and another turn and he found an open area, a grotto really, that would be perfect for calling his troops. His demon army. He dreaded it but knew he couldn't stall any longer.

He hadn't heard from Lacy yet. That was a worry. She'd had time to get to Dani. Had Buster and Bessie put up a fight? He tried to imagine it. With his daughter in the middle. No, the love potion would work. Or the wisteria oil. The two demons would either be gazing into each other's eyes or on the floor, temporarily out of commission. He checked his phone. Yes, he had service. He tried calling Lacy. Her phone went straight to voice mail. No surprise. She'd had to be quiet as she'd approached Dani's room. He'd turned off his while he'd been flying. Had he missed her text? No, but he left his phone on and thrust it into his pocket.

He heard stealthy footsteps behind him. Jerry, a

strange figure in his white gas company jumpsuit and gas mask carried a flashlight and was scanning the area.

"They cut the electricity. Standard procedure during a suspected gas leak. The guy in charge is waiting anxiously where I told him to send all the afterhours personnel. I made them go blocks away as a precaution, in case the gas triggers an explosion. That way the mortals won't hear sounds of a battle. He handed me this flashlight." Jerry clicked it off. "He has no idea I have excellent vampire night vision."

"Where's Richard?" Rafe looked behind his friend.

"He called Ian about that sound machine. We've figured out that using that weapon will put both armies down. Yours *and* Lilith's. Unless there's something about it we don't know. Richard's checking. Since we don't have earplugs we can issue to your side, we're only going to use it as a last-ditch effort." Jerry stuck the flashlight in a deep pocket and pulled out his gun.

"This has the potential to become one huge clusterfuck." Rafe checked his phone again. "I still haven't heard from Lacy. Don't suppose Glory has texted you."

"Not a word. Keep in mind they will have their hands full evading the enemy. Then they must put down the bodyguards and fly the girl here. I would have my phone turned off until I'd landed safely at my destination." Jerry kept looking around the dark area.

"True. But it's been too long. We should have heard by now." Rafe frowned when Jerry punched his arm.

"What are you waiting for, man? You've got to call up the troops. If the girls *are* in trouble, we need to do our part to get this done fast so we can go check on them."

"You're right. Brace yourself. This is about to look ugly." Rafe raised his arms and started the special the chant, the call to arms Lucifer had shown him in that ancient book. It was in an old language and he felt the words come much too easily to his tongue. As he said them, he felt the change in his own body. His horns punched through his skull and scales formed on his frame as it grew and twisted into the grotesque figure that was his demonic self. The gas mask stretched and became a tight fit. He roared as he finished the call, looking around him and feeling the heat of his glowing red eyes. His chest swelled and he clawed the air, eager for blood, the blood of his enemies.

He felt Jerry near his back. He glanced that way, certain his friend would reveal his horror at what Rafe had become. Instead, the man waiting for the war to begin, nodded approval. He raised his gun in triumph and roared his own support of the demon army appearing by the thousands in the halls and chambers leading away from them.

It was no longer dark. No, every man, creature, whatever, sported a shining light in the center of his chest. They each pounded that light, as if to smash and extinguish it. The angry bellowing became so loud, Rafe was afraid the mortals even far outside the gates would hear it.

"Silence!" he ordered. "I need your attention."

A tall demon with a plume of black hair on his wedge-shaped head, stepped forward. "Lord, I am Captain Aamon, at your service." He bowed. "My men are here to aid you in your fight to reclaim your daughter. Lucifer has told us of your worthy cause. And that he wants you to prevail this night." The man's eyes gleamed. It was clear pleasing Lucifer was a bonus he was all for claiming.

"Yes. I am here to make sure Lucifer gets Lilith into Hell and by his side as he wishes. We hope to please Lucifer, do we not?" Rafe's voice had lowered to a guttural growl. Please Lucifer? Whatever it took. An unhappy Lucifer didn't bear thinking about. The bottom line? He was desperate to save Daniela and he was glad the Devil had told these men the objective.

"What is this light on us? We are not happy. It is like a bullseye for the enemy." Aamon produced a shield and slammed it against his black armor.

"It is magic, placed there for your own protection. I have with me vampires who are armed with special potions. The spray they spew can make the strongest warrior demon turn into a sniveling child." Rafe turned to face the seemingly endless lines of men and women who glowed as Abe had promised, like restless lightning bugs in the dark. "We want to reserve that spray for Lilith's traitorous bastards who follow her instead of our master Lucifer."

"Then we will endure the lights. As soon as we

win, they will darken?" Aamon really didn't like what he considered a target on his chest.

"Of course. Now we march!" Rafe looked past him at the rows of warriors behind him.

"Aye!" The sound boomed through the mountain. Fists were raised as were spears and bows.

Rafe wanted to shake someone. Lucifer? Why were his demons armed as if they were in a play about ancient times? Lilith's people carried real guns, assault weapons. He asked Aamon about that.

"The Master likes to see old-fashioned sword play. It is one of his great pleasures and he finds it rare these days. Never doubt he'll be watching this battle. When Lilith's people arrive, they will find their fancy new guns useless." Aamon grinned. "It's close combat this night. An advantage to us." He turned to his soldiers and pulled his sword. "Are we ready to draw blood?"

There was a thunderous clanging of steel on steel. Rafe wanted to join in, but couldn't stop thinking about the mortals a few blocks away.

Jerry must have seen his concern. "Relax, Rafe. There were several explosions last winter up north caused by gas leaks. One whole family was wiped out, including three children. All I had to do was remind the night supervisor about that and he promised to keep every mortal well away from here. I assure you, we will not be disturbed. After this is over, one of us will call him with the all clear."

Jerry was assessing the troops. "I tell you, I would

be shitting my pants if I hadn't seen these kinds of creatures before. Even the women are terrifying." He raised his gun, which would probably be useless unless Lucifer took pity on him. "Are you ready to go toward where the portal might be? Any ideas? Do you think Lilith will be waiting?"

"I have no clue. Aamon is right. Lucifer will be watching and I expect him to make a move to open a portal when he is satisfied with the result of our battle. It's up to us to make sure it's Lilith who is the loser. Now we work our way up toward the summit of this mountain and see what happens." Rafe had been surprised to see the hundreds of women led by an Amazon with a dozen bright red braids crowning her head. As he watched, she flung her head around, whipping those braids like a weapon, each braid tipped with a heavy gold knob that he didn't doubt could kill if it struck a man.

He was ready to lead the columns when Rafe felt a buzzing in his pocket. Odd that, even in his demon form, he could feel his clothes under his scales. He slapped his thigh and finally gave up trying to reach his pocket. He changed back into his mortal form.

"Wait for orders. I have a text coming in. I hope it's from my wife, about my daughter." He pulled out his phone and unlocked it. What he cursed and reached for his spray gun.

"What does she say, Rafe? Are we good to go?" Jerry must have seen something in his friend's face. He walked over and took the phone from Rafe's hand. "What does this mean?"

"They are on their way." Rafe couldn't breathe as he felt his demon rise and take over his body again. He was growing in size. His fury made it almost impossible for him to think rationally. Kill. Find Lilith and drag her down to Hell. Watch while Lucifer subjected her to every horror anyone could imagine. And it still wouldn't be enough to satisfy this rage that made his eyes burn with fire and his gut churn.

"Lacy texted that the plan worked. See you in Austin." Jerry looked puzzled. "Wait. Austin? No, that's not the plan."

"Right. And we had arranged a safe word, you could call it." Rafe's demon growl was back. He had barely choked out those words as he realized what the message meant.

"Safe word." Jerry's face was hard. He looked as freaked out as Rafe was feeling. "So it's not in this text? You don't think the girls and Dani are safe."

"One way to find out." Rafe stared down at his gun. Would it also be rendered useless in the fight to come?

"What was the safe word?" Jerry pulled a knife out of his boot, always ready with his own ancient weapon.

"Kisses. She didn't send me kisses." Rafe raised his gun at the masses of monsters in front of him. "Go down to the bunker. See for yourself. Let me know what you find." He studied the masses of demons waiting for orders. His growl came from deep inside him. "Follow me. That bitch Lilith is on her way here. She may have my daughter and my wife. We will fight until there is not one of her followers left. Until the paths run with their blood. Do you hear me?"

The roar was deafening and the earth shook under his feet. Rafe led the way toward where he planned to make a stand. The final showdown. He had to get there before Lilith did. How had this happened? Somehow the women had been overcome by her demons. What had that monster who had borne him done to Lacy, the rest? He heard the clang of weapons and breathing behind him. The demons were actually trying to be quiet but it was impossible as so many creatures surged upward toward what was near the top of a fake mountain.

"My lord! Someone is coming." Aamon jerked to a stop. "Vampires. Two of them." He pointed to an opening in the ceiling. The mountain was riddled with them. It was part of a railway that allowed train cars to carry passengers in and out of the simulated mining operation. Fake ghosts of miners could swoop down at intervals along with falling rocks designed to make the ride exciting. The cars made their way to the summit with many near misses before plunging down the mountainside in a thrilling switchback trip that left passengers gasping.

"Wait. Don't attack them. As far as I know, Lilith doesn't have vampires in her army." Rafe waited, recognizing the birds flying through a hole in the roof as Richard and then Ian. "Ian! Why are you here? Weren't you supposed to back up Lacy and her crew?"

When the men changed into their mortal

forms, Richard was still in his gas company uniform and mask. Ian had on his policeman's outfit and SWAT helmet. He removed the mask and threw it to the ground.

"It was a trap. I was all set to lock down the hotel when I saw a dozen of Lilith's demons head for the elevators talking about 'the little girl.' No question where they were going. Instead of showing myself as a cop, I shifted like Miguel had done earlier and flew after them. I heard them talking. Lilith had ordered a squad to cover the entire floor where Dani's suite was located. It was clear that the ladies were walking into trouble. I decided to fly to the suite myself and see if I could beat those reinforcements." Ian walked up to Rafe. He looked like he wanted to put a hand on Rafe's shoulder but the presence of the frowning Aamon, as well as Rafe's demon form must have stopped him.

"Well, did you?" Rafe realized this was not going to be good news.

"When I got up there, I could see through the closed balcony doors that Lilith's men had arrived too late to stop our women." Ian glanced at Richard. "The child's bed was empty and there was no sign of Flo or Glory. I'm sure they must have managed to fly Daniela out of there. But Lacy…" Ian did rest a hand on Rafe's scaly arm. "Lilith is obviously very powerful. She had frozen Lacy, made her unable to move. Like we can do to mortals. She couldn't even blink." Ian turned his gaze to Aamon. "Can demons do that?"

"Not most of us. But I'm sure one of Lilith's

station can." Aamon glanced at Rafe. Then he quietly introduced himself. It was clear he was not a fan of vampires, but felt compelled to be polite to Rafe's allies. He did not offer a handshake. Of course, he had such long talons, Ian probably wouldn't have enjoyed one.

Rafe struggled for control. He was losing it. He wanted to scream, hit something, someone. His love, in the hands of his worst enemy. He tried to steady himself and think.

"Captain Aamon's right, Ian. My mother can do things most demons can't." Rafe was almost relieved that his wife was merely frozen. Lilith could have done much worse.

"Son of a bitch! You couldn't get in there and do anything to help her, Ian? How many men did they have?" Richard looked murderous. "What are you doing here? Did she look hurt?"

"She'd obviously put up a fight. Her purse and guns were on the floor as were two demon bodyguards. They'd been knocked out with something. I'd guess the wisteria oil." Ian shook his head. "Flo had lost her flipflops, probably kicked them off before she took off from the balcony." Ian took a step back from Rafe when he growled. "But there were six demons inside and the others arrived as I watched. If I'd changed and charged in, Lilith would have frozen me too. I thought you would need me here."

"You're right. We will need you." Richard had gripped his gun so hard the plastic cracked. Ian nodded.

"Lacy?" Rafe couldn't stop growling. "Besides being frozen, any sign of her being hurt?"

"Lacy had lost her blond wig. I saw a mark on her cheek, her mouth was bleeding too." Ian winced. "Like she'd been slapped around."

Rafe's howl came from his chest. An answering sound came from the men around him. "I don't care if she is my mother. I'll kill Lilith for that." He took a breath for control. His phone buzzed. "You said there was no sign of my daughter?" He had kept his phone out and tossed it to Ian. "Read the text."

"It's Jerry." Ian let out a breath. "They're safe and where you wanted them. He says Dani's asleep and wrapped in a blanket. Flo and Glory are with her and they are ready to lock her in and guard the door." He wiped at his eyes. "Praise God. He's on his way back here. I'll acknowledge the text."

Rafe couldn't relax. Good news but not good enough. There was still Lacy. He didn't doubt his mother would use his wife to get him to either bring Dani to the portal, once one was open, or try to get him to sacrifice himself to save his daughter. He held up his gun again.

"Let's move." He turned to Ian. "Anything else you found out that I need to know?"

"The two bodyguards. Lilith blamed them for the failure to keep Dani safe. She beat them for information and accused them of helping the vampires take Dani away. Nonsense, of course. She was so angry, she wanted to kill them both but the other guards rebelled. They said if she did that, they would not fight for her. That it would prove she did not keep her word and might not pay them at the end of the battle. Bessie and Buster seem to have more friends than your mother has. Lilith finally contented herself with leaving them behind and refusing to pay them. It's all about money with her, it seems." Ian looked at the mass of demons behind Rafe and shook his head. As if he knew Lucifer had probably paid for *this* army.

"I couldn't hear much, but she has spies. Those damned flies of hers. I saw two of them change and report while I watched. Then Lilith pointed here, toward this mountain. I'd expect her and her army to show up here any minute now." He cleared his throat. "If I'd had my sound machine, I could have put them out for long enough to snatch Lacy, but then… who knows if the sound would have even bothered Lilith? I have never seen anyone so powerful. As soon as I realized they were ready to move, I got out of there. Came straight here."

"Yes, she's powerful. There's only one entity more powerful that I know of. I'm afraid it's going to take Lucifer to bring her down." Rafe turned to his army. "On to the summit. We've got to get there before Lilith and her army do. Forward now! We give no quarter!"

Cheers rang out as they moved, walking ever higher into the mountain. Rafe's feet felt like lead weights. He trudged on, trying not to picture what might happen next. His vampire friends behind him were muttering about their own revenge and plans to spray the demons and make them helpless. How foolish it all seemed now. Impossible. Make love not war. Rafe could only hope his guns would still work as they neared the summit. Perhaps seeing demons attacked by the love bug or laid low by the wisteria would amuse Lucifer. It might just persuade the Devil to give Rafe's army an edge in the battle to determine Lacy's fate.

Lacy, his beautiful werecat. She obviously hadn't been able to shift fast enough to escape when demons had swarmed the floor where the suite was located. He should never have let her go with the vampires. But then could he have stopped her? His wife knew how a mother should love her child and would be willing to sacrifice anything for her.

How different from his own mother! It was enough to make him howl again, stirring the men around him to a frenzy of blood lust.

CHAPTER TWENTY-SIX

HE WAS ALMOST at the summit when Rafe sensed another intruder coming from an opening above him. He didn't need Aamon's shout to realize another vampire had joined the party.

"I know him. Stand down." Rafe didn't bother to change. This vampire, like the others, had the power to read his mind and would recognize him despite his hideous form. When the vulture settled next to him and became man, Rafe held out his hand.

Miguel slapped it, palm to palm, not a bit put off by Rafe's long claws. "The werecats and I handled things at the hotel. The wisteria worked like a charm and Lena's protection spell did the rest. I told Lena it would be best if she and her people cleared out before the demons we put down woke up. Then I came here. I figured the demons would take off once they realized the rooms had been abandoned." Miguel's gaze raked the ranks of warriors behind Rafe then he nodded approvingly. "This is a fine force. Any word from the ladies?"

Rafe waited while Miguel pulled an assault

weapon adapted to shoot the wisteria oil out of his backpack. "They got Daniela. She's down below us, safely locked away in a bunker with Flo and Glory guarding her. I just sent Richard down to join them. All three are well-armed." He shook his head. "But three against thousands? We can't let it come to that."

"Wait." Miguel frowned. "There's something you're not telling me." He glanced at Jerry, who had tucked his knife in his belt. Their glances were full of silent communication. "That unnatural mother of yours has your wife?" His fury made him rise from the dirt floor, his fangs long and his cry of rage contagious. The demons waiting for orders behind them echoed it.

"Yes, I'm going mad." Rafe wondered he could talk at all through his clenched teeth. Teeth? They were his own fangs, sharp and eager to tear into enemy flesh. "I expect Lilith and her army any moment now. We must hurry. The plans show this mountain flat at the summit, connected to the buildings on either side and open to the sky. It's a good place for our fight. Unfortunately, we have mere hours until our deadline, a deadline that will make you, my friend, and my other vampire allies, totally useless."

"So we must win before the sun rises." Jerry stepped forward, Ian by his side. "On we go. I can smell the sky from here."

The troop thundered forward, led by the vampires and Rafe. They were soon at the edge of an open area the size of a football field. Rafe gazed at a roof, tar and gravel. He was trying to look for an advantage for his force. Were there hiding places? Air conditioning units, huge metal boxes that were silent without electricity, could provide cover. Covered openings at either end would lead to stairs for the rides in the other buildings connected to the mountain in the middle.

Jerry touched Rafe's shoulder. "I'm changing and flying out to see exactly where they are and how they're set up. We cannot afford to be surprised."

"A good idea." Rafe gave him a fist bump, then the other vampires in turn. He was having trouble thinking beyond saving Lacy before his mother did the unforgiveable. Lilith could well decide that taking Lacy's life would punish Rafe for not being the son she wanted him to be. Lilith could do that with no remorse. As a demon, she had no compassion, no limits to her cruelty.

Jerry landed. "She's here and with more men than I could count."

Captain Aamon pulled his sword. He waved it in the air, uttering foreign words. He spoke commands the demons behind him understood as the clang of other weapons rang through the wide-open space. The ground shook again as Lilith's front line emerged from a passageway at the opposite end of the area. They chanted their own words, making a tremendous noise as Lilith's army marched forward.

"Hold your position!" Rafe realized his mother stood near the front, her body covered in silver armor. It gleamed when clouds scudded across the sky and revealed a shaft of moonlight. She'd even procured a gas mask and looked like a shining version of a famous Star Wars villain. Her spies *had* been busy.

"She has thousands of demons behind her. We should go ahead and shoot, Rafe. We can take down the first few rows of her force with the wisteria." Jerry was eager to get started.

"If we use that, our demons will see that as weakness. Lucifer is watching too. He wants to see some swordplay. We should let them fight first." Rafe wanted to scream in frustration. "Do you see who is beside Lilith?" Indeed, two demons held Lacy next to his mother. His wife was no longer frozen, but her struggles were weak. She must have tried to change into her cat form or run and been punished for it. Her face was bruised and her mouth was bleeding.

"The wisteria won't hurt your wife. Cats aren't sensitive to it. Lena showed me that." Miguel leaped into the air. "But if it will please Lucifer, then let the demons go at it first and we save our spray for now." He glanced at Captain Aamon. "Rafe, he is waiting for your permission to charge."

"Yes, why not? Just make sure everyone knows not to hurt the woman they are holding. My wife." With that, Rafe screamed a command in the old language and the demons ran toward Lilith's army, eager to shed blood. As if Lucifer approved, the sky filled with dark clouds and thunder roared. Lightning struck the field between them but neither force hesitated. They came together with cries of glee as if they'd all been waiting forever to take this thrill ride. Those cries soon changed to howls of hatred and screams of pain as Lilith's demons realized their fancy guns were useless. Very few of the demons carried the blades that Rafe's army used to great effect.

Rafe let the madness take him forward, eager to wet his own blade. Where had the sword come from? Aamon had thrust it into his hand just before the charge. It felt right in his hand. It became an old friend that he knew how to use to advantage as wave after wave of demon berserkers came at them. The field soon became soaked with blood from both sides. His boots slipped but he managed to stay on his feet and surged ahead. He had to get to Lilith and to his wife. He'd seen his mother back away at the first signs of battle, her demon guards dragging Lacy along with her.

His arm was tiring with the weight of that great sword, but he kept swinging, taking an arm here, a head there. As it rolled away, he saw Jerry kick it like a soccer ball, shouting with excitement, his own knife dripping blood as he gutted yet another demon and shoved it away from him. Ian was much the same, an ancient Highlander who was in his element, his own knife ripping into demon after demon.

Lilith's army was forced to fight with teeth and claws. It was an uneven battle and they realized they were losing. Some of them had already run away, muttering about not enough pay for this kind of slaughter. Miguel flew overhead, one of

the few vampires Rafe knew who could fly while
still in mortal form. He'd pulled out his gun and
sprayed wisteria oil on the dark demons. The
lights gleaming on the chests of Rafe's own force
made it easy for Miguel to tell friend from foe.
Rafe had Abe to thank for making that work for
them. He saw the demons hit by the wisteria fall
when they were hit. It was helping tremendously
to cut down the numbers against them.

Still, they were losing men, good demons, who
had come here to help him. The man beside
Aamon went down, his stomach ripped open
by the claws of a giant two-headed demon who
turned to attack the captain.

"Ear plugs, put them in. This has gone on long
enough." Ian had found his computer. "I say fuck
it! They're all going down. Good and bad. Rafe?
Ready?" He waited until Rafe signaled with a
raised hand. The other vampires did the same.
Hopefully Lacy had managed to put her own
plugs in before Lilith had taken her prisoner. Ian
hit some buttons and suddenly every demon on
the field dropped to the ground. Even Aamon
clutched his ears and fell, unconscious.

Rafe stood for a moment, looking around.
Besides the many who had been hurt and killed,
the demons from both sides were unable to
move. He knew it couldn't last long, but the
excruciating pain in their ears had knocked them
out. He shifted into bird form and took to the
dark sky. It was the only way he could get across
the field covered with bodies. He had to find
Lilith and Lacy. Would they both be down?

He realized he was not alone. Miguel, Jerry and Ian were with him, birds themselves. All had chosen dark feathers, to blend with the night sky. Thunder roared again and Rafe was surprised it hadn't started to rain. His heart pounded with his fury and the terror that he'd lost his chance to save the woman he loved. He scanned the edge of the area where he'd last seen Lilith. That silver armor would make her stand out. He landed close to the spot and shifted into his human form, finding demon bodies on the ground but no sign of Lilith or Lacy. Where could they be?

"Let's spread out." Jerry had pulled his knife again. "Ian, any idea how long these creatures will be unconscious?"

"No. I wish I did. Didn't have time to run any tests. I would guess five to ten minutes at the most." Ian pulled his computer from his backpack again. "I can always give them another jolt if I have to."

"Yeah. Keep that in mind. If they stir before you hear from us, do that." Rafe spotted an exit door. "Lilith must have been able to resist that sound or she'd be right here."

"Not surprised. I told you, she's the most powerful demon I've ever seen." Ian drew a small gun from his waistband. "Wonder how this potion would work on her. The love potion."

Rafe choked out a laugh. "On that woman? I can't imagine it." He reached for the door handle. "This is probably an escape route. Stairs. Like for a fire escape."

"Hold on, Rafe." Jerry stepped to his side. "If it

is, it will probably lead to the bunker where Dani is hidden. That's the equipment room, right?"

"Shit, of course it is." Rafe threw open the door and inhaled. "Yes, they went this way. I would know my wife's scent anywhere. Lilith dragged her down with her. She's still after Dani." He picked up something silver. "Looks like my mother got as tired of wearing the gas mask as I did. It's hot as hell." He exchanged looks with the men. "That's a piece of luck for us. If we do catch up with her, we can try the spray on her. See what it does."

"Then what are we waiting for?" Jerry started down the stairs. "My wife is down there. I don't care how strong the door to that bunker is, Lilith could probably figure out how to get through it and she'll take out anyone in her way. With the deadline looming, she's getting desperate. Desperation lends strength. You know that, Rafe."

"Yes, I do." Rafe met Ian's gaze. "Stay here with your sound machine. Like you said, if the demons stir, put them down again. Give me the gun with the love potion. When we get close to the deadline, if I get a chance, I may try it." He took the gun. "I know Lucifer is around here somewhere, watching the action. If he truly wants Lilith, this may give him an opportunity to take her."

He followed Jerry down the stairs, Miguel at his back. It seemed like they wound down the metal steps forever. Truly there were many flights of them into the bowels of the mountain. Rafe was reassured to pick up Lacy's scent. She'd even managed to swipe blood on the wall. He'd know it anywhere. It was a sign she wasn't frozen, but had been dragged along in Lilith's unbreakable grip.

At the bottom, when they came close to the bunker, they heard screaming and smelled the strong scent of wisteria. Richard, Glory and Flo had managed to shoot at Lilith when she approached them. She wouldn't have expected that.

"What is that horrible smell?" Lilith screeched. "You will regret that." She threw Lacy on the ground, set a booted foot on his wife's stomach, then raised her arms at the group gathered behind rocks on either side of the bunker.

"Stop what you're doing, Mother." Rafe stayed a few feet behind her. "Aren't you tired of fighting?"

Lilith whirled around. She rubbed at her wet, flushed cheeks, "My unnatural son. What I am tired of are your foolish tricks! What are they spraying? The smell is disgusting. Most of my body is covered by armor or this would be unbearable."

"It's a little something that makes your lesser demons drop like flies." Rafe forced a smile. "Oh, yes. Some of them do like to turn into flies, don't they? So they can spy on me. That's how you knew what we were planning. But it hasn't done you any good. We are still here and my daughter is safe."

"Is she?" Lilith raised her arm and threw a fire bomb toward the iron door of the equipment room. The heat and roar of it made all of them jump. Glory and Flo screamed and covered their heads. Richard threw himself over his wife. Fortunately, the door held.

"Is that all you've got?" Rafe walked closer. "I see a desperate woman in front of me. Why? Lucifer loves you. He will treat you like his queen once you are by his side. What are you afraid of?"

"You have no idea." She said it quietly. "Fool. You've been to Hell now. Surely you understand why I have no desire to go back."

"Yet you would doom your granddaughter to a life there?" Rafe raised his gun. "What kind of heartless bitch would do such a thing?"

"Are you going to try to kill me?" She laughed. "Impossible. I am immortal. What's in that gun? More of that silly itching oil?" She stepped closer, finally taking her foot off Lacy and kicking her aside. "Go ahead. Take your best shot. I dare you. All it will do is make me more determined to send one of you—your dear Daniela or you yourself, Rafael, to Lucifer in my place."

Rafe closed his eyes. Any last hope that his mother had a care for him was gone. He opened his eyes, aimed and pulled the trigger. Her armor protected her heart. Instead, he hit her right between her beautiful eyes. Her cry echoed in the concrete room. The men stayed close, weapons in hand. Glory ran to Jerry and he wrapped one arm around her. Richard held Flo, his Bible in front of both of them, a shield he obviously hoped would keep whatever was coming from harming his wife.

For a moment there was silence, broken only by Rafe's rasp as he struggled to breathe. He was desperate to go to Lacy but she lay too near Lilith to be safe from his mother's next move. He waited. Lilith didn't stagger, didn't raise her arms or say a word. Finally, she opened her eyes and stared at Rafe.

"My son. Don't you know that everything I did was because I loved you?"

There was a sudden crack as the concrete floor near Lilith's feet moved. Rafe rushed to Lacy. He pulled her away from where a fissure opened and then widened. Lilith stared down at her feet and jumped back, ending up pressed against the metal door. The rest of them were on the other side of the gap opening in the floor. Suddenly a blinding light filled the room. It was coming from inside that hole.

"It's a portal. Just in time, I'd say." Miguel stood behind Rafe. "I hate to remind you that we have less than an hour to get to the plane where the vampires among us can rest when the sun comes up."

"I know. Yes, a portal." Rafe waited. "I think we all know what that means."

Lucifer appeared, rising from a cloud of steam and dust, a ghostly apparition that soon turned into a man. He was dressed in one of his expensive dark suits, his golden hair shining in the light glowing from beneath him. "Well, well, well, here we are, right on time indeed." He grinned. "Lilith, silver becomes you!"

"Oh, shut up." She wiped away the potion that

had run down her face. "I look a mess and you know it."

"But I heard you say you love the boy!" Lucifer rubbed his hands together and sparks flew. "A miracle!"

"I did not." She looked around. "Why are you here? Came to get the girl?"

"No, my dear. It's you, of course. The child is safely behind that door and you couldn't finish the job to get it open." Lucifer turned to Rafe. "Give her another blast of that stuff while she's looking at me. I swear it worked like a charm."

Rafe shrugged. "Why not? You're right. It was a miracle. Though I didn't believe her for a minute. Make sure she's staring at you, Luc. To get the full effect."

Lucifer cackled and grabbed Lilith's chin, forcing her to look into his eyes. "Oh, this is good. Come on, sweet thing. Stare into Daddy's eyes. You love me. You know you do. We will have great times together down there." He glanced at Rafe and nodded.

Rafe aimed and shot again. He hit her cheek this time. Would it be enough? He was doing Lilith a favor, wasn't he? Her life would be happier down there if she loved Lucifer. Happy? He pushed away thoughts of what he'd seen in Hell and slid the gun into his belt. Lilith was a demon after all. It might be the best place for her. Yes, it was.

He held his wife close beside him. It didn't take a glance at her battered face to remind him why he shouldn't give a damn about Lilith's fate.

Lilith blinked, sighed and met Lucifer's gaze. Then she reached out and touched his face. "I can't believe it but you were always the best I ever had. Love? I think that's a silly four-letter word, but I can't resist you. Kiss me, Master."

Lucifer pulled her close and kissed her so thoroughly that the rest of them looked away. He gave a thumbs up to Rafe, then pressed Lilith against him as they descended into the hole and the fissure closed over them. It was soon dark again in the room with only the metal door and the smell of that sweet scent in the air to remind them of what had just happened.

Lacy rubbed Rafe's chest, her sigh loud in the room. They all still wore their gas masks except for her. She looked bruised and broken, but had a smile on her swollen lips and managed a purr.

"Is it really over? Is she truly gone?" Lacy asked. "Can we open that door now? I want to see my baby."

Rafe stared at the smooth concrete, then kissed his wife's bruised cheek. "Of course. We won. I can hardly believe it, but we won. Let's get Dani out of there." He waited impatiently while Richard pulled a key out of his pocket and unlocked the door. Dani came running out and straight into her parents' arms.

"I can't believe it's really over." Rafe pulled his two girls close. "Are you all right, Lacy? What did she do to you?"

"Don't worry about it. She's gone now." Lacy kissed Dani's cheek. "I'm ready to go home."

"What happens to those two demon armies?" Jerry asked that.

"I'm sure Lucifer will make sure they disperse. Lilith's force will realize they won't get paid. Mine is supposed to get a reward from Lucifer since he got the outcome he wanted. I'm sure he'll be generous to Captain Aamon and the rest." Rafe nodded. "You vampires need to go on to the plane. Lacy, Dani and I can head back to the hotel and pack up everything. We'll see you in Austin."

"Love those words." Flo said. "I am happy we are done with this. No more worries. Am I right?"

"I can only hope." Rafe was anxious to get home. He had a business to run. He had a family to love and he was not going to think about his mother rotting in Hell. Was he?

"Did someone remember to call Ian? He's up there with his sound machine, guarding the demon armies." Miguel looked upward.

"I texted him. He's already on his way to the plane." Jerry smiled at Glory. "I think I owe it to Captain Aamon to let him know how this went down. He and his men deserve to know that feeling of victory." He insisted Glory go on to the plane without him. "You really don't want to see those demons, my love. They are the stuff of nightmares. I'll meet you there. As soon as the demons are gone, Richard or I will make a call and let the park manager know the gas leak was a false alarm. We'll give them the all clear."

"Good. I appreciate that, Jerry." Rafe realized he should have thought of that. Thought of a lot of things. Man, he was sick of fighting. Sick of thinking of himself as a demon lord. He hoped he never had to turn into one again. Was that too much to wish for? Probably. He looked down at his sleepy daughter. Flo had already made sure Dani would only remember a trip to Orlando and its theme parks with her parents. The miracle of vampire mind control at work. He was grateful for that.

But in the future, Dani would have to be trained in demon ways and it was his responsibility. Because, while he didn't want any part of that world, it was her legacy. And, someday, other demons or Lucifer might come calling. She had to be prepared to use her powers for good. He was determined she would always make that choice.

Back at the hotel, he was glad to see the room in good order and with no sign of demons, not even Lilith's demon flies. He and Lacy packed up the weapons left behind and arranged transport to the airport. They knew the vampires were already dead to the world in the back bedroom when they finally got on board the plane. Dani soon fell asleep on the couch. Lacy too was exhausted and stretched out on two seats for the short flight. They were in the air and on their way when Abe appeared in the seat next to Rafe.

"Well, my son, you did it. Are you satisfied with the outcome?" Abe spotted a tray of cookies and helped himself. He hummed happily when he discovered they were chocolate chip.

"Satisfied? Not exactly. I got a look at a world I hope never to see again." Rafe took a bite of cookie. It probably was delicious but he couldn't enjoy it.

"You saw Hell. What's bothering you? Don't you think sinners should be punished?" Abe dusted crumbs off his robe.

"Yes, of course. But it's so brutal, so cruel there. And I'm sick of evil and people who have no conscience." Rafe threw down the cookie. "Why can't people be kinder to one another?"

"Good question. Are you worried about your mother down there?" Abe stared at him, seeing into his heart.

"Yes, damn it. And I shouldn't be. She deserves whatever she gets. Look at what she put me and my family through." Rafe grabbed a bottle of water and drank half of it. "Then she said something. Under the influence of that stupid potion. Did it really work, or was it a scam?"

"The love potion? Don't ask me. I've never been in love with anyone but the Lord and that's a much different kind of love. But keep in mind Lilith is a master manipulator. Was what she said about you true? Or was it said only so she can keep you on her string?" Abe sighed. "Am I being cynical? Perhaps. Just enjoy your victory this time, my son. For now, your daughter is safe, your wife is safe and, hmm." He smiled. "There may be a surprise in your future. The love potion did that much for you."

"Abe! Don't tell me!" Rafe had visions of another baby. Would this one be a demon? Or a werecat? Did he care? He loved all his children and would protect them with everything in him. He glanced back at Lacy, asleep a few feet away. He loved her too. And would as long as she'd let him. He'd brought trouble with him. So far, she'd forgiven him for all of it. That was a miracle in itself. He turned back to Abe but the monk had disappeared.

Rafe finished his water and his cookie and decided he'd fretted enough. He'd won this round. Whatever came next? At least he'd had good friends by his side and even help from above. What more could he ask for? He said a quick prayer of thanks for his child's safety, astonished when thinking "God" didn't give him even a twinge.

What did it mean? Had he lost his demon half? Now that was something he couldn't imagine. He thought about testing the theory, trying to change right there in the plane. No, not a good idea. Dani could wake up and it would scare her. But he did search his senses, looking for the demon buzz that was always with him. He poked at it, like he would a sore tooth. No, couldn't find it. Really. There was a void. He could touch his shifter side, no problem. But the demon half? Gone.

Son of a gun. He realized he was grinning as the seatbelt sign came on and he knew they were approaching Austin. No longer a demon. A parting gift from Abe? He looked out the window as the plane parted the clouds and the city came into view. What would his mother think? He laughed and pounded his knee. It was almost worth a trip to Hell to find out. Almost.

He leaned back and closed his eyes as the plane descended. He felt clean, new. Now he knew what real miracles felt like. He glanced back at his beautiful little girl. Somehow, he'd have to make this happen for Daniela as well. That had to be why... He shook his head. He was not going to overthink this. He saw Lacy stir and sit up. One day at a time. He couldn't wait to see what the future held for them. Couldn't wait.

DEAR READER,
   I never imagined when I published *Real Vampires Have Curves* in 2007 that I would still be writing this series in 2023. Can you believe it? But, thanks to loyal fans, it just keeps going.

Rafael Valdez was always a favorite character, especially when he was forced to be Glory St. Clair's sidekick in dog form in the early books. Once he became a hot guy, I knew he had to have his own stories, starting with *Rafe and the Redhead*. In *Rafe Takes the Heat*, fighting the Devil got a little intense. But a Latin lover would be, wouldn't he?

Curious about what happened between Glory, Jerry and Melisandra back in Austin? Check out *Real Vampires Know Size Matters*.

If you are just discovering this series, you might want to see how it all began in 1604. There are four prequels starting with *Real Vampires: How Glory Met Jerry*. You can check the book list for other titles.

Yes, Glory has Olympus roots and now we know Miguel Cisneros is related to her. Hmm. Yes, this is how the *Real Vampires* series grows. Because I think this very hot guy with unusual powers may need his own story. What do you think?

Stay tuned by subscribing to my newsletter on my website gerrybartlett.com.

Thanks for reading and watch out after dark!

Gerry Bartlett

ALSO BY GERRY

THE REAL VAMPIRES SERIES
Real Vampires Have Curves
Real Vampires Live Large
Real Vampires Get Lucky
Real Vampires Don't Diet
Real Vampires Hate Their Thighs
Real Vampires Have More to Love
Real Vampires Don't Wear Size Six
Real Vampires Hate Skinny Jeans
Real Vampires Know Hips Happen
Real Vampires Know Size Matters
Real Vampires Take a Bite Out of Christmas
Real Vampires Say Read My Hips
Real Vampires and the Viking
Rafe and the Redhead
Real Vampires: Rafe Takes the Heat

PREQUELS
Real Vampires: When Glory Met Jerry
Real Vampires: A Highland Christmas
Real Vampires: Glory and the Pirates
Real Vampires: Revenge of the Pirates
Real Vampires: Glory Does Vegas

ROMANTIC SUSPENSE BY
GERRY BARTLETT

TEXAS HEAT SERIES
Texas Heat
Texas Fire
Texas Pride

LONE STAR SUSPENSE
Texas Lightning
Texas Trouble
Texas Reckless

ABOUT THE AUTHOR

GERRY BARTLETT IS the nationally best-selling author of the Real Vampires series which debuted in 2007 with *Real Vampires Have Curves*. She's a native Texan and lives south of Houston where, when she's not writing, she likes to treasure hunt for her antiques business. She's been lucky enough to travel around the world and has collected small boxes to remind her of her favorite places. Gerry is an avid reader of anything with a bit of mystery, some romance and, always, a happy ending. Besides writing about vampires, Gerry has published Lone Star romantic suspense.

You can find her on Instagram and Facebook and at her website gerrybartlett.com where you can sign up for her newsletter.